The Silent Canoe

by J. Philip

Skitt Press

PUBLISHER'S NOTE

This is a work of fiction. Names, places and incidents either are the product of the author's imagination or refer to historical persons or events. Character development and expression of character is fictional.

Published by:

Skitt Press

Toronto, ON
www.thesilentcanoe.com

ISBN: 978-0-9865531-1-0

The Silent Canoe

Author's Note

War, death, love, illness, victory, torture, salvation, … history is dramatic to the core. Canadian history is every bit as sensational as any Hollywood blockbuster, yet we tend to know about it only from textbooks, biographies and fact-based films, the kind you'd see in a high school social studies class. Well researched and presented, they are usually enjoyed only by history buffs.

My intention in writing *The Silent Canoe* was to captivate the reader and give an impression of what it was like to live during those tumultuous times. Rather than focus on a famous figure in Canadian history, I was more interested in writing about an everyday person. What would it have been like if you or I had immigrated to Upper Canada in 1793? What struggles would we have faced? What choices would we have made?

Isaac Devins was one of the first settlers in northern Toronto, a former farming community that has evolved into the largest industrial area in Ontario. Extensive research into the family history book, municipal records, diaries, letters and newspaper clippings has only provided slim and sketchy information.

We know that Isaac Devins and his extended family landed in Niagara, Upper Canada, on April 29, 1793, and were granted free passage by Governor John Graves Simcoe, but we don't know their reasons for coming here. Devins sailed with Simcoe as part of the first group of settlers to the Toronto Bay. He worked as a foreman on the construction of Yonge Street in 1795. We don't know why he was given that appointment or why he chose to accept it.

I discovered that if I wanted to uncover the story of Isaac Devins, then I had to understand the history of Toronto. As I delved deeper, I realized that I also needed to understand the history of Upper Canada, the British Colonies, the United States, and the whole world scene.

Eventually, I gathered sufficient information to complete an Historical Landscape Master Plan and to create fifteen historic signs. But I had uncovered so much more information about Toronto, Niagara and Upper Canada that I did not want to be lost and forgotten again. After much deliberation, I decided to write a book of historical fiction, hoping that it would be detailed and accurate enough for historians to respect and compelling enough for fiction readers to enjoy.

The most important thing for me was to create an accurate story, to be as true to the history of Upper Canada as possible. All the characters in the novel are based on real people, except for Violet, Simeon's wife; Helmut and his family; and Fire Starter and his family.

The underlying question … how much history and how much story? Where biographies of characters exist, such as for Governor Simcoe and his wife, I chose to write about their hopes, dreams, preferences, and prejudices as accurately as I could. For figures such as Isaac Devins, I had to make assumptions and develop their characters. What lies in between the facts—the motivations, the thoughts and feelings, the relationships between characters—has been fictionalized.

The novel's villain, William Jarvis, was a colourful Canadian. Many biographical sketches (see, for example, Toronto's Jarvis Collegiate website at http://schools.tdsb.on.ca/jarvisci/) depict him as a pompous, self-serving wretch who was lazy and arrogant. Other biographies detail his accomplishments as the First Secretary of the Executive Council of Upper Canada and the Registrar General. Many letters he wrote between 1793 and 1823 portray a man who cared deeply about his family. I chose to capitalize on his unsavoury past and make him Isaac Devins' nemesis. Their interactions in the novel are based on fact, except for their first meeting in the woods in Upper Canada and the final scene in the climax.

Certain modern geographical names have been used that were not correct at that time, so that readers won't get lost or frustrated. For instance, Queenston was referred to as the Lower Landing when Isaac Devins was there, until after the War of 1812. The Humber River was referred to as the St. John River or the Toronto River in many historical diaries and letters until the middle of the 1800s. Dundas Street from Burlington to Woodstock was called the Governor's Road, but I use the more familiar names.

As well, a few minor characters were assigned different names. To avoid confusion, I switched Isaac's twin brother's name, Abraham, to Jacob so as not to confuse the reader with Isaac's father. Isaac's sister's name, Elizabeth, was changed to Sarah since there are two other Elizabeths in the Devins family. Likewise, his sister-in-law's name, Hannah, was changed to Rita so as not to confuse with Hannah Jarvis.

The time line for some of the minor historic events was changed to assist in character development and advancing the plot. For instance, Isaac Devins' trial occurred sometime in 1794-95, eight years before the trial in the novel. Most other events leading up to and including the War of 1812 have an accurate time frame.

Finally, the written and spoken language of two hundred years ago was quite different from today. I chose to use everyday language, phrases and idioms rather than historic English.

For inspiring me to do the project and not abandon it, I would like to thank Stanley Fedorowick and Jennifer Sorensen. I would also like to thank Tim and the late Sheila Lambrinos, whose passion for history and the Devins family is exemplary. Thanks also go out to Giorgio Mammoliti, Sandra Farina, Paul Marsala, Caryn Wolfe, Susan Olding, Glenn Bonnetta, Nick Harris, Gary Norris, Anne Birch, Derek Hayes, James Shawana, Karin Braccio and Amie Key. For historical accuracy on the native history and culture, I appreciate the insight of Dr. Shirley Williams.

Finally, my biggest thanks goes to Kevin Philip, who supported me every step of the way, and our son, Shane Philip, for his patience.

for my mother, Helen

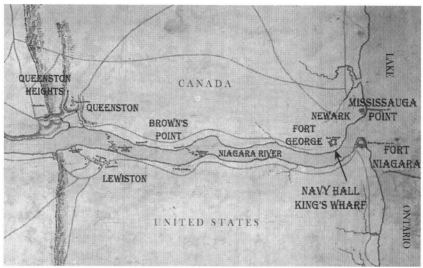

(1814) Map of Niagara Frontier, Library and Archives Canada, NMC-18466-2
(with place names added)

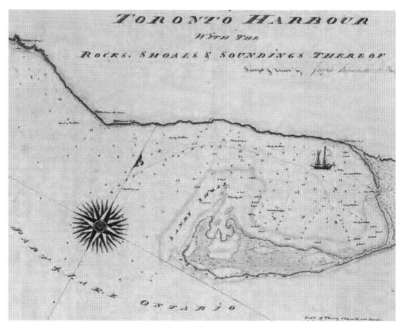

(1792) Joseph Bouchette, Plan of York Harbour, Toronto Public Library, T{1792}/4Msm
Captain Bouchette surveyed the water depth of the harbour the year before the settlers landed.

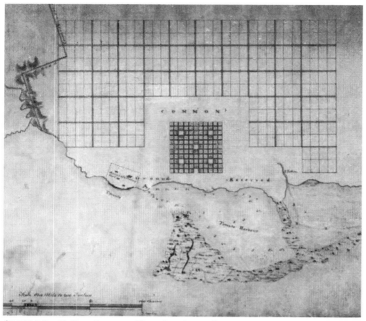

(1788) John Collins, Surveyor, Plan of Harbour of Toronto, Toronto Public Library, T1788/4Mlrg
One of many design concepts for York showing the Peninsula (Toronto Islands), Fort Rouillé,
Garrison creek, town lots for the elite class, parkland (the common) and garden lots on the exterior.

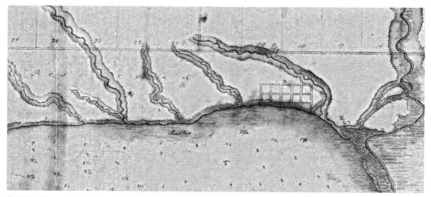

(1793) Alexander Aitkins, Plan of York Harbour, UK National Archives, CO 700 Canada 60
Actual survey of the town site showing Lot Street (Queen Street) in the north, parallel to the lake.

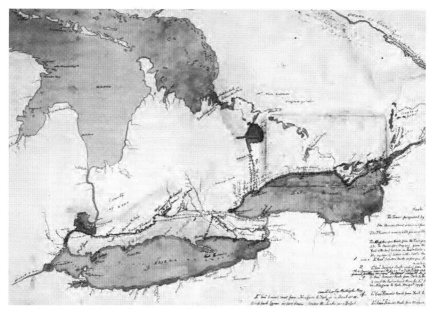

(1795) Sketch Map of Upper Canada Showing the Routes Lt. Gov. Simcoe Took on Journeys
Between March 1793 and September 1795, Archives of Ontario, I0004757
Dundas Road (from Thames River in the west to Kingston in the east) and Yonge Street are shown.

(1814) George Williams, Plan of the Town and Harbour Of York, Library and Archives Canada
NMC 21771
Map shows extent of town and the rebuilt garrison after the Battle of York

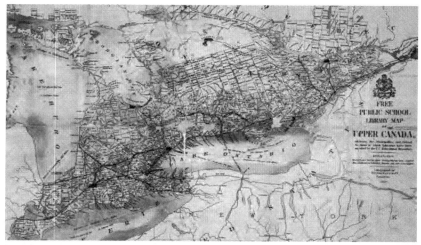

(1857) Free Public School Library Map of Upper Canada, Archives of Ontario, I0004751
Shows extent of development at the time of Isaac Devins' death.

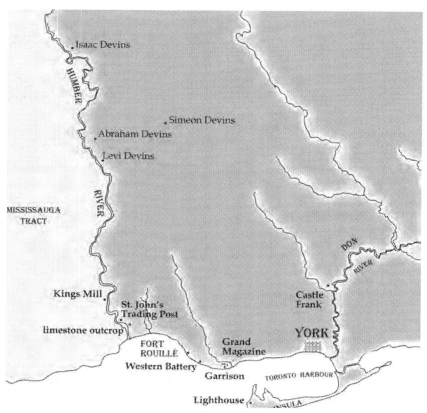

Prologue

Certain he was taking his final breaths, Isaac Devins lay on the featherbed that had been meticulously stuffed by his daughter and grandchildren. Overcome with weakness, he could barely utter a word, such a contrast to his robust, illustrious youth.

He was a man of the river, and to the river he wanted to return. *I must remember to tell Elizabeth to bury me alongside the black oak near the limestone boulders on the riverbank,* he reminded himself, unsure if he had already done so. His daughter, Elizabeth, had returned to the homestead to care for him when he became so ill a couple of weeks ago, alone without his dear, departed wife, Polly. How he missed her. *Soon I will join you, Polly,* he thought, *in heaven or the happy hunting ground, whatever the case may be.*

It was more than four decades since Isaac had last seen Fire Starter. He always said that the Great Spirit helps us to pass to the next life, to complete our journey so that we may be one with the trees, rocks, water and mountains. *A comforting thought,* Isaac had agreed on that cool morning down where the cherry trees leaned precariously close to the river. *Fire Starter was probably the truest friend I ever had.*

Today's generation doesn't even know what a Mississauga looks like, he grumbled, recalling the early days when settlers were scattered like seeds dropped by the mourning dove in the majestic pine forest where the Mississaugas lived.

There was so much more freedom and independence back then, he reminisced, *more hope.* Nowadays, his grandchildren's lives were set. If *you were born on a farm, you would die on a farm. If you were born in the city, you would not venture outside of it. But I suppose that will change, he thought.*

A railway was expected to be built next year, the great Iron Horse. The Upper Canada Gazette said that it would connect Toronto with Detroit and Kingston, reducing travel time from two weeks by stagecoach to less than a day. Isaac pursed his lips and attempted to whistle at the thought but was too weary to let out a sound.

We were the creators of the province, all of us brave enough to throw away familiarity and go north. For the better part of sixty years, he had seen Upper Canada change from a vast wilderness to a land divided by surveys and lot lines, dotted with towns, villages, farms. Governor Simcoe always envisioned that tens of thousands would settle here, even though there were only 420 of us in the township of York when he left.

At the time, Isaac thought that the governor's vision of roads cutting through the province and many towns and cities to be farfetched, even ludicrous. I couldn't see the forest for the trees, he scolded himself.

How he missed the days of being lost in the wilderness, paddling alone down the Humber with towering red maples lining the channel and only ever coming across groups of Mississaugas paddling to their village on the Credit or fishing for salmon at night with fires blazing in the birchbark canoes.

Despite his attempts to immerse himself within the high society of Toronto and become a man of importance, he was always drawn to the river, the only place he felt relaxed, and whole. I bet there was never a white settler who spent so much time on the Humber as I did, he thought.

We fought for this land, not wanting to be consumed and spat out by the American rebels. How ironic that the majority of us fighting against the United States were former Americans ourselves. There must have been something that made us want to defend this country, something that convinced us to sacrifice ourselves and our children. He understood now, much more that he did then, that for him it was not loyalty to the British or even avarice, but his affinity for the Humber River and everything it gave him.

Every day, while the others camped out in the Toronto Bay, he would steal away and walk six miles through the mixed pine forest to make his first birchbark canoe. He always felt at home in the forest, never desiring to cut it down and clear it as so many did when they came to Canada. He left that task to his son, John, who obviously did not want to follow in his father's footsteps. *Funny that I never moved on from here,* Isaac smirked, shaking his head ever so slightly, letting out a small moan.

But here I remained. We raised our eight children along the river, half of them now living far away. *Back then, I wanted to be a Townie, a man of influence, a real go-getter. We were starting a province with nothing to guide us. There were no laws, no industry, no protocols, only the wilderness. And corruption, steeped within the very bowels of the people with influence, the decision-makers. John White could testify to that,* Isaac thought ruefully, *if only he had lived to set things right. His vision of a lawful province based on accountability died along with him, at the hands of lesser men.* Isaac sighed. *So many of the good ones perished while the undeserving reaped the rewards.*

I am tired now, so tired. He felt like he had been tired for the last decade. *It had taken sixty years for the settlers to claim the forest around him. At least half of it is gone now,* he lamented, *stripped bare. We used to be so alone, so peaceful up here. Now there is a plank road connecting Weston and Woodbridge at the back of my lot.*

In my younger days, I would have looked upon that as a great opportunity, as a ticket to wealth and prosperity. Now, I abhor it. Even the ancient trail created by the Hurons centuries ago, the only route through the forest when we first arrived at the Toronto harbour, has all but disappeared. Now it is grown over, absorbed into farmers' fields, with barely a trace left. Fire Starter would be ashamed.

Children today do not appreciate what we had to endure. His lips lifted tentatively at the corners of his mouth, attempting a smile, remembering how his neighbour, Mary Watson, used to walk ten miles along the narrow ancient trail through the bush to the St. Lawrence Market every week with a basket full of butter strapped to her head and return before sunset. *Now that was fortitude*, he nodded to himself. *My grandchildren were born onto homesteads that already had a house, a barn, a shed, horses, livestock and cleared fields. They don't know anything about hardship.*

As his eyes flittered, struggling for a few more minutes of consciousness, he saw Elizabeth come into the room, straighten the bed sheet and put a hand to his forehead. *Such a loving child, so like her mother. Elizabeth understands*, he thought. *Why, she was the first child born of a settler in Toronto. She grew up as Toronto evolved from a dot on a map to a town of more than thirty thousand.* Squeezing his eyes shut, he tried to smile and show his appreciation, but it came across as more of a wince of pain.

At least my children have mostly all married well, none of them into a bad family. We did not have so much choice back then, with very few settlers and townsfolk to choose from. Just look at my brother, Simeon, who might be still alive today if he hadn't fallen for a town girl. Isaac felt his chest tighten. He had loved his youngest brother most of all. They shared a special bond, despite the age difference or maybe because of it.

I can thank the Lord for a long life, even if success has eluded me. Perhaps my children will achieve the prosperity and distinction that I strived for but could never grasp.

As a child he would trudge through the wheat fields with a yoke around his neck hoisting pails of cream to the riverboats and dream of becoming a great man, an important man, a man sought out by everyone for his wisdom and opinions. He longed to leave his mark on the land, in the hearts of the people. Isaac Devins wanted a page in the history books to be written of his achievements.

But here I lie, leaving nothing of value.

There were so many like me who came to Upper Canada with dreams of success and great wealth, but only the privileged and the British succeeded. A few got lucky, but they didn't deserve it. Just look at the mess that incompetent fool, William Jarvis, made of the land grants and how it had affected so many innocent people. I know that I could have done better, Isaac muttered to himself, *if only given the chance.*

I suppose I wasn't as enterprising as some who found a way despite the impenetrable wall that allowed only the privileged to pass through. Polly always said that my disdain for servitude and bootlicking could drive a preacher to drink. I have failed, he chastised himself.

Or did I merely give up?

No matter, there is nothing I can change now, he thought, trying again to smile at Elizabeth, who sat down in the old willow chair beside the bed, the one he had crafted so long ago when they first camped out on the shore of the Toronto harbour. The look of concern and sympathy on her heart-shaped face told him that again he was not successful in showing her a smile. He rolled his eyes in frustration, only to have his daughter gasp, thinking it was his final breath. *Good Lord, I better stop making any kind of expression or Elizabeth will burst into tears.*

I would rather shoot my horse and watch it bleed than see a woman cry, he thought, staring up at the pine rafters that he and his brothers had raised so long ago for the three-room log cabin by the Humber.

The only flow of water that I want to experience is the feel of my paddle dipped into the river as I race through the rapids. How he loved to work up a sweat, paddling hard upstream on a stormy day to one of the calmer pools on the east side, have a rest, and then race back down the river. *There is nothing better than canoeing alone with only the wind, the sun and the clouds to guide you, the fish to feed you, and the animals of the forest as your companions, and silence, pure silence, as your paddle dips into the still, clear water, the ultimate revelry.*

And yet it was his love for the river that ended up being his demise, knocking him down, and laying him out to dry. Some might say that the river consumed him, others swore that Isaac was to blame. *There is no shame in standing up for your beliefs,* he muttered to himself.

Then he thought about that day, so long ago, when fate, or God, intervened and left him with nothing. Every single day, for the last decade, he wondered if he should tell the secret that could finally give him the respect that he deserved.

But perhaps it was too late. Most of the people have been dead for years. Fire Starter would say that nothing good comes of casting shadows on the lone wolf's prey.

Yet, if he did divulge who actually pulled the trigger, his story would be rewritten. I might finally be remembered as something more than just a settler who lived and died in Upper Canada.

Chapter 1 – April 29, 1793

"All ashore!" the ferryman hollered as the battered wooden bateau crashed into the wharf over and over again.

On a calm day, the Niagara River flowed gently down to Lake Ontario with hardly a sound but for the roar of the 250-foot waterfalls a few miles to the south. But when the wind was strong and from the east, nothing could stop the river from becoming a menace. Even the most experienced navigator had trouble cutting through the three-foot swells that made the bow slap furiously against the water, pitching those sitting at the back off their seats. Muffled gasps were heard from nearly two dozen passengers, mostly Americans, about to set foot in Upper Canada for the first time.

"Damn," Isaac said through clenched teeth as he was jostled against the side of the boat and nearly thrown into the swirling river.

The barrel of his Hudson fowler shotgun jammed against his upper thigh, the cold metal pressed down into his flesh. If only my good holster hadn't been left behind, he muttered, cursing the thin leather straps that offered little protection when the waves lurched the boat and forced him into the gunwale. His frustration was echoed by the other men being tossed about waiting for the ferryman to help the women and children onto the dock. Abraham Devins, Isaac's father, pushed his two other sons forward to the gangplank when the crowd thinned out.

Isaac nodded and handed the ferryman ten pence. Quite a hefty price for a quick pull across the river, he thought. Must be five times the amount we paid to cross the Genesee River back home. He had only brought British pence to the northern colony, certain that the American silver dollar, fresh out of the mint a few months earlier, would be rejected. There is no certainty that we will be well-received either, he considered, looking at the sharply dressed British soldiers in their green day coats, white ruffled shirts and grey pantaloons, the colours of the Queen's Rangers, forming a double row along the King's Wharf, standing at attention, muskets pointed upward.

Surely it was not just a ruse, Isaac thought, not some clever trick to lure the Americans here. The advertisement posted at the village square in Genesee, encouraging Loyalists to emigrate from upstate New York, had seemed legitimate. So legitimate that he had convinced his father, sister, two brothers and their families to leave their homes, take all their belongings and go to Upper Canada to seek their fortune.

As he picked up a wooden crate and hoisted it forward to a crew of sailors on the gangplank, Isaac let a seed of doubt enter his mind: What if I have led us into a trap? But he quickly dismissed the notion. It was not his nature to dwell on things that *might* happen. In his twenty-six years, he had always confronted things head-on. That is what sets me apart, makes me stronger, he reminded himself.

He tilted up his black hat with its fashionably rolled-up side rims and surveyed the crowd of settlers shuffling about on the Queenston dock. His family was not hard to spot. They were the only ones looking bewildered, with no particular place to go. They had all dressed in their Sunday best, as per his instructions. Isaac looked down at his own red cotton breeches fastened at the knee with brown buttons and his polished black leather shoes with shiny brass buckles. He wanted to make a good impression. There was a lot at stake.

A proud young man, self-assured, strong and ruggedly handsome, Isaac did not see himself as anything less than an upper statesman, an earl, or even a prince. His greatest wish was to be successful, a man of influence. He lived, dreamed and planned for it every day. He wanted to be a leader, a powerful man, someone making decisions, not meekly following orders. Straightening his back, he leaned forward slightly, unconsciously standing almost at attention. His shoulder-length, sandy-blond hair was tied at the back. His slim, athletic frame and his sharp, intense blue eyes exuded an audacity that was deep within his soul.

Isaac had absolutely refused to follow in his father's footsteps, or those of his grandfather or even great-grandfather. All of them were tenant farmers in New York State. Toiling in the fields, day after day, was only enough to feed their family. He cursed every time he thought of their landlord reaping the rewards of his father's hard labour. But that is how America was settled, he reflected. Wealthy people like William Penn were granted large tracts of land by the British Crown and then sold them to the privileged few who could afford a square mile or two. There was little room for peasants shipped over from Europe to remain anything but peasants. Working as a tenant farmer is no more than slavery, Isaac would often grumble as he loaded sacks of wheat onto his landlord's wagon.

Here in Upper Canada, though, it was all free land. The offer by the British was exactly what he had been looking for. Owning a plot of land would be the first step. After that, he would infiltrate the ruling class and become a man of power. There is a clean slate in the new colony, Isaac had told his brothers. No alliances, laws or politics. Isaac could see that his family would have a chance of becoming more than mere peasants.

"Can we go fishing, Uncle Isaac? The river is full of salmon," called his half-brother, running forward with arms flailing and all the excitement that a five-year-old can generate. Simeon always referred to Isaac, who was more than five times his age, as "Uncle Isaac", a sign of the special bond between them.

The wide-eyed look of anticipation on the little boy's face made Isaac chuckle. He remembered how he and his other brothers used to venture farther and farther down the Mohawk River to find the perfect fishing hole when he was Simeon's age.

Smiling, Isaac affectionately put a firm hand on his brother's shoulder, gave it a squeeze and said, "Maybe after we find a place to stay for the night."

The two walked back toward the crowd, which had spilled over onto the cleared area beside the dock in the dappled shade of willows and silver maples. There was not much evidence of anything beyond the trees, no sign of a town or village, or civilization of any sort, only a footpath leading off into the woods.

Isaac straightened the black silk cravat that Polly had tied so elegantly around his broad neck earlier that morning. It was the only luxury he owned. Polly had fashioned the tie out of a yard of silk that she was given from a desperate highwayman who needed a few halfpence to cross the river back in Genesee. He said he was being chased by a band of Senecas. Sure enough, a dozen natives rode past waving tomahawks and yelling a war cry an hour later. Isaac and Polly's cabin was the last one before the ferry crossing, so they often met travellers looking for change or asking for a place to stay for the night.

Even after he had instructed her to charge the travellers for lodging in the stable and feeding them breakfast, she never did. Isaac would come home from hunting, exhausted and hungry, expecting to see a few pence, but he would only find a handful of candles, a bit of cloth, a bar of soap or some other household item that a wayfarer insisted on giving. She is generous to a fault, he thought now, shaking his head slightly.

We would never have prospered at that rate, Isaac told himself, as he spotted Polly's lithe form bustling about at the edge of the dock, her auburn hair spilling out of her white lace cap and black straw hat. The forest green gown over her black ruffled petticoat made her look stylish, elegant, as if she belonged in the ballrooms of the aristocrats, sipping tea and being led across the dance floor, he thought. He watched her smiling face lift the spirits of everyone she spoke to, admiring her eternally cheerful demeanour.

She is beautiful on the inside and out, Isaac considered, grateful that she was his wife. But she deserves more, he vowed. Here, in Upper Canada, we will make our fortune. Isaac and Simeon slowed down as they reached their flustered-looking family at the end of the dock.

"We will follow the path over there at the edge of the dock," his father pronounced, motioning with a tilt of his forehead, his blue eyes demanding respect. "Surely it must lead to Newark."

Located on the British side of the turbulent Niagara River, Newark was where the Devins, and many other Americans, hoped to find their fortune. Surveyed just two years earlier, only a handful of homes and businesses were scattered on a grid of muddy roads, trying to tame the immense forest that threatened to swallow the intruders. The only other settlers were John Butler's Rangers, who had farm lots along the Niagara River stretching from Newark to Queenston.

Isaac smiled. His father, Abraham, was half a century old, yet still had the spirit of youth. When the War of Independence spread throughout the colonies in 1776, Abraham fought for the American rebels, not feeling loyal to the British due to his German heritage. After the war had ended and America became a country, he returned home to his three children, who were now motherless, his wife having succumbed to the throes of childbirth. Several years passed before Abraham married again and attempted to build and operate a new grist mill. He did not meet with success. Those were not prosperous years, right after the war. Uncertainty and suspicion were everywhere. The population in their village dwindled to almost nothing as many settlers, loyal to the British during the war, were whipped, beaten, and driven from their homes, and escaped to the Dominion of Canada.

When his eldest son, Isaac, approached him, Abraham immediately welcomed his suggestion to move to Upper Canada, with only a hint of trepidation. But the two of them still had to convince Isaac's other brothers and their wives to join them, along with his sister, Sarah, and her husband, Nicholas Miller. Family unity was a deep-rooted tradition for the Devins. Isaac and his father would not even consider moving to Upper Canada if the rest of the family did not go.

"There's nothing there but trees and Indians," his younger brother, Levi, complained. "No roads, no stores, no mills, no livestock. We will be living in the Dark Ages." He stepped away from his brother, shaking his head, dismissing the notion.

"Not at Fort Niagara," Isaac bantered. "It's been there for a couple of hundred years and is well stocked. Five hundred soldiers are stationed there. It is more like a town with stores and warehouses, a shipyard and traders."

"That's fine for a soldier, but not for a farmer," he retorted. "You won't catch me scuttling up with a bunch of Redcoats."

Isaac's twin brother, Jacob, was equally against the idea. "Look around you, brother," he exclaimed, his arm sweeping across the cornfields separated by wide hedgerows and fences. The brothers faced each other on the wooden porch of Jacob's shanty, next to the stable.

"A hundred acres of cleared land with only a few stones to pull. The only thing we will find in Upper Canada is a forest so dense that it will take more than a dozen teams of oxen to haul away the ashes."

"But the land will be ours," Isaac implored. "No rich owner to take away the bulk of the earnings."

"At least here I am sure to feed my family," Jacob shot back. "Even in a bad year we get enough to fill the table."

Despite many attempts at pleading his case, there was nothing that Isaac could say or do to convince his brothers to give up their familiarity, meagre though it was. Frustrated, Isaac paced back and forth, night after night outside the family homestead, too overwrought to sleep. Toiling away as a peasant alongside his brothers in the Genesee valley for years to come was unthinkable. He pleaded with his father, begging him to command his brothers and their wives to accompany them to Upper Canada.

The following Sunday after the family Bible reading, Abraham had his own idea of how to convince his sons.

Clearing his throat, a sign that all were to listen, Abraham looked each of his sons in the eye as they sat around the kitchen table. The quiet chatter of the women cleaning the pots and sweeping the ashes into the hearth did not distract anyone.

"One hundred and fifty years ago, your great-great-great grandfather, Captain Kit, had the strength of mind to leave his comfortable home in Germany and sail to the New World. There was nothing in America then. The pilgrims on the *Mayflower* had arrived only 15 years before, and the only settlements were at Plymouth and a small outpost at Albany. The land was raw, unexplored, untouched."

The brothers had all heard the story of Captain Kit's voyage of 1636 numerous times, but instead of rolling their eyes or looking away, there was something in their father's voice this time that drew them in.

"He paddled upriver with all his belongings, along the same route that Henry Hudson sailed a couple of decades earlier. By the time he arrived at Fort Albany, only a handful of explorers and trappers were wintering in the vast wilderness of America."

As he retold the tale of hardship, adventure, discovery, famine, Abraham's voice became filled with passion, an emotion his sons rarely witnessed. Only when he whipped them for taking the Lord's name in vain had they ever heard it so animated. They could see in his eyes that he had always longed for the same kind of adventure. His desire, his need to break free from a life of predictability, punctuated every word.

"Not only was he one of the original fur traders, but he became an interpreter and friend of the Mahicans. Many settlers were attacked and killed, their women raped and enslaved, but not Captain Kit. Even when he sailed down the Hudson river to what we now call New York to trade furs, the Mahicans never laid a hand on his wife or four children. Captain Kit was well respected, even revered, by both the white and the red men."

Slapping his left knee to emphasize the point, he continued, "His adventures through the virgin forests and the uncharted waters were legendary."

Isaac could feel his father's passion burning inside of him. He had always admired his forefather's journey and longed for a similar quest, where choices made resulted in life or death, where you could find the inner beauty of an untouched world. He looked over at his brothers and could see that they were feeling the same thing.

"Every landlord, every baron, every person in America, owes a large debt to Captain Kit and the first people brave enough to go to the New World." Abraham paused, looking at each of his sons in turn. "If we now travel north to Upper Canada, each one of you can follow in his footsteps. We can honour Captain Kit with our own willingness to take on the challenge."

With a note of finality and commitment, he said, "My sons, we can continue his legacy!"

Abraham's story was so inspiring, so heartfelt, so convincing, that he overturned his sons' fear and doubt.

Whatever the reason, thought Isaac now, looking at his family scattered across the King's Wharf, it doesn't matter. At least we are all in this together. He and his family hoisted all of their belongings onto their backs and trod up the footpath toward Newark.

The leaves were just emerging from the buds of the tops of the trees, emitting a yellow-green glow, but were not out full enough to cast much of a shadow on the unusually warm spring day. Isaac and his brothers grunted as they hauled satchels and bags, four apiece, up the sharp incline, sweating through their heavy woollen daycoats, followed by the women who bore their loads more gracefully, in silence. Young Simeon panted as he dragged a burlap sack full of winter boots and stockings up the foothill, wondering if they would ever reach the top.

"Naysayers be damned," Isaac said and smiled as he slung back his canteen, allowing some water to splash down the front of his neck, his heaving chest grateful for the cool, refreshing cascade. "I don't see a Redcoat anywhere."

"Nor a line of pistols cocked, ready to shoot the Yankees," Levi agreed.

A number of the townsfolk in Genesee had warned Isaac and his brothers. Many Americans were fearful that a war with Canada could break out at any time. Many others would rather die than live under British rule. Isaac Devins would not let tales of woe deter him from achieving his dreams. Once he had an idea in his head, there was little that would stop him from seeing it through.

Finally, they entered a flat stretch and stopped for a rest. "Newark is the gateway to Upper Canada," Isaac explained to Simeon, who was not paying attention and instead was looking for berries along the path. He was hungry and did not know when they would next eat. Simeon knew better than to ask. His father would whip him silly if he dared.

Up ahead were half a dozen British soldiers guarding four ramshackle buildings, known as Navy Hall. Built by the British Navy during the

American Revolution, the long, narrow, low, stone buildings had a wooden interior and served as barracks for the soldiers, offices for the governor and storage for military supplies. As they approached, Isaac's voice trailed off.

A heavy cedar door opened and three soldiers walked out and stood on the wooden boardwalk that ran between the outer stone building and the riverbank. The shortest of the three men had an impossibly straight posture and was wearing the green and gold of the Queen's Rangers. Every fibre of the short man's being exuded an air of authority. He was obviously in command.

Surely that must be him, thought Isaac, the very person I have come all of this way to see, the one who is the key to my success in Upper Canada.

"Governor Simcoe," Isaac called out as he rushed forward along the boardwalk to the open door. "May I have a word, Your Excellency." In his urgency and excitement, the question came out as more of a statement.

John Graves Simcoe, the Lieutenant Governor of the new Province of Upper Canada, a man of great honour and distinction and an experienced war commander, stared blankly at the young commoner approaching at a rapid pace, his shoes clacking on the boardwalk, his three-rimmed hat rolled up at the sides, an obvious sign of his American heritage.

"Devins, sir, Isaac Devins. We met in Genesee when you were hanging the advertisement up on the village post. You were extolling the virtues of the King's Dominion, inviting all who are loyal to the King to venture north."

Governor Simcoe did recall his excursion down to New York State several months earlier, a recruiting mission he had reluctantly been forced to take. In the ten months since he had been in Niagara, in Upper Canada for that matter, the rate of settlement had been extremely slow, almost negligible. There were fewer than five hundred settlers living in the entire province.

The governor knew he had to be convincing, so he offered free land, two hundred acres, to each person brave enough to move north and settle. The only stipulation was that they had to swear allegiance to the King.

Seeing only a hint of recognition in the governor's eyes, Isaac continued, "I inquired whether your offer of free land to all settlers was intended for each family, to which you replied that every man would receive his due."

Isaac Devins had no notion of propriety or class distinction. Perhaps it was his upbringing in the new democratic State of New York, or perhaps it was his disdain for their wealthy landlord, or even his ancestral roots. Whatever the reason, it made him less fearful, less intimidated than the average peasant. Some, like his father, would say it made him arrogant. It was also the reason he expected, no, demanded, that he meet with success in Upper Canada.

"Ah, yes, Devins, now I remember," the governor replied, unsure whether he actually did recall.

Isaac and his father followed the governor into his office in Navy Hall. The well-appointed room had maps and charts plastered on every wall. Sitting on an ornately carved chair behind a grand oak desk, Governor Simcoe inquired, "Three farmers, a miller and a carpenter, you say? All skilled men, we need that here."

With an eagle feather for a quill, the governor made an entry in the logbook, granting free passage to the Devins family. As he closed the bound parchments, he noted that the last entry had been made more than two weeks ago. He gazed up at the young man standing before him, full of confidence, eager to please, not quite gullible but certainly unschooled. Qualities I can use, he thought strategically. I wonder if I can get the young Isaac Devins to ...

"And my brother-in-law, Nicholas Miller, is in fact a miller," Isaac explained, his voice projecting a cheerful candour, like a deer that leaps into a glade full of saplings, unaware of the hunter's arrow aimed at its heart. He was more than grateful that the governor had chosen to waive the tariff charged to all immigrants arriving in Upper Canada, he was ecstatic. I am already making an impact with the governor, he congratulated himself, pleased at his progress. It is a good omen, Isaac thought.

The sun was setting when they finally entered a small clearing with a few log cabins, sheds and barns scattered randomly along twisting, muddy paths. Wisps of smoke from stone chimneys were the only signs of life. A ring of stumps from freshly fallen trees surrounded the clearing. The towering maples, oaks, beeches and pines looked as if they could easily crush the tiny settlement if a strong wind blew.

"Newark is no more than a cowpatch," grumbled Jacob, the more cynical of the Devins brother.

"Now, now," Abraham gently scolded, "I am sure we will at least find an inn here."

◇◇◇◇◇◇◇◇◇◇◇◇◇◇◇◇◇◇◇◇◇◇◇◇◇◇◇◇◇◇◇◇◇◇◇◇◇◇◇

Later that night, Isaac and Polly lay arm in arm on wool blankets strewn across a barn floor. A French settler had generously offered the Devins' family her barn for the night in exchange for an early morning milking.

"There is nothing that can stand in our way," Isaac declared.

Polly lay quietly, listening to her husband's prattle about becoming a merchant or perhaps a miller or innkeeper, of the fine china, tapestries and riches they would have. She smiled, enjoying her husband's enthusiasm. Always the dreamer, she thought, shaking her head ever so slightly, a bemused half-smile curling her upper lip.

On their Sunday walks back at her father's farm, before they were married, she was enchanted by his drive for success.

"We will have a house so grand, Polly, that the Duke and Duchess of Windsor will stop by for a visit, filled with the finest china and overflowing with spices and scents from around the world. You will become a baroness and I will be a most astute businessman, or perhaps a statesman...." Polly would smile and hold Isaac's hand as they walked along the cherry tree lane where they were hidden from view.

Sensible and smart, Polly knew she had married a man who was far more whimsical than practical. She could see that there was an inner joy, an indomitable spirit of optimism and good faith that refused to be quelled by any hardship. That spirit captured her heart two years ago, and would not let go.

Newark and the whole Niagara Peninsula did indeed show some promise, she had to admit to herself. Perhaps they would be able to leave their life of hardship and servitude behind. Polly let the whimsical part of herself share in her husband's optimism, at least for this night.

Please, Lord, she prayed as Isaac raved on about the grand balls they would host and the luxuries that would fill every room, *have mercy and allow us to find the way*. Rolling over, she felt another twinge in her swollen abdomen that made her wince, a reminder of the uncertainty that lay ahead.

Chapter 2 – June 9, 1793

There is gold here in Niagara, I can feel it, Isaac dreamed as he marched swiftly along the path to Navy Hall, the canvas of his necktie flapping in the early summer breeze.

In his short time in Upper Canada, Isaac had watched as the narrow trail along the river transformed into a three-abreast thoroughfare. Newark grew from a few homes to a lively village with an inn, several taverns, trading posts and businesses in a matter of months. Queenston, just below the escarpment, also flourished with an influx of Americans looking for free land.

The gateway to Upper Canada was wide open in the spring of 1793. Isaac was convinced that he would soon reap the rewards. Already he had been introduced to many of the elite and privileged. Soon I will become a member of their social circle, he thought. Then it is only a matter of time before the governor hands me a choice appointment.

His high spirits diminished, however, as he neared Navy Hall. Yesterday, the governor announced that he wanted to move the capital of Upper Canada to Toronto, and Isaac was appalled. Starting again with nothing in the vast wilderness along the north shore of Lake Ontario did not appeal to him in the slightest. Toronto is nothing more than a dot on a map in an endless pine forest. Niagara is so much more civilized, with greater opportunities, particularly if I continue to meet the right people, thought Isaac as he pushed open the heavy wooden door to the governor's office.

He was determined to change Simcoe's mind, and convince him that Niagara was much better suited to be the capital of Upper Canada.

"I don't think the Americans will dare to cross the mighty Niagara River, Your Excellency. The waterfall will stop them dead in their tracks," Isaac urged.

John Graves Simcoe rose from the fine oak chair behind the intricately carved desk and looked around the ramshackle wooden barracks of Navy Hall. He furrowed his thick dark eyebrows that showed only a hint of grey, ran his fingers through his whitish curly wig and straightened his chest and shoulders. Every day he dressed in full military uniform, complete with a white ruffled shirt inside a long green waistcoat, grey pantaloons and black leather boots, and always liked to stand at attention. Although his aging face showed some deep lines, particularly across his forehead, a youthful exuberance shone through.

"Yes, but there are too many possible routes around it. We can be attacked from too many vantage points, I'm afraid," Simcoe said with a note of finality.

Upon arriving in Niagara the previous year, Simcoe had immediately begun his campaign to reinforce British rule. He changed the ancient Iroquoian name of Niagara, meaning "the thunder of the waters" to Newark, the first of many anglicizations. His troop from the American War, the Queen's Rangers, followed him there to strengthen British domination of the peninsula.

The ever-increasing American presence advancing toward Niagara disturbed him. Only a decade had passed since Simcoe defended the British Crown in the American War of Independence. He wanted to stop the Americans from proceeding farther north. Even more, he wanted them gone, period.

Isaac slowly walked toward the governor, stopping to maintain a respectful distance, keeping his wits about him. He had spoken with the governor many times at Navy Hall since that first day. "Still, Your Excellency, I don't think they will come this far north. No one has the desire. Everyone wants to move west and south."

Isaac was trying to prove himself invaluable to the governor as a source of knowledge of American thought, motivation, and culture. In the last few weeks, he witnessed Simcoe assigning high-profile government positions to his contemporaries, something that he wanted for himself. He hoped the governor would view his American heritage as an asset, not as a threat. A man could make a small fortune in a position of power in the untouched new country. His determination and desire for recognition and wealth led Isaac to call on the governor every day.

The governor turned and fixed a steely gaze back at Isaac, noting his keen blue eyes, his straw-coloured hair neatly tied at the back, his well-kept but unadorned daycoat and his youthful exuberance. Simcoe did value Isaac's opinion because of the Devins' long history in the United States. However, he was wary that Isaac's words could be ill-intentioned or deliberately misleading. Little did Isaac know that Simcoe could not fully trust an American, no matter how loyal.

"We have the British forts here, on the southern shores of the Great Lakes," agreed the governor, pointing to the map. "But there are no armed forces to stop the Americans from claiming the Indian territory."

The Northwest Indian War had been raging since well before the War of Independence. Simcoe was strongly in favour of Britain aiding the Indian Confederacy, which claimed the land north of the settled area in New York state and Ohio territory. A large tract of wilderness between the Americans and Upper Canada controlled by an Indian Confederacy was exactly what Simcoe wanted to protect the new province. The governor firmly believed that the fledgling "United States" would fall apart and one day come under British rule again.

Isaac eagerly pointed to the western frontier beyond Philadelphia, the epicentre of migration to the colonies. "When Daniel Boone cut the Cumberland Pass here just before the war, everyone started climbing over the Appalachians and west of the thirteen colonies," insisted Isaac. "More than one hundred thousand people followed him into the frontier over the last fifteen years, spreading west and south. Now that Kentucky has joined the United States, this will drive the Americans farther west still."

True, thought the governor, but the settler's view was a little short-sighted. An order from Lord Dorchester to cede Fort Niagara to the Americans had arrived a few days prior. The British still had control over the French-built forts along the south side of the Great Lakes, even though they were in American territory. Simcoe did not want to give up Fort Niagara or any of the other forts along the Great Lakes. They were vital to his plans to one day invade New York and Ohio and take back the territory the British had lost.

Simcoe rose, shaking his head, and sat down again in the wooden chair, his back straight as a board. "And after they move west, and find any sort of resistance, they will move northward with even greater aplomb," he said.

"Yes, Your Excellency," conceded Isaac, looking at the governor with a steady gaze, "but even if the natives receive support from the Dutch or the Germans, the Americans will not venture north of the Great Lakes, it is the natural dividing point."

At the mention of a greater European presence, Simcoe cast a quick glance over to Isaac. He thought of how to bait the settler into providing details when his manservant rapped on the door, cleared his throat and requested permission to enter.

"Yes, yes, come in, Alfred, what is it?"

"Your Excellency, Peter Russell has just returned from Detroit and requests an audience with you."

Simcoe sighed. "Very well, I will meet him at the stables."

The Governor rose quickly, adjusted his tunic, fanned his wig and with a terse nod strode through the doorway, his back solid and straight, a pose calculated so that he always looked like he was *en guarde*.

Isaac sat and slowly leaned back in the governor's chair, his eyes surveying the rolled-up parchments, stacks of communiqués, and the envelopes on the finely crafted oak desk, transported from Simcoe's estate in Devon. There must be a ream of information here, some of it classified, thought Isaac, fascinated by the chattels of a man with so much power. Although he had sworn an oath of loyalty to the King when they had arrived in Upper Canada, he did not yet feel a sense of loyalty to the British. His motivation for coming to Upper Canada was much more self-serving.

Damn, I had no opportunity to discourage the governor from switching the capital to Toronto, thought Isaac, chastising himself for not being more direct. Over the past five weeks, Isaac had played a carefully orchestrated cat-and-mouse game with the governor. He agreed with Simcoe on almost everything, offering as much knowledge and insight as he could. But when the moment was right, Isaac would casually voice his own agenda. It was a game Isaac was confident he would win.

He leaned over and started to read a letter the governor had just begun to Lord Dorchester that seemed to question the distribution of ships on the Great Lakes when he heard a soft voice clear her throat. Isaac glanced upwards and blurted out, "Good day, Mrs. Simcoe."

He nervously jumped to attention, his abruptness admitting his clandestine intentions. Damn, he silently cursed.

Elizabeth Simcoe, a diminutive, dark-eyed lady with chocolate brown hair and a piercing gaze, stood quietly, hands clasped behind her back, with a slightly alarmed expression.

"Where is the governor?" she inquired, adjusting the fine silk scarf wrapped over her shoulder. She always referred to her husband that way, even in private. Perhaps it was her upbringing as the daughter of a wealthy landlord or perhaps it was a sign of a dry, intelligent humour. Her clever mind knew what she had witnessed. There was no question that she would promptly report Isaac's intrusion to her husband.

Isaac told her about the governor's meeting at the stables and, with a quick bow and touch to his hat, skulked out into the crisp, mid-afternoon sun. The expression on Mrs. Simcoe's face was hard to decipher. The last thing I need is to have the governor question my loyalty, Isaac berated himself. He did not want the long hours spent in Simcoe's office, listening to him strategize about nearly every topic, to be a waste of time.

Lost in thought, Isaac plodded along the path that separated the crumbling barracks from the river's edge. Light glimmered off the mighty rolling Niagara River and danced along the rapids. Suddenly, the sky blackened. Isaac looked up to see thousands of passenger pigeons crossing over to the American side, unaware of the territorial tension below. The pigeons flew so low that Isaac instinctively crouched over, shoulders shrugged, feeling the wind generated by thousands of flapping wings brush over him. He heard a volley of gunshots, and then a second coming from the east. The soldiers at Fort Niagara are in for a feast tonight, he reckoned.

There must be another way to convince Simcoe to stay in Niagara, he thought wistfully. Isaac knew that he had to approach the governor tactfully. He had witnessed the governor's volatility on several occasions, which seemed to arise from a mere pittance. Rumour had it that in England, Simcoe once had ordered a young sentry executed for leaving his post for five minutes. Isaac did not wish to test the governor's patience.

Turning right at the fork, Isaac climbed the steep embankment, his deer-skin boots sending stones careening down the muddy path. The warm spring breeze blew Isaac's sandy fine hair across his face. Soon the unmistakable sound of footsteps and crackling branches resounded through the woods, and Isaac looked up to see a heavyset, well-tailored figure with black leather knee-high boots pounding down the steep incline and a curly white wig slightly askew.

"Have you seen the governor, Devins?" a condescending voice inquired.

Jarvis! Isaac swore under his breath, annoyed to run into the deplorable ass.

"Why yes, he has gone to meet Mr. Russell at the stables. He may still be there," Isaac replied with a show of decorum, despite the fact that he detested the man more than anyone he had ever met.

"I must catch him before he embarks for Toronto," Jarvis muttered as he scrambled down the path followed by a young African – one of six slaves Jarvis had brought from England. Isaac tipped his hat to the young man who did not acknowledge his greeting but kept his eyes locked on the path in front of him.

William Jarvis was an American who had fought under Simcoe's command in Pennsylvania and was wounded in the American Revolutionary War. After his property was confiscated by the Americans, Jarvis followed Simcoe to London. The Governor, who valued loyalty greatly, convinced

Jarvis to accompany him to Upper Canada by offering him the position of Secretary to the Executive Council.

That kind of appointment was exactly what Isaac wanted. Though his father could not afford to send him to Harvard, he considered himself to be as capable as any educated gentleman. If a pompous, dimwitted, snivelling wretch like William Jarvis could gain the governor's favour, reasoned Isaac, surely Simcoe would reward a bright, eager Loyalist like himself.

How unfortunate that we didn't come here one year earlier, lamented Isaac, for the first meeting of the Parliament of Upper Canada. That was when the governor had freely handed out high-ranking positions to almost anyone. Isaac was certain that if they had arrived in Niagara then, he would have been elected to the Legislative Assembly at the very least, and perhaps even appointed a position of power like Jarvis. Instead, he now had to lobby for a position, competing against other settlers who were arriving almost every day, as well as against the British elite that Simcoe relentlessly campaigned to join him in the new province.

Light penetrated the dark woods as Isaac neared the top of the hill, the highest point overlooking Newark and Navy Hall. He entered a clearing on level ground, then walked along a narrow path through the tall prairie grass billowing in the wind. Ahead of him were three brown canvas tents, stiff and sturdy, each one almost the size of a two-room log cabin.

The governor's canvas tents were once owned by Captain James Cook, the famous explorer, navigator and cartographer who sailed around the world three times and discovered more unknown lands than any other.

The governor proudly told Isaac one afternoon that Cook had once served as a master under the command of Simcoe's father, Captain John Simcoe, on board the *Pembroke* when it sailed to Lower Canada. His father helped the British to seize Fort Louisbourg in Halifax from the French. Simcoe's father did not return from that voyage, succumbing to pneumonia when his son was seven years old. The younger Simcoe, forever trying to live up to his father's name, purchased the tents in London at a public auction prior to sailing to Upper Canada.

Isaac stopped for a quick peek into the last tent, the living quarters for the governor and his wife. Polly had marvelled over the fine luxuries in the Simcoes' tent a few weeks earlier when Isaac had brought her up to the plateau without telling her the reason for their visit. Her knees almost collapsed as she gasped with delight, thrilled to see such finery.

"Well, I never," Polly exclaimed as her eyes danced around the room, noting the rich colours of the linens and tapestries, the fine china, the intricately carved patterns on the oak chairs, tables, hutches and bureaus.

"This is a room fit for a king," she declared, "or at least what I expect a royal's quarters to be like."

Polly suddenly felt the urge to sneak inside the tent and feel the soft silks and velvet running through her fingers, taste the fancy pastries left over from afternoon tea, sit on the high back oak chair with plush, soft cushions. She had heard about the elaborate balls that the governor's wife hosted here, the guests consuming fine wines and spirits after an elaborate formal dinner, then dancing under the stars in the midsummer night.

Isaac recalled the look of hurt and anguish that spread across her face as he held her arm, refusing her passage. She had turned and walked away, her long neck gracefully arched downward like a swan searching for a minnow.

Never again, thought Isaac as he reached his favourite lookout, a granite boulder high atop of a cliff on the escarpment.

Sitting down, legs dangling over the high cliff, he stared across the light green carpet of trees stretching toward the American territory far below. The dark brown of the wooden bunkers and blockhouses at Fort Niagara played against the white silhouette of the French chateau at the tip of the peninsula, with sunlight dancing on the shimmering waters of Lake Ontario. Leaning over, he saw the Niagara river far below, the turbulent, blue water providing life to the British colony, only one thousand strong in the province and spread over a huge territory.

Never again will Polly have to imagine finery from a distance, dreaming of a life that she cannot have, vowed Isaac. Yes, he could feel it. Newark, Upper Canada, was where he would make his fortune.

Chapter 3– Morning of June 16, 1793

Polly stirred from a deep, restful sleep, shaking her head back and forth ever so slightly as the first ray of sunlight streamed across her smooth, angelic face. Her green eyes greeted the morning light with curiosity, as they did every morning, then surveyed the two-room log cabin that the family had hastily built on the outskirts of Newark.

She glanced over at her older sister, Rita, sleeping soundly, curled in the arms of her protective husband, Isaac's brother Levi, completely unaware of the cacophony of bird calls that began at first light. She could barely see Isaac's father, Abraham, and his stepmother, Elizabeth, slumbering on a straw bed in the far corner, their sleeping forms rising and falling. Little Simeon slept soundly at their feet, looking peaceful as only a child can. Isaac's twin, Jacob, his wife, Mary, and Isaac's sister, Sarah, and her husband, Nicholas Miller, were sound asleep on the floor in the other room.

How serene and magical the morning is, she thought as she struggled up to her elbows, pushing her long, auburn hair back into her muslin nightcap. She instinctively reached to her right, expecting to feel Isaac's lean, muscular body but instead felt only the cold cotton sheets. He must be up and about early, she surmised, disappointed that she could not feel his warmth.

Polly slowly rolled out of bed and wandered to the window, glancing out at the dirt road and collection of wood shanties hastily erected by other Americans who arrived in Niagara almost daily now. Most settlers, like the Devins, built shanties wherever they could find space.

Yawning, she stretched one arm upward and the other arm sideways, feeling newfound energy enlightening her being. She spotted a tiny figure off in the distance that appeared to be chopping wood at the edge of the settlement.

Isaac let the axe fall where it may, splitting wood randomly and carelessly, barely aware of the black flies that swarmed around him. He grabbed a log from the pile, placed it on the cutting stump and expertly swung the axe downward, splitting the wood with one strike. He then quartered the pieces, making them small enough for Polly to build the morning fire in the little wood stove he had purchased a month ago from a Mississauga trader.

Another breakfast of cornbread, he grumbled as he carried the chopped wood back to the shanty in a twine sack swung over his shoulder. Corn flour was the only grain to be had since their arrival in Niagara almost six weeks ago. The Mississaugas harvested corn along the river banks leading to the Great Lakes, and had a steady supply to trade with the settlers.

Unloading the sack onto the wood pile beside the cabin, Isaac stood and stared into the distance, his mind racing, wondering if his meeting with the Honourable John White today would be enough to change the evening vote. He hoped to persuade White to vote against Governor Simcoe and keep the capital of Upper Canada in Toronto. Every time he heard Simcoe rave about Toronto, it heightened his resolve to thwart the governor's plans.

His silent campaign appeared to be working. He definitely had heard William Jarvis, Thomas Talbot and James Baby voice their approval of staying in Niagara on several occasions. But he still needed to convince Peter Russell and John White. If he could sway just one or two other members of the Legislative Assembly to oppose Simcoe's motion, then moving the capital to Toronto would be defeated; at least, that is what he hoped.

Isaac's trance was abruptly interrupted when he felt Polly's hands at his hips. In a flash he swung around and grabbed her skirts, swinging her up into his arms.

"What are you so lost in thought about?" she asked, laughing, enjoying his playfulness.

Glancing into her sparkling green eyes, Isaac kissed her and said, "Nothing much, just the whole future of our new country."

"You are still against the move to Toronto then," said Polly, raising her eyebrows and frowning slightly. "You know that I want to go, don't you, to start in an unspoiled territory."

In the short time since arriving in Niagara, Polly had quickly realized their "place" in the new colony. Many of the established ladies in their fine linen dresses and feathered bonnets deliberately snubbed her attempts to greet them.

He walked a few paces and sat Polly gently down on a maple stump. "But I also know that we will be better off here. In Niagara, we can build our future, raise our children," he proclaimed as he patted her rounded belly, "and reap our fortune."

Polly smiled, always amused at her husband's whimsical reverie, and guided his hand over to where she felt the baby kicking. "We will at least have a roof over our heads here for the little one," she said cheerily, keeping her doubts to herself.

As they sauntered back to the cabin in the crimson glow of the morning light, Isaac's mind drifted back to his plan to meet with John White later. If he could speak with him first, before anyone else had a chance, perhaps he could plant a seed of doubt. Perhaps he could cast enough uncertainty that White would vote against Simcoe. Perhaps he could persuade him to get the other members of the Legislative Assembly to vote against the move. Perhaps he could ...

"Isaac, would you please be seated for breakfast, you have been standing in the doorway blocking the sunlight long enough," reproached his stepmother as she scurried back to the wood stump in the centre of the room that served as the table, her long black calico skirt billowing behind like a galloping mare.

Isaac sat and stared at the plate of cornbread in the centre of the stump table, ignoring his family's friendly chatter. Swirling a piece slowly in a plate of maple syrup, he wondered if White was approachable, unlike someone like William Jarvis.

Gobbling the last bite, Isaac jumped up from the table, almost sending the maple-stump chair crashing into the earthen floor. "I'm off to the Fort," he informed them as he grabbed his shotgun, canteen and straw hat. He barely heard his stepmother's reprimand as he strode outside into the fresh spring air and headed along Main Street lined with scattered stores, inns and houses extending to the edge of the village.

He reached the King's Wharf in a few minutes, barely aware of the clouds gathering over the horizon, threatening to change the course of the day. Shuffling on board the flat-bottom bateau, the short ferry took himself and five others across the Niagara River to the American side. Passing two pence to the ferryman, Isaac followed the well-worn portage route leading to Fort Niagara.

The trail would surely be wide enough for Little Star, lamented Isaac, as he thought of his cherished black mare stolen on their journey to Upper Canada. The Devins family was only twenty miles from reaching the safety of Fort Niagara that cold, crisp morning. Isaac was shovelling the ashes from the previous night's fire into an old oak bucket when Little Star's whinnying cry pierced the silence of the dawn, warning of danger.

Isaac hurled the shovel down. A burning ember flew upward from the firepit and struck him below his right eye. Shocked, he sprung backward and stepped on the handle of the shovel, catapulting a pile of ashes at himself like a blanket of frost on a cool autumn morning. Shielding his eyes, he staggered forward, gasping for breath, choking. When he finally emerged, he was covered from head to toe with light grey soot. Everything but his eyes was drenched.

Little Star cried out again.

Using the forest for cover, Isaac rounded the wagons where his family slept, crouched down and saw one Mohawk in full warrior headgear perched on his brother's horse and another mounting Little Star, who was prancing and kicking, fearful of the strangers, aware of their ill intentions. Isaac felt his calf muscles constrict, a sign that every nerve ending in his body was alerted and awaiting a command.

Isaac clenched his pocketknife, the only weapon he was carrying. He took aim and cocked his arm backward.

Out of nowhere, he saw five-year-old Simeon scamper ahead and beat the foot of the taller Mohawk, now mounted on Little Star, with a bread pan. Without thinking, Isaac charged out of the woods, arms flailing to draw their attention, covered in ashes like a ghostly mirage, yielding a battle cry so voluminous that it startled the Mohawks and awakened his brothers, who grabbed their guns.

The younger Mohawk reached down, snatched Simeon, and galloped frantically down the trail while the other found a clearing and clambered off through the forest. Isaac quickly aimed and flung his only weapon, piercing the Mohawk in the right shoulder blade.

Then the sound of gunshots ripped through the air.

He turned his head and yelled, "No! They've got Simeon!"

Isaac turned back. His eyes widened. Simeon was reaching for the knife, then he pulled it out of the gaping wound, blood pouring down the Mohawk's back. Isaac's lungs filled with air, his diaphragm contracted, he arched his back. The sound of his unearthly cry, "NO-O-O-O-O-O-O-O-O," resounded through the woods, echoed through the trees, bounced off rocks, reflected off streams and puddles, and overpowered the sound of the horses' hooves, as he feared that the Mohawk would grab his tomahawk and do away with Simeon.

Much to his surprise, the Mohawk pushed Simeon to the ground, wrapped his arms around Little Star's neck and fled at high speed. Isaac's brothers fired off a round of shots but to no avail. Little Star and the brown mare were gone.

Simeon ran back along the trail into his brother's outstretched arms. The little boy's bravado was gone. Tears streamed down his face, his body convulsing.

Isaac patted his mop of curly brown hair, and said, "There now, Simeon, you almost had him. What a brave lad you are."

After a time, Simeon stepped back and looked up at Isaac with his innocent smoke-grey eyes, the colour intensified by tears. "But the Mohawks took Little Star," he whispered.

That's not all they took, grunted Isaac under his breath. With the horses gone, the Devins family now had to carry on to Fort Niagara with all their belongings on their back. They could ill afford to wait for the next group of travellers or soldiers to come along and assist them as the Mohawks were now aware of their exact location in the dangerous, war-torn frontier, the land that the natives claimed as their own. The Mohawks could easily outnumber them, take the women and Simeon, and scalp the men.

"We will leave in an hour," commanded Abraham. "We cannot be more than two days from the Fort. We shall have to make our camp off the trail and not light any fires, lest they find us."

The three brothers stripped the top bunker and canvas cover off the wagon and then loaded it with their feather beds, pillows and tools. Isaac insisted on filling the rest of the wagon with the bags of soot he had meticulously put together. Every evening on their journey, Isaac kept a fire burning through the night so that he could collect the ashes the next morning. He hoped to sell them at Fort Niagara to a merchant who would ship them back to Britain as the English were desperately in need of potash for gunpowder.

"If the merchants won't take the ashes, we can leach them down in the kettle to make the lye, which they will surely take," he explained to his brothers as he hoisted another sack of ashes onto the wagon. "This will be our only source of income or barter when we arrive, and we will need it to purchase seed, horses and oxen. Here, Levi, help me with this last sack."

They quickly resumed their trek along the Mohawk Trail toward Fort Niagara. The men pulled the heavy wagon, meant for horses, and the wives followed behind, carrying the household goods on their backs. Simeon, alone at the rear, was instructed to drive the pigs and chickens with a walnut branch.

"No, this way," Simeon hollered at the chickens that had wandered off into the woods, refusing to follow his lead.

Lagging farther and farther behind, Simeon finally caught up to the rest of his family with fewer than half the animals he had started with. The little boy looked down at the ground, expecting to be scolded, but for once no one took notice. Everyone was pushing and pulling on the wagon that had fallen into a bottomless swamp. They tried in vain for an hour to dislodge it, but the wagon only sunk in deeper.

"Father," Isaac began, completely devastated, as he walked over and put his hands on his father's arms. "The brothers are—"

"Enough!" commanded Abraham, straightening his body, as if Isaac's embrace had renewed his resolve. He thrust his shoulders back and turned around to face all of them.

"We will continue. Now," he said quietly, with strength in his conviction, nodding his head and pushing Simeon forward.

And that is how we arrived in Niagara with only half of our possessions, penniless, and no ashes to trade for food or lodging, thought Isaac with a scowl as he tromped along the portage route to Fort Niagara. Fortune was certainly not smiling on the Devins family that day. Unlike his father, Isaac was not a particularly religious man. Luck follows those who look for it, he instead would say. Though it was not something anyone could rely on, at least fortune was not discriminatory. Even the poorest sop could be handsomely rewarded.

The green canopy thinned as Isaac stepped into a grassy, dry meadow that stretched out to the water's edge. Looking across the Niagara River, he could see Navy Hall on the west side and a few buildings farther north at the mouth that must be Newark. Up ahead was an unmistakable, long, narrow berm, ten feet in height, a burial plot for British and French soldiers, Americans, and Iroquois warriors who fought and died here over the last hundred and fifty years. Beyond this, only the tops of some of the taller buildings in the fort could be seen above the earthworks.

Isaac stopped when he heard muffled voices, laughter and shouts. Never had he seen so many wigwams, row upon row, full of warriors, women and children wearing deerskin tunics, colourful beads, feathers in their hair, hunting knives and moccasins. Many native clans sought refuge at Fort Niagara, escaping the war-torn Indian Territory in Ohio, New York and Michigan. The British allowed any anti-American clan to stay as long as they wanted.

With growing excitement, Isaac's gait quickened to an almost galloping pace when he finally saw the stockade. His heart filled with memories of listening to his grandfather's stories outside the shed, perched on a stump, the hot sun beating down on his shoulders, of the bloody battles won and lost at Fort Niagara.

"Halt ye," a sentry called out, "and state ye business."

Isaac's hurried gait had alarmed the British soldiers guarding the fort, who emerged from an outpost with bayonets pointed straight at Isaac's heart.

Isaac kept his hands steady, and stood at attention as he slowly and carefully replied, "Devins is the name, and I have just ferried here from Newark. I have a meeting with the Honourable John White this morning at the White Chateau. He is expecting me."

Isaac was gambling that the occupancy of the Fort would be near capacity and that the sentries could not possibly know the comings and goings of all the dignitaries.

The sentry glared at him with one eye cocked. "What regiment are ye from?" the sentry demanded as he kept his eyes steady on Isaac's chest, ready for any slight movement, tightening his grip on his weapon.

"I'm not from any at all, sir. My family arrived in Niagara six weeks ago and we were welcomed by His Excellency, Governor Simcoe himself," Isaac stated.

"A colonist," sneered the taller sentry. They confiscated Isaac's shotgun and escorted him to the Fort, one soldier on either side. Marching speedily through the outer gates and stockade, they trod over the wooden drawbridge spanning the steeply sloped moat.

"I swore my allegiance to the King, by the grace of God, two fortnights ago," Isaac added with a steady, even tone, wanting to appear unabashed.

His words fell on deaf ears. The soldiers pushed him forward with their bayonets nudging his back. They marched past the southern redoubt, a large stone building with a pagoda-style roof topped with a copper weather vane, and stomped through a maze of wooden barracks, mess halls, blockhouses, a church and officer quarters. British soldiers, civilians, Mohawks, Mississaugas and Senecas were everywhere. But there were very few Yankees, even though they were on American soil.

Isaac's eyes widened. In front of him was the white-stone chateau he had seen from his favourite lookout on the high cliff near Simcoe's canvas tents. The sprawling two-storey mansion with a mansard roof was the largest building he had ever seen. Massive wooden doors more than double Isaac's height were guarded by two Redcoats. Isaac studied the area below the roof, looking for the hidden cannons that his grandfather told him were used to surprise enemy ships attacking from the north. It was far more impressive than he had ever imagined.

The smaller sentry told Isaac to stop and motioned off to the right. They waited in silence, then the larger sentry cleared his throat and announced, "Your Honour, we have accompanied this man here who claims that he has an engagement scheduled with you this morning."

A tall, dark, handsome, rather stout Englishman turned toward them and placed his hands behind his back. A fine gold pocket watch dangled presumptuously from his morningcoat. His distinguished demeanour gave him the appearance of a much older gentleman than his thirty years of age. Isaac noted that his sharp grey eyes and chiselled cheekbones seemed to contrast with the grandiose, old-fashioned white wig he wore.

He seemed to be a little perplexed as he took one step forward, inquiring, "Have we been acquainted?"

At this, the sentries tightened their grip around Isaac's stiff arms.

Isaac blurted out, "I have the most compelling news regarding the Parliament session this afternoon that you simply must hear."

Intrigued, John White, a London-trained barrister with the distinction of serving in the hallowed ins of Court, replied, "Do continue, sir."

"I fear that His Excellency, Governor Simcoe, will err in his judgment today on a most delicate issue," Isaac implored, "and I believe that you have the wisdom and the power to correct such an error, sir."

White's eyebrows lowered, his eyes changing from inquisitive to calculating. His years in the courtrooms of England and Jamaica had taught him never to dismiss anything. Even the smallest, insignificant scrap may become useful at some point in time.

"Release him," he ordered. The sentries stepped backward, saluted, returned Isaac's gun and withdrew.

Putting his arm over Isaac's shoulder, John White led him toward a hitching post where a black stallion with white hooves was grazing. Although he was an aristocrat and a gentleman, White was a man of the people. He began his discourse in mid-sentence, oblivious to Isaac's intentions.

"I know that Governor Simcoe is equally appalled by the keeping of slaves as I am. He gave me his word that he would support the bill that I put forward today. He knows how dearly I want to ensure that Upper Canada is above that most unsavoury practice. Could anyone else have lobbied him since then? Have you heard, sir, that he will now side with the colonists? I find that most disturbing."

"I am unaware of the governor's position on slavery, though I certainly would support an anti-slavery bill myself," Isaac quickly explained. He had befriended a number of African slaves in Orange County as they worked side by side, erecting a new mill on the landlord's farm. "I was referring, in fact, to the governor's preference for Toronto as the seat of government, rather than this very terrain."

"Yes, yes, I agree that Newark is a far superior location for our Parliament meetings," White agreed. "Why would one want to start again in the wilderness? But what about the slavery issue, man? Did you - what did you say your name was again?

"Devins, sir, Isaac Devins."

"Did you witness any dealings with our governor that could abolish the anti-slavery bill? Has he had any acquaintance in the last fortnight that could in any way be suspicious?" White's voice became agitated, almost accusing.

"Not that I am aware of, sir," Isaac responded in an even tone, trying to cool White's demeanor. "He only met with the Mohawk leader, Joseph Brant, last week at Navy Hall and with none other than the Executive Council during the Parliament sessions."

White's shoulders relaxed. He put one hand under his chin and stared past Isaac at the straw bale that his horse was nibbling on. "Then I still have a chance to push the bill forward," he reasoned, "and I must try to see Talbot and Russell before this afternoon's session."

He walked off toward the white chateau, deep in thought. "William Jarvis and James Baby will not support the bill, they already have slaves. But what about Major Small, he might be approachable. And then there is …"

John White continued to talk until he was out of Isaac's earshot. Isaac thought it best not to pursue him. He is clearly in favour of keeping the capital in Niagara, and that is what matters, he thought. White's opinion will have considerable influence since he is a lawyer and the Attorney-General of Upper Canada, Isaac thought, and seemed like a reasonable fellow.

Isaac hurried back along the trail. As he passed a group of Senecas, he looked for Little Star, as he always did, hoping that the little black mare would somehow be there. He imagined how he would steal her away from her captors, ride off into the woods and take her to Simeon who would be overcome with joy at her return.

Looking up at the position of the sun, Isaac raced to the dock to catch the mid-day ferry. He did not want to miss the afternoon Parliament session.

Chapter 4 – Afternoon of June 16, 1793

Hannah Jarvis pinched her tight bodice at the back, desperately trying to hide her recent weight loss within the billows of her lilac silk skirt. A rotund lady is a well-kept lady, she reminded herself, and Hannah was determined to be viewed as a woman of importance, the matriarch of the colony, or at the very least the wife of a man of great influence.

She vigorously shook her shoulders and leaned forward at the waist in hopes that the gown would fall lower, revealing more of her bosom and less of her hips. Stepping gingerly forward, she keenly observed the flow of the skirt as it swayed to and fro. The tailor in Montreal had assured her that the hoops would last until the summer, but the skirt did seem to be buckling ever so slightly on the left side. Damn the incompetent sentries who had unloaded their belongings at the Queenston dock last fall upon their arrival. Good help was so hard to get in Upper Canada.

Born into a well-to-do family in New York, Hannah Jarvis was accustomed to the finer things in life. She expected nothing less than excellence, and was cantankerous when her expectations were not met. Foolishly, she had wed William more out of love than for position and had lived quite modestly among the aristocracy in London after the American War of Independence. Much too modestly, in her opinion, for the daughter of a land baron to endure.

Governor Simcoe had promised her husband substantial riches if he accompanied him to Canada. Unfortunately, the pot of gold proved to be elusive. Their time in Lower Canada was most unfruitful, and apart from assuming a position in the elite society of Montreal, they hardly increased their fortune. The last nine months in Newark were no better. Her husband's position as the Secretary of the Executive Council did not amount to much. He had not been paid a farthing since they arrived.

Last week's Parliament session, however, changed everything. Hannah's continual badgering had finally paid off. William was appointed the Registrar General for Upper Canada. For every land transaction, he would receive one shilling. Since tens of thousands were expected to immigrate, he stood to make a fortune.

Hannah Jarvis was so delighted that she could hardly sleep, imagining the gowns she would wear, the balls she would host, the introductions she would have, the homes they would own, the jewels she would flaunt. Most importantly, she dreamed of the reverence that would be bestowed upon them by the common folk. They would certainly be regarded as royalty.

A registrar general's wife is only the beginning, she mused. The position would lead the way to even greater appointments ... and one day she would outdo that stuttering little vixen, Elizabeth Simcoe, leave her flat-footed in the dust of her wagon tracks. Oh yes, she would wipe that annoying, smug look off of her wretched little face once and for all. Elizabeth Simcoe may be wealthy and she may be known for her lavish parties, but her days as the "Queen" of Upper Canada would be short-lived.

Now that William was Registrar General, there would be no function that she could not attend, and any attempt to leave her out of it would be viewed as excessively hostile by all. Soon, she would be the *grande dame*, able to choose who to invite to her own lavish parties and, more importantly, who not to invite.

Upon hearing a soft knock, Hannah walked a few paces and swung the oak door wide open. Relieved to see her housekeeper arrive well before the afternoon tea, she quickly ushered her in, insisting that she remove her shoes so as to not track dirt into the house. Polly glanced upward at Hannah Jarvis, offered a brief smile and nodded as she lifted her black muslin dress and entered the fine home.

Several weeks ago, Polly had overheard Hannah Jarvis loudly declare that the only slaves they owned were male and she was in desperate need of a housekeeper. Polly offered her services at once.

The Devins' family was desperately in need of cash and supplies. Isaac and his brothers had been unable to find paid work in Niagara as there were too many other poor souls looking for the same. With most of their possessions left behind in the mud along the trail, the Devins had little they could trade for basic necessities. Polly's salary of eighty shillings per week was a godsend, sufficient to purchase three sturdy axes and a hammer the first week, and a large cast iron pot and a bundle of twine the second. The brothers could now fell trees and make potash for sale or barter.

She removed her shoes as she had been instructed, and followed Mrs. Jarvis into the well-appointed kitchen. Polly refused to curtsey, which was the customary way a servant greeted one's employer. Hannah had to put up with this little act of insubordination just to ensure that Polly would not leave her stranded. Most immigrants were too busy setting up their own homesteads and livelihood to bother offering domestic service.

Polly glanced appreciatively around the kitchen at the many gadgets and contraptions above the hearth and hanging on the walls, many of which she did not yet know how to use. When no one was looking, she would slip into the bedroom and gaze into the looking glass, something she had done only a few times before as a little girl when she had befriended a travelling pedlar who, taking a liking to the rosy-cheeked, sparkly eyed child, allowed her to do so free of charge.

"Polly, dear, could you kindly make some of those delightful cranberry tarts that you made last Wednesday?" Hannah requested. "And please use the rosewood china for the tea. Here is the key."

"Certainly," replied Polly, taking the finely carved maple tea box from the mantle. Tea was so precious that all settlers kept it locked. How she longed to have a nice, relaxing cup of camomile tea. Perhaps she would make a little extra. If only she could take a little home and share it with her family.

She heard a rap on the door knocker and scurried to answer it. "Good afternoon, Mrs. Hamilton," she offered and ushered the guest into the parlour. What a lovely crimson gown, Polly thought, with white lace at the throat and an array of black feathers in the bonnet.

More guests arrived, and Polly flitted about, happily making the pastries and compote in the well-appointed kitchen. She always enjoyed listening to the ladies' gay chatter. They mostly talked of books they had read, balls they had attended, journeys their husband's were taking and the happenings of high society in Montreal and London. Their lives seemed so different from her own, much more extravagant, adventurous.

As she entered the parlour to pour the tea, Polly noted that the conversation this afternoon was much more serious, even sombre. "I do believe that there is absolutely no advantage to relocating to Toronto," declared Mrs. Talbot as she reached across the table to select another pastry.

"Quite right," agreed Hannah Jarvis. "Can you imagine having to begin again with nothing, in the complete wilderness? The thought of foraging for a bed to sleep on makes my skin crawl."

"Here we have our homes, new roads, a prayer hall, a new wagon shop. So many traders stop at Fort Niagara that there is nothing you can't get, if you have the money," added Mrs. Hamilton, whose husband ran the largest warehouse in the Niagara peninsula.

"And your home is so lovely, Catherine," offered Hannah, who was secretly jealous of the elegant, two-storey, stone and lumber ranch overlooking the Niagara River that the Hamiltons had just built.

Robert and Catherine Hamilton had settled in Queenston immediately following the American Revolution. Before long, Robert Hamilton was the wealthiest man in Upper Canada. His warehouse was so large that people travelled many miles to go there for furs, flour, salt, beef, peas, pork and whiskey. His dock on the Queenston Flats was the sole receiver of all British military supplies. To top that off, Governor Simcoe just awarded him the contract to build a new portage trail around the Falls on the west side of the Niagara River, As soon as the road opens, even more settlers would go to his store for supplies.

Hannah glanced around the sitting room of the four-room log home that they had purchased upon their arrival in Newark, having found nothing else that was suitable. Though it was a step up from the two-room shanties that the settlers hastily built upon arrival, it was hardly the home for a registrar general's wife. Her fine oak table with the elegantly carved chairs seemed too large for the meagre sitting room, whose dim light cast deep shadows on her portrait hanging over the end table.

Her thoughts were interrupted by the quiet, assured voice of Elizabeth Simcoe, who always seemed to command attention.

"I am sure that the wilderness in Toronto will not prevent our fine carpenters from constructing the most elegant homes. We shall be able to continue our tradition of holding a ball every fortnight within no time at all. Our social life will not suffer, never fear. I am sure we will be able to continue our Wednesday games of whist as well."

Hannah Jarvis involuntarily sniffed three times while straightening her spine, then replied, "Elizabeth, you have the entire Queen's Rangers at your disposal to clear your land and set up your home, something most of us are not fortunate enough to have. It will be a struggle, to say the least."

"Can you not convince the governor to keep the capital here?" asked Mrs. Talbot.

Isaac overheard Mrs. Simcoe's answer as he strode past the window, the sash open to allow the breeze in. "The governor is as strong in his conviction that Toronto will be the capital as I am in my desire to finish the last pastry," Elizabeth smiled as she reached across the table.

The governor may be strong in his conviction, but his councillors may think otherwise, Isaac mused as he sauntered along the path past the Jarvis home on his way to the Parliament session. He was positive that he had lobbied enough people to ensure that the vote would favour staying in Niagara. So far, Jarvis, Talbot, Baby, White, and likely Peter Russell told him that they would vote against the move to Toronto.

He took the lower path past Navy Hall, then swung around the back and sat himself under the window. Only the aristocrats were permitted into the Parliament sessions. The large room in the stone structure had several tables and chairs, but most of the sixteen members of the Legislature and their cronies were scattered throughout the room. Isaac could hear John White's voice as he began to read the seventh bill on slavery.

"Whereas it is unjust," White stated calmly, "that a people should encourage the introduction of slaves and whereas it is highly expedient to abolish slavery, be it enacted that it shall be unlawful to issue a permit for the introduction of slaves into the province."

White carefully read the legislation, penned after many hours of consultation with Governor Simcoe. His voice became more passionate as he stated the final words: "Furthermore, it shall be unlawful for any contract into which a person is listed as a slave to be binding after the passing of this Act."

John White looked triumphantly around the room, proud of his efforts, and quite certain that such a compelling piece of legislation that righted so hideous an injustice would be duly applauded. It will be the talk of the House of Lords back in London, he fantasized, and my name will become synonymous with the great parliamentarians of Britain.

Instead, dead silence echoed through the hall. Isaac stood up outside the window to get a better glimpse inside. He saw a sea of concerned faces staring intently at a triumphant-looking John White. The gentlemen wore colourful daycoats that extended down to the lower thigh, with white pantaloons and knee stockings. Each wore a white wig with numerous curls falling to the shoulder, an adornment Isaac considered to be pretentious and rather inane. Back home in Genesee, most American frontiersmen snickered at the practice.

"Preposterous!" shouted William Jarvis, the owner of six slaves.

"Unspeakable!" intoned James Baby, also a slave-owner.

"What rubbish!" exclaimed Peter Russell, another slave-owner.

"How can we possibly comply with the law and still proceed to settle this province?" demanded David Smith, the newly appointed Surveyor-General. "There will be no one to clear the forest, work our fields or tend our animals."

"We have paid good money for our Negroes, and have provided them and their children with shelter, food and plenty to drink," declared James

Talbot. "Now you expect us to simply set them free without compensation? What an unconscionable act!"

Hearing such loud voices of opposition, White retaliated, "But it is an un-Christian act to keep slaves, against their will, for the betterment of one's lot. It is entirely without conscience. France restricted the import of slaves nearly a century ago. Other countries around the world are joining them. Our brothers in England considered abolishing slavery at the last Parliament session. It will put us at the forefront of political ingenuity. Our little colony will be the catalyst for Britain to abolish slavery throughout the Empire!"

"I am not interested in what the rest of the world desires," retorted David Smyth, the scent of rum wafting from his clothing. "I am more interested in how I might possibly operate my sawmill without my Negroes to haul the wood. No doubt I would have to close the mill, and how would the settlers fare? Where would they get lumber? The closest mill is in Fort Erie. The whole Niagara Peninsula will suffer. It will stagnate, a slow, agonizing death!" he bellowed as he pounded his fist onto the table.

"Without the sawmill, my tavern in Newark will close, and I won't be able to build the inn that I plan to begin next fortnight," complained David Secord, one of the first to settle in Queenston a decade earlier. "I will have no chance to get ahead."

"And who will shepherd our livestock roaming through the forest? We will surely lose all our swine and cattle. They will no doubt be stolen by the Chippewa, or the Americans who arrive here in droves every day," another raged.

John White interrupted, hoping to quell the ruckus that was rapidly rising to a fever pitch.

"Gentlemen!" he shouted. "Gentlemen. I acknowledge your reluctance, it is duly noted. But surely you join me in believing that no person should be bought and sold? This barbaric act is so beneath us. It is more befitting of the American rebels whose leaders have hundreds of slaves. To not abolish slavery would be to put us in equal company with Washington and Jefferson!" he commanded.

The crowd roared in outrage at the mention of the hated Americans. Isaac peered into the window and saw everyone on their feet, shouting angrily, arms flailing, feet stomping, some almost coming to blows. Bumbling ninnies, he thought. None of them have ever done a day's work in their lives, toiling the way the Devins family had for generations. Isaac remembered seeing the advertisements during the war offering fifty acres of land to Negro slaves who would join the British. And now they want to continue enslaving them in Upper Canada? How hypocritical, Isaac thought, resentment growing inside him.

The raucous noise grew louder, threatening to turn into a brawl. Then the only person still seated, Governor Simcoe, arose and stood up on his chair. He took his pistol out of its holster, cocked back the hammer and casually aimed it toward the window where Isaac was perched. Isaac ducked as he heard a lead ball whistle overhead.

Silence. Simcoe's hand rose and motioned downward, intimating that they were all to listen and obey. "Several months ago, at the Executive Council, our colleague, Peter Martin, told us of the story of the unjust treatment of Chloe Cooley, a Negro slave whose master forced her from her home in Queenston. She was tied and gagged for the ferry across the Niagara, and all the while she was kicking and growling like a trapped animal, desperate to be free. Before reaching the Fort she was sold to an American and taken from her family, never to see her children again."

Simcoe stepped off the chair and walked slowly around the table. "This abhorrent treatment of an innocent woman must not happen here in our new colony. We are better than the Americans. We will not lower ourselves to their level," Simcoe stated, his deep blue eyes commanding the attention of everyone in the room, his arms stretched out as if to embrace them.

The crowd shifted uncomfortably, and several whispered to their neighbour. A few started to speak but held back.

Robert Hamilton finally stood up, cleared his throat and walked slowly toward Simcoe. "All of us here can agree," he responded, "that your example of poor treatment is unnecessary and unjust."

He walked forward and stood at arm's length from the governor. "Those of us here who own slaves—myself, Jarvis, Russell, Baby, Cartwright, and others—treat our Negroes with the utmost respect and dignity. None of our slaves are whipped or beaten, neither are they starved or unkempt. All of them are well fed, live in sufficient comfort, and receive instruction on the basic means of survival, spinning cloth, carding, butchery. Why, I don't think they could survive on their own without us to provide them with food and water."

"Hear, hear!" several members exclaimed.

"Slavery is nothing new here," added William Jarvis. "The French began it long ago, and even the natives have slaves."

"Those of us with property or commerce simply cannot start anew in a vast wilderness without a labour force. There are no hired hands to be had. All the new immigrants are more interested in clearing the land that we are freely giving them than in working for us. We cannot build our businesses here without any workers!" Robert Hamilton exclaimed.

"Gentlemen, I implore you to reconsider," insisted John White.

Simcoe leaned back in his chair and assessed the situation. He and White were vastly outnumbered. The only way to salvage this situation was to suggest a compromise. He could not risk creating any reason for the gentry or the citizens to revolt, just as they had done in America. Better to have a piece of the pie than none at all.

Simcoe rapped on the table. "I understand and respect the general feeling that the development of the colony will suffer by enacting the legislation as it reads," he began. "I suggest, gentlemen, that we amend it to our satisfaction."

"We could legislate that those who already own slaves could continue to do so, but ensure that any newcomers will not be permitted," suggested Richard Hamilton.

"But we should be permitted to have slaves for the duration of our time here, or until our time of death," chimed in James Baby.

As the Legislative Assembly debated the wording of the Bill, Isaac stood up to stretch his legs. The new law does not seem to bear much weight, he thought, since the end to slavery will not take effect until the entire generation passes away. Why bother legislating it at all? He was miffed that White's legislation had to be amended to accommodate the privileged few.

Isaac heard another rap on the table and hurried back to the window. "The last item we will decide today," began Governor Simcoe, "is to consider moving the seat of government for Upper Canada to Toronto. My excursion there several fortnights ago was very illuminating. The natural harbour provides the perfect land formation for defence. With a fort at the entrance to the bay, the Americans will be unable to reach the town. Toronto will be a much safer place to build a new capital city.

"Here in Newark, the Americans are just across the river," he continued. "We will be constantly on guard as the American frontier moves farther north. We will be able to smell their campfires, hear their anthems, watch their military drills, see them stroll along the path on the other side of the river. We need to guard our women and children, and keep them far away from the Americans!"

Simcoe paused when he noticed the blank faces staring back at him. "Do I hear any opposition to the motion of relocating our seat of government to Toronto and establishing our capital city there?"

The room was silent. Isaac expected to hear rousing opposition voiced by the many people he had campaigned. Instead, there was silence.

Finally, John White spoke. "All in favour of relocating the seat of government to Toronto, raise your hands."

Isaac stared into the window. A majority of hands were in the air. Isaac's jaw dropped. He heard White pronounce the names of the supporters: Hamilton, Baby, Jarvis, Secord, Talbot, Smith, and stepped back in disbelief, shaking his head, clenching his teeth and instinctively reaching for his gun.

Astonished, he replayed the conversations that he had with each of them over again in his head, each voicing their objection to moving to Toronto, each person clearly stating their opposition. Not one of them, not one, went against Simcoe, he fumed. He lashed out and kicked the stone walls of Navy Hall with the heel of his boot several times.

Looking up, he saw William Jarvis push the heavy wooden door open and set out toward the stables. Isaac angrily stomped toward him, shouting his name.

"Are you all mad?" exclaimed Isaac, stopping inches away from Jarvis and grabbing his right arm. "You supported the move to Toronto? All your rantings about not wanting to live in a backwater were for nothing? How could you possibly support the bill!?"

Isaac was breathing hard, towering over Jarvis, practically spitting out the words. He wanted to backhand the overbearing imbecile across his pompous face and knock some sense into him.

Jarvis tried to step around him, but his attempts were thwarted. "I already voiced my opposition to the slavery bill. How could I go against the governor yet another time? There is absolutely no way that I could oppose him on the relocation, as much as I abhor the notion of settling in that swamp. My hands were tied. Politics, my dear boy, simply politics," he said, tipping his hat as he strolled around a stunned Isaac Devins, who could barely believe what he was hearing.

Isaac looked back toward Navy Hall and saw John White leave the building. Isaac ran after him, grabbed his right shoulder, and swung him around. White looked upward at his attacker with astonishment. "Not one of you supported staying in Niagara, not one of you!" Isaac insisted. "There was ample time to voice your opposition to the move, and you kept silent."

Isaac pushed White's shoulder away, sending him backward a few steps. "What, in God's name, implored you to support Simcoe's motion?"

John White looked at Isaac, noting his angry brow pulled tight in the centre, his red cheeks tightly flexed, his lips contorted into an angry snarl, his shoulders pointing backward and his broad chest out. Mostly, he saw his furious eyes, laced with a look of pain, yet somehow vulnerable. He had seen that look before, on the faces of slaves being transported by bateau along the Ohio River.

Clearing his throat, he replied, "I had no choice, sir. They were going to defeat my slavery bill until the governor stepped in and resurrected it. How could I go against his motion to relocate to Toronto after he supported a cause so dear to my heart?"

White put his hand on Isaac's shoulder, gave it a gentle squeeze, and led him along the path.

"I can understand perfectly well how you may feel outraged at such an apparent change in everyone's stance. The Parliament sessions drag on for nearly a month, and there are so many compromises that have to be made that it is almost as if you can champion only one or two causes and take a back seat on the rest. Now, my biggest concern was the slavery bill. I put my heart and soul into that piece of legislation. Perhaps if the Toronto motion was not on the same agenda, I could have voiced an opposition to it. But then again, tomorrow I hope to challenge Simcoe on his settlement strategy. There are so many factors that play into the scene, the dance, the music of politics. Did I ever tell you that I once saw the gov' completely dishevelled at a Parliament session in London? He was quite shaken, literally. Come on, I need a whiskey. Let's go to Secord's and I will tell you the rest of the story."

White's straightforward, common sense soothed Isaac's temper. He followed White into the tavern, a ramshackle cabin with a long wood bar and some half-comfortable stools that was a popular meeting place for legislators, settlers and traders.

The two men had the first of many lively, heated debates, passionately discussing the full gambit of issues facing the new colony over a few cups of whiskey. Although he was a member of Simcoe's inner circle, White became fast friends with Isaac from that moment forward. He found Isaac to be a man of integrity, passion and ambition, qualities that he respected.

What neither of them knew was that these attributes would lead to Isaac's demise. Isaac Devins would be disgraced and maimed, and John White would be unable to stop it.

Reflection 1

"Baaaaaaa-a-a-h-h-h," Isaac grunted, waking up.

He nervously scanned the log cabin, unsure of where he was, his blood pounding. A familiar sound filled the room, he was certain he had heard it before. It reminded him of the roar of the waterfall at Niagara, but from a distance, at the top of Queenston Heights, where Simeon had slashed and killed so many Americans during the War of 1812.

Grasping the arms of the rocking chair, he tried to jump up, but he felt paralyzed, unable to move for a moment.

A muffled sound was heard from the other room. Instinctively, he reached down his left side and clutched at his leg but could not find it. How could I forget to put my knife in the holder? he chastised himself. I've never done that before, not since Father gave me my first six-inch blade. His mother thought it dangerous for her six-year-old twins to pick berries in the woods without a knife, with so many wolves and bears around.

Shaking his head, Isaac looked around again, then finally recognized the stone hearth that he and Fire Starter had built so long ago. Every stone had been laid with resentment and hatred of those who tried to destroy me, Isaac remembered. Fire Starter picked the stones and brought them to the clearing along the Humber, and Isaac shaped and stacked them, all the while seething with anger. Damn those traitors, Isaac had raged over and over again as he slapped the mortar down and slammed another boulder on top.

Wrapped in a warm woollen quilt knitted by his daughters, he sat close to the fire, where he must have dozed off. The three-room log cabin along the Humber had been his home for the last fifty years. He never felt the need for anything larger or more extravagant. After the chaos and disappointment of the first decade in Toronto, Isaac chose a simple life along the river.

My time here has given me more faith, more hope, more peace than anything or anyone in Toronto ever did. If only I had known that then, he thought.

His heart was racing so fast he thought it would jump out of his chest. But he did not want to alarm Elizabeth, whom he knew would fret about it for days. How did Polly and I ever raise such a worrywart? he wondered.

Polly was such a capable and resourceful woman. She was never rattled by anything that was thrown her way. She always held a steady gaze, a straight posture and a cheery expression, even when the whole town was cursing my name and wanting me dead.

Why, Elizabeth would not even be here today if it wasn't for her mother's bravery. Tears welled up in his eyes as he remembered how Polly fought back a black bear and two cubs with only a willow branch. She was bending down to fill her canteen on the banks of the lower Humber when she heard a loud snort from behind. It was a case of mother versus mother, Isaac liked to say when he told the tale, for Polly had Elizabeth strapped in the cradleboard and the mother bear was protecting her cubs.

Such a strong, brave woman, Isaac choked, then gruffly swiped his eyes with the back of his hand. He did not like to show any weakness; only the unfortunate did that.

Isaac took a deep, laboured breath and put his left hand across his throat. He frowned, annoyed that his heart was still pounding. Maybe this is finally it, he thought, with a twinge of fear. I will die right here, in the very rocking chair that I made so long ago when we first camped out on the shore of the Toronto Bay. No drama, all alone, no fuss.

He sighed. When did I become so afraid to die? In his younger days, he was not afraid of death, his own death, at least. How can you fear death when you have nothing to lose?

A shotgun had been pointed at his heart a dozen times, and he had been given up for dead in a rotting jail cell. He had waded through a sea of corpses after the explosion at the Battle of York. I was as calm as a cucumber whenever fate put me to the test, he applauded himself. Yet here I am, an old man of eighty-six, shaking in my boots at the thought of passing on.

Isaac had been taught to fear God. His father preached to the family every Sunday morning, there not being a church or a minister within miles. The Devins' family bible was the only book in their home. His mother taught them every day to read and recite her favourite passages. Only when he was older did Isaac start to question whether God truly was there, looking after them as his mother said. How could God choose a life of hardship and labour for me, he wondered, when so many others were better off?

Fire Starter changed all of that. Isaac would listen for hours as Fire Starter told him of the ancient ways, the customs that so many Mississaugas abandoned when the white men came. The spirit lives in everything, he said, the trees, rocks, hills, rivers, stars. Fire Starter's vision of the happy hunting ground seemed as viable as any description of heaven that Isaac knew. As their friendship grew, Isaac came to trust in many of the native beliefs.

Many townsfolk called Isaac "the Indian" because he was so friendly with the Mississaugas. Isaac did not care. His friendship with Fire Starter was more valuable to him than gold. A truer friend and a more valiant warrior you will not meet, Isaac would often say when asked why he preferred to spend his afternoons at the Indian summer camps along the Humber and the Credit.

Isaac helped Fire Starter and his family with the corn and rice harvest every summer before the war, though he would not do the same on his own land. Not once in the last fifty years did Isaac burn a single tree to clear it for farming. All he wanted was to be left alone, live by the river, and be surrounded by the wilderness.

Isaac sighed and stared up at the wood ceiling. *The wilderness has all but gone now.* His own cabin along the Humber was in one of the few forested areas left. Nearly every other property had been cleared for farming.

Back then we forged our own way through the mixed pine forest to find a way to Toronto, often walking in the spring when the ground was too soft for a horse, or we paddled there by canoe. Now there are more roads leading to Toronto than the rows on a cob of corn.

York, it was called back then, Isaac recalled. *How it has grown from a rocky, tree-lined shore with not so much as a building to a thriving, bustling, crowded town of thirty thousand. Governor Simcoe was right,* Isaac thought. *Thank goodness we came up here to the northern wilderness when we did,* Isaac would often declare as he paddled happily along the Humber.

I suppose we could have returned after the war. Much of the town was reduced to rubble and ash and had to be rebuilt. Isaac's skills as a carpenter, as well as a fisherman, were well known. A few folk had even come by on horseback to Isaac's cabin on the Humber, hoping that he would lend his skill to the rebuilding effort.

Isaac thought hard about doing it, for Simeon. He had long ago lost any sentimental ties to the town or to its citizens. But Simeon would want him to do it, he considered, even if it meant sacrificing himself and his beliefs.

He was on the verge of accepting the invitation when a young boy brought him a letter from William Jarvis. Under no circumstances would Isaac ever consider doing anything that Jarvis wanted him to do, especially after the Battle of York.

Jarvis can roast in hell before I would ever consider helping him out, Isaac swore.

There was so much death and destruction that day, bodies strewn everywhere, blood-soaked streets, cries of agony. The townsfolk were in need of a hero. But Jarvis had seen fit to make sure that only he would be recognized, only he would be exalted. Perhaps I would have had a second chance at actually succeeding in Toronto, if only Jarvis hadn't twisted the truth.

But this is where I belong, Isaac told himself, staring at the stone hearth, and hearing the river rush past.

He closed his eyes and let his mind drift, imagining he was paddling in his canoe with nothing to guide him but the wind, the sun, the moon and the stars.

How he loved to sit on the limestone boulder beside the dock at twilight, watching the sky turn shades of orange, red, purple and then black, the sound of crickets chirping and chickadees singing, feeling the wind caressing his skin and hearing the unmistakable sound of sixteen paddles digging into the water as the Mississaugas' long cedar canoes glided by.

Polly was not too happy to come here at first, he remembered, though she knew it was necessary. They had to leave Toronto, there was nowhere for him to turn, no one left to save him.

Strange that my first birchbark canoe affected the lives of so many. Now it lies out behind the shed, covered in moss, rotting away. Soil and seeds have blown in and there are patches of milkweed and oat grass growing in the bottom, threatening to cover it completely, obscuring its existence. Perhaps I should ask my grandson, Isaac Junior, to dig it out. They could bury me in it beside the limestone boulders, right next to Polly.

He imagined lying there, the river rushing past, utterly at ease, no stones to turn.

Chapter 5 – July 29, 1793

BOOM!

A thunderous clap was fired from the cannons at Fort Niagara. The sound travelled blithely through the gorge, caressing the rustling leaves of the sugar maples lining the banks, and was still audible, though barely, all the way to Queenston, even though the mighty Niagara Falls tended to overpower the sound of all else. Then a long whistle blared through the village, turning heads toward the river.

The crowd cheered as the first group of settlers started up the gangplank, relieved to be setting sail for Toronto at last.

Practically the whole town came to watch. The air was filled with the sound of bugles, fifes and drums from the motley crew that Governor Simcoe roused up the night before from Fort Niagara. The military band played noisily from a small clearing on a grassy knoll.

Only a month had passed since the Parliament sessions, after which Governor Simcoe immediately announced the departure date for Toronto.

Isaac's twin brother, Jacob, was the first to jump on the bandwagon. "I think there's a better chance for us there," he insisted as the entire family crowded into the tiny shanty after Sunday dinner. "There will be fewer people and more land."

"I'm not too sure about that, brother," answered Isaac, leaning back in his chair. "The governor plans to take three boatloads, about half the population of Niagara. There will be utter chaos as people fight for the best properties."

Isaac was still against moving the capital of Upper Canada to Toronto, and the Devins family along with it.

"But at least we will be on an even keel with everyone else. Here, the best building lots are taken, allotted to the Governor's best friends."

"And who do you think will get the best building lots in Toronto?" Isaac shot back. "There won't be any for the likes of you and me. All of Simcoe's inner circle, will get their choice, same as here in Newark."

Isaac's younger brother, Levi, chimed in: "Most of the passengers are Queen's Rangers who will be prancing through the wilderness doing whatever Simcoe asks. There will be plenty of prime property left for the rest of us minions brave enough to make the trip. We have nothing here in Newark, nothing to lose."

"But we can get what we need at Hamilton's," Isaac insisted. "He sells everything on credit. We can pay for it later, after the first harvest."

Two days earlier, Isaac had gone to Hamilton's warehouse in Queenston to purchase a knife. Robert Hamilton, the most industrious settler in Upper Canada, had just started the first "bank" in the province, realizing that most settlers arrived in Niagara with no money in their pockets. He offered Isaac twenty pounds, enough to cover a year's expenses, with the stipulation that he would have to pay back twenty-five pounds after the harvest.

"We won't qualify for credit!" retorted Levi. "Robert Hamilton only offers credit to people with a land holding. All we have is an axe and the shoes on our feet."

The person who finally convinced Isaac of the merits of going to Toronto was John White, whom Isaac ran into outside of Secord's Tavern. White pointed out that if getting a government appointment was Isaac's objective, then there was no question that he should follow Simcoe to Toronto.

"Stay close to him, Isaac," imparted White over a glass of corn whiskey, swirling the spirits in the glass several times before downing it, "and it will show him your loyalty. I hear that no members of the governor's cabinet are accompanying him to Toronto. You will become his unofficial second-in-command, his sounding board, his right-hand man. Maybe he will even reward you with a huge land claim."

Isaac knew in his heart that John White, a savvy strategist, was right. The only way he could fulfill his ambition to become a person of importance was to be at Simcoe's side.

Standing at attention at the top of the gangplank, Governor Simcoe enthusiastically welcomed the settlers on board, with his wife, Elizabeth, their three children and their nurses standing dutifully behind. Wearing the bright green and grey colours of the Queen's Rangers, he vigorously shook the hand of the head of each household, slapping the younger settlers on the back and bowing to the women as they stepped aboard. Elizabeth Simcoe, in a regal chiffon gown and red bonnet with white feathers, smiled at the gentlemen and nodded to the women, her hands clasped tightly together.

A half-hour later, the *Mississaga* finally left Niagara in the late afternoon after the final supplies, livestock and gunpowder were loaded into the cargo hold.

Captain Joseph Bouchette steered her through the myriad of merchant and military vessels always bustling around the Niagara harbour, then swung west toward the head of the lake. Isaac smiled as he caught sight of Simeon, one of the few children on board, running excitedly up and down the deck, crawling on the cannons and pretending to fire at the many ships that passed. How fortunate for Simeon, Isaac thought, that he wasn't confined to the first mate's cabin like the Simcoe children.

Wandering over to the captain's lounge, he was invited in by Governor Simcoe, who immediately began telling him about his trip to Toronto a couple of months ago.

"The St. John River on the west boundary is shallow, and there are not a lot of Mississaugas to be found. They have their sacred river brimming with salmon, trout and whitefish just west of there, called the Credit, where they harvest the corn and maple syrup that we get in Newark."

"The St. John River does not seem to give any great advantage then," offered Isaac, who had taken a seat on a stool in the corner.

"On the contrary," began the governor, "the St. John River will become the most important trading route in Upper Canada. I plan to rename it the Humber. A few miles from the mouth, the river is too shallow for a bateau or even a birchbark canoe. But the Toronto Carrying Place trail extends northward for one hundred miles until you reach a large lake. From there, the Mississaugas travel to their homeland on Lake Superior. This footpath is a virtual pot of gold that will bring trade and commerce to our new town."

Isaac's eyes brightened upon hearing that the new town might not be quite as isolated as he originally thought. "So we will be establishing our town site at the mouth of the Humber River then," he concluded.

"Not quite. The town may extend out to the river someday," Simcoe explained, as he gazed out of the side hatch, opened to let in a cooling breeze. "The best site is actually east of there in the shelter of the peninsula. With a new fort guarding the entrance to the harbour, it will be virtually impossible for the enemy to attack."

The governor's voice became louder and more animated as he spoke about his favourite subject. "More forts will be built along the north shore of Lake Ontario to create an impenetrable wall," he continued. "It will be impossible for American ships to pass through."

Simcoe pulled a parchment out of his jacket pocket, unrolled it on the captain's table and pointed to the north side of Lake Ontario at the Toronto Bay. "Here is the grand plan for the townsite that Lord Dorchester gave me back in London, well before the Toronto Purchase."

Isaac looked perplexedly at the map, noting the date of 1788, surprised that the idea to establish a townsite at Toronto had been conceived more than six years previously.

Well, I'll be damned, he said to himself as he realized how futile his attempts were to convince the aristocrats to vote against the move to Toronto. Simcoe and Lord Dorchester had obviously been considering Toronto as a townsite long before the Devins family arrived in Upper Canada.

Scanning the map with great interest, Isaac felt privileged to view the plans for the new town before they even arrived there. All his hard work, conversing and strategizing with the governor day after day, now allowed him certain advantages. He studied the map in detail, trying to ascertain the most strategic building lot for his family's new homestead. Maybe over there, by Garrison Creek, Isaac wondered, or closer to the old French Fort. His excitement grew as he began to envision Toronto as more than just an unending wilderness.

The governor pulled out another map and said, "This lake at the head of the Toronto Carrying Place will be the perfect port to reach the rest of Canada. I plan to name it Lake Simcoe, after my father. I see a large city there, similar in scale to London, that will one day be the jewel of Canada."

The captain leaned over and interjected, "Governor, we still have twenty miles to go and we have lost the light. We will have to trim the sails and bunk down for the night."

Though he was anxious to reach Toronto that day, Simcoe could hardly disagree with the captain. Isaac dismissed himself and wandered out onto the port side, which was vacant, save for the crew lowering the anchor. He lifted a hatch and went down to the lower deck. At the end of a maze of boxes, crates and people, Isaac found his family at the bow.

Tomorrow I will find the best land in Toronto for the Devins family, Isaac said to himself as he drifted off to sleep, leaning against a wood crate filled with sacks of sugar, flour and guns. Jacob's head was on his right shoulder, and Levi's was on the left. Polly and the other wives lay with Simeon in the middle on a make-shift hammock that they had cleverly made out of burlap and twine, while his father lay comfortably on a couple sacks of flour.

Toronto will be a new beginning, Isaac vowed, I can just feel it..

◇◇◇

"Oh my, look at the smoke," Simeon called out, jumping up and down as the *Mississaga* approached the Toronto Bay the next morning. A waft of silver smoke billowed out from the treetops along the jagged shoreline. "Do you think the forest will burn down, Uncle Isaac?"

With a half-smile and a twinkle in his eye, Isaac affectionately placed his hands on the boy's shoulders and replied, "Only if the natives want it to burn. I dare say, they are quite adept at living in the forest." Simeon nodded, looking intently at Isaac, his eyes filled with trust and reverence. "The fire is probably inside the wigwams or close by," Isaac explained.

The ship sailed past the Humber Bay, a low-lying inlet with a gentle curve and a lazy river at the centre. A few miles farther along the rocky shoreline, Simeon called out excitedly, "Uncle Isaac, look! An old castle!"

"That must be the old French fort the governor mentioned," Isaac said. The ruins of Fort Rouillé loomed overhead in a clearing atop a thirty-foot cliff, making it look larger and more impressive. Built by the French in 1750, and burned nine years later as they retreated from the British in the Seven Years War, the buildings were nearly overgrown with vegetation. Isaac pointed to a group of soldiers wielding axes and raising a new stockade with ropes and oxen. They must have started to rebuild the old fort already, Isaac guessed, or perhaps they are building a new one.

As they neared the entrance to the Toronto Bay, the *Mississaga* came to an abrupt halt a few miles short of their destination. A buzz of excitement erupted from the crowd, everyone wondering what was going on.

Isaac entered the captain's cabin and overheard Captain Bouchette insisting, "No, Your Excellency, we cannot enter the Toronto Bay until midday. Winds of twenty knots are coming from the northeast and we cannot risk running aground. The best we can do is set out stone and line sinks every thirty feet to measure the depth, then we can inch our way into the harbour."

Isaac scanned the horizon. Only a narrow, half-mile opening lay between the mainland and the tip of the peninsula. The water was indeed more choppy in the harbour than in the surrounding lake, and looked quite menacing. Isaac sensed the governor's frustration, that his power as the Lieutenant-Governor of Upper Canada on land had little influence on the captain's authority at sea.

"Well, Devins," Simcoe sighed, "we might as well—"

"Your Excellency, I think you had better have a look at this," the captain interrupted.

Simcoe rose and grabbed the captain's looking glass, bringing a small bateau with a French flag into focus. "By the grace of our Lord, it's St. John Rousseau!" he exclaimed. "Captain, lift the sails. We need to rendezvous with that bateau."

Three Mississaugas, recognizable by their brown and red tunics and painted faces, rowed toward them in perfect unison, artfully making the flat-bottomed, cumbersome vessel glide like a birchbark canoe. A robust, husky figure dressed in a deerhide coat was standing at the helm, his long dark hair tied at the back. With one hand on his hip and the other on his bent knee, he held his head high, appearing to have the swagger of a pirate, though he remained at ease. He wore an unusual headdress of feathers and colourful beads, similar to the ones worn by the Mohawk warriors.

"Greetings, my friends," a melodious voice called out with a heavy French accent. "St. John's the name, and trading's the game." He laughed as he gave an exaggerated salute and a bow to no one in particular. "Welcome to my humble abode."

Smiling from ear to ear, he motioned to the shoreline. "That there is my trading post, just a mile up the St. John River," he explained. "I have everything you need right here. I trade with the Mississaugas, the Hurons, the Iroquois, even the Métis if they come down this far. I've got posts all along Lake Ontario, so if you need anything, I mean anything, I can get it," he assured them. "I've got furs, I've got corn, I've got whiskey, I've got sugar. You name it ..."

The governor waited patiently and then greeted him, "St. John, my man, nice to see you again. Come on board."

Three months earlier on his exploratory mission up the Humber River, Simcoe had arranged for Rousseau to guide them through the shifting sands at the mouth of the harbour and was pleased that Rousseau remembered.

One of the crew threw a rope ladder down, and Rousseau mounted it slowly, pausing at each rung to proclaim the attributes of his trading post.

He had been overjoyed when Simcoe told him that he planned to build a town in the Toronto Bay. What a boon to my business, he thought. There will be hundreds of customers living a few miles away, and I will be the only merchant. The closest trading post was twenty miles away on the Credit, and there you had to deal directly with the Mississaugas, something that not everyone fancied. I will become a prosperous man.

Rousseau alighted onto the deck with a loud thump and followed Governor Simcoe into the captain's quarters. The governor motioned for Isaac to follow. Simcoe offered St. John a whiskey, which he drank like it was the last canteen of water on the ship. He downed another half-glass and then sat back in his chair and put one boot up on the table.

"First, Captain, I need to know the depth of the ship under the water," St. John announced. "The entrance to the bay is only one and a half fathoms deep."

"That cannot be," exclaimed Captain Bouchette. "I surveyed it last year." He pulled out a map, dated November 1792, and showed it to Rousseau. "I measured the depth from the western gap to the sand spit. I calculated it to be two fathoms and a half at the low point in the western gap."

Surprised, Rousseau leaned over to view the map more closely. To the best of his knowledge, not a single vessel larger than a bateau had ever entered the Toronto Harbour without himself or his father at the helm. However, the map looked to be quite accurate. The surveyor must have come while I was away at Cataraqui with a load of beaver pelts, he concluded.

Leaning back, Rousseau said, "Then you may have noticed that the shoreline we see here today is completely different than what you show in your map. The ice breakup and the severity of the storms this spring have shifted the sands in a westerly direction, and only I know the route through the harbour."

Captain Bouchette had indeed noticed the different alignment, and it was the reason for his hesitancy. Although he was the son of a commodore,

Bouchette knew that he did not yet have the experience to lead a ship of this size through the shifting sands of the Toronto harbour.

"There's no need to wait, Governor, I can lead her in at once," Rousseau declared.

"Very well," said Simcoe, not heeding Bouchette's advice to wait until midday. "Let's be on our way."

Rousseau instructed the captain to lower the mainsail, which was partially hoisted to maintain the ship's head to windward. He stepped outside the cabin and barked orders to the crewmen. When he was satisfied, he strode to the bow and stood within view of the captain, who was stationed at the wheel, ready to pilot the ship. St. John motioned for Isaac to join him on the deck.

"I need you to relay my orders, Devins," Rousseau explained. "There is no way that the captain and crew will be able to hear me in this wind."

"Aye, aye, Captain," replied Isaac with a mock salute and a grin. Rousseau slapped him on the back, appreciating his humour, and then scanned the shoreline with a copper periscope.

"Ahoy!" he bellowed. "Set about to sail."

Isaac walked toward the stern and shouted out the command. The first mate climbed on top of the scuttlebutt and barked the command to the crewmen within earshot.

"Bring the mainsail aft, mind the gaff," St. John ordered.

Isaac watched as two of the crew, clad in bluish canvas overalls, deftly climbed the main rig and adjusted the tethers. Two of the sails were swiftly unfurled, bringing the ship sharply around to the west. Captain Bouchette, a skilled helmsman, anticipated Rousseau's strategy and angled the rudder accordingly. The *Mississaga* glided through the entrance to the harbour in a graceful backward S-curve, avoiding the shallow sand deposits that could ground the ship.

"Now, Captain," began Rousseau, "just where do you plan to anchor?"

With Simcoe and the captain discussing strategy, Isaac slipped away, heading toward the stern. Now that they were inside the Toronto Bay, he wanted to be by Polly's side. Noticing her leaning against the railing, he put his arm around her, pulled her close and whispered, "I hope Toronto will be a good home for us."

She smiled up at him, appreciating his goodwill. He did not want her to know about the misgivings that still clawed at his heart. Try as he might, he just could not shake a nagging sense that Toronto was going to somehow be his demise.

"We are stopping here?" questioned Simeon, "in the middle of nowhere?"

A wall of gargantuan oak and pine trees seemed to stretch forever along the undulating, rocky grey shoreline, strewn with twisted brambles so thick it was impenetrable.

What will we make out of this vast wilderness, Isaac wondered, and how difficult will it be to carve our future? His mind turned to Polly and their unborn child. How vulnerable will our little settlement be to attack from the Mississaugas, Iroquois or the Americans?

The first mate climbed to the upper deck and bellowed, "The governor wishes to announce that we have arrived in Toronto, and ..." The rest of his speech was drowned out by the blaring of the band who chimed in out of cue. "We will transport all of you to the mainland by ferry. Please line up opposite the galley."

Excitement filled the air as the settlers scurried about to gather their belongings and vie for position in line. Isaac tried to make his way to the front but could not get close enough to reach Governor Simcoe before he boarded the first bateau along with St. John Rousseau, the first mate, and several crewmen.

Damn, Isaac cursed. He had envisioned himself on Simcoe's right-hand side as they alighted onto the sandy beach in the harbour. Instead, Isaac circled back and helped Levi push a couple of crates into the back of the line.

"How did we end up on the fourth bateau? We will never get a choice spot now," Isaac complained. Jacob just shrugged and Levi ignored him.

Isaac scowled and sat down on a coiled rope, preparing for a long wait. He looked to the shoreline and watched with an envious heart as Simcoe placed his arm on Rousseau's shoulder, an obvious gesture of camaraderie. The French trader let out a hearty laugh and thanked the governor for telling him of the Queen's Rangers' need for a steady supply of wine and rum.

"Perhaps you could set up a trading post here in our new townsite," offered Simcoe. "I could give you any lot you want. You could use it as your primary post or as a smaller venue for the townsfolk."

The governor desperately wanted to win Rousseau's favour. Like his father, John Baptiste Rousseau, he worked for the British Department of Indian Affairs for more than a decade as an interpreter and understood many native dialects, including the language spoken by the Mississaugas and the Six Nations—Oneida, Onondaga, Cayuga, Tuscarora, Seneca and Mohawk. Simcoe knew that he would need an interpreter, especially given the uncertain conditions under which they were landing in Toronto.

"Well, now, I don't know about living in town," began Rousseau. "I've lived in the woods my whole life. I would rather sleep under the stars than in a straw bed. My cabin is a meeting place for so many traders, Mississaugas, Senecas, Mohawks. I would hate to lose their business. They might just pass me by and go straight to the Credit."

Rousseau knit his brow and looked off to the right, considering another angle. "I don't think my wife would like it either. She's a woman of the forest, a daughter of Joseph Brant. I can't imagine her drinking high tea and playing cards all day," he said, guffawing at the thought.

Simcoe cordially laughed along with Rousseau, but inside was astounded to hear that Rousseau had a direct connection to Joseph Brant, the powerful and charismatic Mohawk chief and spokesperson for the Six Nations. Joseph Brant was one of the few native leaders that Simcoe respected and feared.

Born in New York State as Thayendanegea, the tall, athletic young man adopted the name Joseph Brant after he attended middle school in

New York. He was one of a dozen native children chosen by the British to learn English so that the British could improve communications with the native clans. Brant later was invited to London, and saw first-hand what a thousand years of British rule could do to the wilderness. He was savvy and sophisticated, worldly and wise, a dangerous combination for the British.

Simcoe needed to have the Mohawks on his side if war with the Americans broke out. Even Lord Dorchester knew they could not defeat the Americans without the help of the Six Nations, the Mississaugas, the Shawnee, the Potawatomi and the Hurons.

I definitely need to nurture a relationship with Rousseau, Simcoe thought. Damn Lord Dorchester for the messy situation he has left me in. The so-called Toronto Purchase of 1787 was never fully ratified. Six months prior in Montreal, Simcoe had questioned Lord Dorchester about its legitimacy.

"But there are no signatures on the agreement of purchase except for a few of our own people," Simcoe argued upon seeing a copy of the deed. "There is no evidence that anyone other than the British were privy to the document."

Lord Dorchester leaned back in his chair behind the mahogany desk, crossing his fingers and laying his hands on his sizable midriff. He gazed at the young Lieutenant-Governor with disdain. Never would he have chosen John Simcoe to be his deputy in charge of Upper Canada. His first choice had been rejected by the Prime Minister, who had appointed Simcoe against his wishes.

"I can assure you," Lord Dorchester began, clearing his throat and lowering his chin so that his eyes stared more intently at Simcoe, "that there were at least five Mississaugas present at the signing. I can also assure you that they readily received our offer of flour, textiles, seventeen hundred pounds in cash and countless barrels of whiskey, although there is probably no remaining evidence of the chattels."

Simcoe stared at the older man, unconvinced. Lord Dorchester may have had a long career as a soldier and administrator in the King's Dominion since the Seven Years War, but he is not seeing the light on this one, he thought.

Placing his two gloved hands on the desk, completely annoyed with the elderly man's staunch ways, Simcoe insisted, "The western boundary is not even clearly defined. Is it at the St. John River beside the Toronto Carrying Place, or is it farther west than that? I can barely read this map."

Simcoe could not help but display his incredulity at Lord Dorchester's ineptness. As someone who prided himself on having a collection of well-drawn maps, he did not place any credence on the validity of the hastily drawn sketch in front of him.

Lord Dorchester, well respected in London for his foresight in the development of the British Colonies over the last two decades, just tutted and replied, "The boundary is definitely west of the river, quite substantially, as noted by this indicator." He pointed to a line on the parchment that appeared to be more of a crease than an ink mark. "The wording in the agreement is sufficient in itself. It distinctly identifies the acreage of the land, which can be confirmed by your surveyor when you go there to settle."

Simcoe pushed his chair back, annoyed at his inability to convince Lord Dorchester, known in London as Sir Guy Carleton, to see logic. In the past three years, we have not seen eye-to-eye on anything, the governor thought. Simcoe was certain that there would be war with the Mississaugas if they realized that the purchase agreement was not valid, and Lord Dorchester was turning a blind eye to it.

But perhaps now he could get St. John Rousseau to find out how upset the Mississaugas are about the Toronto purchase. Rousseau likely has a strong enough ties with Joseph Brant to gain the inside knowledge.

"BOOM! BOOM! BOOM! BOOM! BOOM!"

Cannon shots fired from the *Mississaga* rang through the harbour, silencing the crowd. Then a drill line of Queen's Rangers fired five rounds into the air accompanied by a show of marching. The fife and bugle band played "Rule Britannia," the patriotic song of Great Britain.

Governor Simcoe stood in the centre of a makeshift wooden stage with Captain Bouchette on one side and St. John on the other. The first two stood at strict attention, as was their training and custom, while Rousseau assumed his usual, relaxed, confident stance.

The governor cleared his throat as he surveyed the crowd, the only ones brave enough to accompany him to Toronto. He wanted to ensure that the sovereignty of Britain would be unquestioned in the New World. The governor was absolutely convinced that the majority of the American colonists would favour a return to British rule if the settlement of Upper Canada was successful.

They will come to realize, as he had, that George Washington is nothing but a bumbling, high-handed dreamer with no knowledge or authority to govern a nation. They will quickly find that the idea of democracy imposed by the American rebels is not a viable way to govern, that a nation is best ruled by a knowledgeable, seasoned aristocracy, rather than by a group of radical peasants.

He even imagined the colonists revolting against Washington when they see how successful Upper Canada has become. The King's Dominion would once again include all the land in the New World.

"My fellow Loyalists," Simcoe began. "We are gathered here on the shores of Toronto Bay, this twenty-eighth day of July, the year seventeen hundred and ninety-three, to embark on a most prosperous undertaking, the building of a new capital city for the province of Upper Canada." Simcoe raised his arms at his sides and paused slightly for effect. He wanted to inspire the crowd, to make them feel the same elation that he did. The intense midday heat did not deter him in the slightest.

"Our new town in the Toronto Bay will become the premier place of commerce, wealth and government in the New World. We will build a port over there, larger than the one in Newark, that will receive ships from all parts of the world. Here we will have ..."

Isaac raised his eyebrows listening to the governor's far-fetched plans, begrudgingly standing with his family at the back of the crowd. It was nearly impossible to imagine such a grandiose and successful city when all he could see beyond the tiny plot of cleared land was wilderness. We may have a cabin built by winter, he thought, but there is not much time to do anything else. With no time to sow any crops this year, all of the winter supplies will have to be gathered from the forest, a time-consuming task.

"Hear, hear," chimed out Captain Bouchette, echoed by only a few other voices from the crowd.

Perhaps it was the blistering sun, the lack of a noon-day meal, or a true lack of enthusiasm, but it was not the boisterous reception that Simcoe anticipated. The faces looking back at him wore expressions of discomfort and distress. The governor quickly searched for some encouraging words.

"May I add that the Queen's Rangers will assist you with anything that you need to set up your households."

The crowd erupted into a round of cheers, happy to have the governor's assistance.

The settlers spread out to set up camp for the night. The only place for the Devins family was on the rock beach since all the cleared area had been taken by the first settlers to arrive.

Abraham, a little despondent, said, "Well, it's only temporary, we can move farther back when more of the forest is cleared."

Isaac wasn't so sure. He had seen Simcoe's maps of the new town and they looked quite regimented. There was not a lot of room for people without position, except on the outskirts far from the lake.

"I think we should all fan out, before any of the other settlers do, and scour the area to find the best building lots before night falls, so that we can be the first to approach the governor with a request for a land grant in the morning." Isaac was nervous that their family would not get what they had hoped for.

"I think you are getting a little ahead of yourself" interjected Jacob.

"We have only a couple of hours of daylight to build a shelter for the night," added Levi, "surely this can wait until the morning."

Isaac shook his head, walked briskly toward them, and held his arms out, as if to herd them in. "Father, brothers, do not take this matter lightly. We arrived in Niagara one year too late to obtain a choice lot there. I pray that we do not make the same mistake here in Toronto. The governor has already assigned the best sites to the Executive Council. Our best chance, and maybe our only hope for prosperity here, is to obtain a land grant in the perfect location."

Jacob smiled and bantered back, "The governor told us that there are twenty square miles of land in the townsite." He gestured toward the rest of the crowd. "There looks to be about one hundred and twenty settlers who sailed with us. I doubt that the Queen's Rangers will be granted any building lots unless they are ready to retire from service. Surely we will get a choice location with so few grantees to choose from."

Infuriated by his twin's nonchalance, Isaac retorted, "I refuse to lie back and watch all the choice lots go to someone else, like you seem willing to do."

"Why don't you just go and ask Simcoe right now?" Jacob shouted. "You seem to be cavorting with him like a piglet suckling on a sow!"

The twins rushed at each other, fists first, grappling each other's clothes, tackling and trying to pin the other on the ground, grunting and howling. Abraham calmly walked over and put a hand on each son's shoulder, saying, "Enough!" His authoritative voice was sufficient to separate the two men, who inherently remained obedient to their father.

Abraham continued, "Isaac, I have to agree with the rest. There is insufficient daylight left to wander through the woods when we have a shelter to build."

Infuriated with his family and overwhelmed by the heat, Isaac pushed his brother away. He defiantly yelled back, "Fine! I will do the searching for the entire family myself, with no thanks from you!"

He grabbed his shotgun and stormed off along the shoreline, there being no path to lead him into the woods. How could they not see reason? If you want a good piece of land, you have to act on it, not wait around and hope for the best. Isaac had always stood out from his brothers, the only one who lived in the forest instead of farming the land, who wanted more than to die with a sickle in his hand. He was not about to sit back and be thankful for what happened to come his way.

A narrow, grassy footpath led into the woods and Isaac thankfully followed it, sweat pouring down his back and chest. Chokecherries, raspberries and cinnamon ferns gradually gave way to a jumble of birch, poplar, maple and hackberry trees. The cloud of mosquitoes seemed to get denser the deeper into the forest he went. As he entered the dark forest interior, the footpath faded to nothing. A soft carpet of bronze pine needles filled the forest floor, with no definable tracks.

Relaxing his shoulders, Isaac took a deep breath and felt his anxiety fade away. He always felt at home in the forest, a place he escaped to as a child if he ever wanted to be alone or if he was avoiding a whipping. The warbles of the nightingales, the chirps of the finches, the squawks of the blue jays, the coo of the mourning doves filled the air. He took out his hand blade and made a notch on the north side of the closest tree trunk and stopped to make more notches every thirty feet or so. This type of forest would be only too easy to be lost in, he reckoned, imagining that one could wander for days, even weeks before finding a way out.

Certain that an American would not be granted land along the lakeshore, Isaac walked inland and looked for signs of a stream or one of its tributaries, searching for a source of drinking water. Every family, even the aristocracy, would need water for a vegetable garden, livestock and to grow crops. He finally found a meandering creek of clear water trickling through the woods that seemed to extend for as far as the eye could see. Anywhere along this stream would be ideal, he reasoned.

Crackle, snap, snap!

Instinctively, Isaac crouched down, all of his nerves alerted, and withdrew his shotgun from the holder. Silence. Isaac waited, not yet knowing if he was the hunter or the prey. The silence stretched on and on. Just as he straightened up, he heard a louder crackling sound followed by a low indeterminate utterance, and realized that it was coming from the north. He quickly darted forward, using the tree trunks for cover, stealthily drawing nearer to the source.

From behind a tree, he saw a squad of Queen's Rangers almost directly in front of him in the distance, walking in a straight line, two by two. With great curiosity, Isaac ventured northward to where the soldiers had been and was delighted to see a well worn dirt trail, six feet in width. It must be the Indian trail, the lakeshore road, that he saw on one of Simcoe's maps, the only trail other than the Toronto Carrying Place on the north shore of Lake Ontario. What a find, he whispered, letting out a low whistle.

The land right here is perfect! he thought, with both a trail and a fast-flowing stream. Simcoe told him that thousands of settlers would be coming to Toronto. One day, this land could become part of the city proper, with a row of stores, inns and markets, just like he had seen happen in New York State. He imagined carving up the land into building lots and selling them for a good profit. Perhaps he could open a store, and have a sprawling mansion for Polly and the children.

With a spring in his step, he walked back along the lakeshore trail to the landing spot. The sun had already set, changing the sky to a dazzling panorama of rosy red, orange, yellow and mauve. Isaac barely noticed as he trotted along, anxious to tell everyone of his good fortune.

"By the grace of God, you have accomplished a lot in a short period of time," Isaac complimented his family as he entered a lean-to of stacked logs and canvas on the rocky shoreline.

"The Queen's Rangers brought a dozen logs to each family," explained Levi, "and we cut down a few more from the edge of the woods."

"Listen, everyone, I have made a most incredible discovery," Isaac began as his brothers groaned and rolled their eyes.

The brothers had heard the same words countless times before. Their childhood was filled with Isaac telling them about the adventures they would go on, the riches they would attain, the power they would have, the fine homes, horses and stables they would own. Isaac was always searching for something, even if the objective was not exactly clear.

"I have found the best land for our ..."

A loud gong resounded and was struck over and over again, announcing that the evening meal was ready.

Everyone cheered and walked over to the large communal fire the women had built in the centre of the clearing. Polly and Rita handed out plates of rabbit, duck and squirrel with cranberry preserves and raspberries picked by Simeon. The Devins family devoured the meal, along with the rest of the settlers, all grateful for the bounty of the forest.

Later, Polly took Isaac's hand and squeezed it gently as she stared out across the moonlit bay, the two of them sitting comfortably on a maple stump on the rocky shore. She rested her head against her husband's strong chest as Isaac told her about the land he had found, caressing her arm and stroking her hair.

A good find, she thought, reflecting on their first day in Toronto and the uncertainty of their future. Polly's discomfort with being nine months pregnant and her dread of sleeping on a thin layer of blankets made her stay up as long as she could. Besides, she was enjoying the cooling breeze from the bay that wisped through her wavy auburn mane that she had let down after the others went to bed.

Finally able to sleep, she kissed her husband goodnight and shuffled off to bed, Isaac assisting her to lie down.

The North Star shone brightly, low on the horizon, casting a small beam of starlight on the still water. Isaac picked up a flat stone and skipped it across the water, feeling completely relaxed and pleased to have made the trip with Governor Simcoe. Looking to the west, he saw the last candle snuffed on board the *Mississaga*, and imagined the governor, his wife, and children settling down into their comfortable quarters.

Yet a nagging sense of uncertainty lingered in the pit of his stomach. He thought back to the morning that Little Star was stolen by the Mohawk. Obviously, God's plan for him did not include his little black mare. So did it include a happy, prosperous, fulfilling life here in Toronto?

A glimmer of hope crept back as he remembered the deep connection he felt to the land he had discovered today. He was certain that it would yield an insatiable bounty, riches beyond the imagination, he could just feel it. He picked up another flat stone and sent it skipping across the indigo water.

He stayed like that, long into the night, alone at the landing spot, watching the moonlight shimmer on the lake, their first night in Toronto.

Chapter 6 – August 13, 1793

"We found it, Uncle Isaac!" exclaimed Simeon.

A patch of morning sunlight illuminated the tiny opening in the silver maple trees where the clear, cool waters of the rushing brook carved its way through a sudden drop in elevation. They were only an hour's trek west of Fort Rouillé, the abandoned French stockade between the landing spot and the Humber River, but Isaac and Simeon were already dripping with sweat, their throats parched from the scorching August heat.

Simeon tiptoed out onto a couple of stones and crouched, the creek rushing all around him. Bending over, he placed the top of his head in the water, staying upside down until he could see Isaac's boots at the edge of the stream. Straightening up and flinging his head backwards, Simeon playfully doused his brother with a cascade of water, soaking Isaac's cotton shirt and dungarees. Isaac laughed and grabbed Simeon's arms, playfighting with him on the boulders. Simeon let out a shriek as he landed in the waist-high stream. He splashed back, but Isaac had walked out of range.

Bending down, Isaac filled his canteen next to a young white pine that had been laid across the creek. St. John Rousseau must have put it here, a smart move, Isaac concluded, since none of the settlers had any means to travel out to his trading post by water. Everyone had been too preoccupied during the last two weeks with clearing trees at the landing spot to construct any kind of a boat.

Isaac thought back to what Governor Simcoe had said a week ago as a coxswain rowed them across the bay to the *Mississaga*. "We are making good progress. It won't be long before we have a new town built." The governor's family and servants continued to live in the captain's quarters, waiting for the canvas tents to be set up near Garrison creek. Simcoe seemed oblivious to the sheer volume of work required to chop down the gargantuan oaks and pines at the landing spot that measured six-feet in diameter.

Isaac merely nodded and said, "I am sure we will all have shelter before the snow flies, Your Excellency." Glancing back to the shoreline, Isaac wondered if that would even be possible.

"Look over there, Devins. You can see the new stockade built by my men," Simcoe exclaimed proudly, pointing to the site of the old French fort. "I sent most of the troops to rebuild the fort so that we will be secure before the Americans find out we are here. It should be finished by the month's end."

Isaac pursed his lips slightly, trying to conceal his annoyance. Simcoe's offer of help to the settlers had only lasted for one day, he thought, as the two men boarded the *Mississaga*. Why are the settlers clearing the townsite anyway, when none of us will ever be granted a lot? The Queen's Rangers should be doing it, he muttered to himself. He did not share Simcoe's fixation that the Americans were sure to attack; in fact, he thought the idea quite remote. He would much prefer to have the Queen's Rangers, all one hundred and twenty of them, back at the landing spot felling trees.

"Good evening, Devins," Captain Bouchette said, offering a flask of whiskey, which Isaac gratefully accepted as the governor left the room in search of farther libations.

Surveying the cabin, Isaac spotted a Town Plan for Toronto lying open on a table. It was the same survey he had seen onboard the *Mississaga*. Bringing a candle closer, Isaac studied the map, hoping to find the creek west of the landing site that he had marked by carving his initials in the tree. At last he spotted it – the site appeared to be just on the outer edge of the Garden Lots and had the main east-west route, Lot Street, on the northern boundary.

"Perfect," whispered Isaac. Now, to secure the land for my family . . .

He did not have a chance to raise the subject until after the noon-day meal of salmon cakes, new potatoes and mash, deliciously prepared by Simcoes' servants.

Shortly before dessert, Mrs. Simcoe remarked, "On a short ride westward along the beach I did discover a most enchanting brook. I dismounted and followed the bank for a short spell. The water was cool, almost cold to the touch, such a welcome respite from the heat. The view was so pleasant that I made a quick sketch."

Finding her notebook on a side table near the door, she found the page showing a sketch of a river meandering through the woods with dappled light and deep shade defining the edges.

"My wife is quite the artist," praised the governor, "and has a journal of sketches illustrating our travels in the King's Dominion."

"Quite lovely," admired Isaac as he took the sketch, astounded that Mrs. Simcoe had also discovered his precious bit of land. "I, too, have been to this very site, the first day we arrived. I followed the brook up until the Indian trail in the north, and the land is most suitable for settlement. In fact, I specifically wanted to ask you, Your Excellency, how I can go about securing this very land for my family?"

Isaac put the sketch down on the table and tried to conceal his excitement. He did not want to appear too eager to acquire the land, lest the governor think that he was up to no good.

The governor narrowed his eyebrows slightly, considering the request. "You only have to put your name down on a petition to the Land Board, the same process that has been used in Upper Canada for the last five years," explained Simcoe.

"How much land shall I apply for?" Isaac inquired casually.

The governor cleared his throat. "Yourself, each of your brothers and your father will each receive a two hundred acre farmlot for your loyalty to the King," answered Simcoe. "If you choose a lot at the town centre, it will be considerably smaller, in the range of two to ten acres."

Turning his head away, Isaac tried not to let his disappointment show. Simcoe's offer was so meagre. Almost every Loyalist brave enough to come north to Upper Canada received the same land grant. He had expected a much greater amount considering the countless number of hours he had spent listening to Simcoe's schemes and offering his opinion on what the Americans were likely to do next. Is this the only reward that I get for all the hard work I put in? he wondered.

The governor pulled out the sketch of the Town Plan that Isaac had seen earlier. "Many of the town lots have already been assigned, but there are still a few left."

Just as I suspected, thought Isaac, the governor has already given the best properties to his cronies.

"My heart is quite set on the land with the lovely brook," replied Isaac smoothly, concealing his discontent, "but I don't know how to describe the location for the land claim. Shall I measure the distance from the centre of the landing spot or use the fort as a landmark?"

"No, no," said Simcoe, "there is no need for that. Land claims cannot be made until we have a proper survey of our new town. I have summoned Alexander Aitkin here, and he will set out in a couple of days. He anticipates that it will take a month. Just ensure that you note the proper legal description for your lovely brook in the claim when the survey is complete and you will get the land that you want," promised the governor.

A month, thought Isaac, is an impossibly long time to wait. All my plans will be in limbo until the survey is complete. Isaac resented having to wait so long when he knew he had found the perfect spot for his homestead.

"But how can I ensure others don't claim the same land?" inquired Isaac.

"Just put some boundary markers down, Devins. We passed a law last year that requires everyone to respect the boundary markers. If someone takes or moves them, the punishment is death by hanging."

A few days later, Isaac and Simeon walked eight miles west through the mixed pine forest to St. John's trading post on the Humber River. They knew they had arrived when they saw a log cabin close to the water with a stack of empty whiskey barrels leaning against it and a row of wooden racks for laying out furs and canvas sacks. Three birchbark canoes were lying upside down on the riverbank with paddles next to each. As they rounded the corner of the cabin, they stopped. A boy was squatting in the grass, right in front of them, as if waiting to pounce on an unsuspecting rabbit.

Simeon pushed past his brother, curious to see the black-haired boy, a little older than he was, who dressed in animal skins with strings of green, red and black beads and feathers around his neck. The young boy stood up and looked at the strangers cautiously, not used to seeing anyone arrive out of the forest.

Running up, Simeon said, "Can I see that?" as he reached for the boy's child-sized tomahawk hanging at his waist.

The boy lifted out the finely carved and painted weapon and handed it to Simeon.

"I have never seen one of these," said Simeon, thrilled to be holding something that he had only heard about in his grandfather's stories. He turned it over and over, then cocked his arm back and aimed toward a tree. "How do you use it?"

The boy smiled and took the tomahawk in his left hand, stepped forward with his right knee, evened his balance, and brought it straight up in front to take aim before skilfully flinging it at the birch tree, already riddled with notches.

"Wow, can I try that?" asked Simeon as they both trotted toward the tree to retrieve the tomahawk. The boy yanked the tomahawk from the tree and handed it to Simeon.

"It's really sharp," noted Simeon, "no wonder it can kill a grouse."

Simeon practised cocking it backwards as the two walked back to the totem pole. Turning around, Simeon took aim and launched the tomahawk forward, straight into the ground about ten feet in front of them, only halfway to the birch tree.

"Wait, that wasn't it," said Simeon as the two boys laughed and ran to retrieve it.

Isaac overheard the child explain, "You have to keep your elbow up."

A young woman suddenly appeared in the doorway of the cabin. She had long, dark hair braided on both sides, and wore a golden deerskin dress adorned with colourful beads and feathers. Her dark eyes seemed to caress everything she looked at, as if she could embrace someone with just a glance.

"If you are looking for my husband, he is getting dressed. You can wait for him at the dock," she said pleasantly and pointed toward the river below.

Isaac nodded, looking for an excuse to talk more with her, but finding none, he headed down the steep slope to the river. Surely she is the most beautiful woman I have ever seen, Isaac thought, so lost in a daydream that he did not once think of Polly.

"What have we here? My first visitor, welcome!" St. John Rousseau practically shouted as he came up behind Isaac, startling him. "My wife says you came by foot, good for you, man," he continued. "I can't say I have ever done the same."

Rousseau was a seafarer at heart, more at home in a canoe or schooner than on a horse or walking a trail. Isaac found himself smiling despite himself; St. John's rambunctious, playful enthusiasm was infectious.

"Call me St. John, everybody does. You're Devins, no? We met on the ship."

"Just wanted to come and see your trading post," Isaac bantered. "You've got quite the set-up, a dock large enough for a sizable fleet."

"After the spring melt, the natives come out of hiding. There is a never-ending supply of canoes bringing furs and taking away whiskey," explained Rousseau, "and the dock is not nearly big enough. I haven't seen any bateaux this far up the river, although I hope to soon, now that the British are here."

"It looks like you have been trading here for a long time," observed Isaac, noting the large cleared area cluttered with barrels, racks and canoes.

"I've been here only a year," explained Rousseau. "Before that I was trading all the way from the Grand River in the west to the Bay of Quinte. But my father built this trading post here twenty years ago. In the spring, I come here to get the furs that the Mississaugas bring me, and stay most of the year, making a few trips to Cataraqui to get more whiskey and to Niagara for gunpowder."

Isaac sat on a stump by the dock and Rousseau joined him. Isaac leaned forward, resting his forearms on his thighs, and felt a cool breeze go down the front of the cotton shirt that Polly had sewn after they arrived in Niagara.

"I expect there will be many more ships in the Toronto harbour next year," he said. "You may not need to make those trips to Cataraqui and Niagara any more. The whiskey and gunpowder will be coming directly to you."

Rousseau raised his eyebrows. He had never really imagined that the governor's little town would become a major trading centre, but it surely was possible. "You don't think a dock will be constructed this year?" he queried.

"Not at the rate we are going," answered Isaac. "In the last ten days, we have only downed three of the giant oaks near the landing spot. It is going to take months to clear a spot for the winter, and now we have a huge surplus of timber that the governor has ordered to be burned or floated into the harbour. One of those large oaks could easily make one hundred pounds of potash. I know I could sell it in Niagara for twenty pounds, but I have no way to get it there." Isaac turned his gaze from the rushing river to Rousseau. "If I transport the ashes here, can you sell them to the natives or to any soldiers that come by?"

St. John guffawed and shook his head. "The natives only want the finished product – candles or gunpowder, especially gunpowder. They won't buy the ashes."

"What if I give you some to take along to Niagara or Cataraqui? Could you trade it for me there? You could sell it to the ships bound for Europe. I hear that lye sells at a premium over there. "

Rousseau considered the possibility for a minute, then replied, "I suppose I could, although my bateau is usually packed to overflowing. Perhaps a couple of barrels, no more . . . "

His sentence trailed off as he spotted a canoe heading toward the dock from the north carrying three or four Iroquois. St. John stood up to greet them, saying, "Man-go startalon."

He turned to Isaac and said, "They're Mohawks, my wife's breed. Although she is white, she was raised by Joseph Brant and adopted all their customs and way of living."

Isaac turned and walked to the river's edge. Glancing upstream, he saw Simeon and St. John's boy seated in a tiny canoe looking for frogs and turtles in a sheltered, deep pool. Isaac smiled, then turned south and followed a jagged footpath along the river. He walked for a quarter-mile and stopped at a familiar site – a large, table-sized boulder that seemed to be suspended in the air on a smaller limestone slab at the river's edge. The first time he saw the odd, suspended rock, he was mesmerized. He had felt a driving force compelling him to come to this place, and would spend the afternoon watching the Mississaugas as they paddled up and down the river, almost effortlessly.

Until today, Isaac was always alone at the limestone outcrop, partially hidden by black willow and cranberry trees. However, this morning he saw a single birchbark canoe migrate toward him. He looked intently into the eyes of the approaching paddler, who returned a steady, penetrating and slightly curious gaze.

Steering to the river's edge a few feet away, the man stopped the canoe and sat still. They both stared at each other without a sound, without moving. The clouds parted slightly and a ray of sunlight poked through, illuminating the stranger's long black hair and the red beads around his neck. Eagle feathers attached to his bearskin garment rustled softly and the smell of newly skinned hide drifted over. Isaac assumed he was from the Mississauga clan, the name the settlers called the Anishinaabeg, because of the red and green bands around the man's wrists, but he wasn't certain.

Minutes passed, and then Isaac motioned toward the canoe, back to his chest and then back to the canoe, hoping to convey his desire to obtain one. He repeated the gesture several times and waited. A solemn expression slowly spread across the older man's face. His eyebrows raised. He carefully rolled up his sleeves and then spoke some unintelligible words as he pointed first to himself, then to Isaac, then to the sky and downward.

Repeating the same sequence again, he then looked at Isaac, and said, "Niin bizhaa, bekaa."

He repeated the phrase, and then pointed to Isaac and said, "Waabshkii Mnidoo."

The man then abruptly lifted his paddle, pushed off from the rock and paddled at full speed up the river.

Isaac pondered the significance only for a moment, then excitedly scrambled over the rocks along the riverbank to the trading post. Polly would be pleased with his progress. From the outset, Polly and Isaac knew that it could take years or even decades for roads to be built through the forest. They felt like their future in Toronto somehow depended on the river.

The Devins family did not have the money to build a vessel large enough to travel the turbulent waters of Lake Ontario or to start a mill. However, we could build canoes, just like the natives, Isaac imagined, one for everyone in the family. We could be the first of the settlers to explore the Humber River, Isaac thought, and reap its rewards. His mind filled with images of felling trees, floating logs and trading posts that his family would build.

When he reached St. John's trading post, he called out for Simeon, and the two headed back toward the landing spot at a rapid pace. Sensing his brother's impatience as he ran to catch up, Simeon called out, "Uncle Isaac, are we late for the noon-day meal?" not understanding the need to hurry so fast.

Looking down the narrow, well-worn path, Isaac was too preoccupied to reply. Not only would he be able to canoe swiftly across the Toronto Bay to the peninsula, he could also paddle out quickly to all the ships entering the harbour, reaching them before any others. He could transport goods to and from the ships that would be going back to Niagara or on to Cataraqui and then to Montreal and Europe. Perhaps he could strike a deal with St. John, work as a liaison between the Toronto Bay and the trading post. He barely noticed when they passed Fort Rouillé and crossed over Garrison Creek, with Simeon lagging far behind.

As he turned the corner, Isaac looked up in surprise to see his sister-in-law, Rita, standing on the trail outside the governor's canvas tents.

"What in the blazes – " Isaac began but was interrupted as Rita rushed over, clutched his right arm tightly and looked imploringly into his eyes.

"Isaac, thank the Lord we found you," she said with a shaky voice. "Polly," she said, trying to catch her breath. "Polly is having the baby now!"

"Here?," said Isaac, his voice full of alarm. "What is she doing way over here at the governor's tents?"

"She wanted to look for whortleberries and overheard someone say there were some over in a thicket near the fort," Rita explained. "So we set off after daybreak, just after you left. We only just passed the governor's tents when she gave signs that the baby is coming."

"What a foolhardy thing to do!" scolded Isaac.

Rita nodded in agreement. She also thought it unwise to venture so far away, but her older sister was adamant. Polly had made it clear that she did not want any special treatment just because she was about to have a baby, given the many chores that faced the family. The sisters had just turned back when Polly had her first contraction, stopping them for a moment. Nervously, the two women tried to hurry back to the landing spot but were stopped every minute or so while Polly had another contraction, each more severe than the last. Then her water broke.

"Just tell me when you want to stop," said Rita, certain they could not make it back in time. She felt her knees shaking, afraid that she wouldn't know how to help her sister when the time came. Only once had she seen a birth, when she was a teenager.

They plodded through the forest arm in arm, sweating in the early afternoon heat, Rita lifting Polly's skirt at the front so that she wouldn't trip on the stones along the path. Polly lumbered on, her back straining, her wrists aching, her face flushed. Just when Polly could barely take another step, they saw the governor's tents around the bend.

A woman emerged from one of them. Rita ran ahead and practically shouted, "My sister, she is about to give birth."

Elizabeth Simcoe looked in the direction that Rita was pointing and said, "Oh dear, come in, come in."

Polly and Rita gratefully entered the sizable canvas tent, feeling shy and a little bit frantic. It was a magnificent room, adorned with fine tapestries, lovely wood tables and chairs, portraits, books and maps, all brought over from the *Mississaga* two days earlier and assembled by the Queen's Rangers.

"Over here," Mrs. Simcoe gestured. "Please, yes, lie down my dear, lie down."

Polly sat and laid down on the well-appointed bed, perhaps the Simcoes' own. Elizabeth Simcoe buzzed around the room, looking for items that she knew they would need. The governor's wife was well versed in childbirth. She had given birth to her sixth child only five months earlier in Newark.

"Here are some extra blankets," she announced, and then snapped her fingers three times. "Susan, Martha, bring some hot water, the scissors and make some tea. Don't just stand there, this woman is about to give birth," she said sternly.

The servants scurried off while Mrs. Simcoe pointed to the oak chairs and table.

"Now, make yourselves comfortable, everything you need is here," she said, her compassion for the younger women clearly showing.

Rita looked up at the diminutive, gracious lady, dressed so elegantly in a sky blue taffeta gown with a broad brimmed hat to match. "We cannot fully express our gratitude for you kindness, Mrs. Simcoe," she began.

The governor's wife raised her hand to dismiss the notion. She abruptly left the room, but the two could hear her say outside, "Martha, you stay here and attend to baby Katherine. Susan, please go to the landing spot and inform this woman's family that she is here, and then assist with the birth," she ordered. "And please tell the governor that I have gone to the peninsula to do some sketching," she said as she put her satchel on her back and headed toward the stable. "I hope I have time to capture the *Mississaga* in the harbour before she leaves for Newark."

Polly lay still in the grand, luxurious bed, held her sister's hand, and looked around the spacious room filled with finery and fashionable clothes. She remembered a few months ago when Isaac stopped her from going inside the Simcoes' tent in Niagara, not thinking it proper to enter the home of the governor.

"My, my, my, we have moved up in the world," she joked. She hadn't been in a room half as fine since Hannah Jarvis' home in Newark.

She squeezed her sister's hand. "Rita, you must try this bed. Come. It is as if you are lying on a cloud."

Polly sat up and moved her legs over the bed to make room for her sister. As Rita pensively sat down on the edge of the bed, the next wave of pain struck. She grabbed her sister's hand and laid her back down as Polly gasped and cried out in pain.

"It's coming now, the baby's coming," Polly whispered.

Rita ran out of the tent and practically bumped into Isaac and Simeon, then hurried back inside.

Isaac heard his wife's cry and sent Simeon running back to the landing spot to fetch his mother. He then strode over to another tent and found the Simcoe children's nurses, instructing them to provide assistance. Satisfied that there was nothing farther he could do, he wandered slowly back to the landing spot, where he found his brothers dismembering the branches of a giant pine tree. He joined them, grateful to partake in a physically demanding task that could easily divert his attention.

Later, Isaac sat alone on a log outside of the family's lean-to, as he did most evenings. The ethereal beauty of the sunset, the scattered clouds providing a grey silhouette against the last rays of red, orange, purple and blue, went unnoticed. Everything seemed to move slowly, each second like an epoch. What could be taking so long? Isaac wondered. While others might become agitated or nervous when faced with calamity, Isaac withdrew. His father had often been frustrated with Isaac's deadpan face and lack of emotion when he was younger, especially when he was being reprimanded or whipped for his misdeeds. For Isaac, it was the only way he knew how to cope.

Feeling a tap on his shoulder, he looked up to see Rita standing there, smiling, with a gratified look illuminating her face. "You have a daughter, Isaac," she said with pride in her voice, "as healthy as can be."

Jumping to his feet, Isaac grabbed both of her arms, his eyes showing the worry he had kept hidden inside.

"Polly, how is she?" he asked, fearful that she might not have survived. Many women, including his own mother, died during childbirth.

"She is well, overjoyed at becoming a mother, and sleeping soundly. The governor and his wife have unselfishly offered to spend the night on board the *Mississaga* so Polly does not have to move."

Breathing a sigh of relief, Isaac lit a torch and practically galloped back to the governor's tent. He carefully slipped inside, lit a candle, then took it over to a finely carved maple cradle where the infant lay sleeping, swaddled in a luxurious white, cotton blanket, skillfully folded to cover the baby's tiny hands and feet. Reaching down to touch his daughter's soft cheek, he could not believe anything could be so beautiful, so perfect. Then he was overwhelmed with a sense of apprehension, and knew he would do anything to protect his child, to make sure she has everything she could possibly need.

Snuffing the candle, he crawled into bed beside Polly, placing his arms around her, proud of her strength and courage. She woke up for a moment, whispered his name, smiled, and drifted back to sleep.

Isaac lay awake for a long time, staring into the shadows of the night. He realized that there are two kinds of happiness. First, there is the joy one can have from family and togetherness, the love of a good woman and a new baby girl. He was proud that his daughter was the first of the settlers to be born in Toronto, quite a distinction.

Then there is the happiness that you grant yourself when you have worked hard and accomplished what you set out to do. It was more than just wanting propriety and wealth. He had already concluded that even fools, like William Jarvis, could obtain these things. It was about self-respect. Isaac Devins wanted to prove to himself that he was capable of doing anything that he set out to do, no matter how insurmountable the task.

Glancing over at Polly, her face soft and beautiful, and their child sleeping soundly, Isaac felt animosity and anxiety fade away. A sense of calm and clarity washed over him.

I will not rest until I achieve something great in Toronto, whatever that might be, Isaac vowed.

Chapter 7 - August 18, 1793

A couple of days after his daughter Elizabeth was born, Isaac returned to the limestone outcrop and waited.

Finally, he saw a canoe come closer but was alarmed to see that the Mississauga had bright red and yellow markings painted on his cheeks with black dots on his chin. Isaac's shoulders stiffened and he felt his calf muscles tighten, his whole body alerted to potential danger. On board the *Mississaga*, St. John had said in a drunken tirade that the natives liked to paint their faces but did so for only two reasons – festivities or warring.

Standing with his hands at his sides, Isaac sidled over to the maple tree where he had left his gun, realizing he would have only a split second to grab it, use the tree for cover, aim and fire. He did not want to draw his weapon or duck for cover too early. Neither did he want to show fear. Never let the enemy know that you are weak, his father had taught him as a young boy. Your enemy only knows what you let him know.

The paddler did not stop until he pulled up against the limestone outcrop, a mere ten feet away. The stranger placed his paddle across his knees and said, "Boozhoo," with a pleasant expression on his face. Isaac relaxed his shoulders, exhaled sharply and took a step forward. It was the same older man that he had encountered before.

"Boozhoo," Isaac repeated, recognizing the greeting that he had overheard at St. John's dock.

Swinging deftly out of the canoe onto the limestone outcrop, the stranger looked Isaac up and down, spread his arms wide and said, "Niin bizhaa, bekaa." Isaac had learned from St. John that the phrase meant, "I come in peace."

Then the stranger pointed to himself and said, "Gchi-Bimaashiwin. I am Great Sail."

He then pointed to Isaac and said, "Waabshkii Mnidoo."

Isaac raised his eyebrows, hearing that word again. Not sure what Great Sail meant, Isaac pointed to his chest and said, "Isaac." Great Sail looked at him with an indication of understanding, so Isaac repeated it several times, pleased with himself for communicating his name. The men stared at each other for a while, each with a look of respect.

Glancing down, Isaac noticed that Great Sail wore a wooden totem with an otter carved on it, and bright red beads around his neck. Great Sail must belong to the otter clan, who were found from Toronto to the head of the lake, he concluded. The otter was one of the many animal clans of the Mississaugas, a trait that each child inherited from his father.

Pointing toward the canoe and then to a nearby birch tree, Isaac tried to convey his desire to make one. Two days later, Great Sail returned to the limestone outcrop and introduced Isaac to his son, Fire Starter, who would be his instructor. With a shaved head and a mane of spiked black hair down the middle in the Mohawk-style, the tall, athletic warrior looked fierce, as if he could easily slay a man with one blow. But he also seemed eager to show the white man the knowledge and skills that had been passed down from generation to generation.

Since that day, Fire Starter had come by twice to give more instructions. Every time he placed some tobacco offerings on the riverbank behind the limestone outcrop, which Isaac had learned from St. John was a sacred place.

"The Mississaugas believe that spirits dwell in the rivers," St. John explained, "and they always leave offerings before undertaking a journey."

Isaac figured that there must be hundreds of tobacco offerings left on the banks of the river every fall during the Mississaugas' annual migration to the northern hunting grounds.

"Yes, my friend," St. John told him. "The Mississaugas were curious when they found you at one of their holy places. Other than myself, you are the first white man they have seen on the St. John River."

St. John had a difficult time referring to it by its new name, the Humber. "This is their great migration route that they call 'Cobechenonk,' meaning 'leave the canoes and go back.' They have told me that you have been blessed, and they believe the Great Spirit resides in you. You should be honoured!" he said, chuckling.

Slightly abashed, Isaac could hardly imagine that anyone would perceive him to be spiritual. While his father and brothers believed that God directed your path, Isaac was not so sure. He learned in childhood that justice often was misguided. Did God have a hand in choosing little Johnny Cooper to become the town hero simply because his arrow happened to puncture the heart of the charging cougar threatening to ravage the church picnic? Was it God's plan that the same cougar should carry off his nephew into the woods the night before?

Finally, a canoe rounded the corner, and Isaac was pleased to see Fire Starter heading his way. They greeted each other amicably, then Fire Starter demonstrated how to strip the bark from the birch trunk in long, wide strips by using his knife to make a two-foot long notch and then the blade of his tomahawk to lift the bark off the tree.

Straightening up, Fire Starter uttered a few Anishinaabe words and handed the tomahawk to Isaac. Looking up into the warrior's astute, brown eyes, Isaac was honoured that Fire Starter was handing him his weapon, a symbol of trust. He turned it over and over, admiring the curved shape, the painting of a bear on the two-foot oak handle, and rubbed his finger over the metal blade, honed as sharp as the point of a spear. It would take some skill to use this properly, Isaac concluded. No wonder the Mississaugas wanted guns, a much more effective, though less elegant, weapon.

Looking up again, Isaac said, "Miigwetch," which he believed to mean "thank you."

Fire Starter gave him a nod and motioned for Isaac to begin.

Making the first notch was relatively simple for Isaac, who had acquired some skill as a carpenter. Lifting the birchbark off the tree with the tomahawk was not. Struggling to ensure that it did not tear, Isaac got three-quarters of the way around the trunk before irrevocably splitting it. Frustrated, he ripped the remainder off the trunk and threw it into the brush.

Shaking his head, Fire Starter walked over, picked up the bark and placed it beside the three other strips, saying something in his native tongue that seemed to be scolding Isaac.

On Isaac's next attempt, Fire Starter jumped in and positioned the tomahawk at the correct angles to make the cuts. He is a man of great precision, thought Isaac, and dedicated to his craft. By the third attempt, Isaac barely required any coaching, deftly removing the bark from the tree.

Fire Starter then took Isaac over to the nearest spruce and made a couple of deep notches with his axe, the sap oozing onto his outstretched fingers like soft chewing gum. He pointed to the tree, the birchbark, his own canoe, his canteen and back to the tree. Isaac understood that he was to gather a quart of the spruce gum and Fire Starter would demonstrate how to use it to seal the strips of bark together. Collecting the spruce gum will be a good job for Simeon, Isaac thought, who was still learning to use an axe.

Before he left, Isaac offered Fire Starter some of the sweet bread that Rita had made that morning, which he quickly devoured and then paddled back down the Humber. Such a mercurial way of life, Isaac mused, as he considered the Mississaugas' yearly migration to the northern hunting grounds, hundreds of miles away. The forest truly is their home. The Mississaugas returned to the same location the following year only if the hunting, fishing or farming were not yet depleted.

Looking up at the position of the sun, Isaac realized that it was past midday, so he walked back to St. John's, eager to return the next morning to work on the canoe. Watching the craft take form made Isaac feel a reverence for creation as he honed the birchwood frame and molded it into the perfect form. In a way, he felt like the canoe was part of him.

"Guess what, Uncle Isaac," Simeon shouted as he clambered up the riverbank to join him. "Joseph caught two trout and a whitefish!"

Simeon pointed down to the dock where the fish lay drying in the sun. The young Rousseau boy was about to spear another. The lad must have learned the technique from the Mississaugas, thought Isaac. Often he had seen them spear-fishing at dawn while he quietly observed from the limestone outcrop.

"And look what Joseph gave me," he continued, holding out a three-foot carved stick with a round net at one end. "It's a lacrosse stick," said Simeon.

"So it is," replied Isaac, taking the stick into his hands and examining it with curiosity.

"You take a ball that you make out of twigs, and you throw it so the other person can catch it, or you try to score a goal," explained Simeon excitedly, thrilled to have found another new and fun thing to do.

Isaac had heard of the native game, though he had never seen a match or even a lacrosse stick before. For centuries, all the Six Nations tribes, the Iroquois, and Ojibwe played lacrosse as a means of settling tribal or boundary disputes, and less often to toughen young warriors or for recreation. It was a very spiritual pastime, meant to please the Great Spirit or to collectively pray for someone. Success would bring honour to one's tribe, and glorify the players who brought home victory.

Surprised that St. John's son had given such a treasured object to Simeon, he queried, "You are allowed to keep it?"

"W-e-e-e-lll," began Simeon, "not exactly. I can just borrow it."

Just then, Isaac caught a glimpse through the trees of a shadowy figure striding toward the dock. Stepping out into the sunlight, the boy's mother bent over, her lovely, slender figure showing through the thin deerskin dress, her long black hair tousled by the wind. She seemed to be scolding her son, her words unintelligible and muffled by the distance. Even in anger, her voice sounds like an angel, mused Isaac, admiring everything about her.

"Come on, Uncle Isaac, let's go," Simeon pleaded for the fourth time, tugging at his brother's shirt sleeve, finally hard enough to get his attention.

Breaking away, Isaac dutifully followed Simeon down the path. An hour later they passed a line of trees with the initials I.D. carved on every second trunk. Isaac wanted to ensure that no one else would claim his chosen spot.

Finally, they emerged from the forest a few yards from the Devins' camp on the beach. In the three weeks since we landed in Toronto, we haven't made much progress, Isaac observed cynically. The cleared area for the town site only stretched along the rocky shoreline for four hundred feet and extended northward into the forest for one-quarter of the distance. None of the settlers anticipated how difficult it would be to cut, burn and stack the trees. It was so laborious that no one had time to build a permanent shelter or house. Everyone was still living in the same lean-tos set up the first day.

"We can only do this for another fortnight before we have to build a shelter for the winter," Levi complained, seeing that the sumacs had already changed to a brilliant red.

Simcoe ran a tight ship at the landing spot. Most of the settlers followed his orders and carried out his wishes without a farther thought. Just like a bunch of sheep, Isaac mused. He was one of the few who had dared to wander away and escape the back-breaking task of felling trees to do his own bidding. Hardly anyone took notice, except his brothers.

"Why are you always going off into the wild, Isaac?" asked Jacob, clearly annoyed, glaring out at the floating logs that almost filled the harbour, competing with the waterfowl for the open water. "We could use an extra hand, for sure. The trees are not going to chop themselves down."

"Slacking off, you are," chimed in Levi, looking him up and down, "like a whinny-ninny."

Isaac straightened up and held back the impulse to deck his brother. He explained patiently, as he had done almost every day, "I'm working hard, just like you. When the canoe is finished, and we are the first settlers that can travel across the harbour and over to the river, you will see that I haven't been wasting my time."

On his daily walk to the Humber, Isaac would often meet up with the governor, who seemed pleased to see him, turning him around so that they could walk side by side and discuss his newest plans. Isaac did not mind this at all. In fact, he was elated. *The governor must now think that I am more than just a hired hand,* he told himself.

The next day, Isaac walked along the eastern shore, and the governor ordered, "Devins, I need someone to go out to the peninsula tomorrow. Mrs. Simcoe told me that she spotted white-tailed rabbits out there, hordes of them. You and some of my men can set up traps and shoot some for dinner. I have me a fancy for some hasenpfeffer. Drop by the stable and take a couple horses. I'm sure you will ..."

Simcoe's voice trailed off. Isaac turned and saw Great Sail emerge out of the forest with three other Mississaugas. Ceremoniously adorned with a scarlet broad cloth, leggings, and a black silk handkerchief with silver brooches tied around his neck, Great Sail lifted one arm to his shoulder with his palm outstretched. In a pleasant tone he said, "Welcome. Many days have passed since you come to Toronto, our meeting place." His voice halted after every few words. "We only come now to greet you," he apologized.

"No matter," said Simcoe authoritatively. "I am Lieutenant-Governor Simcoe, the leader."

"I am Great Sail, leader of the Wabakisha of the otter," he said, pointing to the carving hanging from his neck that Isaac had seen a week prior. "He is Golden Eagle, Kineubenae, one of our chief elders."

Great Sail spotted Isaac and came forward, taking Isaac's arm, saying, "Greetings, friend," with a smile of recognition on his well-worn face.

"You two know each other?" Simcoe queried.

"Why, yes, Your Excellency," replied Isaac. "We met a little while ago near St. John's place."

"Come along, then," commanded Simcoe as he led them back to the canvas tents near the fort.

Great Sail brought gifts of beaver pelts, deer skin, moccasins, and sweet bread, Isaac told Polly later when he returned to their lean-to on the rocky shore. Polly rubbed the soft furs and tried on the pair of moccasins he had brought, enjoying the feeling of the soft leather on her weary feet. They felt luxurious compared to her heavy leather shoes that were tearing open on both soles, allowing small pebbles to come in and chafe her feet.

"After a round of whiskey, everyone was rather jolly," Isaac recounted.

Great Sail, a man of some years, swept the Simcoe children up into the air, delighting them and making them giggle. Polly listened raptly, fascinated. Back in New York, she was accustomed to fearing the natives. But here, maybe it was different, she wondered, looking over at her newborn, whom she wanted to protect above all else.

"We are a long way from our sheltered, comfortable life on the farm," Polly noted.

Isaac stood up and padded over to the north corner of the tent, looking down at his infant daughter, Elizabeth, asleep in the cradle under a cheesecloth cover to protect her from mosquitoes. The little one will be safe, at least for the time being. All encounters with the Mississaugas so far had been pleasant, peaceful and profitable. He hoped to forge an even greater alliance with them. If I can gain their acceptance and their trust, reasoned Isaac, they will become my teachers for how to live well in the forest.

Little did Isaac know that the Mississaugas already regarded him as a seer, a spirit of the wind and a friend of the forest. The tale of the white man who they found at their holy place, the limestone outcrop along the Humber, was passed from family to family, clan to clan. How this same white man had arisen out of the forest, like a white spirit, and cried out a sound so voluminous that it shook the trees and made the ground quake. The white man's spirit chased the Mohawk and entered the body of the fine black horse with the little white star, who threw the Mohawk off and into the creek. They found their brother the next day, eyes open and staring up to the heavens, the waters rushing around him, unable to utter a sound or lift his head. All he could do was breathe.

To them, he was Waabshkii Mnidoo. Unbeknownst to Isaac, the tale of Waabshkii Mnidoo would save his life one day, after the white men had all but abandoned him.

Chapter 8 – August 26, 1793

"Atten-tion!"

One hundred Queen's Rangers in green and grey uniforms, with muskets, bayonets and rifles rushed to their positions at the landing spot, facing south toward the lake.

"Forward, slow-march!"

The soldiers marched in unison toward the stage, where the governor and his entourage stood waiting. Knees high and weapons at their shoulders, they paraded past the crowd of settlers. Isaac, his family, and all one hundred and twenty settlers looked on as the soldiers fell into a triple-row formation parallel to the lake, directly in front of the stage.

"Company, halt!"

Clutching their weapons at their sides, the soldiers waited obediently for the next command. Silence. The sergeant then motioned for the fife and bugle corps, who belted out a rousing version of "God Save the King." Quite an impressive display, thought Isaac, for our tiny settlement. In the month since they landed at the Toronto Harbour, only a handful of other settlers had come out to the frontier, so the number of settlers now barely surpassed the number of soldiers.

At precisely noon, four soldiers marched to the side of the stage and ceremoniously raised the flag on a pole that had been erected for the occasion the day before.

"What flag is that, Uncle Isaac?" whispered Simeon, not recognizing the blue, red and white pattern that hung downward on the windless day.

"It's the Union Jack," answered Isaac, adjusting his hat to fend off the midday heat. "I don't think the British would fly anything else." Isaac had only a brief memory of the Union Jack flying at the town hall in Orange County, New York, when he was six years old, before the Revolution.

Isaac glanced back to the stage that he had helped his brothers hastily assemble the day before. Crossing paths with the governor on his way to the limestone outcrop, Isaac had been ordered to return to the landing spot and oversee the construction.

"At once, Devins," the governor ordered. "I need the stage finished by the end of the day. It must be able to hold ten men."

Isaac carefully hid his annoyance at being assigned such a trivial task. He was starting to feel like the governor's whipping boy, which was not how he envisioned his life in Toronto at all.

A trumpet blared, summoning the attention of all settlers and soldiers to the stage. From afar, Isaac watched Governor Simcoe and his entourage with a trifle of admiration and a mountain of envy. Simcoe had invited St. John Rousseau and four members of the Executive Council to join him on stage. *I should be up there too,* grumbled Isaac, considering all the work I've done for the governor. Instead, he watched that half-wit, William Jarvis, along with James Baby, John Small, and John White stand where he felt he should be. *What will it take to impress the governor?* Isaac fumed, impatient with his lack of progress.

"Hear ye, hear ye!" the drill master bellowed. "Let it be known that on this twenty-sixth day of August, in the year seventeen hundred and ninety-three, we are gathered to witness the naming of our new settlement on the north shore of Lake Ontario."

Glancing sideways, Isaac saw that his family was listening attentively. He wondered if naming the settlement York was wise, considering that there already was a settlement on the east coast named New York. The Americans might object since the names could create havoc for anyone trying to send a letter or ship goods, which could easily be left at the wrong port. *I prefer the name Toronto,* he thought.

Isaac was only vaguely aware of Simcoe's political motivations. France had declared war on Britain earlier in the year, on February 1, after sending King Louis XVI and his wife, Marie-Antoinette, to the guillotine. The French Republic then began flaunting the Declaration of the Rights of Man and of the Citizen. Simcoe was vehemently against the French Revolution, just as he had opposed the American Revolution, for it put the power of the King and the aristocrats into the hands of the people. He fervently believed that the King should rule, and was determined that only a limited form of democracy or republicanism should ever come to Upper Canada.

Britain had responded by sending the Duke of York to capture Flanders, an important defensive location. Simcoe chose to name his new settlement York to honour the achievement. He wanted to quell any trace of revolutionary ideas that might linger in the minds of the Loyalists. York would become a symbol of undying devotion to the Crown and against democracy.

Without warning, the military band began to play out of cue, as was their custom, and continued until they caught sight of the drill master, waving his arms and shouting, "Not yet, Not yet!"

Stepping to the front of the stage, Governor Simcoe cleared his throat and began. "Ladies and gentlemen. We are all eternally grateful to King George the Third, who has provided the wisdom and leadership to set our great nation apart, to guide it fearlessly, and to provide for us. Now, we will honour our great King by naming our new settlement in honour of his second son, Ferdinand Augustus, Duke of York."

Pausing for a moment, Simcoe surveyed the audience and detected a hint of dissidence. He could see that a few of the settlers stared at him with tight-lipped faces, their foreheads shrugged as if they were in a quandary. Even one rebellious voice could create a sense of doubt, chip away at the foundation of loyalty to the King, and unravel his plans for colonization.

He tried another tactic. "Together, we will create a town, a nation, as vibrant, prosperous and successful as London, which will be the envy of the American rebels and the pride of Great Britain. The town of York will become the centre of commerce, trade and prosperity in the New World!"

Simcoe looked over at Great Sail and Kineubenae, who nodded in agreement, anticipating the potential for continued trading with the British. He noticed a slight easing of tension in the crowd, and continued.

"All of you will have a voice in the town of York. We will work *together*." Simcoe paused for effect, emphasizing the last word. He knew that he had to appeal to any democratic tendencies that might be lingering in the hearts of the former Americans. "And our hard work and dedication will create a town of prosperity, wealth and prominence for everyone!"

The settlers erupted into applause as they finally heard the words they had been waiting for. Under the direction of the drill sergeant, the Queen's Rangers stood to attention, raised their muskets, pointed them to the sky, and fired a twenty-one-gun salute, the sound resounding off the shimmering waters of Lake Ontario.

"They must have heard the guns clear across at Niagara," muttered Levi to Isaac.

Simeon squatted on the ground with his hands over his ears, squinting. Polly tried to soothe her baby, crying in her arms. "Shhh," Polly whispered, rocking her baby and patting her on the back. "Shhhhhh, Mama's here . . ."

Boom, boom, boom!

Smoke curled from the three cannons on the rocky shore, pointed out into the harbour. A few seconds later, the cannons onboard the *Mississaga* and the *Onondaga* returned fire, the guns pointed toward the peninsula. A final round of "God Save the King" marked the end of the ceremony, and the settlers quickly dispersed.

"I see you have made a bit of progress, considering there was nothing but trees here a month ago," observed John White as he ambled away from the crowd at the foot of the stage. He greeted Isaac in his characteristic style of starting in the middle of a conversation.

"Yes, but we are far from anything even resembling a town," returned Isaac, pleased to see his friend. "Unless you consider a dozen tents strewn at random to be good town planning. Not a single building do we have to offer, as we are too busy cutting down trees."

Isaac could not help but mock the slow pace at which the town was being built. He felt strangely apologetic, as if he were in some way the host who could not offer his guest a place to sleep for the night.

"Distressing news," returned White. "I wonder where on earth we will hold the Executive Council meeting tomorrow."

Simcoe had summoned his elite to Toronto for the meeting but at the last minute ordered them to come a day early to witness the founding of York. William Jarvis complained to everyone during the voyage that he felt like a slave being summoned by his master.

"I doubt the governor will host it in one of the settler's lean-tos, so that leaves either the fort or back on one of the ships," said Isaac. "Unless, of course, you situate yourselves in a circle on any of the stumps jutting out of the ground right here."

He could only imagine how disgusted William Jarvis or Francis Baby would be, accustomed as they were to a wealthy, privileged lifestyle with many comforts.

White chuckled, adding, "Or perhaps in the forest with the wolves. You really are living in such primitive conditions. I can't imagine how you bear it."

The ramshackle lean-tos and tents in the small clearing hardly resembled the streets of London. White considered Montreal primitive when he arrived in Upper Canada several years ago, but at least it had a grid of stone houses, shops, taverns and churches. Even Queenston and Newark had seemed rather stark. Here, there was nothing.

Isaac escorted White to the Devins' lean-to on the shoreline, where Polly and Rita were tending to a pot held over the fire by three branches strung together. The aroma of rabbit stew wafted through the camp as Isaac ushered his guest to his favourite perch on the log. The mosquitoes were gone at this time of year, and the strong wind off the lake was refreshing.

John White felt truly welcomed by the Devins family. Despite having little to offer, their generosity astounded him. Nestled into the eating area under the shade of a cottonwood tree, White admired the workmanship of the maple table and chairs that Isaac and Jacob had designed and built just a week earlier, with only a couple of axes, an adze, and a hand saw. Isaac Devins is obviously a skilled man, White observed.

Although he was a member of the privileged class, he chose to associate with people of honour, integrity and intelligence, no matter their lot in life. He had recognized these qualities in Isaac the day they had met. To those less deserving, he often appeared rude and condescending. But when he saw value in a human being, he was kind, generous and a true friend.

The merriment continued through the afternoon. At nightfall, White reluctantly returned to his quarters on the *Onondaga*, a berth he shared with the other Executive Council members. He declined Isaac's offer to sleep under the stars, saying he wanted to be ferried over to the fort first thing in the morning. White despised the idea of being late for an appointment.

I also don't like to be tardy, Isaac thought as he strode along the path through the woods the next morning, hoping to reach the limestone outcrop well before noon. He needed only another day's work to finish his canoe, hoping to give it a test run before evening. Luckily, the August days were long. Isaac stopped at Garrison creek to fill his canteen and have a quick snack of bread and honey that Polly had packed.

Suddenly, out of the woods came an angry mob of settlers, their voices practically shouting at one another. At the front of the mob was Levi Devins.

"Isaac, do you know where the governor is?" he demanded.

The dozen or so other settlers crowded around Isaac. "He's over at the canvas tent, under the arbour, for the Executive Council meeting."

"Arrrhh!" roared the crowd as they rushed past him. Isaac followed, imploring Levi to fill him in.

The angry settlers stormed into the governor's arbour, demanding to be heard.

"Your Excellency!" shouted Levi. "While you sit here in the comfort of the arbour, sipping tea, we are toiling away at the landing spot, breaking our backs to clear the land for God knows what. We have been here a month, and we still have nothing to show for it – no houses, no mills, no land!"

"You promised us assistance, but we have only seen a handful of Queen's Rangers at our camps," clamoured another settler, gesturing wildly. The initial sense of pride in clearing the forest had been replaced by mounting frustration.

The governor stood and placed his arms behind his back to show that he did not feel threatened. He replied in a quiet, steady voice, "All of my men have been busy rebuilding the fort, for your very protection."

"We don't need protection!" shouted Levi, pushing a fellow settler out of the way and stepping forward to be heard. "We need supplies. We have only a month or so before the snow flies, and we have no adequate shelter. Only two ships have come to this backwater with provisions since we arrived."

"But surely you have gone to St. John's trading post on the river?" said Simcoe, who actually had not been there himself.

"His trading post is fine if you want furs, corn or birchbark ornaments. We need tools, we need grain, we need wool, we need rope. Are we to walk all the way back to Niagara to get these things?" demanded Levi, filled with rage, spitting out his words.

"I tell you, we will not do the like!" steamed another settler, pushing forward to stand beside Levi.

"Why should we even stay here?" yelled another. "At least in Niagara we had a roof over our heads."

The governor had not even thought about the settlers' plight in the comfort of his luxurious canvas tents. Instead, his mind had been occupied with the grander picture of defending Upper Canada from an American attack, constructing roads, opening up the province. The governor was a visionary who had little time for practical matters.

"Gentlemen, gentlemen," interrupted Simcoe in a bland, collected tone. "We were just discussing the urgent need for a sawmill to provide lumber," he lied.

Looking into the crowd, he spotted Isaac's brother-in-law. "Nicholas Miller will start work this afternoon on the King's Mill on the west bank of the Humber. Take as many men as you need. We can have the sawmill operating by the end of the week so that everyone can start building."

"But where will we build our houses?" demanded Levi, not satisfied with Simcoe's response. "We don't have a survey or any means of knowing where we are to settle. I refuse to build a home at the landing spot only to have the very land dedicated to someone else. Just where are we to settle!?" Levi repeated, taking another step toward the governor.

"Aitkins will complete the survey next week, I have been told," Simcoe replied, "and each of you can claim your land grant immediately after that. My promise to you holds firm, free land to all settlers. In the meantime, we will concentrate our efforts on the sawmill so that lumber is ready for building." Simcoe spoke in the collective sense to calm the angry crowd.

"And what will the rest of us do while the mill is being built?" yelled a voice from the back of the crowd.

"I will not fell one more tree at the landing spot," chimed in another, "unless I am assured that the land will be mine."

"Me neither!" and "Hear, hear!" resounded through the crowd. The aristocrats sitting at the table looked nervously up at the governor. The settlers were refusing to carry out Simcoe's orders. The seeds of a revolt have just been planted, thought John White. As a lawyer, White was highly perceptive of the thoughts and emotions of others, far more so than Governor Simcoe.

Simcoe thought quickly. He knew that he had to come up with a fulfilling task that they could toil away at until the survey was completed, after which they would all forget about the frustration of the last month. A diversion would do the trick.

"Gentlemen, one of the reasons that we have had so few ships coming to York is that we do not have an adequate dock. We need to construct one large enough for two or three ships. Tomorrow we will start work on the King's Wharf, using the trees stockpiled along the shoreline."

The settlers seemed uncertain. They shifted back and forth, weighing the governor's plan to determine its worth. Before anyone could voice an objection, Isaac pushed his way through the crowd to the front, nodded to the governor, and then turned to face the crowd.

"I think the governor has a sound plan," intoned Isaac in an optimistic manner. "We need to have a good-sized dock in order to receive goods." Turning to his brother, he continued, "Levi, you said that we desperately need tools and supplies. How can we receive any large-scale quantities without an adequate dock?"

"I suppose we could," answered Levi, mulling over the possibilities.

"At least we would be building something with the trees instead of just cutting them down," said a settler.

"Or burning them," added another.

The settlers all erupted at once, talking among themselves. As they debated who would be in charge and how it would be constructed, Isaac snuck away and resumed his hike to the limestone outcrop. He was pleased that he had been able to assist Simcoe in calming the angry crowd. He hoped that the governor would be appreciative, since the dock would go hand in hand with Simcoe's plans for a shipbuilding wharf next spring.

The next morning, Fire Starter and Isaac sat in their canoes while Fire Starter demonstrated how to paddle and steer. Isaac watched him paddle away swiftly and carve a perfect figure-eight. His movements were swift and sure, almost effortless. Then Fire Starter indicated that Isaac should try.

Pushing off a rock with his paddle, Isaac nearly lost control of the canoe, his weight shifting dangerously from side to side.

"Kaawiin nsastazin," Fire Starter commanded, then motioned how to sit properly in the canoe to keep balance.

Turning and twisting, Isaac guided the canoe in a somewhat circular pattern, with Fire Starter yelling instructions in Anishinaabe and miming the proper technique. Fortunately, Isaac was a quick study. By the third try, he managed to do a figure-eight, but not as elegantly as his teacher.

The next day, Isaac paddled up to the site for the King's Mill, a half-mile north of the limestone outcrop, without any mishap. His brother-in-law welcomed him and said he could use an extra hand. Nicholas immediately dispatched Isaac to paddle over to St. John's trading post to bring more shovels, picks and whip-saws, as well as some feed for the horses.

"A sawmill?" questioned St. John. "I am only too happy to lend you everything you need, my friend. Yes, yes, take the adze too, you may need it for the flue." St. John was pleased to hear of an industry located a few hundred yards south, so close to his trading post.

Nicholas Miller then set Isaac to work with another settler on gathering large boulders to divert water toward the mill. First, they placed a stake in the location of the water wheel. Then they measured twenty feet from the stake in a northwest direction and laid the boulders on both sides, stopping at the river's edge.

"That's a tiny flutter wheel," Isaac remarked when he saw Nicholas trying to place it in the perfect location to receive the water from the flue.

"Why, yes," replied Miller, who had built and operated sawmills and gristmills for most of his life. "For a sawmill, the smaller the better. The five-foot wheel will allow us to have quick, short motions with the blade. A larger wheel would mean that we won't cut as many planks in a day."

Isaac walked around to survey Nicholas' handiwork. "I see where the crank will be attached to push the sash arm up and down for the saw blade," Isaac observed. "But what is the other crank for?"

"It will be attached to a series of gears to provide a sideways motion that will push the log forward toward the saw. With both cranks working together, we will have the most efficient method of sawing wood known to man." Miller had only heard about the second crank just before he left for Upper Canada. He didn't let it be known that this was the first time he was applying the method.

"Quite grand," marvelled Isaac, impressed by the ingenuity of the intricate machinery. "What will be the yield?"

"This type of mill will give us fifty planks a day, about what it would take two men to cut in a week," Miller replied.

At dinner that evening, Isaac informed his family of his prediction. "It will take two days to mill enough lumber for a small shanty. There is no way that all sixteen families in York will have a roof over their head before the snow flies. Father, perhaps we should consider moving back to Newark for the winter."

"Nonsense!" exclaimed Abraham, who was thoroughly enjoying life on the frontier. "If need be, we can build a one-room cabin on our own, without the King's Mill. Levi and Jacob, tomorrow you will find suitable logs for a shelter, borrow an adze and start honing logs so that we are ready." Abraham used his authoritative voice, not allowing any dissension to infiltrate his sons' minds.

"Are we to build the cabin here along the lakeshore?" queried Isaac respectfully. "What if our land grants are much farther removed?" The land that he hoped to acquire was a mile away from the landing spot, and it would be almost impossible to transport the honed logs through the woods to the site. They would have to borrow a team of horses and even then it would be easier to cut and hone the logs right at the building site.

"You do speak with reason, Isaac," responded his father. "We probably should wait until the survey is completed."

Waiting, waiting, waiting, Isaac complained to himself the next morning as he walked toward the mill site, head cast downward looking at the path. So much depends on the survey, and yet the governor does not appear to be concerned. Yes, the governor ordered the King's Mill to be built, but even that gesture won't appease the settlers when they find out that there is not enough lumber to build their homes.

Hearing a sound, Isaac looked up and was surprised to see Simcoe striding toward him. "Devins, I am glad I ran into you," he began.

Uncharacteristically, Isaac interrupted, "Your Excellency, I think we have a problem brewing. The sawmill cannot possibly produce enough lumber for our cabins, and the settlers will protest. I don't think – "

The governor likewise interrupted Isaac, although it was one of his common traits. "The expedition to cut the Dundas Road leaves tomorrow. You will head out with Augustus Jones, a competent surveyor whose work I greatly admire. I need you to act as foreman. It should only take a few weeks."

Isaac started after him along the path. "But, Governor, the survey will be completed next week. How will I ensure that I receive the land grant that I am anticipating?"

Simcoe stopped and turned around, sensing Isaac's reluctance. "Never fear. I will personally ensure that you receive your grant. Just give me a parchment with an adequate description of it, and I will have Jarvis dedicate it to you." Isaac still looked doubtful, so Simcoe offered, "Did I mention this is a paid assignment? You will receive a salary of ten pounds."

Seeing Isaac's doubtful expression change to gratitude, Simcoe turned and continued down the path.

"Thank you, Governor, I am eternally grateful," Isaac called out after him. This was the first time Simcoe had offered him money.

Polly was elated by the news and very pleased that cash would be coming into the household. There were no ladies in need of a server in York, and Elizabeth Simcoe already had her servants. The Devins family still had very little to trade. With some money, they could finally buy some of the bare necessities that they had been forced to leave behind on the trail through the Indian Territory.

Snuggled against her husband, she gazed out over the Toronto Bay from their seat on the log along the rocky shore. Polly leaned her head on his shoulder, knowing that she would miss him while he was gone. Isaac put an arm around her, but his mind was occupied by the adventure that lay before him. He would be going into unknown territory, where no white men had ever laid foot before.

Isaac and Polly were completely unaware that danger awaited them but in very different capacities.

Chapter 9 – October 6, 1793

God speed, prayed Polly, clutching the thwart of the canoe with white knuckles as they cut through the choppy water of Lake Ontario just before noon. The bow of the canoe crashed back down at the bottom of the wave, only to rise on the next crest and crash back down again. A furious wind wailed across the harbour from the southwest, creating three-foot swells where only minutes before the lake had been still. A sudden downpour appeared out of nowhere, the staccato clack of heavy rain almost drowning out the crash of the canoe after every wave.

Polly's heart skipped a beat as the waves broke toward them. Spray washed in, quickly filling the large cedar canoe up to Polly's ankles, her long, blue linen gown floating in the rising water. Terrified, she braced herself for the impact of each wave, expecting the canoe to keel over. Why did I never learn to swim, she scolded herself, certain that she was only seconds away from drowning.

Please, God, begged Polly, *if you choose to take me now, please let Elizabeth get better, please don't let my baby die*. Her heart ached as she pictured her sick infant, left in the care of her mother-in-law, who desperately needed a cure. Days had passed since her child first came down with a hacking cough, fever and chills. She was now so weak that she might not have the strength to pull through.

Polly desperately needed to go to the peninsula that day and return before nightfall. It was her only hope of finding a cure. She was just about to leave on horseback when her sister, Rita, tapped her on the shoulder and pointed to the large cedar canoe that had just pulled into the landing spot.

"I'm sure a canoe would be much swifter than a horse," Rita remarked.

Recognizing two of the natives, Polly greeted them and asked if they could take her across the bay to the peninsula.

"Please, Great Sail, I beg of you. I need to get there as soon as I can. My daughter is sick, dying, and I need some healing for her."

Polly was desperate. She had made a poultice of wheat bran with warm water, as her mother had taught her to do when she was a child, and applied it to little Elizabeth's chest. She had made a tea of raspberry and blueberry, but could only force the child to take a few drops. Her sister had made a vapour of the last of the chamomile tea, but it only seemed to relieve her breathing for a brief moment.

No one at the landing spot could offer anything else. There were no supplies or medicines, let alone a doctor. Everyone had looked through their belongings but no one could provide anything that the Devins did not already have. No turpentine, no epsom salts, no herbal tea. Rita had even gone up to the Simcoe's canvas tents at the fort, but came back empty-handed. There were no boats in the harbour to be sent to Niagara, and it was sheer folly to canoe out into the lake to look for a passing ship.

All the settlers were concerned for the health of the first child born at the settlement. It was as if the fate of baby Elizabeth rested in the hands of each settler, and her death or survival would be a sign of their own destiny. A couple of neighbours immediately left for Niagara on foot, even though it would be a week before they returned.

If only Isaac were here, Polly wailed, he would know what to do. Gone for nearly a month, she did not know when he would return. Damn the governor, she swore ungratefully, and his need to cut a new road before winter. Isaac's salary for building the Dundas Road now seemed insignificant against the life or death of her newborn child.

Great Sail took Polly's hand as he helped her alight onto the rocky shore of the peninsula. "Welcome to our healing garden," he said. "We call it 'the place of trees standing out of the water'. Here, you will find the remedies you seek."

St. John had told them many times that the Mississaugas would go to the peninsula to recover from sickness, gather herbs and perform healing rituals using centuries-old remedies. His wife, Margaret, used more than five hundred plants from the peninsula, forest, swamps, fields and lakeshore for healing, rituals, meditation and magic.

"Fire Starter will show you the way. I must return to the mainland. We are one week away from our great migration to the north for the winter. I have much to do."

Polly stepped back tentatively to allow Great Sail to climb back into the cedar canoe, which looked large enough for twenty passengers. She was more than a little nervous to be left alone with Fire Starter, who spoke very little English and looked menacing with his shaved forehead, long spiky hair at the back, and a yellow and black painted face. She consoled herself by remembering that Isaac spoke highly of Fire Starter as a stern and knowledgeable teacher, and someone he would trust with his life. With a touch of apprehension, Polly followed him, her fear of losing her daughter outweighing all else.

Fire Starter stopped a few feet into the brush that surrounded the shoreline before extracting a fourteen-inch knife from its holster on his deerskin pants. He hacked off four branches of sumac, quickly removing the smaller branches and leaves. Holding one of the branches between his thumb and forefinger, he carved three thin strokes from the bark with a smaller knife.

Pointing to the inner bark with the tip of the blade, he looked up at Polly and said, "Good." He then mimed the removal of the rest of the bark, grinding the inner bark into a powder and applying it to the arms and chest.

Polly nodded her understanding. Fire Starter quickly tied the branches together with some twine and they continued along a well-worn path through a thicket of birch, aspen and cottonwood. The sky cleared as they went and the air seemed light and thin blowing through the saplings, unlike the heaviness of the dense forest on the mainland. A riot of wildflowers exploded at every sunny patch in the thicket, showing a vivid display of autumn yellows, purples and corals, so different from the dark woods at the landing spot.

Before long they reached a fork in the path and swung to the right, toward the tip of the peninsula where the Queen's Rangers were soon to build a lighthouse. They crossed over several logs laid through a small marsh, alive with the song of the red-winged blackbird and the flutter of grasshopper wings. Although it was nearly noon, the call of the loon was a constant symphony played as a backdrop for the tweeting and chirps of hummingbirds, doves and flycatchers.

They stopped to pick some cranberries growing at the edge of the marsh, an important ingredient in home remedies for both the settlers and the Mississaugas. Suddenly, she heard voices and stopped dead in her tracks. Taking no notice, Fire Starter continued along and disappeared into the forest. The voices became louder and more succinct, and then unrecognizable. It must be a group of Mississaugas, thought Polly hopefully, not wanting to consider anything more dangerous.

Hiding behind a walnut tree, she peered around it and could see that Fire Starter was in a serious conversation with another native in front of two wigwams with smoke rising from the centre of each. A handful of people were gathered around him out of curiosity, while others seemed to be preparing the midday meal. A half-skinned deer was hanging by a rope from the lower branch of an ash tree. This must be where the smoke comes from, observed Polly, who had watched it from across the bay as it billowed above the trees on the peninsula for the last ten days.

Unexpectedly, Fire Starter turned and motioned for Polly to join him. As she pensively emerged from the cover of the trees, the voices trailed off to whispers, and then silence.

With all eyes fixed on her, Polly walked slowly to where Fire Starter stood, glancing nervously to the side, thankful that her long skirt covered her shaking knees. Polly had never been this close to a group of Mississaugas before. She had only seen Mohawks, Senecas and Cherokees ride by quickly on their horses on the way to the Genesee River.

She felt utterly alone. No one in her family could spare the time to come with her to the peninsula, despite the gravity of the situation. Rita was only weeks away from giving birth to her own first child. Her mother-in-law was caring for Elizabeth, and all the men, even little Simeon, were busy building a log cabin for the winter. Undaunted, Polly did the unthinkable, driven by the fear of losing her child. She went to the peninsula alone, unaccompanied, placing her trust in Great Sail.

Fire Starter uttered a few words, then a beautiful young woman with long, braided jet-black hair stepped forward beside him. Through gestures, Fire Starter proudly introduced Polly to his wife, Mahima, and their baby. Polly smiled and nodded, admiring the craftsmanship of her deerskin dress and the cradleboard slung over her back.

Curious about the cradleboard, she leaned forward and fondled it, trying to understand its construction. What an incredibly efficient way to transport your child, she thought, observing how the mother's hands were free to engage in other things. She ran her fingers along the edge of the casing, admiring how the willow branches were intertwined to strengthen their mass. The baby sat comfortably inside, nestled in folded blankets, completely secure and content. This would come in so handy, Polly thought, when preparing a meal or spinning.

Her interest in the cradleboard opened the door for the whole group of Mississauga women to come forward and touch Polly's linen dress, so different from their own deerskin garments. She was soon surrounded by curious faces, chattering away, feeling the cotton and stroking the muslin bodice and the ribbons of her bonnet. Some fondled strands of her auburn hair that had escaped from her cap.

Polly felt like a calf on display at the market. She grew more and more uncomfortable with so many hands on her clothing at once, pinching, squeezing, caressing. They are going to smother me, she fretted. She hurriedly took off her bonnet and passed it to the nearest squaw. Her bonnet was passed from hand to hand, mulled over, and tried on by several women. Some of them laughed, others were grim, shaking their heads.

When it was returned, Polly passed it back, miming her intent to give it to them as a gift. The women smiled and some guffawed in reply, which prompted each of them to try it on once more. As Fire Starter and Polly turned to leave, Mahima gave her the cradleboard as a gift.

Polly was touched, and said, "Miigwetch," which delighted the women even more.

Taking a well-worn path, Fire Starter led her eastward for another half-hour. Finally, the forest opened up and they saw a lone sassafras tree, a hundred feet tall, in a meadow of wildflowers and herbs. It looked mysterious and majestic, almost magical. Its leaves were turning from green to yellow and orange, its strong branches pointed upward to the clear blue sky. When the wind blew, it made a shimmering sound, as if it were playing a melody that only the initiated could understand. The sassafras tree was sacred to the Mississaugas.

Fire Starter commanded, "Madabin, madabin," pointing toward the ground and sitting down himself, facing the tree.

Polly sat beside him in the tall grass, prepared to follow Fire Starter's lead. Stretching his arms to the side, then resting his palms on the crumpled grass and wildflowers, he leaned back, closed his eyes and started to chant. Reverence for the healing powers of the sassafras tree emanated from his body and from his humble incantation.

She turned toward the tree, looking for any sign of supernatural power. Her religion did not allow her to worship anything other than the invisible God of the Bible. But so far, her prayers had not been answered, her child had become sicker. Polly decided that God would not mind her trying to use every resource she could to save her child. She mimicked Fire Starter's actions and joined in the singing, hoping that their combined effort would save her baby's life.

Abruptly, the chanting ended. The two sat in silence, staring at the sassafras tree for a long while. Fire Starter then rose and picked some leaves, miming that Polly should help him. After they had gathered a half bushel, Fire Starter indicated that Polly was to sit back down with the leaves in her apron, and remain like that for the rest of the day. He would return to get her before sunset. He then walked back down the path, leaving Polly to continue the ritual alone.

St. John had told the Devins that self-reflection was an important part of the Mississaugas' spiritual path. He said that the Mississaugas believed that one needs to find balance from within, to allow oneself to be open to the Great Spirit, who will guide you on your journey. *Fire Starter must think that I need to pray*, Polly guessed, *or why else would he leave me here alone?*

There was nothing to do but wait. The sun poked through the tree canopy, warming Polly's shoulder, a very pleasant temperature for early October. The breeze was not yet filled with a cold winter chill. Polly ran her fingers over the three smooth lobes of a sassafras leaf that had landed on her forearm, wondering if its healing powers would be enough to save her child.

Why did I ever go into the tent that day? she lamented, cursing herself for being so careless. *If only I had remembered*, she wailed, *Elizabeth would never have gotten sick, would never be on death's door.* She was very much aware of the dangers of going into the tent when the lye was being boiled, but in her haste that day she had forgotten.

For as long as she could remember, the beginning of fall was the traditional soapmaking time. Even though the settlers were still without land or houses, they decided to make soap simply because there were so many ashes from the felled trees. Although most settlers did not bathe regularly for fear of washing away essential oils, soap was still used for daily washing of the face and hands, and for cleaning clothes. The Devins family had only one bar of soap left before winter came and did not want to impose on others.

"It's an embarrassment if we borrow anything else," Polly's mother-in-law had insisted, self-conscious of the implements, ornaments and food that they had been forced to borrow.

The lye was made by slowly pouring water over the ashes until a brownish liquid oozed out from the bottom of the barrel. Polly and Rita collected animal fat from the deer and bear skins and boiled it down with an equal amount of water until most of the water disappeared. Left over night, the fat rose to the top with the impurities remaining in the water solution.

"This has to be the most rancid-smelling task imaginable," Rita complained. "I hate it."

"Almost as bad as skinning a not-so-fresh deer," agreed Polly.

The next morning, Polly stoked the fire and then filled a huge iron kettle with the lye and the fat. She left the solution to boil on its own. Polly only needed to return to add water several times throughout the day and wait until the solution was the correct texture and fitness.

As she washed the iron moulds for the bar soap, she heard gunshots. Pulling her auburn locks back behind her ear, she looked over the top of the well and saw a commotion at the Millers' tent fifty feet away. There were shouts and curses as a half-dozen men pushed and shoved one another, fists flying. She was used to seeing the men fight, something that seemed to happen almost daily, sometimes over a very minor concern.

But this altercation was different, angrier, more threatening. Suddenly, she saw someone with a shotgun point it directly toward Elizabeth, who was peacefully asleep nearby in the bassinet that Levi had made. Without thinking, Polly threw down her wash cloth, grabbed the baby and ran into the tent for cover. Crouching, she prayed that any gunshots would fly overhead.

As she lay on the floor with Elizabeth pulled toward her, she heard a few more gunshots, silence, and then a low murmur of voices, a little less hostile. She left Elizabeth safely on the floor and crept to the doorway to see what was going on. Carefully, she peeled back the canvas door. Seeing no one, she opened the door wider, puzzled as to where the angry settlers could have gone. She opened the tent door even wider so that it was now at its full breadth.

Suddenly, a gust of wind appeared out of nowhere from the south and blew the toxic smoke from the fire pit directly into the tent, where it remained trapped.

"No! Elizabeth!" Polly cried.

She ran inside. Barely able to breathe, her eyes red and itchy from the toxic smoke, she grabbed her baby, then scrambled out of the tent, as far away from the fire pit as she could go. Elizabeth was coughing, choking, hardly able to breathe.

A chill and fever set in almost immediately, and Polly watched helplessly as it grew and seemed to take over her child's little body. If only I had run into the lake or the forest, she agonized.

"I have poisoned my child," she said out loud, heartbroken, as she stared at the sassafras tree.

She looked down to the sassafras leaves in her apron and over to the half-filled basket. The sassafras has to work, she whispered, or my daughter will die and I will never forgive myself.

The longer she looked at the sassafras leaves, the more desperately she wanted to make the tea and lotion, her last hope. How frustrating to sit here with nothing to do but pray and worry and fret, she thought, when there is a potential cure right here in my hands. She waited, prayed, waited and prayed until she could finally wait no longer.

Springing to her feet, she bounded down a narrow path through scrub brush that looked like it would lead toward the harbour. At the water's edge, Polly saw that she could walk around the peninsula, through the marsh, and back to the landing spot in probably four hours, about two hours before Fire Starter would return to the sassafras tree. Without hesitation she dashed along the lakeshore, the sassafras leaves, sumac, and cranberries neatly tucked into the cradleboard slung on her back.

The path meandered through some taller mature trees that cast a cooling shade in the midday heat but it led away from the harbour. Polly hesitated, unsure whether to take the path or to stay along the lakeshore and blaze her own trail. I'm coming, Elizabeth, I'm coming, she told herself over and over again, suspended in time. She envisioned her child lying there, so weak and frail, so close to death. What if I don't make it in time, she moaned, what if ...

Suddenly, she heard voices from the west, along the lakeshore. She clambered along the shoreline toward the sound, hacking away at the reed grass. No thoughts of uncertainty or fear entered her mind as they had earlier in the day. Instead, she pushed her way forward as fast as she could, jumping over the branches, rocks and stumps as if she could actually see where they were. The greater fear, more than her own safety, was not to get back to the landing spot in time.

Flinging apart the last of the tall grasses, she emerged into a clearing and stopped short. The governor's wife, Elizabeth Simcoe, was seated on a boulder twenty paces away, her back turned. She was sketching an image of the landing spot, lost in the beauty of the moment. Mrs. Simcoe looked resplendent, showing a fine posture through her lovely cotton gown blowing softly in the wind. Her sky blue travelling dress almost matched the colour of the water that she was painting so elegantly.

"Dear Governess!" Polly called out, panting, trying to catch her breath.

Her startled listener turned around with a jerk, a look of surprise and shock on her face.

"What in the – " blurted Mrs. Simcoe, who was not used to seeing any settlers on the peninsula. Whenever she came to explore and sketch, there were only a few Mississaugas and no one else.

"I beg of you, please, I must get back to the landing spot immediately. I came out here to get some healing herbs from the Mississaugas since I have nothing else to save my baby, who is so ill that I don't know if she will live another day. I pray, I beg of you, to help me, please!"

Elizabeth Simcoe could sense Polly's distress despite her politeness. She had heard that the Devins' child was dreadfully ill. "How did you get here? Who are you with?" she asked.

"I came across the harbour by canoe with Great Sail and Fire Starter this morning," explained Polly. "But I must return at once. My baby's life is in danger, and I now have a cure. I hope I am not too late."

Elizabeth Simcoe's heart filled with sympathy for Polly, as she imagined how awful it would be to lose a child. "You came here alone?" she inquired.

"Yes," said Polly, impressing her listener, "there was no one else who could come."

She looked at Polly with a new-found respect, remembering the woman who had given birth inside her home only a month ago, who seemed brave but rather plain and simple. This woman must have more character than I gave her credit for, Elizabeth concluded. Not that she would care to socialize with Polly Devins. She never fraternized with anyone who was beneath her social class, unless it helped her husband's political career. Her social life in York so far had been quite lacking since there was no one of gentry who had ventured out to the new settlement yet.

"Mr. Brisbane, please come here and bring my horse," she ordered one of her servants and then turned back to Polly.

"Please take my horse, you will get there much quicker. Just stay on the bridle path until you reach the other side of the swamp. Then you can gallop along the lakeshore since the pebbles are quite small." She gave Polly a look of sympathy and understanding, thankful that her own newborn, six months older, was in good health.

"I am eternally grateful, Mrs. Simcoe," Polly replied, the tension easing out of her voice, neck and shoulders. "You will never know how much I appreciate your kindness."

Galloping along the pebble shore, Polly leaned forward, grabbing the brown mare's long mane for the final tear to the landing spot. She raced to the family tent, but it was abandoned. Everyone must be up at the new homestead, she surmised. She quickly turned the horse and galloped through the forest that led to the Humber River. Levi and Abraham had each claimed two hundred acre lots along its banks ten days earlier after the governor finally produced a survey map. Polly had moved most of their belongings there, not wanting to live alone at the landing spot with her newborn baby.

"By the grace of God, she's still alive," Polly sighed as she saw her mother-in-law sitting at the outdoor table with the baby nestled to her bosom. With only a terse greeting, Polly immediately set to work making the sassafras tea just as Fire Starter had said. She added a touch of honey, hoping that it would entice the child to drink it.

Setting the tea to cool in a pot of cold water, Polly finally was able to hold her baby, kiss her forehead and feel her heartbeat. Elizabeth was just as unresponsive as she had been that morning. At least she has not had a turn for the worst, Polly thought. Holding the baby upright, she soaked a clean rag in the tea and held it to the baby's mouth, putting a couple of drops on her finger so that the baby could taste that it was good.

Polly's heart sang as Elizabeth drank the sassafras tea, slowly at first and then more earnestly. She fed her baby for close to half an hour before Elizabeth drifted off to sleep. Polly watched her intently for any sign of recovery, any hint of wellness, but there was none. Maybe the potion was not strong enough, she fretted. Maybe I should have used more sumac. She lay on a hammock strung between two red oaks, cradling her child, hoping for a miracle. Exhaustion finally overcame her and she drifted into a deep sleep.

When she awoke, night had fallen. Everyone had gone to bed, but the fire was still aglow. Polly added a couple of logs and the orange glow finally illuminated the child's face. She could see in an instant that Elizabeth was much improved. Her eyes were open and she looked alert, watchful and calm, eyes darting around to take in the dancing firelight. Polly gasped, sighed and then whooped out an almost unearthly cry, releasing her stress and tension.

"She's better, she's better! Thank the Lord," Polly chanted over and over again as she danced around the fire with her child in her arms, singing an old German folk song, laughing and cheering.

Like many other Americans, Polly firmly believed in divine intervention. As a child she had seen her uncle brought back to life after he was on his deathbed. Perhaps I am being rewarded for all the good deeds I have done, she wondered. Perhaps it is Providence. Perhaps it is a miracle.

The next morning, rays of glorious sunshine spread throughout the town of York, warming Polly's back as she stood away from the fire with Elizabeth nestled in the cradleboard on her back. How wonderful the daybreak is, mused Polly, when all is safe and sound; no worries or troubles occupying your mind.

"My, oh my, you are a sight," she heard someone exclaim.

Polly turned as Isaac rushed toward her, arms outstretched, so happy to see his wife after a long month in the forest. He kissed her on the forehead, then picked her and the baby up, swinging them around. Polly just laughed and cried and laughed again, barely able to speak.

"Look, Isaac, your daughter is well!" Polly almost shouted, so happy and filled with the kind of joy that only a tragedy overcome can bring.

"Why, yes, she is," agreed Isaac, unaware of the ordeal that Polly had gone through. "And you are looking very well to me too," he said with a playful smile, running his hand along her spine, hoping to entice her.

"I had almost given up, but the Lord was on our side yesterday," Polly babbled. "Perhaps the Great Spirit was watching over us too. Oh, I do hope Fire Starter is not angry that I left without him."

"Fire Starter was here today?" asked Isaac. Shaking her head, Polly filled him in on all that had happened. Her passionate account of their baby's brush with death touched his heart. Gazing at Polly, he admired her tenacity, thinking that his wife truly was a brave woman. As he held Elizabeth's tiny hand in his, Isaac was overcome with a feeling of reverence, for life, for their health, for his good fortune in choosing Polly to be his wife.

"I never gave up hope, not even when the Grim Reaper was hovering over my shoulder. But, Isaac, what has befallen you over the last month? You appear to be no worse for the wear," remarked Polly, pleased that he looked so well. Despite Isaac's filthy clothes, wiry, rough hair loosened at the back and knees protruding through new holes in his dungarees, Polly saw that he seemed somehow fulfilled, as if he had accomplished what he had set out to do.

With a rueful half-smile, Isaac responded, "I can't say that I have come back any farther ahead than where I was before, but it was quite an adventure."

A month earlier, Isaac and Abraham had set out with Augustus Jones and three dozen Queen's Rangers, after being delayed by rain. They stopped at St. John's trading post to get supplies. Isaac felt empowered to be in charge of such an important undertaking, to cut the Dundas Road from the Head of the Lake westward to the Thames River. His father was proud of him and wanted to go along, to the frontier where few white men had gone before.

"If you are travelling by foot, it would be better to walk a few miles north of here," St. John advised. "The Mississaugas operate a crossing there that follows an old footpath all the way through to the Head of the Lake."

The entourage was ferried across the Humber in three canoes, paying for their passage with several bottles of whiskey. The trail was well marked, winding through the Mississauga Tract, a large territory extending westward from York westward to the Head of the Lake and an equal distance north. Lord Dorchester set aside the land for the Mississaugas more than a decade ago, after the Crown purchased the land extending from the Head of the Lake to Kingston, a large portion of the province.

The group did not see any Mississaugas until the trail passed down a steep embankment to the Credit River. Deeper, slower and wider than the Humber, the Credit was so named by the French more than a century earlier as the place where they would trade with the Mississaugas. The French would offer goods to the Mississaugas on "credit" against furs that would be provided the following spring. The Credit was known to the Mississaugas as "Missinihe," meaning "trusting river," and they considered it to be sacred. Here they established many fishing camps during the warm months of spring and summer, harvesting and preserving fruits and vegetables like corn and wild rice, which they would take with them on their annual winter migration to the northern hunting grounds.

"There must be two dozen wigwams down there on the Credit," Isaac's father remarked.

"We'd better camp on the west side, keep some distance," Augustus Jones instructed.

"Let's hope they don't think that we're intruding," added Isaac, a little nervous. He had not heard of any attacks by the Mississaugas since coming to Upper Canada and he had befriended Great Sail and Fire Starter, but nothing with the natives could be certain.

Sitting around the campfire, Isaac and his father listened to the rhythmic sound of drums beating, rattles and rasps shaking and voices singing, the sounds echoing through the trees and dancing on the river. The Mississaugas were paying homage to one of their spirits, Munendoo, whom they believed lived on the Credit River near a deep pool just south of the trail. The Mississaugas revered Munendoo for providing the abundance of salmon, trout and pickerel in the Credit, their sacred river.

The next morning, the crew hiked single-file along the narrow path through the pine forest, known as Lakeshore road. Twenty-two miles later, they arrived at Cootes Paradise, a marshy wetland teeming with ducks, geese and other waterfowl. Captain Coote of the 8th King's Own Regiment settled there after the American War because he was so enamoured with the abundance of game. Located at the Head of the Lake, the area would one day harbour a large city named after George Hamilton.

A few miles farther along they came upon a garrison, a group of tents set up by the Queen's Rangers under the command of Captain Smith. Preparing for an American invasion, Simcoe hoped to build a permanent garrison at Cootes Paradise that would guard access to the Dundas Road that the men were about to cut.

"We started out strong, half of the men felling the trees and the other half clearing the debris and burning the logs," Isaac recounted to Polly. "We widened the existing native footpath to twenty feet and removed the stumps. Augustus Jones wanted to build a turnpike with a crown in the centre and ditches on both sides, but Captain Smith outranked him and insisted on lining the edges with logs instead."

"Thank goodness for Captain Smith," replied Polly.

"Yes," agreed Isaac, "it really did save a lot of time. I did not fancy spending a great deal of effort on a road that leads to nowhere."

Even Isaac, who listened to Simcoe's grand plans and schemes more than anyone else, did not understand the Governor's need for a road from Lake

Ontario to the Thames River. What Simcoe chose not to tell Isaac was that he wanted a connection from Lake Ontario to Lake Huron in case the Americans attacked.

"We met with no resistance cutting through the Mohawk reserve the first time," Isaac continued. "The Grand River is much wider than the Humber or the Credit. We had to hail down some passing canoes to get across as there was no possibility of wading through, and the Mohawks were friendly enough."

The British had granted a six-mile tract on either side of the Grand River to Joseph Brant and the Mohawks, one of the Six Nations, in appreciation for their efforts during the American War of Independence. The Mohawks moved north from their former homeland in the Mohawk Valley in the United States and settled along the Grand River following the dedication of the Haldimand Tract in 1784. However, the Grand River Reserve was still not officially granted to the Mohawks, nor was it surveyed. Joseph Brant was frustrated with the British and with Governor Simcoe in particular for not taking action to finalize the grant.

"The morning we were to return, a torrential rain poured down, turning our newly cut road into a pile of mud. We couldn't even use it. Instead, we had to hack our way through the forest single-file. We were down to ninety men as a number had returned to the garrison stricken with the ague. But thank the Lord we didn't use the new road because the Mohawks were waiting for us. They had set up piles of logs across our newly cut road for fifty feet on either side so that we could not pass or cross the river. At least three hundred of them from Brant's Ford were camped out on both sides of the river, ready to attack."

Polly gasped, "But why would they not let you through?"

"There is a dispute over the ownership of the land at the mouth of the river that has never been resolved," Isaac explained.

Just before the Devins family arrived in Niagara, Joseph Brant had heard a rumour that Simcoe had no intention of honouring the full extent of the Grand River Reserve promised to the Mohawks. Then Simcoe presented a deed to the Mohawks that included only a small portion of the land. Brant was insulted and found the attempts at dishonouring the land claim to be unbearable. He knew that he had some leverage. Simcoe was worried that Upper Canada would soon be at war with the United States and needed the support of the Six Nations and the Mississaugas to defend the border.

"Luckily, they could not see us because we were under the cover of the trees," Isaac continued. "The pounding of the rain and rustling of the leaves in the gale must have concealed our approach. Thank the Lord we were able to retreat without them spotting us. Captain Smith wanted to follow the river south to the lake and continue on to Niagara, but Augustus Jones wanted to go north where the river would narrow. After a heated debate, we headed north along the river's edge, looking for a safe crossing. We stayed back in the forest for fear that a passing canoe would spot us and warn the others."

"Where did you finally cross?" interjected Polly.

"We spent two days walking north but did not cover much ground. It was slow going, hacking our way through the underbrush. We finally saw a set of rapids where the river looked shallow enough. Under the cover of darkness, we waded through the rushing water, grabbing on to rocks for support."

Isaac reached over and took Polly's hand in his. "There was one dicey spot where you had to jump across a chasm from rock to rock, over a small but powerful waterfall. Father tried to cross before me. His hind foot slipped before he could even jump. I grabbed him, and jumped, pulling both of us across. I pushed him forward but then fell backwards, my left foot dangling off the cliff. God must have been smiling down on me because my right foot caught on a rock. Somehow, I was able to pull myself back up to safety. Two of the men behind us didn't make it."

"Oh Isaac, thank the Lord for your safe return!" Polly wailed, throwing her arms around his neck and placing her head on his chest.

Nothing can happen to him, she prayed silently, her vow seeming more like a command than a humble request to God. Despite his wanderlust, Polly loved her husband completely and could not imagine life without him.

Isaac looked down, put his hand under her chin and raised it so that he could gaze directly into her soulful green eyes, glimmering with a hint of sadness. "And I am grateful for my brave wife, who saved our child yesterday."

Polly smiled, her eyes now warm and tender, and rested her head back on his chest. Feeling his warmth, his breath, his life force, she let his essence fill her being and spread to the tips of her fingers and toes. At last she felt safe, as if nothing could harm her. If only I could feel this safe forever, she sighed.

Just then an icy cold wind blew into their tents, a reminder of the dark winter months ahead.

Chapter 10 – December 15, 1793

"Come back here, you silly goose!" Simeon yelled at the top of his lungs, throwing his arms down in frustration, but the bird took no notice as it waddled across the log pile toward the forest.

"Arrrrgh!" Simeon hollered, his knuckles white as he chased it, launching himself off the highest log, his long, curly brown hair flying in the breeze.

Of all the chores he had to do, plucking goose feathers was his least favourite. Sometimes it took five full days just to get enough for a small pillow. He sighed. Simeon had to tend to the geese or else his father was sure to get out his belt and give him a sound whipping. In the Devins' family, children had to do a full day's work, no questions asked. Abraham raised his young son no differently than he had raised Isaac, Jacob and Levi.

It had been Levi's idea to trap some geese from the Humber and bring them back to the homestead. The three chickens they purchased with money from Isaac's work on the Dundas Road did not produce nearly enough feathers. Levi rowed out to the deep pools of the Humber, a short distance north of their new homestead, where a gaggle of geese glided gaily along, unaware of any danger. As the raft slowly moved in, the geese parted and surrounded the craft, curious and not the least bit frightened.

I don't think these fowl have ever seen a shotgun, Levi thought, astonished at their innocent behaviour. He had never seen anything like it back in New York on the Genesee River. All I have to do is wait, he thought.

Sure enough, a goose flew up onto the raft a few feet away. It kept turning in a circle, bobbing its head, as if it were greeting the other watching geese.

Levi carefully grabbed a net, lifted it over the bird's head, and snared it in a split second. As he backpaddled into the main current, the goose stayed still, as if in shock, perhaps because it was terrified or perhaps out of innocence.

"Look what the cat dragged in," bellowed Levi, proud of his catch. His father and brother Jacob held the goose firmly while Levi attached a clip to each wing, something he had fashioned out of wood and an old iron spring he had found at the landing spot. Once released, the goose tottered around erratically, darting here and there, obviously confused, trying to fly and not being able.

Now, Simeon watched the bird wander for a bit, then went back to the clearing behind the cabin to trap weasels, one of his favourite chores. Isaac had shown him how to make a thin rope out of reeds from the river, knowledge he had gained from Fire Starter. Simeon would wait quietly outside a weasel's hole with the rope around it tied into a noose. He would lie still for as long as an hour, and when the animal popped its head out of the ground, Simeon yanked the noose sharply. If he was lucky, the creature's neck would snap and Simeon would whoop and holler in delight. If not, he would take a stone and smash it on the trapped animal's head a few times. His mother and aunts wanted the meat for stew and the fur for leggings and boots.

"Simeon!" Abraham called.

Clambering up from the weasel's hole, he ran over to do his father's bidding. "Yes, Father," he dutifully replied.

"You will now tend to this goose, pluck the feathers, and make sure it does not run off."

"Yes, Father," Simeon repeated.

He turned toward the river where Levi was digging a well, not far from the banks. Now that the river was nearly frozen, they needed a source of water.

The goose and Simeon stood almost eye to eye, each sizing up the other. Simeon took a small step forward, and the goose backed away. There was no fence surrounding the chicken coop or anywhere else in the yard, as no one had found time to build one. They had only received their land grant along the Humber six weeks earlier, and the Devins family were busy clearing the land and preparing for the long winter.

It took Simeon a few days to get the hang of it. Just when he thought he had everything under control and could go back to snaring weasels, Levi brought another goose home. Luckily for Simeon, the second goose was not as eager to escape. When Levi brought home the third, fourth and fifth one, just a few days apart, Simeon's chore became nearly impossible.

"Is that enough to keep you busy, Simeon?" teased Levi as he deposited the last goose at the river's edge.

"It's just you and me," Simeon said to the new goose as he circled it, hoping to drive it back the other way.

"Come on, little fella," coaxed Simeon when he had it cornered between himself and the log cabin. "Come to ... Papa!"

Simeon charged toward the goose. It let out a desperate honk and raced back to the clearing behind the log cabin, vainly trying to flap its wings. Pleased with himself, Simeon sauntered back, happy that he had avoided trouble once again.

"Sim-e-on!"

The voice of his friend Joseph echoed down the river. Simeon rushed to the river edge, straining to see his friend emerge from around the corner. It had been months since Simeon had seen Joseph, or any other children for that matter. No other settlers ventured out this far west of the landing spot. Most had settled within a few miles, just like Isaac, Polly and baby Elizabeth.

"Joseph!" yelled Simeon as his friend came into view, travelling south from the trading post up the river. "Am I glad to see you!"

Simeon heard a whistle from St. John as he steered the canoe toward the landing, a smooth flat rock cleared of soil and moss.

"We're on our way to the Credit," Joseph said as his father steered to the boulder. "Maybe you can come with us!"

Excited, Simeon immediately started to board the canoe, a midsized cedar one that could easily hold the three of them and a huge catch.

"Wait, now," said St. John, smiling, "Not so fast. You will have to ask your father."

Simeon looked around. Where could his father be? At last he remembered that Abraham had gone to the garrison that morning to see if anyone had an extra axe he could borrow. Simeon ran back to the landing and heard St. John bellow out, "Get back there, you varmint!"

Simeon looked downriver and gasped. One of his geese had crossed over the stone and twig barrier he had constructed and was swimming away.

"No!," Simeon hollered as he raced along the river edge as far as the clearing went, then was stopped by a dense barrier of dead branches.

"Don't worry, Simeon," he heard Joseph call out. "We'll catch it."

Simeon watched helplessly from the shoreline. He let out a deep sigh. I hope they catch it; if not, he was sure to get a whipping. Oh no! He had forgotten about the others! He raced back toward the log cabin and chased a couple of chickens back behind the coop.

Dejected, Simeon squatted on the log pile, his head resting in his hands, eyes cast downward. He waited, hoped and prayed. A few large, fluffy snowflakes began to fall in an undefined pattern. Normally, Simeon would be delighted and try to catch the snowflakes on this tongue. But now, he just sat and waited.

Before long the light scattering became a heavy, thick blanket of snow, swirling in the wind and blowing horizontally across the clearing. The wind howled through the trees, roaring like a ferocious animal. Simeon chased the birds into the chicken coop with his willow stick and secured the latch. Turning around, he could barely see the cabin only thirty feet away. He ran inside and was soon warming himself by the stone hearth, drinking a cup of warm goat milk that his mother gave him. He worried, though, and wondering if Joseph and his father had found shelter from the storm.

Isaac was likewise caught unaware by the onset of the blizzard. He was seven miles away, riding through the forest in John White's cutter on the way back from the garrison to his homestead, only a mile from the landing spot on the Toronto Bay. His father and brothers had tried to persuade him to instead claim the land next to them on the Humber, but Isaac refused. His heart was set on the site he had spotted on their first day in Toronto.

"There is so much opportunity for success on the Humber," chided his father. "Only fools will settle near the landing spot. You must join us, your brothers need you."

"When my land becomes part of the growing city, who will be the fool then?" retorted Isaac, weary of his father's lectures. "My land has a small stream, perfect for drinking water and brook trout, so I will not lack for nourishment. I will be close enough to the town to be part of the business there, and close enough so that the governor does not forget about me."

As the wind picked up and whistled through the pines, John White slowed the horses to a trot and then to a walk. Soon, they could see only fifteen feet in front of them, then ten. The tracks showing the trail disappeared into a blanket of snow. There was nothing to guide them now but their instinct.

"Thank the good Lord that I didn't encounter this type of snowstorm on my way here," White exclaimed. "This is pure treachery."

White had made the journey in his cutter from Niagara to York in only two days, stopping at Captain Smith's at the Head of the Lake overnight. All trips from Niagara had to be made by cutter, sled or wagon since the ice in the Toronto harbour would not allow even the best of trawlers safe passage.

"How much farther do we have to go?" inquired White, a trifle uneasy.

"Only a couple of miles," replied Isaac. "I couldn't get a land grant at the landing spot. The governor also made it exceedingly difficult for anyone other than a wealthy man to build there. You can only own a lot on Front Street if you build a large two-storey home using a particular architectural style, Georgian, I think. Only in the back streets can the tinkers and tailors like myself erect a building of their choice on a tiny lot. There was no lumber to construct houses of that size anyway. Simcoe gave all the lumber to the Queen's Rangers to build the dock. Only George Hamilton received some planks from the mill after the dock was constructed. His fancy home is the only one standing at the landing spot."

"Sounds like the governor is undermining his own ambitions to create a robust, bustling town with any degree of haste," observed White.

"Quite correct," agreed Isaac. "You cannot assign all the lumber to the docks in mid-September and expect people to wait and build houses before winter strikes, so most people, including myself, claimed land miles away from the landing spot. Everyone seemed to spread out randomly, like leaves on a windy fall day. So much for the robust town of York that will be grander than Philadelphia."

The wind picked up, blew sideways and circled around. Pellets of snow swirled in every direction, and they could hear the crack of branches breaking, like gunshots.

The horses cried out, startled by the ferocity of the blizzard, and reared onto their hind legs. White wrestled with the reins but the sleigh clipped the hind leg of the brown mare. She fell instantly to the ground, bawling in agony with a broken leg.

White slowly stood up, pointed his rifle, and shot the horse in the heart. He stood motionless for a long time, as if in a trance, then turned to Isaac.

"That was my prized mare, a purebred. I purchased her at Fort Niagara from a trader who imported horses from New York. He said she had an Arabian bloodline, which showed in the way she cantered. What a loss," he said quietly, disheartened that such a valuable animal could meet such an abrupt end.

White had a stable of purebred horses. If there was something that he desired, he spared nothing to ensure that he owned it, regardless of price.

As a result, he was almost constantly in debt, but did not give this more than a second thought. Though he made a fine salary as Attorney General of Upper Canada, he lived as though he were the King.

"Yes, it looked like a fine breed," agreed Isaac. "But can the other horse pull the sleigh alone?"

"We shall see." They removed the harness from the dead mare, then with a crack of the whip, White urged the grey horse forward. Struggling at first, the horse slowly pulled the sleigh, changing direction at the pull of the reins.

"At least we are moving, but I can't say if we are headed in the right direction," Isaac said, searching for tracks. The trail was snowed over and there were no other landmarks to guide them. All the trees looked the same; the heavy snowfall obscured any distinguishing details. Isaac prayed that his intuition would be enough to lead them safely home.

You must always trust in the wind and the willows to lead the way, Great Sail had told him just before he died. *They will always take you home. The easterly winds will show you the direction, and the willows will show you the lowlands.* How he missed Great Sail's sage advice.

Isaac only heard of Great Sail's passing after returning from cutting the Dundas Road. Fire Starter was in deep mourning when Isaac saw him and his family paddling to the Credit. Isaac stared in shock as the lifeless body of Great Sail lay peacefully on a bed of straw in the middle of the canoe. Such a tragedy that a wise, unassuming, charismatic elder would leave this world too soon, thought Isaac. He would often listen to Great Sail's tales of wisdom, astounded by the elder's ability to use animals, plants and nature to explain a powerful adage or one of life's truths.

Fire Starter was particularly heavy-hearted because he had witnessed his father's death.

On the twenty-fifth day of October, Fire Starter and Great Sail had been walking along the shoreline of Lake Simcoe, checking traps they had set the night before. Their clan had already started the great migration to the northern hunting grounds and they were planning to continue their journey after the midday meal. After checking the last trap, Fire Starter followed his father, who had gone on ahead down trail.

He suddenly heard the unmistakable sound of a bear growling and snorting in anger, quite close. Fire Starter crept silently forward. Peering around a tree, he saw his father up ahead, standing still, not moving or gesturing, his arms at his side, facing a giant black bear that was up on its hind legs only twenty feet away.

His father seemed mesmerized and quite complacent. Fire Starter shouted as he pulled out his bow and arrow and watched helplessly as his father allowed the bear to charge at him and take a swipe with a front paw. The blow almost severed Great Sail in half and he doubled over in agony, blood gushing everywhere. The bear then clenched its teeth around his father's neck, shook him and threw him down at its feet. Before the bear could take another swipe, Fire Starter's arrow pierced its heart, With a weak cry, the bear fell over, dead.

"My father did not offer any resistance," Fire Starter told Isaac, with the help of St. John to interpret. "He left his death in the hands of the Great Spirit, who called my father to join him in the spirit world."

Very brave, thought Isaac, to face the angry bear without so much as drawing a weapon. He admired Great Sail's courage but could not imagine such faith. He was much too practical to leave his fate in the hands of God. He wished he could believe in something so strongly.

Fire Starter then showed Isaac the boots that his had mother made out of the bearskin. "I am proud to walk in my father's footsteps, to have this reminder of his life, and to one day join him in the happy hunting ground."

At Isaac's request, Fire Starter took him to Great Sail's final resting place along the Credit River. He asked St. John to accompany them and act as interpreter. St. John was only too happy to do so, having a great respect for Great Sail and also curious to see if the Mississaugas' rituals were any different from the Mohawks. Fire Starter guided the canoe to a number of west-facing mounds grown over with wildflowers and a new one covered in bare earth with birchbark laid on top and secured with stones.

"This place is sacred to us. It is a portal through which the dead and the living can meet. A place to remember our loved ones. Death is a part of living, and living is a part of death," Fire Starter explained. "We buried my father with herbs, medicines, spears and tomahawks. Now we must provide nourishment as often as we can to help him on his journey."

Isaac and St. John stood respectfully beside the grave as Fire Starter placed tobacco, rice, fruit and bread around it. The Anishinaabeg believed that the dead need to be sheltered and fed to not only nurture the departed on their journey but also to ensure that the living were likewise protected.

With a lump in his throat and a tightness in his chest, Isaac bowed his head and prayed, asking that Great Sail continue peacefully on his sacred journey to the happy hunting ground. After many conversations with Great Sail, Isaac believed that the Christian God and the Great Spirit were one and the same, so he knew that his prayer was not in vain. He put his hand on Fire Starter's shoulder in sympathy for the loss of a great man.

"What a tragedy," White remarked as Isaac finished telling him the story of Great Sail's passing. They slumped along slowly through the blizzard, unsure if they were headed in the right direction.

"How long will Fire Starter remain in mourning?" asked White.

"At least one year, that is their custom," Isaac replied.

"We should protect the burial sites and ensure they are unharmed," declared White. Perhaps we could even protect them through legislation, he considered, imagining drafting a bill for the next Parliament session.

After a few minutes, Isaac signalled for White to stop the cutter. "We should have seen a light by now in a window. We may have gone too far. I think we should wait out the storm here."

White grabbed two canvas sheets from the back of the cutter. He unfolded one and put it on the grey mare and then worked with Isaac to secure the blanket around the seat of the cutter, building a small tent around them. They had to shake off the snow every couple of minutes, but it was much warmer than being exposed to the wind.

"Finding your cabin in this storm would be like finding a needle in a haystack. If only we had a candle," said White, imagining the warmth that a single candle can bring.

"Yes," Isaac said in agreement, although he wasn't yet feeling the cold. The deerskin boots, pants and coat that he wore offered better protection, even more so than White's fine woollen cloak and breeches. The Devins family did not yet have a spinning wheel or any wool, so Polly and Rita made a set of deerskin clothes for everyone for the winter. Next year, they would sow flax seed in the spring, harvest it midsummer, spin it in the fall and sew the clothes the following winter.

After a time, Isaac remembered that he had some smerecase in his pouch, a German treat that Polly had learned to make back in New York. The two of them devoured it while debating the merits of building such a large dock at the landing spot.

Daylight faded into dusk before the storm let up enough to move on.

"Thanks be to the good Lord, we are saved!" White exclaimed overdramatically, tongue in cheek. Isaac smiled as they hitched the mare back up to the cutter, and in a short time Isaac could see the light Polly had put in the window.

"Home, at last," sang Isaac, relieved to see the two-room log cabin that he had built with the help of his brothers, Nicholas Miller and a few other settlers. It wasn't much of a home, but it would keep them warm and dry until spring. Polly had a roaring fire going, and the two men pulled chairs to the open stone hearth and warmed their hands and feet.

"My word, this is delicious," White exclaimed after Polly handed him stew she had made from raccoon and squirrel meat. She had flavoured it with dried mint, sage and cranberries, one of many new dishes she was experimenting with in the wilderness.

The three of them enjoyed one another's company until late in the evening, then retired to the wooden beds and straw mattresses that Isaac had finished making a few days earlier.

"You must come and visit us again," Polly said, cradling Elizabeth in her arms, as White set out the next morning for Niagara.

"Indeed, I shall, my lady," replied White, tipping his hat and offering a bow.

John White was not a typical aristocrat. He was equally at home in the company of a pauper as he was in the King's Court. Many in Upper Canada knew him to be approachable and kind, often refusing to take fees for a trial or advice. He sniffed and cleared his throat a few times, feeling like he was catching the ague, but held back any complaints. He did not want to bother these good people with his ailments.

"Do come for the Christmas festivities, and bring your family," Polly invited. "We celebrate all twelve days of Christmas."

◇◇

On each of the twelve days of Christmas, the Devins family had a small feast with special treats, visited other families in York and received guests at their home. For the Twelfth Night celebration, Isaac and his brothers walked to the garrison since they did not yet have a horse or oxen to pull a sleigh. Homes were scattered so far apart across York that meeting at the garrison was the logical choice. Soldiers and settlers bobbed for apples, played cards, and acted out plays and pantomimes. There was music, dancing, singing and drinking the wassail.

Isaac danced twice that evening, once with the governor's wife. But the only dance he cared to remember the next morning was with Margaret, St. John's wife, how her slim body felt in his arms, how her brown eyes smiled up at him, her scent of wildflowers, and how her smile illuminated the entire room. St. John was a lucky man.

Later, alone at the kitchen table, Isaac's mind drifted back over the last year, recalling all the struggles and torments that plagued the family – convincing his brothers to move to Upper Canada, then losing Little Star, their newborn's brush with death. Many hardships had indeed befallen them.

But there were also things to be thankful for. His friendship with John White and Fire Starter. Getting closer to the governor. Polly was pregnant again and, most of all, owning his own land. Although he felt like he was making progress, he still had a nagging sense of uneasiness. He shook his head and sighed. I've become one of the governor's closest confidants in York, but I still have nothing to show for it.

The warmth from the fire faded as the night sky turned from black to grey to blue. The dawn of a new day. Perhaps the new year will bring us a little prosperity, Isaac dreamed as he stretched out his feet and warmed them by the fire. He began to make a list of all the things he wanted to accomplish in 1794.

What Isaac didn't know was that many things out of his control would soon shape his destiny.

Reflection 2

Isaac coughed a few times, then rested his head back on the pillow. Damn, that hurts, he silently cursed, feeling a jolt of pain in his left arm and upper back. He did not like to complain about his war injury. Only the feeble-minded did that. Elizabeth had just helped him to bed and covered him with quilts in the cool spring evening, but it was hard to get comfortable. This damn cough, he swore.

Strange that I wanted so much to be part of the town, but now I abhor it, he thought, staring up at the ceiling. I did everything I could to make my home there but was spat out like a piece of tobacco.

Isaac heard the kettle singing and wondered if Elizabeth was ever going to take it off the stove. Polly had used the small portable oven that he bought from a Mississauga trader in Newark from the time they first arrived in Upper Canada right up until the day she died. I suppose convenience takes over, Isaac sighed. His granddaughters would probably not know how to make cornbread without a modern cast iron stove.

The aroma of sage and mint wafted into the room as Elizabeth flavoured the pot of raccoon stew she was hoping her father would eat. He ate so little now, and she wanted to keep up his strength. She knew there was nothing she could do to bring back the twinkle in his eye. That disappeared the day her mother died, almost two years ago now.

Reminds me of the sweet smell of burning tobacco from the offerings that Fire Starter and the Mississaugas made at the limestone outcrop, Isaac recalled. He would find remnants of the offerings under some carefully placed stones almost every time he went there to rest, to think, to dream. At first it was a place of tranquil repose, where he could be alone and at peace. Then it became a place of reflection, after Fire Starter no longer came. I haven't been there in decades, not since the land was purchased as part of the influx of the Irish in the 1830s.

Isaac found out that someone had purchased the lot with the limestone outcrop while lounging there one lazy afternoon. He had drifted off to sleep, reliving the time when Fire Starter showed him how to make a tomahawk, right there beside the rock. Tap, tap, tap. Isaac was jolted from his slumber. A musket was pointed straight between his eyes. He heard a gruff voice say, "What business have you here? This is my land, and I want you gone."

That was the last time Isaac ever stopped at the limestone outcrop, the sacred place for the Mississaugas. Now it is cleared and used for Sunday picnics down on the river. That is what his son, John C., told him when Isaac asked a few months ago. The people today have no idea they are standing on holy ground. I suppose all this knowledge is lost. Anyone who remembers is dead, except for me.

So much changed after the war. Many say that the War of 1812 brought this country together. I say it separated us even farther.

Any chance I had of working my way into the ruling elite was eliminated by the war. The aristocrats became like a lead wall, impenetrable. They stuck together. Before the Mackenzie rebellion in 1837, they were called the Family Compact. There was no room for someone like me to push my way in, even if I wanted to, which I no longer did.

Hah! Isaac smirked, thinking of how the Family Compact fell after the Rebellion. By 1840, their power and strength were cut in half when the four provinces merged to become Canada West and Canada East. Many of the elite lost their title and positions, never to regain them, when the British colony was restructured.

Isaac had cheered enthusiastically for Mackenzie and the rebels. He helped some of them escape the British soldiers chasing them northward from York. He even transported a few over to the west side of the Humber, to an overgrown trail through the old Mississauga Tract that had been abandoned for decades. His neighbours, the Watsons, were caught assisting the rebels and were jailed. Thank the Lord and the Great Spirit that I did not end up in jail again, thought Isaac, remembering the horrific conditions of York's first prison.

To think that I actually thought I could become one of them. Isaac shook his head. It had all seemed possible back then, but Jarvis got in the way. He was the one who messed up my chances of being successful in York. I blame him for every bad thing that befell me. I suppose I could have returned to York after Jarvis died, a few years after the war, but I didn't have the heart. My dreams of making it in Toronto were over.

Polly would never have wanted to go then. She was happy in our cabin on the river. How she loved to decorate our wood fence with spring flowers that she collected from the woods, and find new scents and remedies from the plants she found deep in the forest. I don't think she would have wanted to socialize with the likes of Hannah Jarvis or Bishop Strachan's wife anyway. She knew that we would always be outcasts.

Through the open door, he watched Elizabeth grinding flour so she could make biscuits for breakfast the next day. She is a handsome woman, Isaac thought, kind and thoughtful, just like her mother. She must be missing her own family, taking care of me. Oh well, she will be with them soon.

Elizabeth walked in and felt Isaac's forehead, pulling the quilt up to his chin, and plumped his pillow. I wonder if Elizabeth remembers how we used to swim in the deep pools of the Humber a mile north, just past the forks, her and I. She loved catching brook trout with the old cedar branch, and trapping rabbits over by the sugar maple bush. I think she loved the Humber as much as I did back then.

Now she loves her grandchildren most of all. I suppose that would never have happened if she had remained a river-child. Polly insisted that her daughter learn to dress and act like a lady.

Polly was right about so many things. She knew from the beginning that Jarvis would be trouble.

Isaac recalled his first encounter with the man along the portage route to Queenston. Isaac could tell by the elaborate style of Jarvis' daycoat and his flamboyant cravat that he came from wealth and likely had a strong connection to the governor. *Here is someone I should get to know,* Isaac had thought at the time.

We didn't even get within conversation range when Jarvis raised his hand and flicked his wrist as if to sweep rubbish off the path. Isaac had slowed, but stood his ground, and watched in disbelief as Jarvis did it again, this time more emphatically, as if Isaac were a fly on a dinner plate. Stunned, Isaac raised his hand to tip his hat. But Jarvis just brushed past him, almost bowling him over with his short, squat, solid body.

Ever since, Isaac hated the man. Not so much at first, but the sentiment grew as the years went by, with every insult and injustice.

He closed his eyes, trying to calm down, and pictured Polly walking along the rocky shore of the Toronto Bay a few days after they had landed in Toronto, sixty years ago. Pregnant with Elizabeth, she had never seemed so beautiful to Isaac, with the wind blowing her soft auburn hair and the sun shining on her beautiful skin. *There was so much hope back then, to live a great life, to become a man of importance, but I failed.*

The only time I could ever find myself was when I was alone, paddling my canoe on the Humber.

144

Chapter 11 – July 31, 1794

Isaac lay peacefully, in the magical light of the half-hour before dawn. He stretched his arms overhead, feeling a wave of contentment fill his body and spread from his head down to his toes. Rolling over, he slid his arm around Polly, who always felt so warm and peaceful. Their two little girls, Elizabeth and Hannah, slept like angels in the trundle bed over in the corner.

Nobody would ever guess that this was Isaac and Polly's first summer on their homestead in York. Their shanty that had been hastily thrown together last fall now was a solid log cabin with a well-tended yard that looked like it had been there for years. Isaac glanced around, admiring the few small trinkets attached to the walls. His resourceful wife had even fashioned dinner plates out of tin and glass. While Isaac and his brothers chopped trees and burned stumps, Polly had turned the house into a home.

Outside, she had planted a vegetable and herb garden with the seed that Isaac received in exchange for a couple of days of solid work at a neighbouring building bee. The rows of corn Polly had planted were six feet tall already, and the carrots had nearly gone to seed. Little Elizabeth followed her mother around the yard, copying her every move, and pretended to water the seedlings while Polly carried Hannah around in the cradleboard that the Mississauga woman had given her on the peninsula.

The half-acre clearing surrounding the log cabin was smooth and passable now that Isaac had finished burning the stumps. Polly boiled the ashes down into lye, and he transported it to St. John's trading post in his birchbark canoe. They were able to sell the potash in exchange for a couple of goats and pigs, which they let wander through the thick, mixed pine forest. Isolated, with no neighbours for miles, there was no need for fences to keep the animals in. They still had another four months before he was required to put one up.

Isaac smiled contentedly, blissful in the new morning. He was proud of his homestead. He knew the land he chose had great potential and would one day make him a wealthy man, he could just feel it.

"Chop, chop, chop!"

Who could possibly be felling a tree within earshot of our cabin, wondered Isaac. His closest neighbour was George Hamilton, whose fine two-storey home was within the townsite two miles away, and the Hamiltons were rarely there. The industrious George Hamilton was too busy building an empire from Newark to the Head of the Lake to bother much with the few settlers in York. Isaac rolled out of bed and quickly put on his dungarees, breeches and a deerskin tunic that was a gift from Fire Starter's wife, Mahima. Grabbing his gun, he crept outside, hoping not to alarm the intruders.

He paused and listened for any indication of where the sound came from. Spotting a flash of sunlight that reflected off an axe blade, he estimated the intruders were a few hundred yards downstream along the creek. Isaac crept softly through the trees and soon could see five or six men chopping down a couple of hardwoods near the creek.

What the devil? thought Isaac, miffed that the intruders were taking down the timber, as if they had a right to do so. They seemed oblivious to the boundary markers that were almost within plain sight, or they had chosen to ignore them.

Great Sail had chastised Isaac because he placed so much importance on the desire to conquer and own land. "All is one, each leaf a living entity, as vital to the health of the tree as the roots which anchor and nourish it," Great Sail had reminded him a few months before his death. "So, too, are we who live under the trees. We have invited the white men to come and share our forest with us, and you have moved in and settled. While we travel with the seasons, you do not. That we cannot understand. Why would you stay near Lake Ontario during the winter when the bounty of the forest has moved north? And why do you fight among yourselves over small pieces of forest, placing undue importance on owning it? We all own it, and we do not, for Mother Nature decides who she will favour and who she will punish."

Isaac recognized the wisdom in Great Sail's words, and even tried to live by it. He graciously opened his home, tent and lean-to for every Mississauga or weary traveller that ventured past. Polly would offer them nourishment, and they could eat and sleep in comfort until they were ready to depart. But somehow the idea of living communally could not overtake Isaac's basic instincts. Sharing land with his neighbours and friends was just as foreign a concept to him as land ownership was to the natives.

Isaac strode toward the intruders, his weapon drawn. "Stop, thieves!" he shouted. "This here is private property, you will have to find another source of timber on unclaimed land!"

Although some settlers were grateful that others were chopping down the forest, Isaac viewed each tree as a source of income and was perturbed that someone was stealing it.

The men stopped working and stared over at Isaac, seeing a fierce, intent young man with a penetrating, unfriendly gaze, dressed in beads and feathers like a native. One of them muttered something in what sounded like a French accent. Another man approached Isaac, ignoring the rifle pointing at his chest. He withdrew a piece of crumpled yellow paper from his pocket and showed it to Isaac.

"I have a certificate here for Lot 5, Con 2, in the town of York. You, sir, are on my land."

No, that cannot be, fumed Isaac as he read over the document. The lot and concession number on the certificate matched the description of his own land. There must be some mistake, he thought.

"Governor Simcoe himself assured me that Lot 5, Con 2, East half, is mine," countered Isaac. "The governor submitted the petition himself to the Land Board."

"Can I see your certificate then?" inquired the stranger a trifle smugly.

Isaac pressed his lips together and glared back at the intruder. He didn't have a yellow paper. Almost every week following his return from cutting the Dundas Road he had written to William Jarvis, head Registrar of land titles, requesting that the petition be processed but had not received a reply. He was too busy to travel all the way to Niagara to see Jarvis personally, the demands of setting up a homestead being paramount.

Jarvis! Why, I ought to strangle his fat, ugly neck and throw him in the Toronto harbour, Isaac swore under his breath.

Studying the certificate in detail, Isaac saw that it looked to be in order. Damn. How could this have happened? The governor had promised him that he would see to it himself. Still, he needed proof.

"I need to take this with me to show the governor," Isaac began.

"Not on your life," interjected the tallest of the men. "This yellow paper is like gold. How do we know that you won't throw it away or burn it?" Although the strangers had not drawn a weapon, they seemed confident, unabashed, perhaps because they outnumbered Isaac.

There were many tales that circulated among the settlers of deeds mysteriously disappearing and miraculously being replaced by others with different owners. The Land Board was not yet a smoothly operating government machine. It often seemed to create more problems than it solved. Many people were frustrated with William Jarvis. He could not keep up with the unending crush of petitions that grew larger every passing day with more and more settlers arriving in Upper Canada.

"Then I will respectfully request that you refrain from any more activity here until I have a chance to speak to the governor," Isaac demanded, gesturing with his rifle that they should all leave at once.

"Very well," replied the eldest, turning away from Isaac. "Let's go back to the town. See if we can round up a couple more axemen."

Warily, Isaac watched them disappear into the brush but kept his rifle cocked, just in case they circled back. He could not believe that someone was claiming the land that he had worked so hard to improve. Stomping along the footpath to the town, he cursed Jarvis for being such an incompetent fool. The soft pine needles caressed his deerskin clothes and the wind whispered, a welcome companion to the hot midday sun. But Isaac was oblivious to his surroundings, he was so enraged.

Months ago he had solemnly sworn his oath of allegiance, the first step that the British required for someone to receive a free grant.

"I, Isaac Devins, do promise and declare that I will maintain and defend to the utmost of my power the authority of the King in his Parliament, as the Supreme Legislature of this Province."

He then made a petition to the government requesting his land. Since he had to leave for the Head of the Lake the next day to work on Dundas Street, the governor had promised to submit the paperwork for Isaac himself.

In November, Isaac had gone to the town hall office at Market Square, the first government building built in York, to check on it. Fortunately, or so he had thought at the time, Jarvis was there on a short trip from Niagara. Like many members of the Executive Council, Jarvis refused to settle in York, viewing it as a muddy backwater full of mosquitoes.

Isaac had politely inquired whether his petition had been granted, and was told by Jarvis, "Never fear. Your petition has been received and will be processed in due haste."

The New Year celebration for 1794 had come and gone, spring turned into summer, and still Isaac did not have his yellow paper. There was such a backlog at the Land Board that many settlers were in the same predicament. Most families decided not to wait for the yellow paper before settling their land because the growing season was short. If they waited, they would face autumn and winter without a harvest.

Isaac, likewise, did not delay and began carving a homestead out of the forest. The yellow paper is just a formality anyway, Isaac thought at the time, to place a hold on the property until the deed could be issued.

Pushing a large wooden door open, Isaac strode into St. John's store, one of the first structures built at the landing site. Barrels of flour, seeds and sugar, cords of rope and twine, and piles of axes and adzes filled the room. By chance, he found the governor there in a heated conversation with St. John.

"That I cannot do," Simcoe stated. "I do not have the manpower for such an undertaking."

"But surely the Queen's Rangers can lend a hand," insisted St. John. He had asked Simcoe months ago for a dozen soldiers to assist him in cutting a new road from his store east to the Don River. Such a route would divert traffic from Asa Danforth's newly constructed east-west road to the waterfront. Only one-third of the settlers in York came frequently to trade at St. John's store, and he wanted to increase the flow.

"They have new orders now," replied Simcoe. "Lord Dorchester has insisted, against my better judgment, to send all the Queen's Rangers to Niagara, leaving me without a labour force! How am I to build roads, buildings, mills, docks, a town, without any men? How can he possibly think that supervising the transfer of Fort Niagara from British to American hands would be so pressing, more important than building the capital of the province?"

Simcoe pounded his fist on the table, then turned abruptly and saw Isaac waiting to speak to him. "Devins, just what, pray tell, are you doing tomorrow? I need someone to accompany me to the Head of the Lake. There are . . . "

Isaac listened patiently to the governor's plans for extending the Dundas Road to Lake Huron and Detroit, his favourite subject. When he could finally interject, he said with indignation, "Your Excellency, I need to bring a matter of grave importance to your attention. Do you recall submitting the petition to the Land Board for my homestead along the creek?"

"Why, yes, I gave it to Secretary Jarvis the following week when I was in Queenston. What of it?" inquired the governor.

"Several people confronted me today holding a yellow paper indicating that they are the rightful owners of my land. How is this possible?" inquired Isaac.

Right on cue, two of the men who had been cutting trees on his land stomped into the store, also looking for the governor.

"Here are the culprits who are claiming my property!" Isaac shouted.

"And this is the varmint who is squatting on our land!" exclaimed the taller of the two.

"Gentlemen, gentlemen, let's discuss this matter rationally and with respect," Simcoe commanded.

Knitting his eyebrows together, the governor scanned the yellow paper. He turned it over and held it up to the light streaming in from the giant windows. Counterfeiting was a common practice in the colony. After several minutes, the governor pursed his lips and frowned ever so slightly. He seemed to be staring blankly over the tops of their heads.

Land speculation is rampant, thought Simcoe. Landjobbers were penetrating the system, pledging allegiance to the King, then immediately selling their property and returning to the States. The petitions were piled high in Jarvis's office, and Simcoe did not have the manpower to assign anyone else to help.

"The yellow paper appears to be in good standing," declared the governor. Isaac's heart sank while his opponents cheered wildly. "However, I cannot be sure until I verify the transfer of title back at the registrar's office in Newark. For now, nobody will occupy the said property until I return."

Simcoe strode toward the door in his characteristic style, leaving a room full of flabbergasted and annoyed people behind. Isaac said "What?" under his breath, not quite believing what the governor had just decreed.

"But, Governor, my crops, my livestock. Who will tend to them?" Isaac cried out in anguish, running after Simcoe. "I should at least be able to harvest them."

Without turning around or looking back, the governor shouted, "Of course, Devins. You can return at threshing time. But you must vacate your premises for the time being. I don't want a civil war to break out in my own backyard. I leave for Niagara on the morrow."

Enraged, Isaac turned back toward St. John's store and saw the four men on the veranda. "Sons of Satan!" Isaac bellowed, his blood boiling, his face contorted in anger. He charged toward them, ready to tear them apart.

The men stood their ground, arms at their sides, waiting to draw their pistols. Knowing that they outnumbered Isaac, they appeared calm and focused. "No, you are the scoundrel, squatting on our land!" yelled back the younger one. He took a step forward, but the eldest one held him back.

"Stinkards! If I catch you in my house or on my land, that day will be your last!" Isaac shouted, chest leaning forward, hands at his side, ready to draw.

"And you better stay away from the boundary markers, Devins. We will surely turn you in if you move them even a pinch," promised the taller one. The punishment in Upper Canada for any vandalism or movement of the stone boundary markers that demarcated lot lines was death.

"May your table be rotten and your horses be shot dead!" cursed Isaac, almost frothing at the mouth.

Hearing the commotion, St. John burst through the door. He strode between them, holding his arms up on both sides as if to push the men apart.

"What have we here?" he questioned. "Surely nothing worth killing for."

Turning toward Isaac, he grabbed his arms, saying, "Isaac, my friend, let it go, you can't solve it here." Although he had no idea what the skirmish entailed, he knew that Isaac was outnumbered and did not stand a chance if guns were drawn.

"These bloody scoundrels are trying to snatch my land, right out from under me," cursed Isaac, "and they have falsified papers."

St. John listened to Isaac's story as he led him along the path, his hand resting on Isaac's shoulder as they walked briskly toward the disputed land. He had heard many similar tales of woe. Many people blamed William Jarvis, and cursed his name. St. John himself had requested a sizable portion of land surrounding his trading post on the Humber River but had yet to receive any written letter of approval.

St. John's practical, sympathetic manner and tone of voice helped Isaac to calm down, and he walked back to his homestead with less anger than when he left. He was surprised to see the front door ajar. His heart skipped a few beats and he grabbed his rifle. Could those land-stealing demons have returned here and terrorized Polly and the girls?

Creeping closer with his gun drawn, he stopped at the sound of voices. Isaac felt a flood of relief wash over his body when he heard Polly speaking in a normal tone. Looking through a window, he saw three Mississaugas with painted faces and deerskin clothes, one with a headdress, and one with a papoose, seated around the table watching Polly as she bustled about the kitchen preparing the noon-day meal. He relaxed and went to the door to greet them.

"Boozhoo," Isaac said, nodding his head and smiling as he entered.

Isaac's greeting was returned, and then followed by a flurry of words that he could not understand. Shaking his head, Isaac held up his hands and said, "Kaawiin nsastazin?" asking them to explain what they said.

The eldest stood up, nodded, and spoke at length using expressions that Isaac did not know. Isaac listened patiently out of respect, then shrugged helplessly, indicating that he could not understand.

"I don't think they speak a word of English," Polly exclaimed as she removed a steaming-hot pot from the metal arm that swung over the fire. She carefully used the ladle to apportion some out into the wooden bowls that Isaac had made last winter.

Composed and at ease, Polly was used to having Mississaugas at her table. It was their custom to walk into a settler's house unannounced and sit for hours on end, without ever seeming to want anything other than companionship. Closed doors and boundary markers meant nothing to the Mississaugas. They believed that they were sharing the forest and its harvest with the white people.

Polly offered the three of them some rabbit stew and creamed onions, which they gratefully accepted. The young boy was more interested in playing with Elizabeth, who had toddled into the room in a tiny deerskin dress, a smile beaming from ear to ear and a look of wonder illuminating her face. Elizabeth walked right over, plopped herself down on the floor, clapped her hands and laughed. The lack of a common language was not a barrier between the two children. The adults watched with fascination, perhaps a little envy. The mother spoke a few words, encouraging her son, and smiling all the while.

Isaac went outside to the chicken coop, still agitated that they might lose their homestead. He strolled over to the woodpile, where he had just begun to saw a fence post that morning, hoping to begin constructing it the following week. Well, no need to continue with this, he grumbled, or anything else around here, for that matter. I suppose our homesteading will be on hold for a few months.

An hour later, the Mississaugas came to the woodpile where Isaac still sat, contemplating his next move. "Aaniish nda noozwin?" the young mother inquired, wanting to know Isaac's name.

"Nda zhinkaaz," answered Isaac, finally able to understand a simple phrase.

"Ahhh," he heard them say as they began to talk rapidly, looking Isaac up and down, excited. "Waabshkii Mnidoo!" they called out as they turned and walked on the trail leading to the fort. Isaac still had to remember to ask Fire Starter what those words meant.

Several months later, Isaac walked in his snowshoes to St. John's store in York, where a letter was waiting for him from Niagara. Although they had lived at his father's homestead on the Humber, Isaac had stolen back to his own land on several occasions to harvest his vegetables, and to ensure that no one was squatting. He even dared to sow a small field with early spring vegetable seed, so certain was he that the land would be his.

St. John's wife, Margaret, handed him the envelope with a shy smile and a flip of her long black hair that fell loosely past her waist, making her look exotic and tantalizing. Isaac smiled back and reached for the letter, their hands briefly touching, sending a spark of energy flying between them. Stepping back, he grinned and stared into her dark mesmerizing eyes.

"Well, aren't you going to open it?" Margaret asked, smiling.

"Quite right," Isaac replied as he removed the letter. "Dear Mr. Devins," he began, then read silently to himself. Margaret watched his cheerful expression slowly disappear and be replaced with a look of concern, shock, disbelief, then rage.

"Arrgghh!" Isaac growled. "How could they ... " He stormed out of the store, too angry to remember his manners.

Up ahead he spotted Governor Simcoe approaching in a cariole. Isaac jumped in front and waved it down, exclaiming, "Governor, this is outrageous! My land has been stolen away from me!" He waved the letter frantically.

Handing it to the governor, Isaac hoped Simcoe would take the matter into his own hands.

"I say, Devins, it does look as though the land legitimately belongs to the Lamberts. This is an outrage!" Simcoe agreed, shaking his head. "Unfortunately, there is nothing I can do once the deed has been granted. There is no system set up to deal with any disputes. I suppose you could take it to the District Court, but that could take months, even years."

Beyond frustration, Isaac seethed with anger. How could this have happened?

"Jarvis!" Isaac exclaimed so violently that the governor did a double-take. It could only be that incompetent louse, Isaac silently raged, cursing his very existence.

"All is lost for me and my family. We have nothing now, " muttered Isaac, still seething, ready to kill.

Simcoe breathed in sharply and cleared his throat, his face reddening. Isaac's despair hit home. The governor had recently experienced a disruption in his own life. Last June, his infant daughter, Katherine, succumbed to illness and was buried just outside the garrison, sadly defining the first cemetery in York. His wife, Sophia and Francis then departed to Niagara for an unknown length of time, his wife not trusting that York was a healthy place for her family. He did not want to leave Isaac Devins quite so downtrodden.

"Cheer up, Devins. I will grant you any other two hundred acres, anywhere you can find in the township. I also have another commission for you."

Isaac looked up with a glimmer of hope. Maybe this will be the big appointment that I have been looking for.

"I need you to go up to the Yonge Street project and act as a foreman. A group of settlers took over the construction after the Queen's Rangers were called away to Fort Niagara and Fort Detroit last fall. They have a capable leader, William Berczy, who hails from Germany, but I need to ensure that they are not lagging behind. I need you to confirm that they are constructing it up to the same standards as the Dundas Road. I will double your salary for this one, pay you twenty pounds."

That amount is what most farmers hoped to make in a year, thought Isaac, and can go a long way when you have to start all over again in the bush without a home, seed or any fields to grow them in. He accepted, but was bitterly disappointed. It was not the important government position that he was expecting. That will come, he sighed. He just had to be patient.

Two months later, after New Year's Day of 1795, Isaac set out to join the Yonge Street crew. He kissed Polly on the doorstep of their new cabin along the Humber, next to Levi's farm. They chose a 200 acre lot next to the family this time, at Polly's insistence. After taking all of their possessions out of their former homestead, Isaac had set the cabin ablaze, ensuring that the new owners saw him.

He stopped at St. John's to fill his water bottle and get some tea, flour, dried pork, beans and salt. Now that the Queen's Rangers were no longer part of the crew, Isaac was told that the settlers had to supply their own food.

"Well, Devins, you are far better off heading inland, what with practically the entire British Navy armed and patrolling Lake Ontario," declared St. John, who had a clear view across the lake to Fort Niagara from his front door. "It looks like we are already at war with the Americans."

"Lord Dorchester must be concerned that the Americans will attack, now that the French Republic is keeping the better part of the British Army busy."

"Good thing you are going to open up Yonge Street, my friend, just in case they do attack," observed St. John, somewhat envious of Isaac's latest assignment. "The defeat of the Shawnee, Wyandot and Ojibwas a few months ago in the Battle of Fallen Timbers has opened the door for the Americans to push northward all the way up to Detroit. Now there is nothing to stop them from coming."

"Yonge Street will provide a critical link to Lake Huron and Detroit," agreed Isaac, who had heard the governor talk about its advantages on many occasions. "It will be a crucial route if the Americans invade and take over Niagara."

Isaac set off and by mid-afternoon reached Nicholas Miller's new homestead, one of only two houses built along Yonge Street past the York boundary. Miller had left York not long after building the King's Mill, hoping to take advantage of an even greater offer of free land. He quickly built a grist mill and livery, and hoped to add a sawmill and tannery. Isaac admired his brother-in-law's industriousness, hoping to one day follow suit, and was pleased that his sister was well taken care of.

"You need to continue northward for another six miles," Miller advised Isaac. "There you will see a path leading to the east that will take you to the Berczy settlement. If you continue north along Yonge Street for another twenty-five miles, you will find the Berczy construction crew. Perhaps they are farther along than that, but I doubt it."

Just past the Miller homestead, the cleared path dwindled to a mere ten feet in width and followed its own course according to the slope of the land. Tramping along on snowshoes, mile after mile, Isaac moved swiftly across hills and valleys, rivers and ponds. The towering trees were so immense that they blocked the sunlight, even when the noon-day sun was overhead.

At dusk, Isaac was overtaken by three men on horseback who offered him a ride on one of the steeds they were leading to the Berczy settlement.

"We have forty families there, all Germans," said one of the men. "You will not want for anything."

"Well," said Isaac, "as my grandfather used to say, 'Man soll das Fell des Bären nicht verteilen, bevor man ihn erlegt hat!'" (Don't count your chickens before they hatch).

The three strangers chuckled, amused that Isaac knew their mother tongue. "You are from Prussia, then?" inquired the youngest one, named Helmut.

"My family first settled in Albany, New York, more than one hundred and fifty years ago, but we have kept the language and customs of our heritage," Isaac replied. "We moved from town to town throughout New York and last hailed from Genesee. I hear you are also from the area."

"Yes," answered Helmut, "but we were only there for a short while. We landed in Philadelphia two years ago and were offered free land if we cut a road from there to Genesee. One year later, we finally finished, only to discover that we would not become land owners, as promised, but would become tenant farmers, the exact situation we were trying to escape from."

Isaac nodded. He remembered quite well how it felt to be a tenant farmer. Although he didn't get the piece of land that he wanted in York, at least he owned two hundred acres along the Humber River and didn't have to answer to a landlord.

"Then we heard about the free land offered in Upper Canada, so we came north last summer and set up camp on Yonge Street. Last September we started cutting the road at Eglinton. When we finish, we have been promised one thousand acres per family, as a reward."

That's quite a prize, thought Isaac with a hint of envy, thinking of his

200 acre lot along the Humber. William Berczy must know how to handle the governor.

Isaac was indeed treated like royalty as Helmut's wife served him a meal of rabbit and venison with sauerkraut and pretzels. His glass of spirits was kept full by his host, who drank copiously, telling tales of life in Prussia and how it had changed when the French Republic attacked. The two young children who played by the hearth reminded Isaac of Elizabeth, and he fell asleep that night missing her, Polly, and Hannah.

At daybreak, Isaac and his host took a cutter through the woods over freshly fallen snow. Travelling north along Yonge Street, they had to veer off into the woods ten miles short of their destination. There were too many stumps blocking the way to allow safe passage.

"We will have to remove the stumps in spring when the ground thaws," explained Helmut. "It is too treacherous to burn them in the dense woods without fear of starting a massive forest fire."

Two hours later they reached the camp south of the Holland River. "Has anyone seen Bertzie?" called out Helmut.

They found him at the frontier where a group of men were chopping down a towering, one-hundred-and-fifty-foot white pine that looked like it was dangerously close to falling in the wrong direction.

"Over to the left! No, not that far!" Berczy barked out in German.

As Isaac drew closer he saw a medium-built, dark-haired man with a long thin beard wearing a bearskin jacket and a raccoon hat speaking to several workers. He had a commanding presence but seemed somewhat reserved, confident, but approachable.

"Mr. Berczy, may I introduce to you Mr. Isaac Devins, from York, an assistant to Governor Simcoe," Helmut said.

"So the governor has sent someone to check up on me, I see," Berczy said with a half-smile and a shrug. "Maybe he does not trust that an artist like me actually has some engineering skills."

In Europe, William Berczy made a living as a portrait artist, capturing the likenesses of dukes and duchesses in Tuscany and even King George III just prior to sailing for the New World. His artistry and ingenuity were later combined as he designed some of the early buildings in Toronto – including the home of Peter Russell, known as the "Abbey." Berczy would later be called one of Toronto's first architects.

"I wouldn't call myself a spy," replied Isaac, trying to keep the tone light, extending his hand in greeting. "Instead, I've come here to offer assistance. I worked with the Queen's Rangers cutting the Dundas Road at the Head of the Lake, so I was sent here to ensure that Yonge Street is built to the same standard."

"Where I come from, we call that tyranny," snapped Berczy, the half-smile changing to annoyance. William Berczy had his own way of doing things. He had fled his homeland to avoid being taken over by the French Republic and did not like to be under anyone's authority.

Raising his eyebrows, Isaac was surprised to hear words challenging the governor's supremacy. Not wanting trouble, Isaac replied, "Those are strong words, sir. Just think of me as a second-in-command. Someone who can manage the workforce and assure that the road is built with quality. You can assign me to any post, and I will gladly do my share."

William Moll Berczy, a man of unyielding faith and integrity, appreciated Isaac's honesty and dedication. He put his arm around Isaac's shoulders and led him to the uncut edge of the forest so that they could turn around and gaze down the finished portion of Yonge Street. Not that there was much to see beyond a flurry of workers.

"When do you predict you'll be finished?" inquired Isaac, quite impressed that they had progressed this far in such a short time.

Berczy stopped and turned toward Isaac. "We have to reach the wooden lodge along the Holland River by September to receive a land grant of 64,000 acres. So far, we have cut out thirty-five miles, and we have eighteen to go. I have no doubt that we will meet with success."

"I will be only too glad to help," Isaac offered.

For several days, he observed the intricacies of the German's road-building techniques. "I have examined the last fifteen miles from here south to the Berczy settlement," Isaac told Berczy later one evening outside his tent. "The route is clearly defined with only a few slight deviations from Augustus Jones's survey marks. Quite an admirable job you have done."

Isaac wanted to lead slowly into his critique, not having any real authority other than Simcoe's quick decision to send him up there.

"There are just a couple of areas where the road edges are not lined that need attention," he said diplomatically.

The next morning, Isaac set out with five men and a team of two oxen to line the road with trees wherever there were gaps. They reached the first site and had just started to unhitch the oxen when a snow squall struck, appearing out of nowhere from a clear sky. The blinding snow swirled in the wind, allowing a visibility of only a few feet. After an hour of huddling together with no possibility of lighting a fire in the ferocious wind, they trudged back to camp, plodding through almost a foot of snow.

By evening, the storm passed and the men emerged from the tents, hungry and restless. The fire used by the camp cooks had long been extinguished and had to be relit before anyone could eat. A handful of workers were ordered to check the traps, bringing back a half-dozen rabbits and several raccoons, hardly enough to feed one hundred men. Fortunately, the camp cook had sufficient wheat flour to make dumplings that he added to a broth made from the meat.

"The hunters must have been unable to go out today because of the snowstorm," Helmut advised as they approached one of several campfires set up to warm the workers.

"It may be hours before we eat," grumbled another.

"If we get any at all," added another.

Isaac walked over to Berczy's tent through crowds of crewmen huddled together. Lifting the deerskin flap, Isaac went inside to warm himself.

"Don't get too comfortable," warned Berczy. "There are still a lot of men that will need to come in and do the same thing."

Unlike Governor Simcoe, who always kept a noticeable distance between himself and his minions, William Berczy made no such distinction. He treated each of his workers as if they were equals.

The next morning was clear and crisp. Isaac, Helmut and four others set out with a team of oxen back to the repair site. They unhooked a log from the oxen's harness, and all six of them rolled it into position using tree branches as levers. I never fancied myself to be a lumberjack, Isaac silently complained, thinking that Simcoe's description of the job was quite misleading. It is ironic that from the very beginning I did not want to spend my time chopping down the forest, but that is what I seem to be doing most since coming to Upper Canada.

Chop, chop, chop. See-saw, see-saw. Hack, hack, hack, hack. Isaac's crew worked diligently, in surprisingly high spirits, placing ten logs into empty spots along the cleared road edges over a two-day span, before another storm struck. Luckily, they were only a half-mile from the camp and were able to make it back within an hour.

No one went hungry that evening, as the cook had instructed the hunters to bring in double the amount of game. Three new wigwams were constructed so that the cook could prepare meals and bake bread while the snow pelted down outside. But the storm raged for three days, and the food supply dwindled to nothing. By day four, all that the crew had to eat were two small cornmeal biscuits apiece.

Isaac tried to lift the men's spirits. "I understand your frustration, as I am also lacking a proper meal," he began sympathetically. "But I am sure we have seen the worst of Mother Nature, and can expect clear weather to guide us through the rest of the winter."

No sooner had Isaac finished his sentence than the wind swelled to a howl and another blizzard struck, the worst the crew had seen so far. Blinding snow pelted across the land, threatening to bury the tents and all their equipment. There was no chance to hunt for game, and the traps had snared only a few rabbits and squirrels.

Real starvation set in and with it, illness. At first, a couple of people, weak with hunger, contracted the chills, fever and aches, but the malaise quickly spread. Berczy walked from tent to tent offering words of encouragement.

"Cheer up, men. The blizzard can't last all winter. We will soon be out of it. Some people have the fever, so I advise you to stick to your own tent, just in case."

The storm was relentless. Whenever the weather letup, even for an hour, the men would hitch a sleigh to a team of horses and transport the sick back to the main settlement. Soon there were more people working to evacuate the sick than to construct the roadway. Some didn't make it. Isaac and Helmut, still perfectly healthy, hoisted a couple of dead bodies onto a sleigh to be taken to base camp.

"Shouldn't we all be heading back to the settlement until the winter subsides?" questioned Isaac, concerned that he, too, would soon fall ill.

"Nonsense," insisted Berczy, not used to having his command questioned. "We will proceed according to schedule."

"Very well," replied Isaac, masking his misgivings.

Although the snow let up for a couple of weeks, the illness did not. More and more workers became sick and had to be transported out, and more died. Berczy was relentless, insisting that the diminishing crew continue, despite only moving forward fifty feet or so per day.

"At this pace, we will not reach Lake Simcoe until next Christmas," complained Helmut, wiping his nose and coughing.

A few days passed before Isaac also fell prey to the illness. He continued his duties for as long as he could, until he became so weak with exhaustion that he could barely take a step. One morning, he stumbled into Berczy's wigwam, then tripped and fell down face first, his head hitting the side of a chair. He was knocked out cold.

"Quick, remove his coat and lay him by the fire," commanded Berczy, "and pass me my hunting knife."

Wiping it off on a cloth, Berczy took the knife, rolled up Isaac's sleeve and laid the point on Isaac's muscular forearm, toward the inside. He quickly drew the knife downward and made a three-inch-long gash that immediately filled with red blood, the excess oozing in trickles down Isaac's arm.

Berczy then made another three-inch gash that mirrored the one on the right. In Berlin, a doctor had showed him where to cut an ill person's arms to purify the blood and release the toxins. He recalled that the doctor had made similar incisions on the calves of both legs, so he sliced each of Isaac's legs accordingly.

Silence. Stillness. Isaac saw Polly walking through a field of purple asters and golden rod, a bright pink bonnet on her head, looking regal, serene. She stopped and turned, smiled, then nodded her head. Isaac obediently stepped forward, walking stiffly, like a soldier, but eager to join her. She stretched out her arms and suddenly there were five children on each side holding her hands. They each had a lit candle and held it up toward the sky. The flames grew higher and higher, stretching up to the heavens.

A massive arching white light, stretched down from the sky, illuminating an image of Captain Kit and his grandfather, who beckoned him forward. The white light was peaceful, the white light was serenity, the white light called him. He reached for it, as if to grab a giant white hand with its palm open, so smooth and peaceful. He knew he would be safe there.

He reached out again . . . and . . .

Chapter 12 – March 1, 1795

Isaac opened his eyes, then shut them immediately to block out the sunlight. He faintly heard William Berczy's voice in the background, saying something about a new wagon from the settlement. Groaning, Isaac tried to clear his throat, and reached out as if to grab a flask of water.

"You are finally awake, my friend," said Berczy.

"How . . . long . . ." began Isaac, his voice low and gruff.

"You have been sleeping, in and out, for the last three days," explained Berczy. "We kept you hot by the fire so that you could sweat out the impurities. We almost lost you, but by the grace of the Good Lord, you came back. As soon as this squall lets up, we will send you back to the village for recovery. Here, drink this hot toddy, it does wonders."

Later that afternoon, Isaac was taken to the Berczy settlement, still weak with hunger and fatigue. Isaac asked to be taken to Helmut's cabin, and found that Helmut himself had not yet recovered and had spread the illness to everyone in his family except for his two nephews.

"Aye, we are no better here than at camp," Helmut told Isaac, "except for the decent shelter. The sickness has spread to every cabin here and I believe there are more people racked with fever than healthy and strong."

All Isaac could think of was to get home, see Polly again, put his arms around her, toss little Elizabeth in the air and hear her squeal with delight, and tickle Hannah under the chin. But he was too sick to make the journey, too weak to walk more than a half-mile or so. Besides, the illness spread like wildfire and he did not want to infect anyone in his family, have them suffer and die.

Before a fortnight had passed, William Berczy and the remainder of the crew returned to the settlement to wait out the storm, and the construction of Yonge Street was put on hold until spring.

With so many ill, there were only a few able to hunt or set traps and fewer still to make bread. Just as many people died from hunger as from the illness. In a moment of clarity, Helmut's wife, raging with fever, gave Isaac the last piece of cornbread, her deep-seated sense of propriety demanding that her guest receive the best that they could offer. Isaac thanked her and tried to share it but was vehemently refused by his righteous hosts.

Two days later, she was dead. Helmut followed her the next day, begging that his children be looked after with his dying breath. Grim, gaunt and lightheaded, Isaac was so weak that he could barely mourn the loss.

Fortunately for Isaac and the remainder of Helmut's family, the hand of death released its hold a few days later, and most started to make a slow recovery. Isaac soon was strong enough to check the traps with a few of Berczy's men and give the catch to the women to prepare. Berczy organized a feeding system for the entire settlement so that all survivors received a daily ration.

It was weeks before Isaac had a chance to catch a lift down to York. He had no remorse abandoning his assignment to oversee the construction of Yonge Street. His brush with death made him realize that nothing was better than holding Polly in his arms or paddling alone down the Humber in his canoe.

Finally back at York, Isaac slid weakly out of the cutter and rapped softly at Levi's door, hoping not to arouse any sleeping bodies. Polly answered and almost fainted at the sight of her husband.

"My sweet Jesus, thank you," she exclaimed, throwing her arms around him, squeezing a little too hard. Isaac smiled like a boy who had snared his first rabbit. He could not believe how incredible it felt to hold his wife in his arms, to smell her sweet-scented hair and see her radiant face. Polly finally backed away, her smile fading, when she realized how pale and frail Isaac looked.

"You have the fever," she stated, her hand reaching up to feel his forehead and cheeks. "Come, I will make a remedy," she ordered, leading Isaac toward a chair next to the hearth. She returned with a hot drink of the same ingredients she had used to cure baby Elizabeth after her trek to the peninsula.

"Drink it slowly," she advised. "Within a few days you will feel like new."

Sure enough, the ancient healing techniques from the Mississaugas again proved their worth, completely curing Isaac within a few days.

"Most of the Berczy clan are giving up and going back to Niagara to wait it out," Isaac informed Polly. "I don't think Berczy will have enough workers to continue, the project will be abandoned."

"I am just content that you are here, Isaac, where you belong," said Polly, still marvelling at her good fortune that her husband had returned. "The girls missed you so much."

Isaac put his arms around Polly, grateful to be alive and well.

◇◇◇

The spring of 1795 began as a promising season for the residents of York, a welcome relief after the harsh, unforgiving winter. Colourful buds burst out of sleeping grey twigs, creating a pale yellow-green glow. The forest floor came alive with clumps of pink and white trilliums, ferns, trout lilies and mayapples. Tulips and daffodils, imported from Britain, were grown near the front door of many of the homes in the town centre. Everything in York seemed to be starting anew, except for Isaac Devins.

By the end of May, his brothers had already cleared five acres on each of their properties and were intent on clearing two more so that they could get a late crop in. Isaac, on the other hand, did not. He had never intended to come to Upper Canada to be a farmer, clear the land and sow seed. Instead, he went to the river every morning and stared out, mesmerized. There is something about the river that draws me here, almost like a magnet, he thought. It was as if an unseen force held him, captivated.

His father reproached him, telling Isaac that he was wasting his time and should be providing for his family, but Isaac ignored his pleas. The twenty pounds from his work on Yonge Street would carry himself, Polly and the two girls comfortably through the winter. He wanted something more, but he was not sure just what it was.

Isaac was restless. There was little he could do to advance his position with the governor, who had already left for Niagara for the summer. No one else of importance was residing in the muddy little village of twenty buildings clustered along the lakeshore, extending up Yonge to Lot Street. None of the aristocrats had moved to York, preferring to stay in Niagara, which had everything that one could ask for. He thought about opening another sawmill, but there were not enough settlers in York to justify it.

For a fee of ten pounds, the governor hired Isaac to keep watch over the Humber while he was gone, certain that American spies were scouting out the Toronto Carrying Place. In his birchbark canoe, Isaac paddled past the King's Mill to the mouth every day, then returned past his own homestead and continued up to the start of the Indian trail. He felt an overwhelming sense of peace and fulfillment every time he dipped his paddle into the cool blue water. Many times he would meet Fire Starter or other Mississaugas, who invited him to their meals and meetings of the elders. In a few months, Isaac had a good grasp of their language and customs.

One August afternoon, Isaac came upon a handful of settlers standing on a log laid across a streamlet near the King's Mill, bent over with wooden clubs in hand. Curious, he paddled over and saw them attempting to catch some of the larger fish. He joined them, bashing at the sturgeon as they swam by, then removing them with a net. Isaac was pleased to bring home a few three-footers for his family.

Fire Starter shook his head, almost laughing, when he saw Isaac out on one of the logs with a wooden club in hand. "You will make the fish angry," he said, his English vastly improved since they had first met two years ago.

"Come here when night falls, I will show you."

They met at the limestone outcrop at Fire Starter's insistence. He wanted to leave some tobacco offerings for the river spirits in hopes of a bountiful catch. Loading the equipment into the canoe, they set off upstream as the red sky turned to mauve, violet and finally to black.

Finding a deep pool, Fire Starter backpaddled, slowed the canoe, then turned it perpendicular to the shore. He took out a metal jack, a circular iron grate on pivots, and placed it in the centre of the canoe, then piled some pine chips no more than one foot long on top. It took him only a few seconds to create smoke after rubbing some pieces of flint together. Isaac whistled in approval when Fire Starter had a three-foot flame burning within a minute. I can see how he got his name, mused Isaac, leaning back in the canoe.

Fire was such an essential to both the settlers and the Mississaugas. Many kept a fire going all through the night in their hearth, wigwam or fire pit to avoid having to start one the next morning, a cumbersome task. Abraham would send Simeon over to Levi's property next door with a lantern to bring a flame back to the homestead every time their fire went out. That would not be necessary for Fire Starter who could probably ignite a flame with a blade of grass, thought Isaac.

Slowly and deliberately, Fire Starter stood up in the canoe with the flames burning brightly in front of him, motioning for Isaac to keep still. The canoe wobbled, but the fire held steady. They waited and waited. Finally, with a swift but sure motion, Fire Starter struck, piercing the neck of a three-foot-long trout. Hoisting it over the side, he placed it on a flat-bottomed tray made of dried reed grass.

One after another, Fire Starter expertly speared and hauled the fish, some of them almost four feet long. Isaac could see that the fish were much more plentiful during the night and were drawn to the flickering firelight. If a shoal passed by, Fire Starter could easily kill forty or fifty in an hour.

"If the fish is here," explained Fire Starter, pointing to a location toward the surface of the water near the canoe, "you must strike here." He indicated a spot closer to the boat than the fish would be. "If the fish is deep and far, you must strike nearer still."

Within minutes, Fire Starter filled the canoe.

"Why don't you take more, try to sell it to the settlers?" questioned Isaac, thinking that it could be quite a lucrative venture.

"We only take what we need," explained Fire Starter. "The river is a spirit. It blesses us with fish. We do not want to make Munendoo and the other spirits angry."

Paddling back to the limestone outcrop, they could see other fires scattered along the riverbank, surrounded by fishermen. Until that evening, Isaac was unaware that the Mississaugas came to the river at nighttime. They later salted and smoked the fish, and transported it by canoe to the northern hunting grounds every winter.

The summer passed pleasantly for Isaac, who joined Fire Starter almost every night for fishing. By mid-October, Isaac had caught and smoked enough fish to feed the entire Devins clan throughout the winter.

The rest of the settlers did not fare so well. Massive crop failure struck the town of York in the summer and fall of 1795.

There hadn't been a day of rain past May. Many settlers traded all their supplies for seed that did not yield a viable crop and were left with nothing. With 450 people in four isolated pockets – the townsite, the Humber, the Don, and Yonge Street – the settlers were too spread out to be able to rely on one another through another tough winter. Facing a real threat of starvation, many packed up and went back to Niagara, where supplies were much more plentiful, leaving less than half the population in York.

The Devins family did not have that option. With no money or connections in Niagara, they were just as well off in York. The only thing that got them through the long winter of 1795–96 was Isaac.

Every night, he went to the Humber and caught two dozen fish, more than double that on a good night. Although the salmon run was over, the river still abounded with brook trout, pike, pickerel and whitefish. When the river froze over in January, Isaac built a wooden shelter, then dug a hole in the ice and continued fishing until spring.

The fish were so bountiful that Isaac did not know what to do with the surplus until one afternoon when a few settlers overheard Isaac outside of William Allans's new shipping warehouse close to the dock.

"There's so many, I only keep the four-footers now and throw the rest back," Isaac told Allan.

"I would pay a good price for a load of fish, if you have it, Devins," interjected a settler from Yonge Street. "We don't have enough food to get us through next week."

So began his fishing business. Every Friday, Isaac loaded a small wooden sled with dozens of fish, strapped a yoke over his neck, and pulled it a half-mile to Levi's homestead. On Saturday mornings, he hitched up the oxen, loaded his brother's sleigh, and took the load to the dock at the foot of Yonge Street.

When the news spread, the townsfolk would wait on the dock for Isaac's arrival. Some travelled for miles to buy the fish to feed their starving families. When they heard the jingle bells ringing down Yonge Street, the starving settlers would cheer and clear a path for him.

Isaac soon became known as the Guardian of the Humber. The settlers were truly thankful. Many had already killed their horses or oxen and eaten the meat, and scrounged the frozen forest for any plant that could be ground and baked. If the need was great, Isaac gave part of the catch to a starving settler or family who promised to repay him in the spring. William Allan bought the leftovers to sell at his warehouse.

"We were down to our last rabbit a week ago," one settler explained, "and the traps were bare. This will at least last us for another fortnight."

Isaac felt like a hero and was treated like one. He hoped that the governor would hear of his success while he was away that winter at Fort Detroit, Kingston and Montreal. Not until the spring of 1796 did Isaac meet up with the governor again at St. John's former store, lying abandoned.

"I hear you have become quite the riverman," exclaimed Simcoe, patting Isaac on the shoulder, "and have saved many from certain starvation, quite remarkable."

Not skilled at self-promotion, Isaac merely said, "I just used the skills taught to me by the Mississaugas. They have many things that we can learn from."

"You can tell me all about it tomorrow," replied Simcoe. "I need you to take me up the Don River to Castle Frank."

Although the Simcoes' cottage was only a few miles northeast of the townsite, no roads were yet built and it could only be reached by the river. Isaac had not ventured east of Yonge Street and was pleased to discover a new part of the township. He asked his brother, Levi, to accompany him.

They transported Simcoe and his estate manager, John Scadding, from the dock east through the marshes at the mouth of the river in Isaac's little birchbark canoe, something that the governor requested. They passed by Scadding's cabin near the mouth on the east side and canoed under the wooden bridge he had constructed. The Don River was not as steep as the Humber, so it was easier to paddle up through the shallow runs.

The governor invited Isaac along under the pretence of showing him his summer home that had just been completed. However, his deeper motivation was to learn about the Mississaugas' recent declaration of conflict. Isaac was known as someone who was friendly with the Mississaugas, knew some of their language and was almost considered an extended family member. Simcoe could no longer consult with St. John on native affairs as he had moved on to Ancaster, so Isaac was his next best choice.

Strangely enough, St. John's last day in York was Isaac's first day back from the Yonge Street commission. Isaac arrived in a cutter from the Berczy settlement, grateful that there was still deep snow in April. Thank the good Lord that I didn't wait a couple more weeks, thought Isaac, as Yonge Street would be nearly impassable until the drier days of midsummer. It could take a horse and wagon almost two weeks to trudge through the mud for the twenty-six-mile trip to York in the spring, whereas it took only a day and a half by cutter.

"You seem a little low on supplies," observed Isaac, who stopped in at St. John's store to pick up a gift for Polly before going home. Polly did so love to have a cup of tea, but Isaac only saw a few bags of flour and oats.

St. John stood up, stroked his dark beard, put one hand in each pocket of his rusty brown daycoat and declared, "The rest of the merchandise is already packed away on the bateau. We are sailing for the Head of the Lake today, never to return. I've had it with Simcoe's broken promises. He's a two-faced, good-for-nothing liar!"

St. John's land claim must have been refused, thought Isaac, who was all too familiar with the shortcomings of the Land Board. "Five thousand acres on the east side of the Humber I was promised," continued St. John, "Don't you remember, Devins, on the ship coming into the harbour, the very first day we arrived here?"

Isaac could barely remember, perhaps due to the copious amount of wine the three of them had consumed that night. But he was not surprised. Many settlers, other than Simcoe's Executive Council and Legislative Assembly, had similar complaints. The governor made many promises that he later denied or did not keep.

"I've got my eye on a few thousand acres near Cootes Paradise. You should drop in if you are ever passing through," said St. John as he boarded the bateau. He turned and did not look back. Isaac saw Margaret strolling toward him, noting her always fresh beauty, lovely and surreal. She smiled at Isaac, but her eyes betrayed a sadness.

"So long," she said, looking up at him with her intoxicating green eyes.

Isaac took her hand and kissed it, as only a gentleman could, but would have preferred much more. Margaret bowed her head and joined her husband at the stern. Isaac felt a tug on his sleeve, looked down, and smiled as Joseph handed him a pocket-sized curved knife with a short, wooden handle, painted red, blue and yellow, and a blue feather.

"Can you give this to Simeon?" asked Joseph, "I couldn't find him on the river yesterday." The boy had carved the initials S.D. into the handle along with an image of a willow leaf and a bird, possibly a raven.

"Sure thing," said Isaac, patting him on the shoulder as he ran to join his parents.

The governor just lost his best interpreter and intermediary with the natives, observed Isaac, as he watched St. John's bateau disappear beyond the rocks and birch trees on a small jetty. He was surprised that Simcoe did not do more to keep St. John in York, particularly since the Mississaugas had recently begun to show signs of exasperation.

When Isaac met up with Fire Starter and Kineubenae just after they had met with the governor. Kineubenae rambled on with annoyance and disgust, which Fire Starter translated for Isaac.

"He told the governor that we have shared our land with the settlers, but they drive us away like dogs," related Fire Starter, equally appalled by the settlers' actions. "They destroy our burial sites, steal our offerings and dig up our graves."

No doubt they are referring to a particular incident involving Hannah Jarvis, concluded Isaac, who had heard about it from John White. Unlike Isaac and Polly Devins, many settlers did not react kindly when the Mississaugas entered their homes without asking, often staying for hours on end or even over night. The Mississaugas did not understand the idea of property lines and single-family dwellings. It was a concept as foreign to them as living communally was to the settlers. They would only become proprietary if they were at war with a neighbouring clan.

The Jarvis family was one of the first of the elite class to move to York, at Governor Simcoe's insistence that the registrar general be situated closer to the seat of government. Their home was built at the corner of Duke and Caroline Streets, one of the prestigious lots in town. William Smith, the same British contractor who later constructed Castle Frank, laid the last brick on the rear facade of the Jarvis home in the spring of 1795. At last, Hannah Jarvis had a home grand enough for her liking, although she continually snubbed York. She was often heard saying that it was better suited to a frog pond than a city.

A few days after reluctantly arriving in York, Hannah Jarvis was sorting things out in the parlor, trying to decide which room should have the silver candleholders and which should have the brass. She did so want to make a lasting impression when Elizabeth Simcoe came for tea the following week. Finally, she would be able to show her superiority without even trying. Imagine, Elizabeth Simcoe still hosting balls and tea parties in a canvas tent.

She was just about to open another crate of housewares when two Mississaugas opened the door and let themselves in. They walked through each room, searching for food and water.

Startled, Hannah let out a shrill cry and backed away.

"Why, the nerve!" she exclaimed. "Don't you know your manners?"

She was astounded. Nothing like this had ever happened in Newark or Montreal. What an unsophisticated backwoods settlement York is, she muttered, where natives come striding in unannounced. The Mississaugas looked equally startled, not understanding her indignation. They shrugged and walked into the pantry, looking for food, scraps, anything. One of them took the lid off of a pot boiling over the hearth and then sat down at the table opposite Hannah Jarvis.

"Hmmgh!" she snorted.

Rising to her feet, she searched the parlour and found the witchhazel broom, then beat the intruders in the arms, chest and head, bellowing, "Leave, at once!" over and over again.

The Mississaugas backed away, but then one of them yanked the broom out of Hannah's hands. He mimed her actions, swinging the broom toward her, letting out a half-hearted warrior cry, the two of them mocking her. Incensed, Hannah backed away, scuffled about, and found William's pistol lying on the night table. She came out of the bedroom and pointed it toward them, her hands shaking, her eyes wild, motioning toward the door.

When they didn't move, she closed her eyes and pulled the trigger.

She opened them, and saw the backs of the two escaping through the doorway, running as fast as their feet would carry them.

"Oh, my brand-new door!" she cried, upset that it now had a bullet hole. The natives will know to stay away from this house now, she thought proudly, pleased that she had fended them off.

Annoyances like this between settlers and natives were not specifically what troubled the governor, however. He had just received word that Joseph Brant issued a proclamation denouncing the government. Brant represented not only the Six Nations Reserve along the Grand River but also the Mississaugas and most of the land claims in Upper Canada. He was one of the few whom the British considered capable of uniting all the many tribes to oppose the Crown.

The tension between the British and Brant escalated after Brant sold a large tract of land in the Grand River Reserve, the size of a township, to private settlers. Brant could see the enormous profit potential in selling land to settlers and resented the British for not allowing it to happen. Many native families were leaving the Grand River Reserve and moving back to New York where they could sell land; Brant wanted to keep his people in Upper Canada, and knew that he needed to offer them a good reason to stay.

"We are not slaves to the British," Brant wrote. "Why should we not sell what is ours?"

Governor Simcoe and Lord Dorchester were the most vocal opponents of allowing the natives to sell land.

"Why should we allow our Loyalists to purchase land from Joseph Brant when we could be making the profit from it?" Lord Dorchester declared in writing and at meetings of the Executive Council. "After the War of Independence, we purchased all the land north of Lake Ontario from the Mississaugas. Then we granted the Grand River Reserve to Brant's clan so they could come here from the Mohawk valley in the States. Why should we bother giving the Mohawks land that we already paid for if they are going to turn around and sell it?

"We should be the ones rendering the profit," Simcoe strongly agreed. "We need the revenue to build roads, docks, mills, all things that the natives benefit from. They don't have the skills or wherewithal to build a province the way that we do."

176

"The natives are not British subjects," John White agreed. "They have no right to sell land."

Now that Brant had publicly expressed his outrage and disappointment with the British, Simcoe was worried that perhaps he had gone too far. He feared that the skirmish might be enough to push Brant to align with the Americans, or with the French and Spanish in the Mississippi Valley. He knew that it was often only a minor incident that tipped the scales, causing alliances to shift or war to be declared.

"What we don't know is how infuriated Joseph Brant is because we are opposing the land sales or whether it is all just talk," Simcoe explained to Isaac as they paddled up the river.

They passed under another bridge at Lot Street that provided a connection to the Danforth Road. Isaac was silent, unsure yet of the governor's intentions.

The lone canoe was a rare occasion for the governor, who usually had an entourage of staff tagging along. However, he wanted to impress upon Isaac the importance of his mission. Devins had spent the majority of his time on the Humber over the last year, pulling away from the aristocratic society, and Simcoe wanted him back in the fold.

"I do believe that the natives are interested in adopting some of our British customs, particularly in the area of farming," Isaac replied, thinking of a recent conversation with Fire Starter. Without breaking the rhythm of the paddle strokes, he continued, "Perhaps that is why they are up in arms about not being permitted to sell land."

Treading softly, Isaac did not want to present a view contrary to Simcoe's well-known position; neither did he want to betray the Mississaugas.

Fire Starter had told him, "Chief Wabakinine says, we have become reliant on the white man for so many things. Clothes, tools, guns. If we can't find sufficient pelts to trade for them, we will surely be lost. Perhaps an easier way would be to sell our land for greater profit so that we can meet the needs of our people. Perhaps we should be clearing the land and farming like the white man does."

Fire Starter had leaned forward and taken a long drag on a pipe, then had handed it to Isaac. "But I do not agree. We are people of the forest. That is where we belong."

Arriving at the landing spot below Castle Frank, the four men climbed out of the canoe and started the ascent up the steep wooded hill, the governor taking the lead, followed by Isaac, Levi and Scadding. A cool spring breeze rustled through the emerging greenery, fresh, crisp and new. Simcoe contemplated his next words, to steer the conversation toward his original intent.

"You have close ties with the Mississaugas," the governor began, his tone light and engaging. "Perhaps you could find out their stance on land sales."

Since Joseph Brant had become the spokesman for the Mississaugas, Simcoe assumed that any information he could gain from the Mississaugas would also apply to Joseph Brant and the Mohawks. The security of Upper Canada depended on it, and he felt that Isaac Devins was the most likely of the 432 settlers presently in York to become an informant and provide crucial intelligence. Spying, as he learned during the American Revolution, was a critical military tactic that often determined victory or defeat.

"I have very little contact with the chief or elders," replied Isaac, not sure exactly what Simcoe was asking him to do. He could not envision the sort of espionage that Simcoe was intimating. He did not have any direct connection with Chief Wabakinine or with Joseph Brant, and did not know how he would be privy to classified information.

Not another word was spoken until they reached the top of the steep incline and had a chance to catch their breath. Walking through the edge of the forest, they entered a clearing. An attractive, large wood cabin was at the far end. It had Greek columns that supported a triangular roof over the front entrance, making it look like the grandest building in the town of York. The Simcoes built Castle Frank as a summer cottage, enjoying the spectacular view toward the lakefront and across to Niagara. Named for their son, Francis, it was Simcoe's first and only house built in Upper Canada.

The governor brought up the subject again just as they sat down to tea with Mrs. Simcoe, who arrived with the children, nurses and staff only minutes beforehand. The intricately carved, dark oak table seemed a trifle luxurious for the unfinished log house, which did not yet have proper interior walls.

Taking a seat on a comfortable oak chair opposite Isaac, Simcoe queried, "Do you suppose that Joseph Brant would revoke his alliance with the British and side with the Americans or the French if we continue to thwart their attempts to sell land?"

Before Isaac could reply, Elizabeth Simcoe joined them, nodded to Isaac and handed her husband a letter that had just arrived from Montreal. The communiqué must be at least three weeks old, Isaac calculated, as that is the time it took for a letter carrier to walk from Montreal to York. The roads were still too muddy and gouged for any efficient travel by horse and buggy.

Scanning the letter quickly, Simcoe cleared his throat, then remarked rather stoically, "It's final, then."

Sitting back in his chair, he tucked his left hand under his chin and put his right hand across his chest, a common mannerism when he was deep in thought.

"My request for a leave of absence was accepted in London. I cannot say that I am saddened or disheartened. Instead, I find it a relief not to have to deal with Lord Dorchester's inane policies any longer. The man is insisting that we prepare for a defensive war with the Americans and does not want to take any direct action. I find it infuriating to sit back and let that happen. We should be attacking them now, while they are more vulnerable and do not expect an offensive from us. If we could cut them off from support from the French, we will most certainly be victorious."

Rapping his fingers on the table, the governor continued, "I have written communiqués, I have spoken with him directly. Nothing will change his mind. There is nothing more I can do."

Simcoe seemed resigned, worn out, acquiescent. He coughed and sniffed a few times, a sign that he was suffering from the ague.

"When will you depart?" asked Isaac, shocked that the governor was leaving. For the last three years he had operated under the premise of befriending the man to advance his own position, and had so far received only a few small appointments.

"In six weeks we set sail," replied Simcoe.

Blast! uttered Isaac to himself. He never anticipated that Simcoe would leave. Once he's gone, I will have nothing. All my hard work, all the strategy meetings with the governor, all the jobs that I have done for him, will be for naught. Simcoe has enemies in this town, and Isaac knew that his support of Simcoe would not win him any favours with the next governor. Isaac imagined himself at the bottom of the pecking order, again.

"Who will take over your position while you are away?" he asked quietly.

"I have recommended that Peter Russell take command temporarily," replied Simcoe, dusting off his daycoat as if he was wiping himself clean.

Damn, Isaac cursed to himself, unsure whether Peter Russell would become a friend or foe. He had very little to do with the elder statesman, whom he considered to be extraneous and a two-bit player.

Simcoe advised that he still wanted Isaac to be an informant for the Mississaugas, even though he did not yet know when he would return to York. "I expect to have regular correspondence from you shipped to England so that I can keep abreast of the situation and advise the King," Simcoe commanded. "I don't want to lose Joseph Brant's support while I am away."

That was the last time that Isaac Devins saw the governor. Two days later, the Simcoes sailed to Niagara and did not return. Isaac was distraught but kept up his end of the bargain, writing to Simcoe one month later to inform him of an extremely delicate situation that had arisen. Chief Wabakinine, head of the Mississaugas of the Credit, was killed by a British soldier.

The chief had been fishing all night, then went with his wife, sister and a few others to the wharf in York to sell some of the excess. They purchased some rum and headed over to their encampment. On the way, a soldier stopped them and offered the chief's sister some more rum and a dollar to grant him certain favours. Later that night, the soldier went by the encampment but everyone was sleeping. Wabakinine's wife awoke, startled, and prodded her husband, saying that the white man was going to kill his sister.

Half-asleep and stumbling, the chief confronted the intruder, threatening him. The two men fought. The quarrel ended when the soldier struck the chief over the head with a rock, and he died a few days later. Within a few weeks, the chief's wife was also dead and rumour spread that it was because of mistreatment by white men.

"My brothers in the eagle clan are extremely angry," Fire Starter told Isaac a few weeks after it happened. By September, Fire Starter had usually left for the northern hunting grounds for the winter, but this year, the otter clan and many others held back, in case there was warfare. "Her brother wants revenge. He has already stopped Augustus Jones from completing his survey on the Grand River, and I am sure that more action will follow."

Isaac diligently wrote to Simcoe, advising him that there could very well be a confrontation. That winter, the tension escalated when the soldier was acquitted of murdering the chief due to lack of evidence. None of the Mississaugas had shown up for the trial.

"This is an insult to my people," Fire Starter told Isaac, with sorrow in his eyes. "I am truly saddened that we will soon be at war with you, my friend," he said, putting an arm on Isaac's shoulder. "You should take your family to Niagara while you still can."

The Mississaugas had two hundred warriors assembled at their settlement along the Credit River, ready to attack at any moment, a force that could easily decimate an army of a thousand troops if fought in the forest. The garrison at York had only one hundred and fifty troops that winter, and any reinforcements from Niagara, Kingston or Montreal would take weeks to arrive. Peter Russell quickly ordered that a new battery and blockhouse be immediately constructed west of the garrison, to increase the number of soldiers stationed at York.

"Joseph Brant sent a wampum belt to our new chief," Fire Starter explained.

The wampum belt of the Mohawks was a call to action. It had white and purple shell beads strung into a pattern depicting a confrontation and was painted red, the symbol of war.

"He would like us to join their four hundred warriors and attack the British for all their terrible acts." Brant wanted to capitalize on the tragedy affecting the Mississaugas to further his own cause – the right to sell land from the Grand River Reserve to settlers.

To think that a war against the Mississaugas was pending because of a senseless act of lust was infuriating to Isaac. The tension could very well have been prevented, Isaac thought, by making the British soldier pay for his crime. He sympathized with Fire Starter and the Mississaugas. Isaac denounced the British, though not publicly, for fear of being called a traitor.

On four occasions during the standoff, Isaac wrote to Governor Simcoe, advising the British to make peace with the natives, but did not receive a reply. At first he assumed that he had the wrong address, so he checked with the postmaster, who verified that it was correct. He then suspected that there had been some sort of foul play in mailing the letter. Or perhaps something calamitous had happened to Simcoe. He finally learned the following spring that Simcoe had been sent to Haiti to fight the French, although he was still officially the Lieutenant Governor of Upper Canada.

So now the governor is off fighting another war, Isaac complained to no one in particular, kicking a stump. Where does that leave me?

The only thing I have accomplished in Upper Canada over the last four years is setting up a small fishing business and acquiring land of my own. I have not acquired a high-ranking position. I have not acquired any riches. I am only the "Guardian of the Humber", he grumbled.

Isaac wanted more, but now that Governor Simcoe was gone, he did not know where to turn. He bent down, picked up a stone and threw it, hearing the sound echo through the woods.

It leaves me nowhere, he knew, absolutely nowhere.

Chapter 13 - May 30, 1796

With Governor Simcoe absent, Isaac's chances of infiltrating the ruling elite in Upper Canada faded to nothing. Where Simcoe welcomed debate and discussion with anyone who had an opinion, the next administrator, Peter Russell, did not. Isaac tried on several occasions to start up a conversation with Russell regarding a possible American attack. He even lied and declared that he would spy for Russell on the affairs of the Mississaugas and Joseph Brant, but received only a quick nod and a dismissal.

"I no longer have a voice or an opinion that matters," he grumbled to Polly at their homestead along the Humber, when he finally accepted that Simcoe would not return. "I do not see why we should continue to support a government that mistreats the Mississaugas."

The only people I trust now, thought Isaac, are Fire Starter and his family. Fire Starter had never betrayed him, and Isaac knew he could trust him with his life.

Polly listened quietly as she wiped the table after the evening meal. She had heard Isaac bemoan the British for weeks now, his frustration mounting each passing day. "You cannot take on the whole British government on your own," she gently reproached. "You would need a bigger army than just the Devins clan, I'm afraid."

"Perhaps we should join forces with the Mississaugas then, live a nomadic life in the forest," replied Isaac. "I hear – "

"And give up our land grant that we have righteously earned?" interrupted Polly, alarmed that Isaac would consider such an idea. "We would have absolutely nothing, and I do not want to become a tenant again for a wealthy land baron. I refuse!"

Isaac was startled by Polly's passionate outburst. She was usually so even-tempered and supportive.

The next morning, he paddled upriver to the junction, portaged briefly along the Toronto Carrying Place trail, and placed his canoe back in the water. He got out the map that St. John had given him just before he left York. Must be only a mile farther, he decided. The map showed two more sets of rapids, a straight stretch and then a series of bends. He could barely make out the chicken scratch that St. John had penned after that. He would have to rely on his instinct to lead the way.

Maybe the river has always drawn me away, Isaac considered. He wondered if his father felt the same way about the wilderness. His brothers certainly did not. They were happy to own land, clear it, cultivate it and reap the harvest, but Isaac was not. Perhaps it was his need for something greater. Perhaps it was just fate.

He paddled hard around a series of eddies, then snaked along the shallow side as close as he could get to the edge, the dappled shade of silver maples providing a reprieve from the blistering sun. He now was at the northern limit of the townsite, on the eastern branch of the Humber, a half-mile north of the first fork.

The view opened up and he saw the perfect landing spot, a low limestone shelf on a deep bend. The black willow trees framed the rock, making a corridor, as if to welcome him in. This must be it, thought Isaac, checking the map again.

He secured the canoe, then walked along the riverbank, admiring the view across the river. There seemed to be something familiar about this place. The shore was lined with soft, low grasses, and he could imagine his children playing there happily, jumping from rock to rock, making a daisy chain from the wildflowers scattered about the bank.

He squatted and snared a grasshopper, holding it in his cupped hands. Fire Starter said that grasshoppers were to be revered. "They provide food for the frogs, which then provide food for the hawks. If any living being is killed, you must make a sacrifice to the Great Spirit to honour it."

Isaac's grandfather had always told him to catch and squash as many grasshoppers as he could because they ate the grain he was trying to grow.

Looking down, Isaac slowly opened his hands and allowed the grasshopper to jump to the nearest leaf. He then called upon the Great Spirit to bless the trees, water, soil, rocks and animals around him. A feeling washed over him as he surveyed the steep riverbank on the opposite side and how the curve of the river carved a flat bank below his feet, a feeling of home.

That afternoon, Isaac told Polly of his plan for them to buy the two hundred acre property along the Humber at the northern limit of Toronto. "We will be secluded enough that the politics and prejudices of the town of York will not touch us, and close enough to the Toronto Carrying Place to be close to the Mississaugas."

Although she would have much preferred to stay close to the family, Polly put her husband's need for change above all else and nodded her head in agreement. By the end of September, Isaac and Fire Starter set the last stone on the hearth of the new three-room log cabin along the Humber River, at the northern limit of the town of York.

"Nothing can harm us here," Isaac said as he and Polly watched the girls throw stones into the river from the front porch. "Only the Mississaugas come up this far, and they usually take the Toronto Carrying Place trail, which cuts through the far east corner. No one would even know that we are here."

Polly smiled and went inside to start the fire. She knew her husband was despondent but did not know how to fix it. *At least our new home is one room larger*, she thought, not wanting to succumb to bitterness or woe at being so isolated.

Isaac let out a sigh and shook his head. *I didn't accomplish what I set out to do*, he scolded himself. *All the time I spent strategizing with Governor Simcoe did not amount to anything. What a waste of time. Without the* governor, he did not have the heart or the tenacity to continue. My dreams of wealth and position are over, he mourned. He picked up a twig, snapped it in half and tossed both ends into the river.

That fall, Isaac spent many nights with Fire Starter on the Humber fishing for trout, talking long into the night.

"You've acquired quite the reputation," John White told him when they ran into each other at William Allan's warehouse at Christmas. "I hear they call you 'The Indian.'"

Isaac grinned and replied, "That is something to be proud of, then."

Although he was content to live in the wilderness away from the townsfolk, there was still a small part of him that longed for something more. Maybe that is why he agreed to go to the first York township meeting in the summer of 1797, instead of his father, who was ill with lake fever. Rumour had it that a family would be fined fifty pounds if not a single member showed up to be counted for the census.

Isaac and Levi jumped off the wagon at the tavern along Yonge Street but could barely find a place to hitch the horses. It was a hot, humid late-July afternoon, the kind of day when sweat gathers in beads on the nose and drenches the back of the neck, even while sitting still. Settlers jammed the parlour and overflowed into the hallway and the day room. All guns had to be left at the door.

"All those in favour, say 'Aye.'" A round of "ayes" filled the room.

Isaac nodded, accepting the nomination, not entirely sure he had made the right decision. He was now elected to be the Constable of the Humber. Every person raised their hand, Isaac noted, surprised that there were no dissenters in the crowd. Not that he had made many enemies in the last four years. Unless, of course, you counted the disdain some of the Executive Council held toward him because of his close association with Governor Simcoe.

It was no surprise that Isaac was elected to watch over the Humber at the first Town Meeting. Last year he had caught a handful of newcomers taking lumber from the west bank near the lakeshore road. He informed the magistrate and the people were punished, one of them flogged and the rest banished from York. The constable's job seemed like a natural fit.

By a show of hands, the crowd elected a town clerk, assessors and tax collectors, six pathmasters to regulate the construction of roads, a poundkeeper to ensure farm animals did not run free and six constables for the various settlement areas. All positions dealt with policing and local matters.

"What about the squatters?" yelled out William Berczy, the newly elected pathmaster for the German settlement. "Surely we can whip the louts and send them back to the States!"

Berczy never did receive the huge grant of land he was promised since he had been forced to abandon the construction of Yonge Street. He was concerned that squatters would come and cut down the trees, burn them, sell the potash and move on before his people could get legal title to the land.

"Gentlemen, gentlemen, let us not get ahead of ourselves. Pathmasters do not have the authority to deal with squatters, only with landowners," said the magistrate.

"But our British common law does deal with theft," interjected John White, who had been standing at the back of the room unnoticed. Everyone turned to look his way, recognizing that a man of the law had spoken. Striding forward through the crowd, he continued, "Anyone who takes real property, including trees, without permission from the owner can be committed of thievery, which is punishable by flogging or banishment."

No one questioned White's authority or wisdom as the Attorney General of Upper Canada. Peter Russell asked him to attend the Town Meeting and ensure that it did not escalate into a brawl. Russell questioned if the citizens were capable of governing themselves. Many on the Executive Council did not believe that the settlers had the wherewithal to make decisions or debate issues, and needed the British elite to do it for them.

"So the pathmaster, or anyone else, can identify the squatters to the magistrate, who will then decide whether to indict them," suggested Isaac, always curious about the procedure of the law. Since he was now appointed to be the constable for the Humber, he also wanted to know the extent of his own authority and the procedure for turning in criminals. His grandfather always said that God would punish those who committed a cardinal sin, but Isaac wanted to have a more practical solution.

"That is absolutely correct, sir," answered John White. "There will be recompense for squatting but as a matter of common law."

The crowd erupted, everyone gesturing and talking at once. When the magistrate brought the meeting to order, George Playter, the newly elected tax assessor, asked, "Will there still be a tax on corn whiskey, given that we do not yet have a road to the Bay of Quinte or a wharf at the townsite?"

The summer of 1796 was a banner year, following the year of drought that sent many settlers back to Niagara. The corn crop was so abundant that the only thing the settlers could do with the excess was to make whiskey.

"Better not be!" hollered Levi Devins. "No one will pay it!"

After the meeting, a number of the newly elected settlers stayed at the tavern for a round of whiskey. Isaac raised his cup to cheer Playter for his appointment as a tax assessor. Arriving in 1795 from the Bay of Quinte, George Playter had likewise tried to break into Simcoe's inner circle. But his strong, unyielding Quaker beliefs barred the way since the governor wanted the Church of England to be the only religion in Upper Canada.

Isaiah Skinner was another Scottish settler who was burned by Simcoe's abrupt departure. "Now I can barely scrape together a lease to continue operating the mills. Every time I apply, I am refused," Skinner ranted.

Isaac nodded, an empathetic half-smile on his face. He knew only too well how one's power can be snuffed without warning. "No one on the Executive Council or the Legislative Assembly has any sympathy for my welfare," Isaac said. "I don't think there is anyone who cares to strategize the way that Simcoe did, something that I thoroughly enjoyed doing on every occasion."

"But at least you have now been elected the Constable of the Humber," responded Skinner, sensing that Isaac's level of frustration was equal to his own.

"And you the Pathmaster for the Don," Isaac bantered.

"Ha, but what good is that?" Skinner replied, his voice agitated. "Don Mills is on the river, not on the roads. Let the farmers be the pathmasters. How will I ever be able to monitor whether the farmers are maintaining the road in front of their property, much less fine them? I think I'll move back to Niagara, at least there may be fresh faces there."

"No, we need a good miller like yourself on the Don," chimed in John White, stepping in to join Isaac for a drink. All four men clinked their glasses and toasted the King, then shot back the whiskey.

Isaac scanned the rest of the crowd scattered throughout the drawing room. This group here – Isaiah Skinner, John Dennis, George Playter, John Ashbridge and the others – are all set to become wealthy, powerful men in York, simply by the virtue of their appointment to positions of authority at the first Town Meeting. Shall I join them? he asked himself, realizing that his appointment as constable put himself in their company. Shall I start again from scratch, lobbying my way into a higher position? Shall I spend countless hours courting Peter Russell the same way I did Governor Simcoe?

After a few glasses, John White strongly encouraged Isaac to do just that. "Stick close to him, Isaac, and see what good will come of it."

"You told me that about Simcoe, and look where that got me," retorted Isaac.

◇◇

The next day, Isaac set off in his birchbark canoe up to his cabin in the north, grateful to be away from the townsfolk. He dipped his paddle into the warm summer stream and almost touched bottom on an outside corner. Every riffle, run and bend he knew like the back of his hand. Though he was alone, he never felt lonely on the river. The pines, cedars, willows and silver maples, the birds, rabbits and coyotes, the robins, blue jays and warblers, all seemed to welcome him.

He decided right then and there that he was not going to heed his friend's advice this time around.

The first five years in Upper Canada had taken a toll. Isaac Devins was no longer a young, ambitious pup hoping to claw his way through the high society of Toronto. He had tried that, but the wall was too strong and interwoven with decades of partisan politics and prejudice.

He sighed. No matter, thought Isaac, as he turned his canoe leeward. At least I don't have to keep company with the likes of William Jarvis or any of the other high-handed, lazy aristocrats.

Over the next few years, the people he kept company with the most were Fire Starter and John White. During the salmon run, Isaac paddled down to the King's Mill to fish and later sell the catch at the market block in York, satisfied with his small fishing business. He also kept up his winter ice-fishing, for which the townsfolk were grateful.

Ambitions to be a great man of importance in the high society of York no longer plagued him.

Isaac was content to be a man of the river, or so he thought.

Reflection 3

Never thought I would live to see my eighty-seventh birthday, Isaac considered as he watched his family close the gate and walk down the lane. *Nice of Lucy and James to show up, they live so far away. Too many grandchildren though, and great-grandchildren. I'm glad they don't come here all at once.*

Polly would love it if she was here. Nothing would make her happier than to be surrounded by her children, especially the ones she fought so hard for. Isaac closed his eyes and leaned his head against the back of the rocking chair, too weak to do anything else. *She was a saint.*

They say that war breeds war. I don't think we knew back then how true that is, Isaac thought, staring out the window at the Humber flowing past. *The river was high and turbulent for this late in June, but not nearly as high as it was fifty years ago. Burning the forest and replacing it with farms took its toll.* Isaac had to rebuild his dock three times over the last half-century, each time a yard lower.

All of us who fought in the War of 1812 can blame Napoleon and the struggle for democracy. If the British and the French were not battling in Europe, the Americans might never have declared war on Canada. The Yankees would not have had a chance against the British if most of them weren't already fighting the French. Strange that the politics of those days still interests me, he thought.

He coughed and leaned forward slightly. Today was a good day. He got out of bed himself and made it to the rocker. Elizabeth will be surprised. Such a good daughter. I don't know how she ended up with such a mouse for a husband. I guess I can blame a lot of things, but mostly because we were isolated up here, away from the townsfolk. There were only two other families within five miles of here just before the war. None of them had men of marrying age. I suppose if we had stayed with the rest of the Devins miles down the Humber or had moved to town, she could have done better.

Isaac shook his head. Polly had taken the girls to a building bee in 1811, a few months before the war broke out. At nineteen years of age, Elizabeth was almost too old to be considered for marriage. Polly hoped that her daughter would meet someone; otherwise she would have to move to town until her daughter was engaged. Polly had become so accustomed to their life in the wilderness that she dreaded the thought.

Isaac did not attend the building bee, or any other community affair, not since 1802. After he had been publicly humiliated and left for dead, he did nothing further to help the town of York. None of them, not one of them, stood up for me, only Fire Starter. He was the most loyal friend I ever had, Isaac reminisced, a tear welling in his eye. Damn, he cursed, why am I missing Fire Starter so much after all these years?

I suppose I wouldn't have even bothered to fight in the war if it wasn't for him. Not after everyone turned on me, he muttered, a strain of bitterness woven into his words. But when Fire Starter asked for help, Isaac could not refuse.

Now I never see a sign of a Mississauga anywhere, Isaac lamented. It had been decades since any canoed past his cabin. The Mississauga Tract that stretched from Toronto to Hamilton was sold before the War of 1812, and any stragglers left the area after it looked like a civil war would break out in 1837. Isaac often thought to paddle up to the northern hunting grounds in Lake Superior and see if he could find Fire Starter's wife or children but he had been too disabled in the last two decades to do it.

They used to call out my name, Waabshkii Mnidoo, as they canoed past, he reminisced. Isaac and Polly would smile and invite them in for refreshments or to stay the night. The Mississaugas are more trustworthy than any townsfolk, he often said.

192

My children all think I am a bitter old man. None of them have followed in my footsteps – they all are farmers – none of them became a carpenter, fisherman, a drover or a hunter. None of them have canoed to Toronto or up to the forks of the Credit. None of them have portaged along the Toronto Carrying Place to Lake Simcoe. Isaac sighed. *They grew up in different times, after the war. I guess those early days are gone.*

Progress, such a misleading word, Isaac thought. *Hard to believe that I wanted progress, to conquer the wilderness, when we first came to Upper Canada. It had all seemed so within my grasp, to shape the province, to be an important man. If only Governor Simcoe hadn't left.*

But the river became my home, the wilderness my solace, and the Mississaugas my family.

Isaac looked out the window and saw Elizabeth, dressed in a cheery blue cotton dress, come around the bend, stroll up the rocky path to the porch, knock on the door a few times and let herself in. *She seems happy that I am up and about today. Of all my eight children, she and Hannah are the only ones who knows what we went through, when Upper Canada was struggling for its identity.*

There was no stopping what Simcoe had started in 1793. A decade after the war, immigration to Upper Canada exploded. The lots around Isaac and Polly's homestead were quickly bought and cleared for farming. *At least I kept seventy acres so that I have a semblance of wilderness, even if the bears no longer come to the door, the wolves no longer howl, and the salmon have all but disappeared.*

The east half of Isaac's two hundred acre lot was cleared by his son, John C., in 1835. Isaac reluctantly let him do it when Polly insisted, "John C. needs to get a good start. We don't have the money to help him buy a lot. Ours is one of the last forested lots left. Please, Isaac, please help our son."

Isaac grumbled but did not want to disappoint Polly. He knew he could not stop the wheels of change, though he wished otherwise. *I suppose if Upper Canada had been conquered by the United States,* it would have been worse. The wilderness around him would have disappeared even faster.

Elizabeth was only ten years old when he had been whipped, beaten and scourged. I wonder what she and Hannah remember when I finally went home, delirious, close to death, wounded from head to foot. He instinctively put his hand over his shoulder, the deepest wound that took months to heal. How could I possibly want to defend the people, ten years later, who had inflicted such torture?

Yet there were many former Americans, both the elite and the peasants, who were committed to defending the British colonies from being swallowed by the United States of America. Simeon, only twenty-two at the outbreak of the war, got caught up in the excitement. I think he joined the York militia not so much to defeat the Americans but to prove his own worth.

Elizabeth smiled at him, and said she was going to fill the milk pail. Isaac watched his daughter stroll down the path, and wondered if she ever felt the way he did, that God, or the Great Spirit, did not have a grand plan after all. Although he was content with his place in the wilderness, far away from the townsfolk and their backstabbing, elitist ways, there was something still inside him, a nagging feeling, that he wished he had done more. But if I had, would it have made a difference?

Jarvis! If only he had not opened his big mouth. He glanced over to the spot where his birchbark canoe lay rotting, thinking how once again it had saved his life.

With Polly and Jarvis gone, only I know the secret now. Isaac tried to lift his head, but fatigue overwhelmed him. Instead, he closed his eyes and drifted off. Only the three of us know who pulled the trigger.

I suppose that will be another secret that will die along with me.

Chapter 14 - December 31, 1799

The turn of the century was a cause for tremendous celebration in York. In seven years, the tiny, forested landing spot had transformed into a town with a grid of streets, a wharf, stores, taverns, businesses and houses scattered throughout. York was a lively village with many balls, tea parties, whist games and socials for the aristocrats who lived there. Everyone, young and old, wealthy or not, was anticipating a week of merriment leading up to the Twelfth Night gala. But it turned out to be a catastrophe for Isaac Devins, John White and the entire town.

The afternoon of December 31, 1799, was mild and clear as Isaac canoed down to the mouth of the Humber, then headed east toward the fort along the lakeshore. Just around the next corner, Isaac told himself as he paddled hard into the bitter, unrelenting wind. Leaning forward, he used short, choppy strokes to counteract the pull of the wind that seemed to be following its own path, oblivious to the hardship it caused.

Isaac's canoes were still his most prized possessions and his preferred means of travel. Others chastised him for not having a horse and buggy, but he simply did not see the need. Their homestead was so secluded with no roads or settlement for miles around that he did not see the need for horses. In the four months of winter when the rivers and lakes were frozen solid, they just did not leave their homestead. Sometimes his brothers would hitch their horses to the cutter and come for a visit. Otherwise, Polly and Isaac were content to be on their own with Elizabeth, Hannah and baby Sarah.

Quite a crowd had gathered at the Market Square for the New Year's feast put on by the military and merchants. Everyone came from miles around. Isaac found the rest of the Devins family at a hitching post. They lined up behind Nicholas Miller, who had arrived with a large group from the Yonge Street settlement. The smell of roasted deer, porcupine, squirrel, rabbit and partridge spread throughout the market as the settlers crowded around tables of hot potatoes, carrots and squash. Kegs of rum and wine were plentiful, and the settlers drank cup after cup.

"I just remember that the cannons were so loud," Simeon told Isaac when asked if he remembered the ceremony for the founding of York only seven years earlier on the shores of the Toronto Bay.

Now that he was thirteen years of age, Simeon wanted to look older and self-assured, like his father and brothers. No more mollycoddling or crying for him. From now on, he would be as cool and collected as a grown-up. He was proud that his father had included him on the New Year's trip to York along with his half-brothers, Isaac, Levi and Jacob.

Isaac glanced around and was pleased to see William Berczy, John Dennis, William Allan, and others whom he had not seen since the first Town Meeting. But he was equally saddened that two of the people he conspired with the most when York was merely a dot on the map, Governor Simcoe and St. John Rousseau, were not there. Not to mention Fire Starter, who was somewhere in the northern hunting grounds for the winter.

"Pretty good stock for us peasants," bantered Levi, laughing, clinking glasses with whoever was close by.

"Too true!" agreed Berczy, relieved that he had opted not to attend the Governor's Ball.

Most of the Executive Council members and their cronies had gathered at Peter Russell's residence earlier in the afternoon to celebrate the New Year. The Governor's Ball, complete with dance, music, supper and toasts, went on in spite of the absence of the new governor, Colonel Peter Hunter, who was in Niagara. Isaac's friend, John White, attended, though he later would wish that he had stayed as far away as possible.

John White's status had spiralled downward in the last two years, right after one of his greatest successes, the creation of the Law Society of Upper Canada. He co-authored the bylaws and set the protocol for the organization that issues a standard of conduct for lawyers in the new province. He excitedly agreed to be the first president and treasurer.

Within months, White became disillusioned and cut himself off from the very association that he had created. Many of his superiors did not share his vision of how the law should be administered in Upper Canada and loudly objected, making White look like a halfwit. William Osgoode, in Lower Canada, and the Governor General preferred an exact interpretation of British law, while White believed that British law should be adapted to the unique circumstances of Upper Canada.

Even more dismaying, one of the first bylaws that the law society passed was absolutely abhorrent to White. It allowed the sixteen lawyers in Upper Canada that Simcoe had appointed in 1793, who did not have any legal training, to continue to practise law.

"Blasphemy!" John White had exclaimed. "The law in Upper Canada must not be administered by paupers and peasants!"

He passionately did not want unqualified people to practise law in Upper Canada, but the law society that he created now allowed it to happen. This offended every one of White's principles, and he defiantly quit. He did not want to be part of a society that allowed untrained lawyers to practise in Upper Canada.

Wallowing in the futility of his efforts, John White grew despondent, erratic and narrow-minded. He became embittered, blamed his wife for his debacle and even sent her back to England, although his sons remained in York. Disillusioned, he cut himself off from society, preferring to become more of a criticizing backbencher at the Executive Council than an active participant. He soon became known as a dissenter and someone with unpredictable behaviour.

After the Governor's Ball, White joined Isaac at Market Square, relieved to see a familiar face that was not caught up in the backstabbing of York society. "Isaac, my old friend, I had to accept, my honour was at stake," he began, hiccuping, obviously drunk, putting an arm around Isaac's shoulders. Isaac chuckled, always amused at White's habit of starting a conversation in the middle, and placed his arm over his shoulder so that his friend would not keel over.

"Friday morning at ten o'clock, at the back of the Government House," White continued, "it will be settled once and for all."

Isaac directed them toward the lakeshore, where they could wait for the fireworks display, the two of them staggering along together. Finding a log, Isaac sat White down, took out his flask and handed it to his friend, then took another drink himself, the rum warming him, protecting him from the strong, bitter winds blowing in from the lake.

"I can't say that I have ever fought in a duel before," began White as Isaac reeled back, unsure if he heard his friend correctly.

"Did you say a duel?" questioned Isaac. "With whom, and for what purpose?"

The events leading up to the challenge actually began seven months earlier during an afternoon tea at Government House. Though he did not attend, White was livid when he heard that his wife was snubbed by John Small's wife, who walked right by her without so much as saying a word. In the elite society of York, the utmost form of indecency was to be condescending toward someone at a social gathering. It was an even greater insult not to acknowledge another person's presence in public.

Contrary to his refined character, White retaliated by going to his neighbour's home to ask Mrs. Small to explain her behaviour, which she could not do to his satisfaction. Even more angry, White continued on to Surveyor General David Smith's home with the express purpose to undermine the lady that had snubbed his wife.

"You cannot mean that, I am sure," exclaimed Smith, dumbfounded that White was revealing such a lurid tale about John Small's wife.

"Oh, yes," replied White, his arms clasped behind his back, wearing a fine satin daycoat with pantaloons, dressed rather formally, pacing as if he were in a courtroom. "Though I am remiss to repeat it, Mrs. Small and I did in fact have an affair of the most sensational kind."

Smith's eyes widened, the corners of his mouth turning upward, quite shocked to hear such a tale. "When did this happen? For how long did you have the affair?" he inquired, eager for details. Gossip was almost considered a pastime among the elite. Many, including Smith, thrived on its shocking stories.

"Why, not very long at all. I had to break it off for, how do you say, medical reasons." White lowered his eyes and looked at Smith in an intense, all-knowing way.

"You don't mean ..." began Smith, a little horrified.

"Yes," replied White, lowering his head in resignation. "She gave me the clap, the vixen. I suspect that I certainly was not the only one she infected."

Stupefied, White requested permission, over and over again, to relate the story to Judge Elmsley's wife to inform her of Mrs. Small's poor character. White finally agreed, but under the caveat that neither of them repeat the story to anyone else. Satisfied that he had successfully besmirched the character of Mrs. Small, whom he did not consider to be on the same social level, White thought that nothing further would come of it. That will teach her to be deprecating toward me, he huffed, almost forgetting that it was his wife who had been snubbed.

Everything changed at the Governor's Ball on New Year's Eve. David Smith not only told the tale to John Elmsley but also retold it to almost anyone who would listen. White was oblivious to the betrayal, twirling on the dance floor with an array of partners. When the story finally got around to John Small, he was furious. Marching over to White, he grabbed his arm, pushing Mrs. Talbot out of the way, and knocked White on his chest, sending him reeling backwards.

"How dare you insult my wife!" raged Small, his face red with anger, teeth clenched, leaning forward with fists clenched at his side.

As the Clerk of the Executive Council, Small was also one of Governor Simcoe's hand-picked members of the elite class, and the two had been acquainted for more than seven years. Small and White became next-door neighbours in York when they both reluctantly moved from Niagara, the one common thread between the two men. Until this evening, the two had been polite to one other, if not cordial.

"And you mine, sir!" White retorted. "Though I dare say that yours is by far the greater humiliation."

Grunting and pounding his feet to the ground, Small's face turned even redder, furious that White dared to imply superiority. The music and the dancing stopped as all revellers gathered around the feuding twosome, curious to see the conflict unfold.

"I will not stand for this!" roared Small, his chest barrelled out as far as it could go. "I demand satisfaction in the field of honour!" he bellowed, spitting the words into his opponent's face.

White did not flinch. He just stared back at Small, rather intrigued. He looks like a fool, White mused, with such a flamboyant display of anger. I don't even have to say anything more, he thought. John Small is going to self-destruct all on his own.

Taking a long white glove out of his pocket, Small threw it on the ground at John White's feet. "Friday, at ten o'clock, in the field behind the Government House," hollered Small, clenching his fists at the end of each word for emphasis. "I challenge you to a duel!"

The ladies in the crowd gasped and clung to their husbands. The gentlemen all started to talk at once, saying that such a practice was not necessary and that other means could settle the dispute. White raised his eyebrows, cocked his head, and was quite amused by the whole affair. So John Small wants to defend his honour, does he?

Still feeling superior and doubtful that Small would even turn up, White answered with authority, "I accept."

The crowd erupted as everyone talked at once, horrified and intrigued at the same time. Gentlemen of the elite class sometimes used duelling as a means to resolve their disputes but so far there had been no need. A duel had not yet been fought in York.

"You could not have just taken a swing at each other and battled it out right there?" questioned Isaac, worried and concerned that his friend had bitten off more than he could chew. Isaac had settled many disputes with his fists, thankful that guns or knives were not involved.

"Not when a gentleman's honour is at stake, apparently," chuckled White, not overly concerned with the procedure. The goal of a duel was not usually to kill the opponent but to restore honour, and White intended to do just that. He did not want to have any opportunity to feel inferior to someone like John Small, who was merely the clerk of the Executive Council.

John White was a lawyer, which designated him as a gentleman. He was one of the few barristers in York who had trained in London's Inns of Court, and had been called to the Bar fifteen years ago. Small, on the other hand, was one of many British subjects whom Simcoe had granted the position of justice of the peace just before he left York in 1796. It burned White to the core that an untrained justice like Small could feel superior to an honourable gentleman like himself.

"You will be there on Friday, won't you, Devins?" he inquired, slurring his words.

Before he could reply, the first firework was set off with an ear-splitting bang, shot into the air, and burst into a spectacle of orange lights, the brilliant display reflecting off the water of Lake Ontario. Cries of "ooh" and "ahhh" were heard from two hundred citizens who had gathered on the beach. The elite society, who had just arrived after leaving the Governor's Ball, politely clapped while whoops and calls were heard from the rest of the crowd. William Allan, the new store owner, had acquired some that had been shipped over from China. Most of the settlers had never seen fireworks before.

Cheers of "Happy New Year" resounded all along the beach as people embraced and clinked glasses. After another minute, a second firework was lit, with an even greater response. Isaac turned his head as he heard John White start to sing:

Should auld acquaintance be forgot

And never brought to mind

Should auld acquaintance be forgot

And auld lang syne

Everyone in high society knew the song that had been written twelve years earlier by a Scotsman, Robert Burns, and had quickly spread throughout the British Empire. Before long, everyone in the town of York was singing the festive tune, the sound of the revellers becoming louder every round.

"Yes, my friend," said Isaac when the singing died down a little, "I will be there."

With a delighted grin spreading from ear to ear, White pounded Isaac on the back several times before stumbling back and tripping over the log. Isaac helped his friend up and realized he needed to get him back home. On the way, he encountered his father, Levi and Simeon, who helped him drag the semi-conscious lawyer down Princess Street to Duke.

"How did you like the fireworks?" Isaac asked Simeon, who replied, "Spectacular! It was like the whole sky was on fire! At first I thought it was going to attack me, but then it just seemed like magic."

Simeon walked along beside his brothers, pretending to shoot the cannons, wall guns and artillery, mimicking the sound of the gunshots and cannon fire. Isaac grinned, remembering his own fascination with weaponry when he was Simeon's age. He used to tie together a couple of large branches with some twine to make a catapult, and would fire stones, acorns, apples, potatoes, or anything else he could find, pretending to shoot the British. Of course, that was during the American Revolution, when his father was fighting for the rebels. How times have changed, mused Isaac, and how thin are our allegiances, wondering if Simeon now pretended to shoot Americans.

Eventually they put White to bed. Isaac and Simeon lay down on the floor of White's home for the night while Abraham and Levi opted to sleep on the straw bales in the stable.

For the next two nights, Isaac tried to talk his friend out of going through with the duel, but White was adamant. He would not bow down to John Small, particularly when there was an element of truth to the rumour. Mrs. Small had been so naughty when they had tea together several years ago, bending over so that her breasts popped out. Why, I would have been a fool not to take advantage.

John White greeted the morning of the duel with exuberance. He was a little lightheaded from the last few late nights at the tavern with Isaac, but otherwise in high spirits. The Devins brothers and Abraham met him at the field behind Government House fifteen minutes early, along with his second, Baron Frederick de Hoen.

Isaac tried one last time to convince his friend to back down, but to no avail. White was determined to go through with it.

"I doubt the scoundrel will even show up," White laughed.

Try as he might, Isaac could not get John White to take the duel more seriously, and realize that he might not like the outcome, especially if he is maimed or worse. Gossip around town indicated that Small seriously wanted John White dead. Frustrated with his friend's nonchalance, he shrugged and asked de Hoen if he had brought duelling pistols, a rifle and a sword, not knowing which weapon Small would choose.

At precisely ten o'clock, John Small and his second, Sheriff Alexander Macdonnell, made their entrance and took a position at the opposite end of the snow-covered field. Small was smartly attired in the white, red and gold colours of the York militia, with a pin denoting his position as a Lieutenant Colonel, a new appointment he had attained a month earlier. Despite this rank, Small had virtually no military experience. He received the position for his leadership abilities rather than his military skills.

Facing his challenger, John White was still dressed in his evening clothes from the night before, everything looking a little frumpy and wrinkled. The opponents walked toward each other with their seconds by their sides, slowly, for the snow was more than a foot deep. They stopped about ten feet apart, sizing each other up.

"Mr. Small's weapon of choice is a duelling pistol, single barrel," declared Small's second, holding a fourteen-inch wooden pistol with a metal grip forward for inspection. Baron de Hoen examined the pistol and handed it back.

"They will only have one shot then," declared Isaac to his brothers.

The Devins brothers stood on the sidelines along with a handful of other spectators. Duels had been fought for centuries before the one in York, but it was not a practice favoured by many. A duel was seen as contrary to Christian values, and reserved for those who could not control their anger. At the end of the eighteenth century, duelling was largely relegated to the military and shunned by high society.

"Speed and accuracy will be necessary to win," added Abraham, who had witnessed two duels in Genesee after the war. Neither had ended in death. One defender chose to apologize before the duel began, and the other ended up with both duellists firing into the air.

After the formality of examining the weapons, Sheriff Macdonnell declared, "Each will take ten paces. You may then turn and fire."

"Ten paces!" Isaac whispered to his father. "John Small must really mean business. Most duels are fifteen paces, a much greater chance to miss your opponent."

Clearing his throat for emphasis, Small proclaimed in a determined, ugly tone, "To the death."

What!? thought Isaac, stunned at the severity of the terms.

Turning his head, he saw that his friend remained steady and had not moved a muscle. A slightly raised eyebrow was the only indication of the wave of shock and bewilderment that spread throughout White's body, almost paralyzing him. He had not really considered that the duel would be more than a show of bravado, two cocks strutting through the barnyard, ruffling their feathers. "To the death" implied that someone would be killed, which was much more than he had bargained for.

Baron de Hoen frantically searched for more bullets. Both men would keep shooting until the other fell. Not finding any, he called out to Isaac and his brothers, who emptied their own guns and handed over what they had.

White studied his opponent with a lawyer's eye, looking him up and down, observing his shorter stature, stocky frame, reddened cheeks, stubby fingers, perusing Small intently for the first time. He is probably fifteen or twenty years older than I am, concluded White, who was a couple of months shy of thirty-eight, though it was difficult to assess because of the white wig. Likely quite strong, he observed, noting his barrel chest and tree-trunk legs, although that should not be a factor. My youth and agility will give me the advantage, he concluded, assessing the situation as only a lawyer could.

With a renewed sense of confidence, he nodded to indicate that he was ready.

Standing back to back, both men began pacing while Sheriff Macdonnell counted. White looked to the ground, then up at the sky. Fight to the death! he screamed inside. Why did I ever agree to this barbaric, ludicrous, asinine showcase for male bravado?

"Two … three," counted the sheriff with a prolonged pause between each number.

This is supposed to be about restoring honour, fretted White, eyes darting back and forth, not about killing! Most duels did not actually result in a slaying but rather in the victor merely maiming his opponent or even choosing not to shoot. Often one opponent would not show up, fearful of the other's shooting skills. Why did he choose the most deadly outcome? he fretted. Does he really want me dead that badly?

"Six ... seven," counted the sheriff.

I should have insisted that we wait for a week, passions do cool off, White nervously thought, feeling his heart racing, clenching his teeth, breathing fast and shallow.

"Eight ... nine," continued the sheriff, his voice louder with each count.

Isaac watched his friend's back, his strong, confident gait carrying him forward, appearing to be calm, collected, not a hair out of place. Glancing over to his opponent, Isaac saw that John Small looked equally confident, although his steps were shorter, more calculating, resolute.

An image of his wife twelve years younger walking through a cherry orchard all in pink bloom flashed through White's mind, and suddenly he saw his two sons, aged eight and ten, walking over a log laid across the river, both of them falling in and being sucked down in a whirlpool. Fortunately, God was with us that day. He had pulled them out of the water, sputtering and choking, eyes wide with fear, grateful for the strength and fortitude of their father. They need me, thought White. They still need me. God, be with me now!

"Ten!" bellowed the sheriff, wanting to ensure that there was no confusion.

With total clarity, knowing exactly what he must do, White spun around so quickly that he almost kept going. Raising his pistol at the same time, he fired, too soon, well before he faced his opponent, the bullet bouncing off an oak tree and careening into the forest. His narrowed eyes, protruding jaw and look of intensity softened in an instant as the full realization of his fate washed over him.

Small heard the shot before he was halfway through his pivot and turned to see White standing there with a smoking pistol in his hand, feet frozen into the ground, a look of foreboding cast upon his face. Well, well, well, Small thought, it looks as if there is only one shot remaining, and that would be mine. John White, prepare to die.

White looked back at his opponent with shock and curiosity, as if time had slowed. He seems to be suspended in a cloud, thought White, every split second playing out profusely, each one seeming like an eternity. He watched with fascination as the corners of Small's mouth quivered, moved downward, then upward ever so slowly.

He is smiling, thought White, his last thought, one that would stretch into eternity.

In a flash, Small raised his arm, narrowed his eyes and shot straight.

He watched his opponent fall back, blood spattering from his right side just below his ribs, his hand coming up to cover the wound. White tried to stagger backwards but collapsed instead, his legs paralyzed. His limp body landed in the snow as Isaac ran toward him, unable to get there in time to lessen the fall.

Satisfied with the morning's outcome, Small held the pistol to his lips and blew away the smoke from the shaft, handed it to his second, then turned away abruptly and walked back toward Duke Street. Thoughts of sparing White's life came across his mind for only an instant but were quickly replaced by the towering rage bottled up inside of him, needing an avenue to escape. That will teach him for insulting my wife!

Isaac rushed to his friend, who had fallen like a dead buck and was writhing in agony. The bullet ruptured his spine and splayed his nerve endings. Blood from the gaping wound gushed everywhere, turning the lily-white snow to crimson and pink. Covering the wound with one knee, Isaac ripped a strip of cloth from his scarf and stuffed it into the hole, then stripped off several more to tie around White's waist, eventually slowing, then stopping, the flow of blood.

Carefully picking him up, Isaac, his brothers and de Hoen carried the blood-stained gentleman to the front of Government House, his body convulsing in an inhuman way. He moaned and whimpered, in complete agony. Soon, they were surrounded by a dozen men who all grabbed an arm or a leg.

"Simeon, I need you to go and get Polly, she will know what to do."

Ever since the day that Polly cured baby Elizabeth with a remedy from the Indians' sacred healing grounds, she had become known as an authority on healing. There were still not any physicians who resided in York permanently, so people had to rely on each other's wisdom and ingenuity. But before Simeon could leave, a number of town women rushed over to see to the wound. They immediately started to make preparations, even before they reached Peter Russell's house, the closest one to the duel site.

That was the last time that Isaac saw his friend alive. Thirty-six hours later, John White died of the gunshot wound, his kidney and liver irrevocably damaged.

The whole town went into mourning. An unseasy quietude descended, hovered and lingered over York.

Twelfth Night celebrations were cut short. Balls, whist games and teas were unattended. Taverns and inns were unusually tranquil. Even the robust streets were empty, most people opting to quietly stay at home. People assembled for the service at St. James Church, or in homes or stables for the Methodists and the Quakers, but otherwise kept to themselves.

The editorial in the *Upper Canada Gazette* decried the loss of a professional gentleman, a sincere friend, an honest and upright man who was highly esteemed.

The funeral was held one week after the duel on a bitterly cold afternoon. It would be weeks before White's wife received a letter informing her that her husband had died trying to defend her honour, chivalrous to the end. His two sons were sent to Montreal and then on to England, alone and fatherless.

Isaac's initial shock was eventually replaced by waves of anger and sorrow. The establishment had defeated John White, Isaac raged as he sat on a log in his wooden ice hut on a frosty winter evening. The fish were not biting yet, but he did not notice or care. Isaac spent every night in the hut for the remainder of the winter, alone, reflecting on the loss of his friend.

"First Governor Simcoe, then St. John Rousseau, and now John White have all been beaten, by the politics, the system, the power of the chosen few in York," Isaac eventually said to Polly a few months later after the girls had gone to bed.

He sat with his elbows on his knees, warming his hands by the fire, though it was a warm spring evening. Polly just listened, relieved that her husband was speaking his mind. He had been quiet, sullen and detached ever since the funeral. She had tried every way she knew to reach him, and help him return to the optimistic, unaffected man she once knew.

"What kind of country has been created here? One where only British law and British rule are acceptable and must dominate above all else, where only the chosen few have any say in what is good for the people, where the King must reign supreme, where the elite are rewarded while the less privileged have to struggle to survive?"

Polly took his hand, but he shrugged her off. Isaac wanted nothing more than to be having this very discussion with John White over a glass of ale at the tavern, like they usually did.

"We came here, to Upper Canada, seven years ago, when there was nothing. No towns, no roads, no laws. I wanted nothing more than to work my way in, so that I could have an influence on shaping a province and, yes, reap the rewards. I could not break down the walls. My best hope was Governor Simcoe, and even he was defeated by powers greater than himself. I think he just gave up in the end."

Isaac sat back, then went over to the window and leaned on the sill with both hands, staring out at the river flowing past, the water higher and more turbulent in the spring. He unconsciously shook his head back and forth.

"John White was killed not because he started a rumour but because he was driven to it. No one wanted justice more than him. He could never accept the fact that people untrained in the law would become the basis for a new law system in Canada. He could not accept it, and it drove him mad."

Isaac stared down at the windowsill for a long time, then looked out at the river, feeling on edge but numb at the same time. Polly walked over and put her hand on her husband's back. She knew that watching his friend die, be killed by a lesser man, and not stepping in to prevent it was torture for him.

Stepping back, he violently shrugged off his wife's gesture again, and walked down to the river. He paddled upriver to a deep pool where the water swirled softly in eddies outside the turbulence of the main stream, and stared deep into the river. Minnows darted and schools of larger fish swam together, oblivious to the lone man in the silent canoe.

"Fire Starter says that the Great Spirit calls a mortal to join him in the spirit world when one's life is complete," Isaac said out loud to the trees, insects and birds.

"How could John's life be complete?"

His voice echoed softly through the trees laden with buds about to burst open, but no answer came. Leaning back in the birchbark canoe, Isaac just drifted.

His eye caught a white-tailed deer at the edge of the river where it bent down for a drink. The deer noticed him, stood frozen, then decided there was no threat and continued. Isaac felt a wave of energy rush through his body.

He could easily send a bullet through the deer's heart. He chose not to, this time.

Chapter 15 – November 6, 1800

Isaac paddled alone down the Humber as he usually did, but this time with fire in his eye and his shotgun loaded.

He had to stop them.

Fire Starter asked him to look after the river before he left for the winter migration, and Isaac intended to do just that.

"My people mourn because the fish are dying," Fire Starter complained several months back as they rested side by side at the limestone outcrop. "They cannot swim because there is too much wood floating in the river. Soon they will no longer return. Our agreement with the British says we will give up the land on the west side, but the fish must be protected."

The Mississaugas from the beginning were assured by Simcoe that the fishery in the Humber would be preserved. Despite his promise, the governor ordered the King's Mill to be built along the Humber. Then he turned a blind eye to any illegal activity, save for felling trees. It was as if anyone could do anything they wanted along the Humber.

"We complained about the white men's fishing nets many times. Governor Simcoe promised us that they would not be permitted. Not one of the British officers have made them stop," Fire Starter griped.

Isaac no longer had the authority to arrest anyone, but he still preached wherever he went that nets should not be used. He put up signs along the river at favourite fishing spots and even placed an advertisement in the *Upper Canada Gazette* imploring citizens not to deplete the fishery. Consequently, Isaac was never appointed Constable of the Humber again.

Undeterred, he continued his efforts to protect the salmon, trout and pickerel without having any official status to do so. But as the township grew, there was more and more illegal fishing.

Fire Starter thanked Isaac many times for defending the river. "Without you, my friend, there would be no more salmon for our children and their children," he said before he paddled his wife and four of his children upstream toward Lake Simcoe.

Polly chastised him for devoting too much of his attention to the matter. "Do you think we will have enough to eat ourselves for the winter?" she would question him at breakfast, the only time she ever saw him during a day. Lonely and tired of the extra chores she had to take on, she wished that her husband would sleep at home instead of patrolling the Humber for fishing nets.

"I know, Polly, that is why I must do it."

Five years ago the salmon were plenty, and there was enough for everyone. He was worried there would not be enough to feed his growing family in the years to come.

His father, Abraham, lambasted him for segregating himself from the rest of the community. "You look like you are after everyone in town, from beggar to statesman. You are ruining any future chances you may have, making enemies instead of friends. No one is going to do you any favours at this rate."

Isaac pressed on, and at last there seemed to be some progress. Fewer people were fishing along the Humber and even fewer were using nets. As his reputation as the "Guardian of the Humber" grew and his message spread, many settlers realized that fishing nets on the Humber just might not be worth the trouble. Isaac relaxed and spent less time patrolling the river and more time at home, which Polly was grateful for.

The first bridge built across the Humber at Lakeshore Road in 1798 changed all that. It replaced the ferry operated by the Mississaugas near the King's Mill, providing a quicker and more reliable way to cross the river. Within a year, settlers realized that there was nothing to stop them from crossing to the west side of the Humber in the Mississauga tract, and travelling upriver to fish, particularly after the Mississaugas left for the northern hunting grounds.

Settlers whom Isaac had once charged and taken to court now taunted him as they laid the nets out on the west bank.

"Now what, Devins?" laughed a fisherman as he slapped his thigh and guffawed. "This here is Indian territory. There is nothing you can do to stop me."

Boiling with anger, Isaac contacted the magistrate and was told that there was nothing the government could do. "Sorry, Devins. It is out of our jurisdiction. Maybe you could take it up with your Indian friends."

Since it was already November, Isaac would not see any of the Mississaugas until spring. He just could not sit back and do nothing. Justice had to be done. Isaac devised a plan to secretly paddle across the river at night and cut the culprits' fishing nets while they slept.

"You are a regular Robin Hood," Levi remarked when Isaac told him of his nightly activities. Isaac felt like Levi was the only one he could trust who would not judge or reprimand him. Levi applauded his older brother for taking action against those who were ravaging the fishery against the law.

But almost every other citizen of York, from farmer to aristocrat, hated the fishing net bandit and vowed to catch the delinquent at all costs. The fishermen were angry, and the merchants, too. William Allan's store at the townsite often did not have a supply of fish in stock. The price of fish inflated rapidly, such that many settlers had to do without.

Some of the illicit fishermen brought dogs to guard the nets at night, but Isaac always found a way to sneak in and slash the nets, even if he had to wait until daytime to do it.

Thou shalt not steal..... Isaac was whipped by his father for many a childhood prank, but never for taking anything that was not his. Yet the years of backstabbing and unmerited rewards had changed him, and led him to believe that he must justice into his own hands.

He had tried sitting as a juror at some of the trials, but found that money and favouritism were stronger than truth or justice. He tried laying a personal charge so that he could show up in court and shame the offenders in public. Despite his heartfelt testimony of how illegal fishing hurt all the citizens of York, the court most often ruled in favour of the defendant. Soon, every one of the Justices regarded Isaac Devins as an annoying radical who was disrupting the court. Every way that he tried to work within the rules of society, society failed him.

Isaac was proud to be the Fishing Net Bandit. He finally felt like he could make a difference. It was the only way he could stop the illegal fishing by the settlers, protect the fishery, and help Fire Starter, his one true friend. Every time he slashed the nets he felt like the Great Spirit was watching over him with approval. God is smiling on me, he would say as he glided away, alone in his canoe, silently into the night.

"Hear ye, Hear ye. On the charges of petty larceny, destruction of property and assault, we hereby pronounce you guilty as charged."

Isaac hung his head in the prisoner's box. He heard Polly softly cry out, her quiet weeping showing the frustration and terror that she felt for her husband. Oh, Isaac, she thought, please God that they spare you. Isaac had already spent three weeks in the York jail awaiting trial, and he looked so pale and thin. Polly prayed that he would not be sent back to jail, or worse. Our three daughters need you at home, she wept.

William Jarvis, Chairman of the Home District Council, pounded his gavel on the wooden desk, signifying the final judgement. The court room in Government House was silenced. He looked over to the prisoner's box and attempted to keep an impartial face, but the corners of his mouth turned up slightly, and his eyes betrayed how truly delighted he was.

Isaac glared up at Jarvis, the most despicable, miserable excuse for a human being he had ever encountered, and let out a deep, exasperated breath. Just my luck to have Jarvis pronounce the punishment. He looks like he is thoroughly enjoying my misery, the bastard.

No one could say that spending time at the York jail, opened in 1799, was a pleasant experience. It was a tiny, primitive structure of squared logs with a central peaked roof on the east side of Market Square near the lake. The only adornment was a bell at the entrance to the jail so that the custodian, Hugh Cameron, could be hailed.

Isaac was in one of three dark, rancid cells with two other prisoners and only one small window, six inches by six inches, over the door. The window was perched high to prevent any disgruntled settlers from pointing a rifle in and taking a shot at the prisoners.

The sweltering heat of late summer made it hard to breathe. Isaac often stood and tried to put his face as close as possible to the tiny window to get some fresh air. They were fed only one canteen of water and one pound of wheaten bread each day, placed on a tin plate and passed through the window, usually spilling all over. Most days, Isaac did not care, his hunger got the better of him and he ate the meagre fare right off the mud floor. After a few days he no longer noticed the foul, rank aroma of the chamber pot that was emptied only once per week.

On his second day in jail, Isaac heard the faint sound of Polly's voice, calling him. At first he wanted to call out, but refrained, not wanting to get her hopes up, or the other prisoners to hear. Polly came back the next day, and the fourth, and the fifth, hoping to hear her husband's voice, praying that he was not ill or mistreated. Then she gave up, hurt and dejected. Isaac was relieved that she didn't come back. He did not know when his trial would be held and did not want Polly to make the long journey every day. The girls needed her at home.

How could it have come to this? Isaac asked himself. If ever I needed my friend, John White, it is now. Isaac defended himself at the Court of General Quarter Sessions of the Peace, not having money to hire a lawyer. There was still a shortage of lawyers in York, and the few that did practice charged an exorbitant fee. Not that a so-called lawyer would be able to put together much of a defence anyway, he grumbled, recalling White's contempt for the untrained laymen appointed to the Law Society of Upper Canada.

"Probably the worst you will get will be a public whipping," sneered one of Isaac's cellmates, a hardened criminal chained to the floor. Awaiting execution, the convict did not consider flogging to be much of a sentence.

"Maybe they will give you a branding," bawled the other cellmate, lying on a pile of straw that served as a bed for the inmates and as a nest for the numerous field mice running rampant throughout the jail. He rolled up his sleeve and revealed the scars on his forearm left by the hot poker, his punishment for stealing horses. Although it was not a common sentence, Isaac did not want to be left with a constant reminder of a crime that he still felt was justified.

"At least you won't be put in the stocks," the first criminal added. The Home District had no funds for something as extraneous as a pillory. The taxes collected would not cover it.

"If they don't brand you, then they certainly will banish you," bantered the other, enjoying ribbing Isaac, who tried to maintain a stoic expression. The last thing he wanted to do was to show any sign of fear or weakness. Both men were in jail for murder, and he did not want to provoke them.

"All prisoners move to the back!" bellowed the turnkey, unlocking the door. "Devins, come with me. Your trial is today."

Rising from the dirt floor, Isaac followed the jailer to a holding room, his shoulders drooped, his head cast downward. He shielded his eyes from the bright sunlight. Isaac was washed down from head to toe to remove some of the grime and stench from his clothes. Then he was told to comb his hair and adjust his appearance to look presentable.

As he entered the courtroom, the first person he saw was Polly. Intense worry was written across her face and she leaned forward as if to embrace him. He gave her a small, encouraging smile even though he felt anything but confident. As the chairman, William Jarvis, sat at a separate table to the right of the Justices, Isaac took his place in the prisoner's box to the left, hands shackled in front, facing the audience. Anything could happen in this free-for-all court, he thought.

Raising his head, Isaac looked over to where the three justices of the peace were seated. John Small was making notes on a parchment with a long grey quill. He had been appointed as a Justice of the Peace shortly after his acquittal for murdering John White. A great injustice, Isaac had loudly declared in Market Square half a dozen times. I'm sure he remembers that I stood up for John White at the duel, and hates me for it.

The second judge, William Allan, probably detests me the most. Every Saturday, at Allan's general store, Isaac heard him cursing the fishing net bandit, vowing to rip him apart limb by limb.

The only one who does not harbour open resentment toward me is John Elmsely, fidgeting and looking bored. That leaves William Jarvis, and he hates me as much as I hate him. I have no hope, Isaac thought.

"What say you, in defence of the aforesaid crimes?" demanded Jarvis.

"I only cut the nets to ensure that there will be fish in the river for many years to come, to enforce the law that was enacted in 1792," Isaac replied evenly, a little surprised at how firm is voice sounded. "Every time a net is cast, it depletes the fish population. Soon, there will be no fish left for our children and our grandchildren. Is that what we want, a river without fish?"

"What we want is fish on our table!" yelled someone from the crowd of angry citizens who crammed the courtroom to witness the trial of the fishing net bandit. The remark opened the floodgate for the rest of the crowd to scream out against Isaac Devins.

"Order in the court, order in the court!" Jarvis pounded the gavel over and over again on the oak desk.

The crowd eventually quieted, and Jarvis turned to Isaac. "Do you have anything further to add?"

"No, your Honour, just that I hope that true justice will prevail and you will see fit to grant me a sentence that befits someone who had good intentions, who wanted to secure a future for his family and for the rest of the citizens in York," replied Isaac, looking at each of the judges in turn, then slowly sitting down to await their decision.

In hushed voices, the three Justices began their deliberations, never looking over at the prisoner's box. That is not a good sign, thought Isaac. He glanced at Polly and smiled weakly, thinking how beautiful she looked even when she was tormented. Levi held his hands clasped together to indicate that Isaac was in their prayers. It will take more than prayer to save me from the wrath of the Justices, bemoaned Isaac.

The minutes ticked past. Small finally waved to the Chairman and passed him a folded piece of paper. Jarvis read the note, raised his eyebrows, cleared his throat and tugged on his wig.

Polly gulped and started to tremble, unsure whether to laugh or cry. Please, God, don't let it be banishment, she whispered. Even though we only have a cabin in the woods, she thought, many hours were spent tending to the garden, digging a well, building a stable and making it into a home with so many happy memories. Please don't take it away from us.

"Considering the nature and seriousness of the crime, and the many people affected by his actions," began Jarvis. Thomas Ridout, the Clerk of the Peace, furiously wrote on a piece of parchment.

"We find it necessary to impose the maximum penalty."

The night that Isaac was caught started out like any other. After sunset, he paddled down the river to just north of St. John's old trading post. Perhaps it was the full light from the harvest moon that was his downfall, because he barely got out of his canoe when he heard a twig snap.

Alerted, Isaac remained low, crouching on his haunches on the river bank, prepared to jump in. He turned his head sharply in the direction of the sound. Hearing nothing further, he took his six-inch blade out of its holster, pulled the fishing net up onto the shore and slashed it in choice locations, rendering it useless. He was only part way through when he heard a loud voice behind him.

"Hands up!" He felt the cold end of a double barrel rifle jut into his back.

"Stand up, slowly," the voice commanded.

"Now turn around, nice and slow," the voice continued, sounding ever more confident, ever more cocky.

Isaac did as he was told, keeping his hands at shoulder level, and shuffled his feet. Just as he made the last turn, his foot fell into a small depression in the earth, jerking his body backwards. His arm hit the gun barrel forward. The gunman fired but the blast went off into the woods. Instinctively, Isaac punched his assailant in the gut, then jabbed him with an undercut to the chin that knocked him backwards. Wrestling the gun from him, Isaac pummelled his chest, head, gut, until he could feel no more movement and hear no more sound.

Breathing out a low whistle, Isaac slowly stood up. In an instant he was tackled by two burly men who had circled around the other way unnoticed. They punched and kicked him over and over again, then tied his hands behind his back.

"Please stand, Mr. Devins," commanded Jarvis, gesturing with his right hand.

All ears strained to listen. Of all the people that Isaac did not want to have pronounce his punishment, it was William Jarvis. He had resented the inept, bungling fool for more than a decade. First he snubbed me, then he screwed up my land claim, now he is sentencing me.

"For the crimes of theft, destruction of property, and assault, you will be confined for one month to the York jail in the Home District".

An unusual punishment, thought Isaac. Jail time was normally only for those on death row, the criminally insane or those awaiting a trial. Then he noticed Jarvis' eyes grow wider and a look of satisfaction, almost pleasure, spread across his face. Here it comes.

"The term will commence and end with a whipping of thirty-nine lashes on a bare back. In addition, you will be fined twenty pounds even. Should you be unable to pay such a fine, you will remain in custody until it is paid."

The crowd gasped. Isaac stared at Jarvis, dumbfounded. Any trial that he had ever attended either as an accuser or as a jury member resulted in fines, usually no more than ten pounds. Jail time and two whippings, thirty-nine lashes each, was an extreme punishment, considering the crime. Damn, he whispered, they decided to slay me.

Polly cried out, horrified. She put both hands over her mouth, imagining the pain as his body is ripped apart by the crack of the whip. Not only that, how would they raise the money to pay the fine? Twenty pounds was what most farmers made in one year. Polly and Isaac lived off the land, more so than most, and had only a smattering of shillings.

"The court is now adjourned," the bailiff said flatly.

Walking away with his arms still in chains, Isaac felt desensitized, as if the punishment was for someone else. Whipping, a month in prison, and a fine? It seemed unreal, like a bad dream.

The next afternoon, Isaac was taken at gunpoint by two of the Queen's Rangers to Market Square and tied to the whipping post with leather straps. A raucous crowd gathered to witness the punishment of the fishing net bandit. Abraham and Levi positioned themselves at the front of the crowd, facing Isaac so that he could look over and see his family there to support him. Polly did not come. She could not bear to watch her husband be tortured. She stayed at home with the girls, hugging them harder than necessary most of the day.

The Sheriff, Alexander Macdonnell, directed the Rangers to cut Isaac's shirt open. Stepping back a couple of paces, he frowned, not altogether comfortable with this part of his job. Appointed by the Lieutenant-Governor, the Sheriff usually spent his time implementing the governor's wishes. Only a small portion of his duties involved overseeing capital or corporal punishment.

Isaac mentally built up an impenetrable wall that he hoped would carry him through the next five minutes, the length of time he guessed it would take. Standing tall, steady and straight. He blankly stared out into the crowd wearing a mask of fierce determination. Above all, he was a confident man, proud of what he had done, and prouder still of his family whom he did not want to disgrace. No one would see him plead for mercy. No one.

The crowd jeered. Those whose nets had been removed and slashed yelled the loudest.

"Look! It's the fishing net bandit!" someone called out and mimicked a fisherman casting a line out to sea, drawing laughter from the crowd. He did it again while others pretended to be the fish being reeled in.

Isaac stared forward. Nothing would tear apart his resolve.

"Indian lover!" cried another. Everyone knew Isaac Devins spent more time with the Mississaugas than with anyone else.

"Republican!" yelled others, laughing and jostling each other.

To call someone a "Republican" was the ultimate insult in Upper Canada. Equating someone with the American rebels could lead to the person being charged with treason for which the punishment was hanging. It was so offensive that Levi became unhinged. He turned and lunged at the nearest man, shoved him to the ground, and bashed his knees into the man's chest.

"One!" the Sheriff bellowed, silencing the crowd, as the guard cracked the whip down the centre of Isaac's bare back. Jerking his head back and tightening his lips, Isaac closed his eyes and shut out everything. He arched his back to cushion the blows, but the pain mounted with every blow.

"Nine!" shouted the Sheriff, wondering why the Justices felt compelled to inflict such a stiff sentence. Most other floggings were twenty blows at the most.

Abraham watched with tears in his eyes. The pain of seeing his eldest son suffering was unbearable. Why didn't he listen to me and stop that unnecessary policing? I should have stepped in and stopped him.

"Twenty-one!"

Perhaps the Justices ordered thirty-nine lashes to reinforce the idea of a "Christian moral order," thought the Sheriff, thinking abstractly now. He did not want to think about the pain that Isaac might be suffering.

"Thirty-three!"

Isaac's body was limp and no longer responded to the whip at all. The pain was beyond imagination. A memory played in his head over and over again, when he was a boy and his father was teaching him to ride a pony.

"Get up, Isaac," his father said after he slipped off the saddle for the umpteenth time. "The pony is trying to figure you out. Let him know that you are in control."

Isaac did not even notice when the whipping stopped, the pain was so complete. Back in his cell, he lay on the straw bed, moaning, falling into and out of consciousness. Polly, he thought. Polly, I did not break. He lay motionless, oblivious, unresponsive.

"Ahhhh!" gasped one of Isaac's cellmates.

The man backed away and called the custodian for a shirt, a blanket, anything. A handful of field mice had crawled on Isaac's back, drawn toward the gaping wounds.

Two days later, Isaac was able to crawl out of the straw bed and rise to a hunched-over kneeling position. He rose unsteadily to his feet, anxious to take a couple of steps. Parched, he drank the last few sips from the canteen, then called for the custodian to bring more, banging a tin cup against the wooden door.

After a month, his wounds were healed but he was extremely feeble. Isaac left the jail again in shackles, and once more was led to the whipping post in Market Square. This time, only his father, brothers and a handful of bystanders watched. At first the pain was more intense than the last time. Then the Sheriff seemed to strike him with much less force. Perhaps he is feeling sorry for me, Isaac thought, wincing from the force of another blow. After all, I was only stopping an illegal activity, something the authorities were unable and unwilling to do.

Isaac's father watched as his son was whipped again, blood dripping from new welts, his back raw and scarred. Abraham paid the jailer the twenty-pound fine from money he had collected from friends and neighbours. Many remembered how Isaac had saved them from starvation that cruel winter of 1795 and gave whatever they could.

Abraham and Levi carried him to a wagon and laid him on a bed of straw, then went to the wharf and rowed back to Abraham's homestead by bateau so that he would not be jostled about on the bumpy roads.

Polly almost fainted when she saw her husband's weak body laid on his father's bed, then attended to her husband lovingly and with competence.

A few days earlier, she had gone to the Mississaugas' healing grounds on the peninsula to collect some of the herbs she would need. It was no longer an untouched paradise teeming with waterfowl. Now it was heavily used by settlers and Mississaugas. In the summers, the natives would hold horse and pony races, and the settlers would have cariole races in winter, both having to fend off the goats that roamed freely through the fields. Storehouses and barracks had been built by the military close to the lighthouse at Gibraltar Point.

Polly mixed the ginseng root she unearthed from the sunny meadow around the sassafras tree. She combined it with rabbit fat and smeared it over her husband's raw back, then covered his wounds with a sheet of cotton covered in turpentine. She made a poultice of whiskey, corn meal, ground lilac bark and wild ginger, and soothed him with her gentle, caring voice. But the infection that had begun in the filthy jail cell started to spread.

As night fell, Isaac became more and more delirious, and Polly did not know if he would live to see the morning. She lay awake all night long and prayed. *Please, Almighty God, do not take my husband away.*

The next morning, Fire Starter walked into the room. Word had spread all the way to the northern hunting grounds that Waabshkii Mnidoo was dying. Fire Starter had immediately left and journeyed south, bringing a tea that his wife had made of cedar and ginseng, excellent for healing wounds.

"After the Creator breathed the spirit of life into us, he asked our Grandmother Cedar to give us her medicine and make us pure," he explained to Polly as he helped her to prepare it. "By drinking her remedy, Isaac will be cleansed, and everything that he does not need on his journey will be left behind. We pray that the Manitou, the unknown power of life and the universe, will shine on Isaac Devins."

The cedar was one of four essential healing herbs that the Mississaugas had used for centuries. After forcing Isaac to drink it, the two of them waited by his side, in silence, each praying that he would live to see another day.

Polly looked at Fire Starter and said, "Ten years ago, we prayed together for baby Elizabeth, who was healed by your nurturing potion. I pray now that we will again be so blessed."

Fire Starter merely nodded.

A few hours later, Isaac opened his eyes, weak but lucid. "You ... are ... here?" he questioned Fire Starter.

"Yes, we arrived at the Credit Village yesterday from the northern hunting grounds. I must go now and make an offering to thank the Great Spirit for allowing you to continue your journey with us a little while longer."

At the limestone outcrop, Fire Starter took his leather pouch with the sign of the otter, got out of the canoe, and stuffed some tobacco leaves, mint, meadowsweet and feverfew into a crevice. He struck his flint on the limestone, a spark flew, and a sweet smell surrounded him. Placing his hands on his heart, he bowed. *We thank you, Great Spirit*, he whispered softly.

Isaac's return to health proceeded miraculously quick and by the end of May, 1802, he felt as strong as he had ever been. His disposition, however, was not so quick to recover.

Resentment filled his being. Resentment of the injustice of the legal system, resentment of having to take the law into his own hands, resentment of the elite class that rejected him and left him there to die. He was grim, introspective, and aloof for months. Only the birth of his fourth daughter, Rebecca, lifted his spirits slightly.

That winter, Isaac wanted more than ever to retreat from the unbending politics of York. He found work as a drover in the United States under the condition that he be paid in currency rather than goods. He needed to make enough money to pay back the twenty pounds that he owed his father, brothers, and their neighbours. Nothing could convince him to return to his life of night fishing in the summer and ice fishing in the winter. He swore that he would never again sell fish to anyone in York.

Alongside a crew of a dozen men, Isaac drove cattle and oxen from New Jersey to Niagara through the Indian Territory so that the livestock could be shipped to the rapidly expanding western territories. Travelling through the Indian Territory was still fraught with danger. Many drovers had to give up one or two of their animals to the Chippewa, Mohawks or Senecas in order to pass safely through. Others were attacked, their cattle stolen and the drovers killed.

On their first trip through the Mohawk Valley, Isaac's group stopped suddenly when they were surrounded by Chippewas on all sides, just a few days south of Fort Niagara. The Chippewas looked fierce with war paint all over their faces and bodies, and each had a gun pointed or a tomahawk raised.

The head drover tried to speak with the leader, but was barely able to communicate. One of the warriors tackled the head drover to the ground and held his arms behind his back, while another put a pistol to his ear and yelled something in Anishinaabe.

"Stay down, stay down," Isaac shouted.

He felt the cold metal of a tomahawk cut the side of his neck, as a Chippewa threatened to scalp him. Without moving a muscle, Isaac greeted them in their own language, telling him the name that the Mississaugas had given him, Waabshkii Mnidoo. He told them the story of how he tried to save the salmon and his imprisonment through words and gestures.

The warriors withdrew and told Isaac they could safely pass. Twice more, he repeated the story to other marauding bands before he became known as the fishing net bandit and was granted free passage every time they passed through. Promoted to head drover, he led many excursions safely through the Indian Territory.

Though he was away from his family, the days passed peacefully for Isaac. He was relieved to be away from York. His intense anger and hatred of William Jarvis, the justice system, the impenetrable aristocracy, and the unforgiving crowd at his whipping slowly subsided.

But he did not know if he could ever forgive the settlers who destroyed the Mississaugas' fishery, or the political system in York that allowed it to happen. He knew that one day the salmon would be gone forever.

Isaac finished the year away from York much calmer, more humble and focused. His employers rewarded him with an ox and a cow in addition to his salary. He traded the cow for twenty pounds and repaid the money his father had borrowed to pay his fine. Soon, he insisted on working for only several months at a time so that he could spend time with Polly and the girls.

While Isaac spent less time in York, the town expanded. In the spring of 1803, a grammar school opened as well as a formalized market at the square. Isaac and Polly chose not to send their daughters as the girls would have to walk twelve miles on a trail through the forest every morning, and return by sunset. Elizabeth had only two more years to study anyway. Instead, Polly continued teaching her children to read and write at home, the same way she had been taught so many years ago. Besides, the school really was a place for the well-to-do, who could afford the costly tuition.

Isaac, Polly and the children lived contentedly, alone at the north edge of Toronto at Emery, the name his wife gave to their homestead. There was no one that Isaac trusted or even wanted to befriend in the town, so there was no reason to go there except for specialty supplies. They socialized with their relatives in Weston as often as they could, and spent the summers with Fire Starter and his family.

The seasons passed and Isaac and Polly watched their family grow. Finally, a baby boy was born on New Year's day in 1809. They decided to name him John Chapman Devins. "Chapman" was Polly's family name, while "John" was chosen in memory of Governor Simcoe, who Isaac learned had passed away in 1806. He still held the Governor in high regard, fondly remembering their strategy sessions and lively debates on how to create a new province.

All that seemed far removed now, almost as if it had happened to someone else, or had all been a dream.

Chapter 16 – April 1, 1812

Ding-dong! ding-dong!

The bell of St. James church rang out merrily as the happy young couple were congratulated with hugs and kisses just outside the tall, elegantly carved wooden doors. It was a fine April morning, crisp and clear, any signs of winter eradicated by a cascade of spring flowers in the gardens of the many fine homes in York. The enduring aroma of pine needles emanated from the forest surrounding the town, augmented by the scent of spring blossoms. The fresh, clean air whiffed through the streets and in through the windows of the fine homes, shops, and stables, refreshing and new.

The bride had chosen to resist tradition and have the ceremony at the church mainly because her father was an active member of the Board. Besides, her parents' home was too small and plain for the kind of ceremony she wanted. St. James was a fine church, the first one constructed in York five years ago. The bride's father demanded that the new minister, Rev. John Strachan, officiate the wedding.

Shaking the groom's hand and slapping him on the back, Isaac congratulated Simeon, happy that his little brother had found a suitable wife. He was fortunate, too. Along the Humber where Simeon's homestead lay just north of his father's, there was little chance of meeting a potential spouse. York, in contrast, had over five hundred people in 1812, and many teas, balls and funerals held regularly. Unless young people living in the outskirts went into town for an event, their only prospects were their neighbours' sons or daughters.

By happy chance, Simeon met Violet eight months earlier at a building bee held at William Allan's new tannery. As the principal merchant in York, Allan was someone that the young Simeon Devins wanted to impress. Isaac did not follow through, Simeon often thought. He gave up before he could accomplish anything in York, but not me. I am going to be somebody in this town, he vowed, and I will not give up.

Many of the other thirty-five young men at the building bee had the same intention, to impress one of the most powerful men in York. His father, Abraham, decided to leave the back-breaking work of raising a stable to his sons. Isaac likewise did not offer his assistance. He did not feel any lingering resentment toward William Allan, he just did not want to be involved. Isaac was content to live his life in relative seclusion on the Humber, with Fire Starter and his family for company, and not be involved with anyone in York.

After the men raised the roof and secured it in place, they all retired to the lawn of Allan's exquisite park lot. Leah Allan, with assistance from other wives and servants, prepared a spectacular feast of wild boar, goose, and mutton with rhubarb pie, pound cake and raisin cheesecake for dessert. Competition was fierce among building bee hostesses, and Leah Allan did not want to be outdone.

Ale and spirits were plentiful and the men were thirsty. Games of football and tennis were played with vigour, followed by music and dancing that stretched long into the night.

Simeon was drinking ale and laughing with his buddies when he was lightly tapped on the shoulder. He turned and his eyes widened in surprise and awe. The most beautiful girl he had ever seen was standing right in front of him. She smiled, her full red lips parted, her raven black hair caressing her smooth cheeks. Her slim but shapely figure was bewitchingly dressed in a scarlet gown with white lace at the throat.

"Shall we dance?" she inquired.

Without a word, Simeon offered his hand and led her to the dance floor. His step-mother, Elizabeth, always remarked how elegant Simeon was,

228

a natural dancer, as she taught him to reel and step, and how to treat a lady. By the look of appreciation on her face, Violet Johnson was enjoying Simeon's gallantry. She also noted his confident stature, inviting laughter, his smooth brown hair, and firm jaw. His grey eyes seemed to smile at everyone he met. There was something about him that had made her walk forward and boldly ask for a dance, something she had never done before.

Simeon began to call on Violet whenever he was in town, to her father's dismay. James Johnson was in shipping and owned a warehouse near Allan's wharf. He did not fancy the son of a farmer calling on his daughter. After their fourth Sunday afternoon stroll, Johnson declared there would be no more such encounters. Simeon was devastated. He had completely fallen for Violet, and could not imagine a day without her.

"Isaac, what should I do?" asked the love-struck 23-year-old, trusting his older brother to understand and provide sound advice. Simeon had often heard the tale of how Isaac secretly married Polly, not telling anyone until months later when their fathers could better handle the news.

"All I can say is that if your heart tells you it is right, then you will find a way," Isaac replied.

Simeon began attending St. James church every other Sunday, even though he had been raised Methodist, knowing that Violet and her family were avid church-goers. He passed her a note and they began meeting secretly in the field behind Government House, knowing that nobody would be there on a Sunday. Although she was from a privileged family and he was not, neither cared. Holding hands and dancing barefoot through the meadow, laughing and embracing, their love could not be denied.

When they broke the news of their intention to marry, Abraham and Elizabeth were delighted, but Violet's father was livid. Fortunately for the glowing couple, James Johnson was distracted since a war with the Americans was imminent. Major General Brock had just announced that York would become a naval yard and Johnson was concerned with how it would affected his shipping business. When he could not persuade his daughter to change her mind, even after threatening to cut her off from his fortune, he tried another tactic.

"There is only one action you can take that will win my favour," he told Simeon one afternoon after cornering him alone at the dock. "Join the York militia, and I will give consent for you to marry Violet."

The call to join the militia was rampant throughout York in the spring of 1812, and many young men signed up. Simeon had previously considered it, seeing the military as a way to increase his prosperity and to travel to exotic places. The next morning, he walked to the garrison and enrolled.

"Congratulations, son," James Johnson said loudly for all to hear as he patted Simeon on the back, wanting to keep up appearances.

His daughter beamed, elated that her father was finally accepting Simeon as her husband on her wedding day. Johnson just smiled and nodded to all the wedding guests. Now that my son-in-law has joined the militia, he thought, he will be sent off to war for God knows how long, and who knows when, or if, he will return.

"All the best, old friend!" chimed out Joseph Rousseau, who happened to be in York on his friend's wedding day.

The two young men embraced. Simeon reached into his pocket and pulled out the curved dagger with the wooden handle and the blue feather that Joseph had given him so long ago, and handed it to his friend.

Grinning from ear to ear, Joseph exclaimed, "You still have it!"

"I brought it along today for luck!" answered Simeon, slapping him on the back, happy that he could see his oldest friend on his wedding day. "What brings you to York?"

"My father was just appointed as the Lieutenant-Colonel of the 2nd York militia, and I will serve under him," said Joseph, proud that his father had earned such an important position. "Perhaps we will train together at the York garrison."

"St. John Rousseau is a Lieutenant-Colonel in the militia!" interrupted Isaac who overheard the two friends talking. "I would never have imagined that. He was always so independent, so pragmatic."

St. John moved his way up the ranks, going from interpreter for the Indian Department, to Superintendent, to tax collector and now was appointed to a high-ranking position in the militia. While Isaac had dropped out of society, St. John had become fully integrated.

"My father does indeed have his own ways, but he is foremost and truly a Canadian," said Joseph, putting his arm around Simeon's shoulder, who nodded in agreement, feeling equally patriotic.

The two young men had grown up in Upper Canada and felt a strong bond toward their country, particularly now that it was being threatened by the Americans. While Joseph, Simeon, and many other young men joined the militia that spring, others, like the "Blackguards," supported annexation to the United States. That spring, many Canadians moved south to live in a country with a political ideology they could believe in. Likewise, many Americans fled north to join the British colony, not happy with how the new concepts of "democracy" and the "republic" were crudely administered and seemed to favour a chosen few.

Simeon proudly introduced Joseph to his new wife who looked radiant, thrilled to meet her husband's oldest friend. "I have heard stories of the two of you playing together along the Humber, the only two young lads in the whole settlement. It is hard to imagine now, almost twenty years later, that both of you knew our lively town before it even existed."

"Yes, Simeon was on the ship that first arrived at York harbour, and my father paddled out to meet them. We were destined to become friends."

How times have changed, Isaac thought as he listened to the young men reminisce. The spirit of conquering the wilderness, of braving the elements and the harshness of pioneer life was nowhere to be seen as the colony faced the certainty of war with the United States. Everyone spoke about it, and knew that the Yankees were coming. Most assumed the Americans had a better army and would win.

"The apathy of the Canadian people is the biggest threat to the Canadas," Major General Isaac Brock proclaimed often, to anyone who would listen.

As far back as 1807, Brock voiced his opinion that Canada would be defeated in a war against America because most of the people did not have the courage to believe that they could win.

"Canada will become another state in America simply because of the low morale," he said to Henry Bathurst, Secretary of War for the Colonies, while he was stationed in Quebec. "The defeatist attitude so prevalent here will sadly lead to the country dissolving without even a struggle."

At the beginning of 1812, there was no doubt to anyone, Canadian or American, that war would be declared. One of the principal reasons, as reported in the *Upper Canada Gazette*, was that the Americans objected to the British naval blockade on the European coast that restricted trading between France and the United States. The British argued that they needed to cripple the French economy in their war against Napoleon. The United States countered that as a neutral country, it should be able to trade with whomever it pleases.

"The British are not respecting our rights as a sovereign nation," President James Madison declared. "We are no longer a colony of Britain!"

"The Americans also object to the impressment of former British sailors," Isaac said to Simeon during one of many discussions on the topic of war. "What right does Britain have to force civilians into service with the Royal Navy?"

A centuries-old law permitted the British Navy to reclaim any sailors who deserted. The highly unpopular press gangs would search the taverns and inns in New York city, take able-bodied men with any kind of seafaring or river-boat experience, march them up the gangplank, and shackle them to their posts.

"We are short of qualified seamen during wartime, and we need to man our ships in order to defeat Napoleon!" answered Simeon, enjoying the debate with his brother. "If Britain falls, there will no longer be a Canada."

"Well, there may not be much of a Canada if America is permitted to continue to expand west and north, swallowing up the Indian Territory," observed Isaac, who always supported Simcoe's idea of creating a separate, sovereign Indian Territory between Upper Canada and New England. "The

Americans have made it clear that they want to acquire all the land up to the Pacific coast, and where will the natives live?"

Everyone knew that Isaac's close ties with Fire Starter and the Mississaugas made him sympathetic to preserving their culture and their land.

"Yes, and where will the Loyalists live?" conjectured Simeon. "There is no longer any doubt that the Americans want to make our British colonies disappear so that they can take over the entire continent!"

The words of former President Thomas Jefferson recently printed in the *Upper Canada Gazette* made it quite clear.

"The acquisition of Canada this year will be a mere matter of marching," Jefferson wrote.

Even the Secretary of War, John C. Calhoun, predicted, "In four weeks, ... the whole of Canada will be in our possession."

Such blatant, unequivocal, words of intent had a profound impact on the settlers that spring, an impact that Major General Brock hoped would incite a call to action, a shedding of the cloak of apathy for the armour of Canadian sovereignty.

Many, like Simeon, were incensed at the audacity of the Americans, the sheer arrogance of assuming that Canadians were such easy pickings. "They must think we are blockheads, birdbrains, half-wits," Simeon pronounced to Isaac after reading the newspaper. "How can they be so bold? A generation ago, we were all living together, side by side. Have they forgotten that British blood runs through their veins?"

For others, particularly the older generation, apathy and resignation only deepened. "The President is correct," Abraham said, "Canada will not win the war. There are only five hundred thousand Canadians and seven million Americans. What chance do we have?"

Abraham had fought against the British during the War of Independence and did not believe the British would win the second time around. He was well aware of the American fighting spirit, and knew that the British were no match..

"The British are too busy fighting Napoleon to worry about the Canadas, the same way that they were too busy fighting a continental war to worry about the Americans," he continued, spreading his arms. "Perhaps we should not even bother putting up a defence. There is so much bloodshed that could be avoided."

He did not want to see his sons fight in a senseless war that he felt they had no chance of winning, perhaps never to return.

"But Father, we must fight for our homes, our property, our country," urged Simeon, incredulous as only youth can be at his father's caution. "We do not want to be absorbed into their fledgling attempt at government. The greatest empire in the world is our protector. Our loyalty should be to the King, not to a stooge like Madison."

Abraham shook his head. "We will not lose our homesteads when the Americans take over, if we are aligned with them," he replied, recalling how his alliance with the Americans had spared him thirty years ago. "If you insist on joining the York militia, you will have nothing when the Americans defeat us. I hope you are smart enough to switch alliances before the British are defeated."

Abraham had no preference between a monarchist or republican system, as long as there was no blatant tyranny. Isaac, likewise, felt that either form of government was fine as long as people were free to go about their daily lives. It did not matter to him whether he lived in a British colony or an American state. As war grew more certain, many other citizens were also undecided.

Simeon, on the other hand, strongly believed that Canada must be defended. He argued this point over and over again, before, during, and after his military drills, with anyone who would listen. His passion, youth and fitness caused him to be posted to one of the flank companies of the 3rd York Militia. He trained as a loader for 5- to 18-pounder guns, and excelled in armed combat with the musket and bayonet, hoping to one day be promoted to major, lieutenant or even general.

The flank companies were created because General Brock did not trust that all 13,000 men who volunteered for the militia in Upper Canada were loyal to the British Crown. He feared that arming that many volunteers could lead to a mass revolt in favour of the Americans. Providing arms to only a small group of flank companies allayed Brock's angst, and allowed him to provide a select group with special training and equipment.

"I think you will be fighting an uphill battle to get promoted beyond Corporal," Isaac told Simeon when he heard of his brother's ambitions. "The only people who become officers are members of the upper class with wealth or power."

Isaac had observed that the people who had positions of influence in the Executive Council and Legislative Assembly were appointed as officers in the militia, regardless of whether they had any training or experience with military operations.

"How could an unorganized, inept, ignorant fool like William Jarvis get appointed as a Lieutenant-Colonel?" Isaac asked rhetorically. "Simply because he knows people in the right places."

"Then I better get to know some people," retorted Simeon, a little put off by his brother's constant lectures on the impossibility of penetrating the elite class. Simeon was tired of hearing Isaac's stories of rejection and intended to prove his brother wrong.

"As long as you don't join the British military," warned Isaac, afraid that his brother would trade his freedom as a volunteer in the militia for the regiment and structure of the regular army.

Recruitment teams paraded through York, at least a half dozen times a year, enticing young men with tales of excitement, travel, adventure, and glory. The colourful uniforms of the Redcoats were attractive to both the women folk and the young men who wanted to impress them. Many a tale was told by the recruitment teams to wide-eyed young men, who would sometimes run off to enlist in the army after a few pints. The romance of war and soldiering was enticing to many young men whose only other prospect was the daily toil of pioneering from sunrise to sunset.

Like the militia, the British Army awarded high ranks on the basis of money, rather than merit. Many commissions as officers were bought and sold. Lieutenant, captains and majors came from the middle class, while major generals, lieutenant generals and generals came from the wealthy elite or nobility. Filling the lowest ranks were farmers, tradesmen, labourers, and beggars, along with criminals who chose military service over other sentencing options after being convicted in a courtroom.

"Are you sure you want to join a bunch of low-lifes who may want to do away with you?" questioned Isaac, worried that his brother was not considering the realities of life in the army. "You would have to live at the York garrison for a mere one shilling per day amongst a bunch of thugs and thieves."

"Under Major General Brock's command, I certainly do," Simeon replied adamantly.

Brock had an extraordinary reputation throughout Canada. He was known to place the needs of the common soldier in high regard and often used kindness as a means of instilling loyalty and bravery. Simeon was attracted to the honour and fairness that Brock exuded wherever he went. He was drawn in by the charisma of a great leader.

Isaac watched his brother dance with his bride in the garden outside the church after the wedding, momentarily forgetting his misgivings about Simeon's career in the militia. Surveying the crowd around the newlyweds, his eyes locked on Polly who still looked beautiful, wearing an attractive purple gown, a few grey steaks highlighting her long auburn hair tied loosely at the back. She was talking with Elizabeth, their eldest daughter, who had just turned 19, and was due to marry next month. Their other seven children stayed at home, Isaac not having sufficient transport for them all. The trail through the bush was as impassable as ever, and more easily travelled on horseback than by wagon.

Raising his glass, Isaac made the first toast of the afternoon, praising his brother for his choice of a bride, and playfully chiding him for joining the militia.

"I am just not certain," Isaac concluded, "why Simeon would join the militia, then marry such a beauty on the brink of war. Perhaps he has his mind half-cocked!"

The crowd burst into laughter and joyously toasted the couple. The final toast before the couple sped off on their honeymoon was reserved for the bride's father.

"To my darling daughter, and her most fortunate groom," Johnson began. "May your lives begin today with great satisfaction, and Simeon, may you be dutiful when your country calls and honour the King, as my sweetheart waits for your safe return."

And may she wait for you in vain, Johnson smirked to himself, all the while smiling and keeping up appearances. He did not want his daughter to know his true feelings.

Polly, Elizabeth and the other women threw white petals as the bride and groom dashed out of the garden gate, climbed into a buggy, and trotted off.

"They are staying at Violet's sister's home this evening," Isaac informed Polly and Elizabeth on their way home. Simeon had only told his father and Isaac the secret location since he did not want to be a victim of a charivari, where local people, mostly not invited to the wedding, would put on masks and harass the newlyweds on their wedding night.

When Violet's father was informed of their plan, he casually let it slip to Samuel Jarvis, son of William Jarvis. The younger Jarvis had wanted to marry his daughter but she had turned him down. Johnson would have been happy with that match even though William Jarvis had managed to lose much of his wealth, to his wife's great displeasure.

Samuel Jarvis, an intern for the Law Society, of Upper Canada, invited a number of his upper-crust friends to the couple's hideaway. They sat on a fence outside an open window and threw rocks at the walls of the fine brick home.

Samuel Jarvis shouted out, "Fine union, if you want to marry a farm boy!"

He downed a shot, then passed the whiskey along.

"Hey, farmer boy," yelled another, "shouldn't you be out counting sheep or baling hay?"

The friends snickered and guffawed, each one secretly envious that an unknown farm boy had landed arguably the most beautiful girl in York.

They kept up the banter for an hour, throwing rocks and rotten food, clanging chains together to make a ruckus, whistling, jeering, yelling insults at Simeon, all feeling superior. The friends had attended Reverend John Strachan's grammar school in Cornwall, the first and finest school in the province. All of them looked down on those who could not afford a formal education. Simeon was a mere private in the militia, so they did not consider him to be worthy of a beautiful girl like Violet.

Samuel Jarvis finally went to the window and looked in. Most people would be quite willing to pay them to stop the disturbance at this point, and he intended to ask for a bundle. He walked around to the front door, pushed his way in, and walked from room to room, not finding a soul. Simeon and Violet had slipped out a back door, taken one of her father's horses, and galloped off to Simeon's property on the Humber where they knew they would be safe, a full moon guiding them along the meandering trail through the forest.

Heading home after the ceremony, Isaac and Polly had almost reached their cabin when they met Fire Starter, two of his sons, and six others along the Toronto Carrying Place trail, with a large cedar canoe on their backs, heading upriver. Dismounting from his horse, Isaac passed the reins to Polly and took a place behind Fire Starter, his neck and shoulders now bearing part of the weight of the canoe and the deerskin hide that was packed in bundles on its way north.

"Greetings, old friend," said Isaac. "Why such a hurry?"

The men carried the heavy cedar canoe at a brisk pace along the portage route. "We are going to a special pow-wow. When the war comes, we must be ready. Our brothers in the south, the Shawnee, have tired of being pushed west as the Americans take over our land. Tecumseh has vowed to fight and reclaim the Ohio territory that they lost at the Battle of Fallen Timbers. He asked us to join him, for all clans to fight together. Tecumseh says that the forest, rivers, lakes and plains are owned in common by all clans."

The Shawnee were the southern-most clan in the Algonquin tribe, speaking a similar language to the Mississaugas. Much of the Ohio territory was ceded to the Americans at the conclusion of the Northwest Indian War in 1794. Tecumseh, the leader of the Shawnee, wanted the Americans to rescind the treaties, not believing that the land should be divided, especially three million acres that the Americans acquired at Fort Wayne in Indiana without even consulting his clan.

"Sell a country!" Tecumseh had exclaimed, "Why not sell the air, the great sea, as well as the earth? Didn't the Great Spirit make them all for the use of his children?"

Fire Starter was equally appalled. "I do not understand why our leaders continue to trade our forest for money or weapons," he said. "Many years ago, I thought the white men foolish when they gave us tools and weapons to use the forest and the rivers. We did not own them, yet the white men gave us gifts. Now we know that the white men did not intend to share the land, but instead they destroy our forests, dirty our rivers, kill our fish, harm our children, rape our women, make us ill with small pox and other diseases. They do not share with us, but force us away."

Isaac thought about how much had changed for the Mississaugas since the settlers arrived twenty years ago. The Mississaugas' sacred healing garden on the peninsula was abandoned, wildlife was no longer abundant, river levels had dropped as more land was cleared for farming, fish were dwindling, the huge volume of waterfowl in the Toronto harbour was no more, many native cemeteries and holy places had been destroyed. But most of all, their ability to go anywhere they wanted had all but disappeared. Homesteads where the Mississaugas were not welcome dotted the landscape like the holes in a block of cheddar cheese.

"Tecumseh wants you to join the Shawnee in Ohio?" questioned Isaac, wondering if there would be a resistance against the Americans within their own country.

"No, Tecumseh and three thousand warriors of the Shawnee, Miami, Wyandot, Potomac and Delaware have already arrived in Detroit to join the British. Tecumseh is calling for all clans to join together to stop the Americans who destroyed his headquarters and his family at Tippecanoe."

The slaughter at Tippecanoe in Indiana began when the American General William Harrison requested a conference with the Shawnee, waiting until Tecumseh was weeks away. He secretly planned to destroy the command post. Tecumseh's brother, known as The Prophet, incited his warriors to attack the British, saying that the white men's bullets would not harm them. Dozens of Shawnee warriors were killed, and the rest were disbanded, angry at the Prophet, and threatened to strip him of his power and kill him. When Tecumseh returned three months later, he found his alliances fragmented and his people despondent.

"Brothers, the white men are not our friends," Tecumseh declared at a pow-wow. "At first, they only asked for land sufficient for a wigwam; now, nothing will satisfy them but the whole of our hunting grounds, from the rising to the setting sun."

In the years leading up to the 1812, Tecumseh travelled extensively throughout the northern states to convince the clans to come together in a common goal. The idea of a native confederacy had been promoted sixty years previously by the Ottawa war chief Pontiac. Joseph Brant had tried to unite the clans, right up until his death in 1807. Tecumseh likewise believed that the only hope was for all native clans to unite. With his powerful, convincing oratory skills, Tecumseh could move an audience to rage, sorrow or contentment, whatever he wished. Of all the native leaders, the Americans and the British feared him most of all.

"Brothers, my people are brave and numerous," he began at one of his recruitment drives, "but the white people are too strong for them alone. I wish you to take up the tomahawk with them. If we all unite, we will cause the rivers to stain the great waters with their blood."

Tecumseh wanted to kill all white men, dig up their graves and throw the bones into the ocean from which their boats first came. However, he knew that the First Nations would have to ally with either the Americans or the British, that the Natives alone were not strong enough to defeat either one of them, let alone both.

In the spring of 1811, Isaac met Tecumseh on one of his drives to the Genesee when both groups camped on opposite sides of a river for the night. Three of Tecumseh's warriors paddled over to Isaac's camp, requesting through sign language that he give them one of his pigs. When Isaac answered in near-perfect Algonquin language, the warriors smiled, greeted him and invited him to their side for the evening meal. Word had spread amongst the tribes of the white man who drove the cattle and knew their language and customs.

Immediately upon entering the wigwam, Isaac was impressed by Tecumseh's demeanour. His very presence commanded respect. Fire Starter told him that Tecumseh was both a fierce warrior and a humanitarian, someone who would spare a life if there was no reason to kill. Word spread that Tecumseh would instruct his warriors not to rape and pillage a settlement after a battle, only to gather and bury their own dead.

"The Six Nations here want to remain neutral," asserted Tecumseh. "What of their northern brothers?"

"The Grand River nations are definitely aligned with the British," answered Isaac, pleased to pass on valuable information. "Their Chief, John Norton, is part Scottish, and continually presses the government to create an independent territory. They want a unification of all tribes to fight together."

"We must be united," agreed Tecumseh. "We must smoke the same pipe; we must fight each other's battles; and more than all, we must love the Great Spirit. He is for us; he will destroy our enemies and make all his red children happy."

Isaac was impressed with Tecumseh's intelligence, directness, and charm. His compelling way of speaking, drawing each person in to his cause, was infectious.

He passed a pipe to Isaac. After a while, Tecumseh asked, "But what of the Mississaugas?"

"Unknown, at this time. Some would prefer to remain neutral, others want to align with the British. The Chief, Kineubenae, does not trust the

British. They reneged on their promise to give the Mississaugas the rights to the river mouths and the fisheries. It was supposed to be part of the deal when they ceded over the southern part of the Mississauga Tract in 1806. The Chief was pressured by the British into handing over the land for an ox, some flour, a keg of rum and the promise to build cabins for the 200 Mississaugas who survived the small pox epidemic, a mere pittance. The British destroyed their cornfields, even one of the Chief's. I don't know if they will align with the British or join the Americans."

Tecumseh knitted his brow, breathed out heavily, then said, "The only way to stop this evil is for the red men to unite in claiming a common and equal right in the land, as it was first, and should be now, for the land was never divided before the Long Knives came."

As he trudged along the trail behind Isaac, Fire Starter shifted his hold on the canoe and said, "I am fearful, my friend, that we are losing our traditions, our way of life. We need more men like you who want to help us preserve it."

Isaac smiled and nodded. That was as close to an endearment as Fire Starter would ever give.

"It is hard to trust General Brock's words, that they will create a territory for us when they win the war."

"I cannot tell you if he is to be trusted," said Isaac, who only heard of Brock coming to York once in the six months since he became the Lieutenant-Governor of Upper Canada. "But I think you have a greater chance for independence with the British than the Americans - not much, but greater."

The men stopped, bent down and rolled the canoe over into the river. Fire Starter stood up and put a hand on Isaac's shoulder. The two men embraced, both with heavy hearts at the thought of the Mississaugas' destiny.

Walking back through the forest with Polly and Elizabeth, Isaac could not help but feel dismal, despite the happiness he had felt earlier at Simeon's wedding. War was coming, likely sooner than expected, and he could not share the patriotism coursing through Simeon's veins. Neither could be feel Fire Starter's urgent need to choose an alliance.

Perhaps remaining neutral, like the Six Nations south of the border, was the best option. At least it would not ruffle any feathers. It was also a position that he could live with. Thankful that his isolated homestead on the Humber would not possibly be the target of an attack from either side, Isaac breathed a long sigh. At least Polly and their eight children would be safe when the war came.

Two months later, as Isaac docked his canoe at William Allan's wharf he heard and saw a commotion on the east side.

"War!" and "Victory!" were heard above other shouts as people embraced one another, argued and debated with animated looks of resignation, worry and excitement. News had just arrived from Niagara that the United States had declared War on Britain.

"When did it happen?" he heard someone ask.

"The official date shown here is June 18, 1812," was the answer.

"But that is tomorrow's date. How is that possible? The declaration must be false."

"The official messenger sent by the U. S. Congress has yet to arrive," declared the courier who brought the message. "John Jacob Astor, a retailer in Washington who I might add has a vested interest in our Canadian fur trade, sent me word as soon as he received the news. I galloped at break-neck speed, transferring from exhausted horse to exhausted horse, stopping only for a few hours to sleep, and brought the news here today, one day ahead of the official announcement."

The Yankees have finally made it official, thought Isaac.

His resentment toward the British elite still lingered. In many ways, he would love to see the likes of John Small lose everything they had, and get what they deserve. He imagined William Jarvis trying to lead a battalion to defend York, then being shot down by a pimply private, falling face first into a sea of blood. Perhaps war would not be so bad after all.

He tied his canoe securely, then climbed out and walked to William Allan's store, his preferred place to buy square nails and rope, despite the fact that Allan had been one of the Justices at Isaac's trial. Isaac learned that Allan had tried to have the sentence reduced, but was overruled by Jarvis and Small, so Isaac did not harbour any ill feelings toward him.

"Incredible that we received the news before the Yankees declared war," Allan said.

He had joined the York militia six months earlier after General Brock offered the elite members of society a ranked position, regardless of whether they had any military experience. William Allan, York's most important businessman, was made a Lieutenant-Colonel.

"I suppose that does give us an advantage," Isaac replied, sorting through different sizes and materials of rope he wanted to use to bundle branches and twigs together for the winter months. He did not want to reveal how he felt, that he secretly hoped that York would fall.

"I hear that we have already detached our navy and army to secure the Great Lakes. The Americans hardly have any ships, and are no match for the British Navy," Allan said excitedly.

Nodding, Isaac left the store and wandered over to Market Square where a crowd had gathered, discussing the war.

"We don't stand a chance," said one settler, while another exclaimed, "I hope we surrender before the fighting comes to York!"

"We should crush the Yankees, rub the arrogant smiles off their faces," a man yelled in a heated debate outside a tavern, while someone hollered, "Damn the Yankees!"

Within days, paranoia crept into York. Word spread that General Brock immediately had arrested and deported American citizens in Niagara who had yet to take the pledge of allegiance to the King. He also deported long time residents who were even slightly suspected of siding with the

Americans. Since the vast majority of those living in Upper Canada were formerly Americans, many people were suspect. Neighbour began suspecting neighbour.

Soon Isaac had a target on his back because of his many trips to the United States, driving livestock every winter for the last ten years. Healthy and only 44 years old, Isaac was a perfect candidate to join the militia, but had declined to do so.

"Watch out for Devins," he overheard someone say as he walked past the hitching posts near the wharf one afternoon. "He's probably a spy for the Americans. Just watch your mouth around him."

A week later, William Allan approached Isaac with a proposition when he came into the store for a new axe. He asked if Isaac would secretly monitor the traffic along the Humber, particularly on the road from Weston up to Vaughan Mills, along the old route of the Toronto Carrying Place.

"In effect, you will be a spy for the Canadians, but will appear to be someone who is sympathetic to the Americans. As the only settler living close to both the Humber River and the road, you are in the perfect position to monitor any activity approaching from the north. We hope you will use your contacts with the Mississaugas to get information for us," explained Allan.

Isaac asked to be given the colours of the York militia to wear so that he would no longer be suspected of treason every time he came to town. Allan refused. He wanted Isaac to appear to be against the British so that anyone considering a treasonous act would think he was aligned with the Americans. Allan was confident that Isaac Devins, though he was treated badly a decade earlier, was loyal to Upper Canada.

Isaac still did not see any reason to help the British, but after some deliberation, he accepted the proposal, on the condition that he would not be forced to join the York militia.

He had no intention of actually helping the British and passing on valuable information. Instead, he intended to provide false information, if he felt it necessary.

"I suppose we are now working for the Canadian government," Isaac lied to Polly that night, as they lay together after the children had gone to sleep. "My only way of staying free of the York militia is to stay put and ply them with information on any nefarious plots that may arise from the north."

Isaac did not tell Polly that he planned to undermine the British. She would not understand.

"I am truly thankful for that," said Polly, placing her arm across her husband's chest as she lay her head on his left shoulder. She did not want Isaac to run off to fight in a war and leave her alone to care for her brood. Nor did she fancy him coming home injured, an arm missing, a leg mangled, a foot crushed - or not come back at all.

She leaned over and rocked the cradle of their youngest daughter, Lucy, born only two months ago, and hoped that she would one day canoe with her father past their homestead as all the other children had done.

As she drifted to sleep, Polly's thoughts became a little more philosophical. What will become of our children should the Americans win the war, she wondered.

Isaac's thoughts turned to Simeon, wondering if he had already been sent to battle.

Chapter 17 – July 27, 1812

"Left, right, left, right, left, right ..."

Simeon marched with his head held high, clutching his musket with his left hand. His red day coat, made by his mother, Elizabeth, melded into a long line of red stomping through the forest, single-file. The white crossbelt on his chest supported the cartridge pouch and bayonet slung over his right hip. On his head he wore a black shako hat given to him by Levi, and he wore his old grey wool trousers. Simeon's uniform may have been somewhat crude, like many in the York militia, but his determination made up for it.

Under the command of Captain Duncan Cameron, the 3rd York Militia flank company raced toward Fort Detroit. For two hundred miles they trudged westward along the muddy Dundas Road with muskets, pistols, bayonets, and iron spears weighing them down in the sweltering heat of summer. The white bandana tied onto Simeon's left arm swung back and forth as they climbed up hills and valleys, waded across rivers and trampled through the mud.

A month after war was declared, General Isaac Brock received news at his headquarters in Fort George, Niagara, that the Americans had taken the village of Sandwich across the river from Fort Detroit, as the first battle in the war. He sprang into action, despite orders from the Governor General, Sir George Prevost, who cautioned Brock to maintain a defensive strategy.

Like many other top British officials, Prevost believed that the skirmish with the United States would not amount to anything, and would almost resolve itself. Knowing that control of the Great Lakes would determine who wins the war, Prevost concentrated most of the British regulars in

Montreal and Quebec. These two locations already had strong, well-built forts, and were sited to guard the entrance to the St. Lawrence, the gateway to North America. Prevost did not want them to fall into enemy hands, and was prepared to sacrifice the rest of the British territory to safely guard them.

However, Prevost's strategy left a long, unprotected border in Upper Canada. With no additional British soldiers available to fight because they were battling Napoleon in Europe, the armed forces in Upper Canada consisted mainly of volunteers in the militia and a handful of regulars. The British were counting on assistance from native clans, many of whom they had been supplying with arms for the last few years.

Prevost's plan was to maintain position, then sit back and wait for a diplomatic solution to be reached.

Major General Isaac Brock, on the other hand, did not want to wait. He saw the American capture of Sandwich as a call to action. A courageous and aggressive leader, Brock knew that Canada needed an early victory to boost morale. The more time spent acting defensively, Brock wrote in response to Prevost far away in Lower Canada, the less chance of success.

A week after hearing of the defeat at Sandwich, Brock received a communiqué from James Baby, one of Simcoe's trusted elite who had moved to Detroit, that the Americans had invaded, pillaged his home, confiscated his horses and sheep, and converted his uncle's home into a military headquarters. Energized by the easy victory, the American General of the Army of the Northwest then wrote a proclamation and posted it throughout Sandwich that encouraged all Canadians to join the Americans in their war against the tyranny of British rule:

"The army under my command has invaded your country. To peaceable inhabitants it brings neither danger or difficulty. I come to find enemies, not to make them. I come to protect, not to injure you. Raise not your arms against your brethren. ... The United States offers you peace, liberty and security. If you put up resistance, there will be war and destruction. No white man found fighting by the side of an Indian will be taken prisoner, they will be immediately killed. Choose wisely ..."

General William Hull, like many other Americans, was blindly confident that Canadians would choose democracy over being ruled by the King.

Just as Brock had feared, three hundred former Americans in Sandwich immediately sought protection from the American army. Other militias refused to take up arms, afraid that the Americans would kill them.

Brock sprung into action. He worried that if this news spread to other parts of Upper and Lower Canada, it would have a snowball effect. The majority of the people in Canada used to be American, and he wanted to ensure that no one else defected.

Without waiting for a reply from Governor General Prevost, which could take weeks, Brock sailed to Toronto for the Legislative Assembly, and asked them to invoke martial law. He was afraid that even more settlers would flee to the United States or help the Americans within Canadian territory. Knowing he did not have the full support of the Grand River First Nations, who chose to remain neutral, Brock wanted the power to stop any resistance to the defence of Canada before it escalated to a fever pitch.

"General Brock is brilliant," Simeon said to his family at the dinner table at his father's homestead after the morning drills at the garrison. "I have every confidence he can outwit the Americans."

While waiting for the Legislative Assembly to make a decision on martial law, which they were highly reluctant to do, Brock made the rounds at the garrison and chose Simeon's troop as one to accompany him to Detroit. His encouraging, uplifting words were enough to instill a profound sense of dedication to the defense of Upper Canada, and Simeon and the rest of the young men lapped up every word.

Simeon was excited to be going to battle. His flank company became known as the Grenadiers because of their size, strength and special combat training. It was a tribute to the 150-year-old British Grenadiers, the fiercest fighting unit in the British Army. Marching toward Long Point, where his troop would meet up with General Brock, he imagined being in the front of the line of fire, slaying Americans, taking prisoners and pounding the enemy with cannon fire. When they stopped for the night, the men would rile each other up and curse the Americans.

"The Yankees think they can just march in here and we will bow down? Balderdash!" jeered one volunteer.

"They think they are so powerful, let's see what happens when they see our bayonets," yelled another.

"The only white flag we will see will be American," chimed in Simeon.

Twelve days later, they met up with General Brock. Simeon could barely see the dozen horses carrying Brock and other high ranking officers until he was at the top of a hill. General Brock looked strong and fierce on his black stallion, Albert, shouting commands and marshalling the troops.

Born on the small English isle of Guernsey off the coast of Normandy in 1769, Isaac Brock was the fourth son in a family with a history in the military. He purchased a position as a lieutenant-colonel in 1797, and after service in the Caribbean, Germany and Holland, was assigned to Lower Canada in 1802.

Spending nearly a decade in Canada without any action, Brock was seeking to be transferred to Europe to fight against Napoleon when President Madison openly declared that the United States would take the Canadas. Brock quickly changed his mind and asked to stay on, exhilarated by the prospect of defeating the Americans. He received the rank of Major General in 1811, and stationed himself at Fort George in Niagara.

Immediately, he began to prepare Upper Canada for war, a year before it was declared. He reinforced the defences along the border and set up a warning system along the Niagara River from Fort Erie to Fort George. He passed legislation that formalized recruitment to the militia and drastically increased military training.

From Long Point, Simeon and the York militia travelled with Brock's ensemble in a scattered fleet of small bateaux, many of them flat boats that farmers used to transport corn and oats to market. The General did not want to alarm the Americans by the sight of large schooners full of soldiers and provoke an attack too soon. For five days and five nights they battled a ferocious storm and bitterly cold winds, rowing the small boats through three-foot, crashing waves. The rocky shoreline and two hundred foot cliffs did not offer any place to moor. They only stopped once for a few hours before the wind picked up again. The tenacity of the 3rd York Militia, who battled the extreme weather and rough conditions but with a sense of cheer and optimism, impressed the General.

At midnight, they finally reached Amherstburg and were met at the wharf by the Lincoln militia, civilians, and a clan of Shawnee who fired muskets in the General's honour. Brock quickly put an end to the celebration, reminding the warriors to save their ammunition for the enemy.

The General met Tecumseh and his warriors for the first time that night. Brock was impressed by Tecumseh's strong physique, keen intelligence, and calm demeanour. With his head shaved at the front and three long black braids at the back, Tecumseh looked fierce but at the same time wise. Brock could tell from his coppertone complexion, oval face, ornaments hanging from his straight nose and the long fringed buckskin jacket and moccasins he wore that Tecumseh was a brave warrior. He could see that Tecumseh was likeminded, and that he commanded his people with only a few words and gestures, the mark of a true leader.

"I have led many expeditions in Europe and Central America, and have defeated many enemies of the King," declared General Brock. "But now, I wish for my soldiers to take lessons from your warriors, that we may learn how to make war in these great forests."

Tecumseh paused for a moment, then stepped forward and stretched out his hand. "This is a man," he said, and the warriors cheered.

The next morning, the two men met at James Baby's home in Sandwich to devise a plan of attack, as the home was no longer in American hands.

The Yankees had retreated across the river to Fort Detroit after learning that a huge force of native warriors captured Fort Mackinac. Hull feared that the mighty warriors would travel south and slaughter them as well.

Brock looked Tecumseh in the eye and said, "I definitely am overstepping my superior's orders by being here. The Governor General cautioned against taking the offensive, but a direct attack is needed. His defensive strategy is not sound or relevant to the political situation."

Tecumseh and five hundred warriors had been fighting in the Detroit area since the American invasion but had little support or direction from the British so far. Along with chiefs from the Wyandot and other clans, Tecumseh and two dozen warriors attacked and dispersed more than two hundred American soldiers near Brownstone, Michigan. He welcomed General Brock with enthusiasm, happy to have an experienced military commander at the helm.

"Here are General Hull's letters that we confiscated from the schooner," said Thomas Talbot, handing them to Brock.

The British had seized an American schooner, the *Cuyahoga Packet*, and with it a bag of Hull's personal correspondence. Brock noted the fear in Hull's writing, the sense of uncertainty about how, and if, the Americans would continue their offensive.

Brock passed the letters to Tecumseh. "You can see that General Hull overestimates the size of our army here in Sandwich. He also is extremely wary of your warriors. The man is writing like a frightened dog with his tail between his legs." Weeks ago, Brock sent a phony letter, which the Americans intercepted, implying that there were numerous troops waiting outside Amherstburg, and the Americans believed it.

Tecumseh looked appreciatively at Brock's sturdy, towering frame as the general stood with one leg perched on a stump around the campfire, two curved pistols in holsters dangling from his waist. "Yes, we must attack, and soon," he agreed, "the Americans are now isolated and suffering. Last week, they retreated from Sandwich and crossed the river to Fort Detroit. The Americans are fearful, and we must make that fear multiply."

Although they had not stopped the Americans from taking Sandwich, Tecumseh and his warriors did cut off the supply lines which limited the American's ammunition, and left them anxious and starving. Tecumseh's success fuelled Brock's notion that the American morale was low. He also knew that mounted American troops were quickly advancing northward, closing in on them.

All eyes were on General Brock as he paced back and forth, one hand clutching his chin and the other pointed straight downward, in a stiff, military position. Brock stopped abruptly and turned to face his listeners, arms spread at his sides.

"We must attack immediately. Since their greatest fear is the Shawnee, Tecumseh should lead our attack from the north, in full view, accompanied by a British offensive from the east and south hidden by the cover of the trees. Tecumseh, your warriors will frighten the enemy and direct their attention northward while we bombard them from the south."

"We will be honoured to lead the way" replied Tecumseh, pleased that Brock was a man of action.

The two devised a plan of intimidation, to outwit the Americans. The British troops would stand twice as far apart as normal to make their numbers appear greater, and the Shawnee would attack multiple times.

Two days later, a flotilla of bateaux ferried Tecumseh and his warriors across the Detroit River under the cover of darkness. They hid in the forest until the appointed time, while the boats returned to the east side of the river so as to not arouse suspicion, and to transport the next group of soldiers and militia.

That evening, Simeon and the other privates in his troop were ordered by Captain Cameron to prepare for an attack at dawn. Since Fort Detroit lay inland half a mile, Simeon and four dozen other Grenadiers would attack on foot, without artillery, and use their bayonets in one-to-one combat when they infiltrated the Fort. The remaining troops in Captain Cameron's company would transport the 18-pounder guns and ammunition close to the south of the Fort and fire on command.

Exhilarated, Simeon could hardly sleep, envisioning the combat zone and himself taking down a horde of enemy soldiers. He acted out the drills for loading and firing the bayonet, imagining artillery booming, fire and smoke everywhere. Simeon had no fear or regret, only anticipation. He was confident in his decision to fight for Canada, to stop the American invasion.

"I think our surprise attack will confuse them and divide their forces," Simeon remarked to James Finch and Cornelius van Nostrand, two privates lying beside him in the bushes. All thoughts of Violet and his family were pushed to the side as the excitement of confronting the enemy took over.

"We just have to make sure that the Shawnee do not mistake the Redcoats for the Bluecoats," replied Finch, wryly, "or we will have a bigger battle than we thought."

"They outnumber us for sure," said Simeon, repeating information he had overheard two majors discussing, "but I am positive that we will outwit them."

"We'd better," added Finch. "My father would be happy if the Americans win, and I don't want to hear him boasting if I'm taken prisoner or sent back to York under house arrest."

At four o' clock in the morning, Simeon and the others received instructions.

"We will be marching with one militia man between two soldiers," said a commander to the volunteers. "If your lieutenant falls, take his place. If you captain falls, take his place. If your colonel falls, take his place."

Simeon boarded a crowded bateau, secretly crossed the river, and hacked his way through the forest to wait fifty yards outside the fort until morning. The square-shaped fort had parapets twenty feet high and was protected by an embankment, a dry ditch, and a double row of pickets. It could withstand a siege from the land but not from the river. The summer night was warm, and Simeon took off his redcoat and waited. General Brock had arrived and was positioned in front of the troops, waiting in silence.

Dawn broke.

Tecumseh and his warriors charged toward the fort from the north, hollering war cries, their shouts resounding through the forest and fields. With painted faces, warrior headdresses, fringed deerskin clothes, tomahawks, knives and muskets, they were a formidable, frightening force. After passing through a meadow visible to the Americans, Tecumseh directed them to sneak back through the forest and charge through the open field again and again.

"Good Lord, there must be two thousand of them!" remarked a stunned American soldier on watch monitoring the open field.

At that moment, cannons were fired from the *Hunter* and the *Queen Charlotte,* two British schooners anchored on the Detroit River. Five hundred militia and British soldiers crossed the river in bateaux, guns firing to announce their arrival. At the same time, Simeon and four hundred others marched to the fort from the southwest with General Brock in the lead, and immediately began firing. The General was an imposing figure in his scarlet coat with a double row of gold lace and buttons, cocked hat, white trousers and glistening black Hessian riding boots.

The brilliantly orchestrated attack had the Americans convinced they were surrounded by thousands of fierce Shawnee warriors and a vast army of British soldiers backed by a dozen schooners; an unbeatable force that seemed to grow and multiply. Before a single shot was fired by the Americans, a white flag of surrender was hung on the fortress walls, and the message was relayed to General Brock.

Elated, but also disappointed, Brock ordered a cease-fire. Simeon and the other soldiers stood at ease. Messengers were sent to Tecumseh, to the schooners and to the artillery to halt the attack. A few minutes later, the gates of the fortress opened and General Hull emerged carrying a white flag. The look of defeat on the aging man's face showed his fear that the 2,500 soldiers stationed at Fort Detroit would be slaughtered by the better trained and more numerous British army that had joined forces with Tecumseh and his warriors. In actuality, the nine hundred British soldiers and militia were equally inexperienced, save for their leader, General Brock.

Taking Hull prisoner, Brock ordered Captain Cameron's flank company and two hundred others to enter the fort and secure it. The American flag was lowered and replaced by the Union Jack. Simeon marched in with his bayonet ready. Hundreds of American soldiers stood with their hands behind their backs. Captain Cameron directed half of his company to lead the prisoners out of the fort, while Simeon and the other half gathered weapons and piled them according to type.

Tecumseh ordered his warriors not to scalp the surrendered Americans. The warriors joined the soldiers in looting the fort, the spoils of victory.

Simeon found an amethyst brooch in an officer's quarters and snagged it, thinking to give it to Violet. He also took four shotguns, some doubloons and an intricately carved wooden tea box.

The next morning, Brock ordered a victory parade around Fort Detroit to celebrate the easy capture and remind the Americans of their humiliating defeat. The 2,500 surrendered soldiers watched helplessly as an army less than half their size filed past. Simeon marched in line, confident in the British ability to defend the country. He wished that Violet, his father and Isaac could be there to share in his success.

"Gentlemen," began General Brock, addressing Hull and the American soldiers, "as your captors, we will treat you with the utmost respect that is inherent in the customs of the British people. We assure you of your safety and the protection of your life, property and religious freedom. You will be returned to your homes and property outside Fort Detroit, but all soldiers and officers will remain under house arrest and not be permitted to carry arms or engage in any battle."

After a rousing rendition of *Rule, Britannia!* from the military band, General Brock removed his scarlet sash and fastened it about Tecumseh as a symbol of their alliance, then handed him a pair of silver-mounted pistols. Nodding in appreciation, Tecumseh removed his arrow-patterned sash and tied it about Brock. The two men shook hands, turned and faced the troops and warriors. The British, Canadians and warriors were proud of their first victory, in a war that many predicted would be easily won by the Americans.

For Tecumseh, the victory was sweet. He led the Shawnee and other tribes triumphantly back into Michigan territory, reclaiming their lost land. Tecumseh hoped for more victories so that he could recover the lost Ohio territory and finally avenge his fallen warriors at Tippecanoe.

One week later, news of the battle at Fort Detroit reached York via courier, the thrill of victory spreading like wildfire. Just as General Brock had predicted, the victory transformed the hearts and minds of citizens, soldiers and militia, who began to believe that perhaps the King's Dominions would have a chance of defeating the Americans.

Levi Devins, whose regiment was not selected to go to Fort Detroit, remarked for all to hear, "We showed the proud, boastful Americans just what our colony is made of!"

Others excitedly remarked, "Perhaps we will gain back some land lost when the Americans announced their Independence!" A few others predicted a short end to the war. Even the naysayers applauded the victory.

Isaac read about the battle in the *Upper Canada Gazette* a week later, and marvelled that the Canadians could win with no loss of life, especially since they were so greatly outnumbered. "Simeon must not have seen much action," remarked Isaac around the kitchen table at his father's house in Weston, thinking how eager his brother had been to spring into battle.

As if he had heard his name being called, Simeon appeared in the doorway, his tall black shako hat extending to the door header, his redcoat and grey trousers dulled with grime, with a smile of contentment and joy for everyone. Violet let out a shriek, then rushed into her husband's arms, relieved to see him uninjured and looking healthy. Stretching his arms around her tiny waist, Simeon picked her up and gave her a passionate kiss in front of everyone. The public display of affection was not his style, but he was so enraptured with seeing Violet that he forgot everything else.

Abraham, Isaac, Jacob, and Levi embraced him, pounding him on the back, eager to hear his tale. Simeon excitedly recounted his adventure and continually applauded the brilliance of Brock's strategy and leadership.

"Everyone, from private to colonel, civilian to warrior, is dedicated to his service,"said Simeon, marvelling at Brock's ability to make every soldier feel important and courageous. "With General Brock at the helm, I have no doubt we will send the Americans running back south of Lake Erie, with their arms dragging on the ground."

The success at Fort Detroit elevated Isaac Brock to hero status. Editorials in the *Upper Canada Gazette* lauded him as the protector of the settlers' homes and properties, and the protector of justice and British values. The success at Amherstburg generated a sense of national pride, provoking people to vow to defend the King, the country and their homes to the death. Brock's victory had converted apathy into allegiance.

"It is almost as if General Brock should be crowned as King," Isaac said sarcastically, not caught up in the wave of patriotic sentiment that swept the country.

Simeon guffawed, amused that his brother was still not wholeheartedly supporting the British cause. "Nonsense. He is merely a courageous and brilliant leader who will defeat the American republic and their experiment in democracy. Perhaps Brock will become the adopted son of the King!"

"Or he will become a prisoner of the Americans. No matter. Whoever wins, we will still have taxes to pay, whether it is to a King or a pauper."

By the end of August, news arrived in York that General Hull had been court-martialled upon his return to Washington, for surrendering without so much as firing a single shot. He was charged with treason amid public outrage that the soldiers had just given up. The *New York Post* reported that an American soldier who had been stationed at Fort Detroit remarked, "General Hull had men enough to have this place three times, and he still gave up his post. Shame to him, shame to his country."

Shame was felt not only by the defeated Americans that summer. Paddling down the Credit River on a bright and sunny afternoon, Isaac met up with Fire Starter who looked devastated.

"My people are divided, my people are broken, my people are lost. We have defeated ourselves," he woefully declared. "The Great Spirit has abandoned us."

Isaac was alarmed. Never before had he seen him so overcome with emotion. "I sense there was a great loss," Isaac said, putting his hand on his heart to show his concern.

"I am afraid for my people, now," Fire Starter said. "One month ago, Kineubenae met with death."

The Chief of Fire Starter's otter clan of the Mississaugas, Kineubenae, had been leading the Mississaugas of the Credit for two decades. He was the Chief who reluctantly signed over the southern part of the Mississauga Tract, under great pressure from the British. By 1812, Kineubenae was nearing the end of his life. With the Americans invading the land north of the Great Lakes, he knew the Mississaugas were frightened and needed reassurance. Kineubenae wanted to inspire his clan with an example of the strength of their beliefs and traditions.

"At a meeting of the elders, Kineubenae told us that he had fasted, and that the Great Spirit had provided him with protection against arrows, tomahawks and bullets. He then took a tin cup and walked slowly away from us and turned back toward the circle. 'Fire Starter,' he said, 'when I lift the cup to my face, you must fire your rifle. The Great Spirit protects me, and I will catch the bullet in the kettle. Do not fear, no harm will come to me.'"

Isaac involuntarily raised his eyebrows, alarmed at the story he was hearing. "Kineubenae lifted the kettle to his face, and I stood up and fired. Kineubenae fell to the ground. The bullet went through his left eye. Blood was everywhere. I killed my chief."

Overcome with sorrow, Fire Starter bowed his head and shoulders, closed his eyes and clutched his hands together. "He wanted to teach us, so that we would believe in our traditions. But where was the Great Spirit?"

Isaac put an arm over his friend's shoulders. "Perhaps the Great Spirit intended for his life to end that way," he said, groping for words.

Shrugging off Isaac's arm, Fire Starter spoke with rising anger.

"No, that cannot be! The Great Spirit would protect such a valuable servant. Now, my people question the old ways, our traditions, our beliefs. I am ashamed of my people. The young ones do not come to the elders, instead they talk to the white men. Kineubenae's son does not believe in our traditions, and will spread this message. Maybe he should not be chief. Half of us want him, half do not."

They spoke long into the night, both concerned that when the Americans invaded and took over, the Mississaugas would be left with nothing. "The British are no better at keeping promises," Fire Starter said, "but at least there is a slight chance they will ensure there is a territory for us if they win the war."

Paddling back up the Humber with the light of the waxing moon, Isaac thought of all the times that the British gentry had undermined him. They bungled his land claim, rejected him, mocked him, scorned him, jailed him and tortured him. At the centre of it all, Isaac fumed, was William Jarvis, the most undeserving lout who now has a position of power in the militia. The injustice burned him.

He got out of the canoe at the limestone outcrop. Leaning back against the rock, he relaxed and watched the water glimmer in the moonlight as it made its way quietly to Lake Ontario, like waves of music playing a triumphant song. The sound of leaves rustling and the coolness on his face and hands soothed him, made him feel whole.

Isaac reflected for long into the night, and realized where his loyalty lay – with Fire Starter and the Mississaugas. If a British victory was the best outcome for the Mississaugas, Isaac decided he would support the British.

The next morning, he made his way to the wharf in York harbour, and walked over to Allan's store. He informed him that the Mississaugas could no longer be counted on as a defensive force in case of an attack on York.

"They are divided," he explained. "Some of them may fight for us, but they cannot be relied upon as a military unit for us or for the Americans," Isaac explained.

William Allan walked out from behind his desk and shook Isaac's hand, saying quietly, "Good work, Devins. This is important information that General Brock will be pleased to know."

Walking toward Market Square, Isaac tipped his hat to a few people, some of whom responded in kind, while others ignored him. Isaac chuckled to himself, amused that many people thought of him as a traitor or at least sympathetic to the Americans. No matter.

He would keep his ears open and spy for the British, now that he was dedicated to ensuring they won.

Chapter 18 – September 14, 1812

All was quiet for the next six weeks on the Niagara frontier, while the Americans and British regrouped and planned their next strategy.

Simeon, Levi, Jacob and the other volunteers in the York militia enjoyed the break, grateful to spend time with their families and friends. The York militia had to report to the garrison every morning and perform drills, but were otherwise free by midday to assist with the local war effort.

Many soldiers helped the farmers as it was threshing time. Most farmers kept only a small portion of the harvest and donated the rest to the grist mill where it was ground free of charge. Soldiers' wives then used the flour to make bread and biscuits. Keeping the army fed during wartime was a formidable challenge, the heroes of which were the farmers, millers and the women who toiled without complaint.

By the first of October, Captain Cameron's flank company of the 3rd York Militia was called to Fort George in Niagara. General Brock was convinced that the next American attack would be along the Niagara frontier. Spies who had infiltrated the American headquarters had confirmed his suspicion, and he wanted to be ready.

"One last kiss," Violet said to Simeon, placing her arms around his neck, pulling him so close that she could hardly breathe. He smiled, then bent and kissed her long and hard. Looking at each other, their eyes locked, they both felt empowered, a new energy radiating between them.

Simeon reluctantly backed away, feasting his eyes on his beautiful wife for one more moment. How did I ever get so lucky, he asked himself, to have such a lovely, kind, enchanting creature in my life? I will have to keep her beautiful face in my mind, until I return. He turned to join Levi and Jacob, who were waiting at the stable, when Violet rushed forward and whispered softly into his ear, "Simeon, I think I am with child."

"What?" he exclaimed, elated and shocked at the same time. He turned back and clutched her arms, looking deeply into her green eyes.

"Yes!" she replied, with a smile so tender he could hardly bear it.

With a whoop and a shriek, Simeon picked her up and swung her around, laughing and hollering with joy. He could not believe that he was going to be a father so soon. Simeon had always wanted to have children, perhaps because of the isolation he had known growing up in the wilderness. He had only one other child to play with, Joseph Rousseau, who lived miles away at St. John's trading post. After the Rousseaus moved to Ancaster, there were no other children within walking distance for the next decade. The closest person Simeon had to a friend was Isaac, who took him along on as many walks through the forest and trips down the river as he could.

Violet watched her husband, Levi and Jacob walk away and turn the corner down the footpath. She sighed and stared at the empty path as if in a trance, a soft smile on her lips. He is going to be a good father, she thought. Her hand automatically moved down to her lower abdomen, feeling only a slight bulge on her trim waistline. I hope he will be here at York when the baby comes.

Three weeks later, Violet was at home contentedly making yarn at the spinning wheel, a task that she had recently learned from Polly. Growing up in a privileged family, she had often seen women spinning, but had never been permitted to do so.

She was eager to learn, as she was artfully inclined and enjoyed using her hands to create things. Polly showed her how to spin and card wool, and then use the loom to create colourful patterns. How thrilling, thought Violet, who did not see spinning as a chore, but as a most enjoyable pastime.

Hearing a knock, she opened the door, smiled, and invited Isaac and Abraham in, offering them a chair at the kitchen table. She eagerly took the letter that was passed to her, instantly recognizing her husband's handwriting. She ripped it open.

My beautiful Violet, she read aloud.

"He always calls me that," she said happily, while Isaac and Abraham nodded rather uncomfortably, lines showing across their foreheads.

It is with much regret that I am writing this letter, for it means that I am not there in person to tell you the same. My flank company is stationed here at Brown's Point, a low-lying outcrop that juts out into the west bank of the Niagara River midway between Fort George and Queenston. Were it not for the War, I would much admire the view, the fast-flowing, deep blue water of the Niagara River rushing past on its journey to the mouth, with gaggles of geese and flocks of seagulls, terns and herons flying everywhere.

The view towards Queenston to the south is quite attractive, with fine homes and businesses on the flats and the lush green forest of Queenston Heights towering above. I remember Isaac taking me up there when I was quite small, and looking at the finery in the Governor's canvas tents. Hopefully I will have some time later to find the same lookout over the river that was Isaac's favourite place to sit and daydream. I remember thinking that you could see the whole world from up there.

Gazing blankly at the wooden table, Isaac smiled to himself, remembering how youth and determination had engulfed him as he sat upon that rock hundreds of feet above the mighty Niagara River, dreaming up strategies to obtain power and wealth in the new province. Twenty years ago, he had been sure that making himself indispensable to the Governor would lead to riches and fame. How naïve I was, he tutted.

To the north, I can see the enemy at Fort Niagara, but views to Fort George and Newark on our side are blocked by trees and the curvature of the river. Lewistown, on the American side, a sleepy little village, is located to the southeast. I can just see a few scattered roof tops amongst the trees. The enemy struts along the river bank directly across from us, sometimes a single soldier, and sometimes a sea of blue. I am certain they see us here, camped out at Brown's Point.

We are guarding two guns, a nine-pounder long gun and a huge 18-pounder that it takes eight of us to fire. It is quite an involved procedure, one that we practice every day. First the sergeant in command aims the wall gun. On the right side, the sponge man wipes it out with a damp fleece on a wooden staff to remove any lit remnants of the previous shot. Then the loader on the left pushes the ammunition into the muzzle while the sponge man rams it down tight. The vent man then fills the hold with finely ground gunpowder, a dangerous job because if he lets air in too soon, any remnants of fire from the previous shot would be instantly ignited, killing all of us.

After the wall gun is fired, the force pushes it backward by twenty feet, so everyone must stand clear or be killed. I imagine a lot of soldiers are lost just firing the gun, without the enemy having to lift a finger. Captain Cameron has ordered his troops to be spread out in pairs surrounding the point to make sure that the enemy cannot capture the guns. Today, I am stationed with James Finch, who lives over on the Yonge settlement, a likable fellow who I have a pint with over at Brown's tavern when not on duty.

Captain Cameron has observed signs that a major offensive is imminent. The Americans are amassing near Lewiston. We see the smoke from their campfires during the day, and the flame at night. There must be thousands of them. Tensions are high, everyone is on edge. I ran into Samuel Jarvis yesterday at Adam Brown's tavern. He was looking for a fight. Grenadiers, he sneered at us, where are your grenades? Maybe he was jealous, since his troop has no such distinction.

Like father, like son, thought Isaac. The Jarvis family has always thought they are better than everyone else, and for no justifiable reason. If Simcoe had not given William Jarvis such grand appointments, the Jarvis clan would be struggling like everyone else. Their entitlement always frustrated Isaac, who considered himself to have more common sense, wisdom and capability in his little finger than William Jarvis could ever hope to have. Maybe Upper Canada would not even be at war with the Americans, considered Isaac, if not for the handful of bumbling fools running the colony.

Cornelius van Nostrand, a private in Captain Chewitt's regiment whom I shared a trench with in Detroit, stepped in, even though Jarvis is his superior, but Jarvis just pushed him out of the way. Come on,

Grenadiers, sneered Jarvis, show us your stock. Then he looked over and singled me out of the crowd. He walked over, took out his shotgun, slammed it down on the bar, and offered me a challenge. From five paces away, whoever could get the gun first, would be the winner.

This is sheer madness, I thought, we have an enemy across the river who is going to invade at any second. Come on, Devins, he sneered, be a man, show us what you are made of. I resisted because of the sheer folly of a confrontation. It did not make any sense to go after one another when we need all our soldiers to fight the enemy. But then I thought of how he orchestrated the charivari on our wedding night, and I felt that I had to defend your honour, so I accepted. Jarvis looked as if he had downed a few pints, so I figured I would have the advantage anyway.

Violet looked up at Isaac and Abraham with fear in her eyes. She did not want to imagine any harm coming to Simeon, particularly from her old suitor, Samuel Jarvis. "Dear God, you don't suppose..." she began, but Abraham just motioned for her to keep reading.

On the count of two, Jarvis set off but I reached the bar at the same time. We struggled for the gun, pushing the other away. He started playing dirty, poking me in the eye, choking me, but I held on, not willing to be outdone by a knave. We were going at it for only a minute when Jarvis gave out, lost his strength, so I elbowed him in the chest and pushed him, turning as I did. The gun went off. The fool had left it loaded on the bar. Fortunately, no one was hit. Two captains then came into the bar while I was pointing the gun at Jarvis' chest, but the lads covered it up and we all went about our business as if nothing happened.

"The frustration of waiting for the Americans to attack must be getting to them," remarked Isaac. Abraham nodded in agreement.

The tension at camp is now so thick you could cut it with a knife. Hopefully the enemy will attack soon so we can take our aggressions out on them. I expect the next time I write will be after the battle. Hopefully we will be sent back to York soon. I can't wait to...

"Well, the rest is just a salutation," said Violet, blushing. Later, when she was alone, she read .....

I can't wait to hold you in my arms, my beautiful Violet. Have you told anyone that you are expecting yet? I remain, your loving husband, Simeon.

Reading that last sentence over and over again became a daily habit, one that Violet could not help but do to reassure herself that her husband would be safe, and would return home soon. She tried to distract herself with more spinning, hoping to make some warm clothes for the coming winter, but the solitude made her stop and think too much.

Polly dropped by and suggested she join her at a quilting bee, a popular wartime activity for women to make blankets and coats for the troops. The winter cold was as much of a threat to the soldier as a musket aimed straight at the heart.

Stitching a plain red square of linen together with a grey one, Violet sewed furiously, along with the other soldier's wives. The women who gathered every afternoon at the home of Cynthia Dennis in Weston decided at the beginning to stitch red and grey or white patches together to emulate the colour of the British uniforms. They chose to forego the intricate patterns of a typical quilt, and instead opted to speed up the time for completion by keeping the design plain and simple.

The conversation that afternoon was filled with both gay chatter and indignation. "I do not think that the Reverend actually meant it that way," explained Amy Farr, quite indignant that anyone could doubt the pastor. Reverend John Strachan of the Anglican Church lectured many parishioners on the roles that men and women should play during these difficult times. "I think he meant that women should be duty-bound to defend their country first, rather than promote their own social advancement."

Violet listened with keen interest. She had only once met the illustrious Reverend Strachan on her wedding day, just a week after his arrival in York. He quickly established himself as a man of influence, propriety and kindness. In a few short months he had become a leader in the community, with social standing equal to the top-ranking officials in the militia.

"We had better not speak about our neighbour then," chimed in Polly, drawing a laugh from all who were listening.

266

Polly attended the quilting bees against her husband's wishes, out of a strong sense of duty. Isaac did not see the necessity for the women to make quilts when they could be tending to the fields and livestock while the men were away. For the women, quilting together was more than a means of helping the war effort. It was a chance to vent their frustration at being left alone, the resentment of being forced to do their husband's chores, the fear of their men being killed, and the dread of living under the American flag.

Violet was relieved that most of the talk did not involve the war, a welcome distraction. A knock was heard at the door, and a servant opened it to usher in a soldier, dressed in full military colours.

The room fell silent, and all stitching halted. Each woman could see that the soldier was carrying a letter, which could only mean one thing. Looking nervously at their hands, at the ground, at each other, the women waited, for what seemed like an eternity.

Violet grasped Polly's hand, squeezing so tight that Polly almost cried out in pain.

Finally, the soldier lifted his arm and said, "I have a letter for Jane Collins."

A gasp was heard, followed by a cry and a sob. Violet put her arms around Jane who was sitting next to her, while others gave her a handkerchief and squeezed her shoulders. Although each woman grieved for Jane, an air of relief filled the room as the others thanked the Lord that their husbands were safe, at least for the time being.

A couple of weeks passed with no further news from Niagara. Every person seemed to be on edge, not knowing when or if the Americans had invaded. Finally, a messenger arrived on a ship with the news that Queenston had been assaulted, taken over by the Americans, then recaptured. The British had won the Battle of Queenston!

The news spread from the wharf, to the town and then to the garrison, and two days later to Weston along the Humber. Violet, Abraham and Hannah were filled with relief, although they were still uncertain of Simeon, Jacob and Levi's fate.

Ten days later, Isaac brought another letter to Violet, which she opened with a flourish and quickly began to read...

My beautiful Violet, by now you must have heard that we were triumphant and sent the Yankees home with their tails between their legs.

We were awakened as dawn broke on October 13th by the men on watch who spotted artillery being fired at Queenston from Fort Gary across the river. Flashes and streaks of orange lit the dim morning light as the deafening claps of bombs and gunfire echoed through the gorge. The thundering cracks and bangs were so much more voluminous than any of our weekly drills at the garrison. I remember thinking that perhaps you could even hear it in York.

The fleet of bateaux crossing the Niagara must have caught a strong current because most of the Yankees landed just north of Queenston at Hamilton Cove while some of them landed a little farther south. Fortunately for us, none of the bateaux landed before we heard counter fire coming from our side.

All the soldiers at Brown's Point watched helplessly as the entire battle unfolded, until about half an hour later when the wind blew the smoke from the guns our way, cutting off our view. James Finch and I walked out toward the Captains' tents, hoping to find out what to do because our guns did not have the range to do any damage from here.

We should probably stay here and defend the battery, Captain Cameron remarked, frustrated that they had not been given any instruction of what to do if Queenston was attacked. Captain Heward agreed, saying that General Brock always assumed that the Americans would attack Fort George. The Captains were still debating the decision to maintain their position when the sound of the fighting intensified considerably. A few minutes later, thirty of us were summoned to go assist the soldiers in Queenston, and the remaining troops were ordered to stay and ensure that the guns did not fall into enemy hands.

No sooner had we begun our march down the river road when we heard a horse galloping madly, and along came General Brock on his beautiful black stallion flying down the path. To Queenston! he shouted without slowing his gait, And push on the York volunteers!

Captain Cameron immediately picked up the pace and we reached the north end of Queenston in just under an hour. We were sent to the shore where a double line of soldiers were firing at the last of the Yankees still in their bateaux, struggling to land. With our extra guns added to the foray, we soon defeated them, most of them surrendering. Even the American Brigadier General, Stephen Van Rensselaer, was taken out of action, hit six times as he stepped out of his boat. What an easy victory, someone remarked, considering they outnumber us 6,000 to 2,000, but little did any of us know that the battle had just begun.

After the prisoners were marched to Fort George under guard, we were ordered to walk down the beach and look for injured soldiers who had a chance at survival. The beach was littered with bodies, some dead, others wounded, arms and legs missing, heads blown off, bowels lying on top of the belly. With no hospital and very few doctors, anyone with even a moderate injury would be left for dead.

Si-me-on, I heard someone call as I neared the end of the beach. I glanced all around, and finally saw a body splayed on the ground, one hand reaching forward, trying to grab my coat. Joseph! I exclaimed, thrilled to see my oldest friend but then immediately alarmed that he must be injured. Indeed, he had dislocated his shoulder and cracked his foot in a couple of places. I hoisted him up and hauled him to the river road.

The battle scene was horrendous, Joseph said. His father, St. John, also was fighting at the beach, but he had yet to find him. Eventually, a half-filled wagon drove by going north, so we stopped it and asked if he could transport some of the injured to Fort George. Let my father know I am well, he hollered out as the wagon drove off.

I met up with my troop north of Queenston at George Hamilton's house overlooking the river. Guns were being fired from Lewiston and Fort Gary, a couple of the cannon balls wounding our soldiers. A single 18-pounder shot tore off Andrew Kennedy's leg and ripped open Thomas Major's calf, the remainder of us running for shelter.

Boom, boom, boom, boom, boom! The guns on Queenston Heights were firing directly at us, which could only mean one thing, the Americans had made it across the river farther south and captured the escarpment. The Yankees had turned the guns on Queenston Heights away from America and aimed them toward us, and were destroying homes, businesses, streets and parks in Queenston.

We were then ordered to ascend the western side of the escarpment at Queenston Heights to assist General Brock. We found a path up the escarpment and joined Captain Williams and the 49ᵗʰ regiment partway up who were sheltered in the trees. We numbered about eighty men, compared to four hundred Americans. There we met up with a number of companies of the York militia who were regrouping to charge back up the mountain. James Finch and I ran into Cornelius van Nostrand, who told us that a sharpshooter had gunned down General Brock. He lay lifeless in the field on the west side, covered in blood, having taken six shots.

"Good Lord!" exclaimed Abraham, "We have lost our great commander, a true visionary and humanitarian. How did we possibly manage to take back Queenston without General Brock?"

Violet mimicked her father-in-law's concern, shook her head, then read on …

Apparently General Brock dismounted, climbed over a stone wall, and waved all fifty of the soldiers forward, his sword in hand, leading the charge. It was not long before he was grazed by a musket ball, then sniped down, an obvious target in his general's uniform. A young lad ran up to the General, saying, are you much hurt, Sir, to which he received no reply. During the retreat, a number of soldiers pried a dead body off of General Brock and then transported him down the hillside to Queenston, hiding his body in an unknown house.

Our company, half of the 3ʳᵈ York Militia, then accompanied Van Nostrand's unit and the other soldiers for a second time up the western flank, most of the soldiers filled with rage and vowing to avenge General Brock's death. We slowly crept through the trees, using them for cover, and reached the summit with the Yankees only one hundred yards away.

We charged the Yankees with rifles and pistols firing and bombarded them with grenades, causing them to make a fast retreat. They quickly reorganized and came back fighting, with an even greater line of fire. Captain Dennis, judging the strength of their troops, decided that we should withdraw. The smoke from the guns was so thick that we could barely see or breathe. We rounded up the prisoners and the wounded, scrambled back down the escarpment, and continued northward to the home of James Durham, abandoning Queenston at approximately 9:00 in the morning.

The Yankees quickly moved in and took over the village, plundered the fine homes, knocked down chimneys and hearths, and peppered the walls with shot. Secord's tavern and many other businesses were destroyed, as well as George Hamilton's fine home. We were astounded that the Americans did not immediately send over more troops since the Queenston landing was now open to them. We found out later that the Americans had lost the bateau carrying all the oars during the initial crossing, so they could not safely return.

"Ha ha", laughed Isaac. "A bateau has no use without the oars to row it. The Americans must have been trapped on our side. Any that could be found would be as precious as gold".

Violet nodded, recalling that it took nearly a week to carve a new pair of oars from oak or hickory.

General Roger Sheaffe, now the commander in charge, and his troop of highly trained officers arrived from Fort George, their minds set on recapturing Queenston. Even though the Americans had launched an attack on the Fort from across the river, the greater degree of artillery fire and hand-to-hand combat seemed to be coming from Queenston. General Sheaffe correctly surmised that if the British could retake Queenston, the rest of the assault would be withdrawn.

John Norton, Chief of the Grand River Mohawks, led the counter attack, approaching Queenston Heights from the south. Hiding in the forest, they sniped away at the American soldiers. Strangely, the Americans made more noise than the Mohawks, shouting and hollering at the top of their lungs, while the Mohawks calmly and with deadly precision executed them with tomahawks, pistols, rifles and knives. The warriors looked fierce, covered with war paint, and adorned in deerskin, colourful headdresses and feathers, their muscular, toned bodies ready to strike. When they got closer, they scalped the Americans.

A mass hysteria struck and many frightened soldiers retreated, deserting the American army. They snuck down the escarpment into the gorge, jumped into any boat they could find and set back toward Lewiston, many without oars, desperately paddling with their hands, praying that the river currents would bring them safely across.

General Sheaffe then decided to mimic the advance of the Mohawks, and ordered seven hundred militia, including myself, James Finch and Cornelius Van Nostrand, to travel undercover through the woods to the south while the British army would attack from the west. It was mid-afternoon, 3:00 precisely, when we finally set out. Captain Cameron ordered us to advance, stop and fire, then march. Before long, a sea of thick white smoke from the gunfire blew in, and we were unable to see anything more than ten feet away.

A structured sort of chaos then ensued, as all of us started firing at once - the Mohawks, the southern troops and the western companies — with none of us able to see or hear orders. We all then pushed for the summit simultaneously, and handily captured it after a brief resistance from the Americans.

Surrounded and frightened, the Americans stood a few moments, then fled by the hundreds down the escarpment. With the river far below and nowhere to retreat to, they lined the edge of the sheer cliff. Many were pushed off the edge by the mob of soldiers, and were ripped to pieces as they crashed through the jagged rocks and trees. Others just dove right into the Niagara River, attempting to swim to safety. We fired at their heads bobbing in the river, picking off as many as we could.

Soon after, Captain Cameron ordered us to cease fire after a white flag was waved.

After the surrender, the British rounded up 436 regulars and 489 militias. Dead bodies were everywhere, all through the town and Queenston Heights, some stripped of clothing and supplies and others with their skulls split open by the Mohawks' scalping knives and tomahawks. The walking wounded were sent back across the river, followed by the American soldiers who were honour-bound not to take up arms until formally exchanged for British prisoners. We rounded up a considerable number of American rifles, muskets and shotguns, and brought them back to our posts.

Victory is sweet, tastes like honey, remarked James Finch as we strolled leisurely back to Brown's Point. We all gathered outside of the tavern, grateful that the Americans had not reached there and made off with the whiskey and the rum. He told me he wants to open a hotel south of the Yonge Street settlement. Hopefully we can go for a visit after the War.

Our victory cheers and celebrations were not as joyful as they could have been. I am truly saddened that we have lost such a brave, strong, noble General. Although the war claimed a great leader, his replacement proved to be equally adept at the tactics and strategies of warfare. I was quite impressed by General Sheaffe, and look forward to fighting under his command at the next battle.

We are now stationed here at Brown's Point for an indefinite period of time, and are on guard in case the Americans launch another attack. I hope Captain Cameron's company is ordered back to York soon. Though the taste of victory may be sweet, nothing compares to you, my beautiful Violet. I cannot wait until I hold you in my arms again, and hear your soft, uplifting voice...

Again, Violet chose to keep the remaining words to herself.

Isaac whistled, nodded his head, and remarked, "Our little Simeon was right in the thick of it, and came out unscathed. I thank the Lord and the Great Spirit for that," he added and Abraham agreed.

A few weeks later, many members of the York militia returned, but not Simeon. Violet's patience began to wear thin. She desperately wanted to see her husband, to share with him the joy of the coming baby, to talk with him, to comfort him. Not even the lively conversation at the ladies' quilting bees distracted her. When will I see him again? she asked herself.

Despondent, she went to their special meeting place, a circle of birch trees just outside of St. James church where Simeon had proposed, just to feel close to him.

The leaves had all fallen from the trees by then, the bare twigs merely silhouettes of the summer's glory. Violet knelt in a pile of crimson, gold, and orange leaves, some of them starting to turn brown. She usually enjoyed the fall, the cool winds and radiant colours a marked change from the heat of summer, but this year she was blind to its beauty. Tired and weak, she lay down, not caring who saw her.

Joseph Rousseau found her there. He walked over and sat down, taking her hand. Alarmed, Violet sprang up, and saw a look of pain on his face that she did not want to see.

"No," she said softly, looking at him to confirm or deny her suspicion. Joseph could only glance back, helplessly, grimacing, almost looking guilty.

"No," she said again, a little more loudly, pulling completely away from him.

Violet shook her head and said slowly, "He made it through the battle." She was trying to convince Joseph and herself, that it could not be so. "I have the letter. We have not heard of any other assaults since Queenston."

Clearing his throat, Joseph reached into his pocket and pulled out the curved knife with the initials S.D. and the blue feather that he had given Simeon so long ago. Handing it to Violet, he said softly, "Simeon would want you to have this ....."

"No," whispered Polly, shocked to hear her husband referred to in the past tense. "No," she said with a trifle more conviction. She paused, feeling strangely numb while the seconds dragged on for minutes. Finally, the realization came over her.

"NO-O-O-O!" she screamed as loud as she could.

Joseph extended his arms to comfort her, but Violet beat him off, pounding his chest with her fists. Her body convulsed and she began to weep, gently at first, then completely. As if in a trance, she screamed out "No!" over and over and over, her body writhing.

Joseph leaned forward and pulled her close, giving her a shoulder to cry on. She wept for what seemed like an eternity, unable to talk, think, or listen. All she felt was pain, and an immeasurable loss.

Guiding her to a wagon and lifting her to the seat, Joseph kept one arm around Violet's shoulders so that she wouldn't fall off. At the homestead, she broke down again as she realized that Simeon would not ever walk through that door again. She could not bear to go inside yet, so they remained in the wagon for a long time, side by side, joined in immense sorrow.

"Good day," greeted Isaac, who had noticed them seated in the wagon from the rocker on his father's porch. He was curious why the two did not dismount from the wagon and go into the house or garden. Observing their raw emotions, he instantly knew. He blankly said, "Simeon," as if to confirm it to himself.

"He fell ill a few weeks after the battle," said Joseph. "An illness spread throughout the camps, similar to the ague but stronger. Some of the soldiers recovered, others did not."

Apart from the enemy, disease was the number one killer in the war, with few doctors or other healers around to offer a cure.

"Simeon fought for his life, a valiant effort, but did not make it. Neither did my father."

"Good God, man!" exclaimed Isaac, shocked and outraged by the loss of his brother and his old friend.

"How many more?" he asked rhetorically, a tear welling at the corner of his eye, his voice cracking on the last word. He turned away to fetch Polly and Elizabeth who would know what to do for Violet.

That evening, Isaac's outrage intensified. Not only would an American victory end any possibility of Fire Starter and his clan securing a separate Indian territory, but the war had now destroyed his family. The outrage turned to hatred, of the Americans, the gentry, the President, the King and nearly every other thing that threatened his existence.

The next morning, he rode to York and requested an audience with William Allan, who had just returned to his store on the wharf from the garrison.

"I want to join the militia," Isaac said, "we must stop the Yankees before they kill us all." He thought of his children at home in their cabin on the Humber. He needed to protect them and the land that they would one day inherit.

Allan looked up at Isaac with curiosity, wondering what had changed. He rose from his desk in the office at the back of his store, walked around and leaned against it as if he wanted to conspire with Isaac. "Well, now, I think we have plenty of men to defend York," he replied, "but few who can get us the information that we need to win. Wars are not won by the size of an army. Wars are won by information. If we know what the enemy will do before they do it, we will win the war."

"But I want to fight the enemy, to protect our homes, to kill the Yankees," insisted Isaac, uncharacteristically showing his anger and frustration.

"No, Devins, we need you to keep an ear to the ground. You are far more valuable to us as an informant than just another soldier in the field."

Frustrated, Isaac wandered onto the wharf, kicking stones that got in his way, staring across the bay to the peninsula. Maybe if I tell him that the Mississaugas no longer confide in me, he will let me fight, he thought. But perhaps Allan is correct. I would be just another bloke with a musket.

A cold wind blew in from the bay, a chill reminder of the coming winter. He turned back toward the shoreline, resigned to remain as a spy in York.

As he climbed onto the east side of the wharf, Isaac noticed a thin skeleton of a warship under construction at the dock. Governor General Prevost recently ordered that a new frigate, the *Sir Isaac Brock,* be constructed. Prevost considered York to be a secure location and well guarded against a surprise invasion, particularly in the winter when the harbour was frozen. Isaac stopped to admire the size of the ship under construction, amazed that so few workers could ever complete a ship of that size.

"Devins, can you lend us a hand?" someone shouted.

Isaac walked over and grabbed the end of a plank the men were hoisting onto an overhead platform, and helped them push it up. Half an hour later, he was still helping with various tasks, enjoying the comradeship.

"You know that this is paid work," one of the hands offered. "You should get on the payroll, Devins."

The British military was the mainstay of the economy of York, being the principal purchaser of goods and hiring people for various jobs. Now that much of the labour force was either training or fighting in the War, there was a severe lack of workers for many essential tasks.

"Perhaps, but this ship will be a tad larger than the canoes that I am used to building," Isaac declared, his dry humour drawing cackles from the men.

Though he belittled the notion, Isaac was actually intrigued by the thought of joining the crew and being able to learn the intricacies of building a 30-gun fighting ship. He recalled the day he had helped Captain Bouchette and the crew dislodge the *Mississaga* from being stranded at the entrance to the harbour, and what a thrill it had been to explore the mighty ship and help Bouchette crank the wheel. Before long, a supervisor came and offered Isaac a job, observing his carpentry skills as he handily sawed a curved section of a plank.

For the next eight months, Isaac dedicated four days a week to the *Sir Isaac Brock,* and returned to his family on his days off. There was no news to report on the activities of the Mississaugas. Instead, Isaac was grateful to be doing an important task in the war effort, one that could make a difference to the outcome. If Upper Canada could produce another fighting ship before the Americans, it could mean domination of the Great Lakes. Most wars, including Britain's war with Napoleon, were determined not on land but by the might of the navy. Control of the waterways in the Canadas meant control of the supply of food, weapons, ammunition, raw materials and machinery, and could alter the course of the war.

All winter, the supervisor pressed the construction crew to work faster, longer, harder. "We need to get her done before winter ends," he explained. "As soon as the ice breaks up, the Yankees will come barging in. We have to finish her, and sail her on to Kingston before the Americans can take her."

There was little doubt in anyone's mind that the Americans would launch an attack in the spring. It was the topic of conversation at every dinner table, in every tavern, on every street corner. Isaac discussed the pending attack with his father almost every evening at dinner, before returning to Simeon's house to sleep.

Isaac had moved there after Violet left so that he could be closer to the wharf, and would return to his own homestead on the weekends. All the Devins encouraged Violet to stay on in Weston, but after she lost the baby she was so distraught that she returned to her family. Her father welcomed her with open arms, happy that his girl was home again, with little thought given to his departed son-in-law. Simeon's death from illness did not even qualify him as a hero, Johnson sniffed.

The first of April passed, but the late spring did not bring about the melting of the ice. Tension mounted, as all citizens tried to prepare for a battle, but there was nothing to do except for stockpiling food, water, guns and ammunition. Many took comfort in the fact that York was protected by the garrison and the peninsula so that the enemy could not assault the town.

Isaac worked furiously on the *Sir Isaac Brock*, the task obliterating thoughts of all else. It was almost as if he and the shipbuilding crew were deep inside a cocoon, working madly away, oblivious to all else. Unbeknownst to the citizens in York, they would be besieged by the might of the American military in less than two weeks time.

"Come on, fellows," Isaac cheered aloud to his co-workers as they began the final work on the port side, "we must finish before we are attacked. Then we can get us some Yankees!"

Chapter 19 – April 26, 1813

"Captain, you better take a look at this!" burst out the young sergeant as he handed the looking glass to his commander with a shaking hand. "There must be a dozen of them headed this way!"

Standing on the high bluffs east of the Don River in York, Captain Duncan Cameron held the dark brown looking glass in both hands to steady it in the early light of the morning. Peering out across Lake Ontario, he could just make out a flotilla of schooners approaching from the southeast. There was no reason to suspect that they belonged to the British, they could only be American.

"Aye, likely a few more," affirmed the Captain, who had been stationed with a portion of the 3rd York Militia at the bluffs since the first of April, specifically to watch for an invasion.

"Quick, flag the signal and sound the guns at once!" he commanded.

It was midday, just one week after the ice had broken away from the Toronto harbour allowing full access by enemy ships. Over the winter, the Americans had considered attacking Montreal or Kingston in order to capture the St. Lawrence River and close Upper Canada off from the rest of the British Empire. But an easy victory at York was too tempting.

With just an isolated village and a garrison with a make-shift shipping yard, York did not offer much of a military advantage if taken. However, the Americans desperately needed a victory. Most other attempts since the outbreak of the war had ended in failure. The President's political opponents in the border states were ridiculing the war effort, calling it Madison's war.

"If we do not obtain a victory in our next campaign, our war effort will collapse," Major-General Henry Dearborn passionately related to his superiors in Washington. "We need a victory to ensure that the States of New England do not turn against us."

The new U. S. Secretary of War, John Armstrong, sat back in his chair, nervously tapping the table, with a stern look on his chiselled face. He had just taken over from William Eustis, who famously declared, "We can take the Canadas without soldiers. We have only to send officers into the province and the people ... will rally round our standard." Armstrong did not want to be fired like Eustis, such a disgrace.

"A victory at York will be all the incentive we need," continued Dearborn. "It is an easy target and our sources say that the British have only a few hundred troops stationed there."

The impact that news of a victory would have on the mindset of the American people was considered to be so critical that the Americans published an announcement of a victory at York long before they even set sail. Dearborn hoped to influence the outcome of the election, and did so successfully since a majority of Republicans were elected that spring, before the Battle of York was even fought.

"Now we have to make good on our promise," said Armstrong.

"We must capture their ships at the wharf, then we will have more stationed on Lake Ontario," added Dearborn who wanted to close the entrance to the St. Lawrence and cut off supplies that the British received from overseas. Seizing the *Sir Isaac Brock* and the *Prince Regent* from York could put control of the Great Lakes into American hands.

Upon hearing the signal from the bluffs, the citizens of York, soldiers, militia and Mississaugas were warned that the Americans were approaching. Everyone scurried about under General Sheaffe's command, who happened to be in York on other business. Anticipation and excitement filled the air. Previous victories had lifted the spirits of the Canadians, and they were quite assured that they would win again, not yet aware of how vastly outnumbered they were.

Isaac awoke abruptly, the sound of distant cannon fire stirring him. The cool spring air was warm inside the wigwam heated by the coals from last night's fire. He sat up quickly and saw that Fire Starter was also alerted. They heard another volley of cannon shots and then silence. Looking each other in the eye, they both knew that the Americans were coming.

Fire Starter and his family had just returned from the northern migration and set up their wigwams near the marsh at the mouth of the Don River to take advantage of the spring brook trout run. That winter, only a small group of Mississaugas had left for the northern hunting grounds, with the majority opting to remain on the Credit to assist in the war.

They dashed off toward the town after downing mouthfuls of sausage and cornbread, paddling hard in their birchbark canoes. At the wharf, they encountered a chaotic scene of civilians, militia and soldiers all darting in different directions amid cries of panic, aggression, elation and confidence. Isaac spotted William Allan standing on a chair just outside his store, shouting out orders.

Making their way to the front, they heard that General Sheaffe had ordered all troops to be divided into east and west defensive units until they knew exactly where the Americans would land. Fort York in the west was already occupied by British soldiers, militia and fifty or so Mississaugas. The eastern blockhouse and Market Square were likewise guarded.

Families were sent northward along Yonge Street or east along the Danforth Road and told to camp far enough away to avoid gunfire. The more well-to-do members of the aristocracy either went to the officer's quarters in the garrison or they hired a bateau to take them westward, trying to outrun the advancing American ships.

"I repeat, all members of the 1st York Militia report to the garrison. All members of the 2nd and 3rd York Militia, report to the blockhouse. Devins, and all of you standing over there, report to the east."

Isaac, Fire Starter and the surrounding crowd tromped along at a reckless pace, almost tripping over one another. The thrill of being under attack, of defending one's territory, was infectious, since there was still no visible sign of the enemy and no real indication of battle.

When they stopped and dispersed, Fire Starter whispered to Isaac, "I must go warn my family to move inland so that they won't be seen," and slipped away without notice.

Isaac was assigned to guard the blockhouse along with a dozen other civilians and sixty members of the militia. He received a few looks of disdain for not having a uniform, but the majority appreciated any citizen who had a gun and was willing to fight.

"Ha ha, Devins, good to see you here," chimed in George Playter, Isaac's former compatriot from the first Town Meeting when he was elected constable. "Though it is strange to see you this far east of the Humber," he chided. Playter wore the uniform of an officer, an appointment he had acquired not long after arriving in Upper Canada.

"And you this far west of the Don," retorted Isaac with a half smile, referring to Playter's homestead near Castle Frank.

They soon got into a lively debate on where the Americans were likely to land, how many there would be, and what types of artillery they would bring. After a glass of whiskey, Playter revealed a secret to anyone who would listen. That morning, he had been entrusted with a set of critical government documents, including the Town Records and the Archives of the Province of Upper Canada, and instructed to hide them at his property which was well removed from the townsite. The Magistrate did not want them to fall into enemy hands.

"I hid them in the butter churn, I did," declared Playter with a cocksure smile on his broad face. "Then my wife hid the churn in the rose garden." The Playter homestead had become well known for its beautiful rose gardens, prompting the family to later name it Rosedale.

"Surely they won't think to look there," agreed Isaac.

Boredom spread throughout the ranks after sunset when everyone realized that the Americans would not be attacking until the following morning. Isaac made a bed for himself out of oak leaves and pine needles, alongside many of the militia who did not have a home in town. All beds in the blockhouse were filled with soldiers and militia of higher rank. Isaac reassured himself that no one in his family would venture away from their homestead along the Humber. His family would be safe.

Ding-dong! Ding-Dong!

The church bell at St. James rang out at five in the morning, alerting the town that the Americans were coming. A strong westward wind raged across Lake Ontario that morning, indicative of the battle about to unfold. Captain Cameron kept a watchful eye on the American squadron as fourteen warships sailed past the bluffs and approached the peninsula. He dispatched a messenger to the garrison to report that there had been no landing in the east, and sent a signal by flags that the enemy was approaching.

Guards and soldiers stationed at the lighthouse watched the fleet approaching. As the flotilla passed by the tip of the peninsula, they prepared to engage in combat. Surprisingly, no attempt was made to turn into the Toronto Bay. Instead, the ships sailed on, the relentless wind forcing them westward. The Americans were too shrewd after all to pass within firing range of the garrison that guarded the harbour, or perhaps too fearful. A landing far west of the garrison proved to be a better option for them.

"Dear Lord, it is the whole Yankee fleet!" shouted several citizens as the sails came into view beyond the harbour. To a trained eye, there were only two decent sized fighting ships and the rest were refitted cargo schooners. But the sheer number of ships sailing together was more than had ever been seen in York before.

Gazing through a looking glass at the garrison, General Sheaffe watched the Americans sail past and concluded that the enemy would land at the old French fort since it was still partially cleared, an obvious choice. He immediately dispatched one-third of his men to join forces with the Mississaugas and the Glengarry Light Infantry whom he had already sent to thwart the landing attempt. Sheaffe believed that the only advantage they could seize would be at the point of landing where the Canadians might outnumber the Americans as they rowed in.

The race was on to see who would arrive at the landing site first. The Mississaugas, in the lead, ran rapidly along the Lakeshore Road but were soon fired on by cannons from the American ships sailing alongside them.

"Hurry, use the trees for cover," Fire Starter advised his brothers as they retreated into the dense foliage, considerably slowing their progress. Fire Starter watched helplessly as two men were struck by hot shot.

"No, save your weapons for when we meet them face to face," he advised some of the younger, less experienced warriors who fired at the ships with their muskets. He wanted to ensure that no ammunition was wasted. As one of the few Mississaugas who had a good command of English, Fire Starter acted as an interpreter for Major James Givens, whom Sheaffe assigned to lead the Mississaugas.

The sound of cannon fire echoed down the lake to the eastern blockhouse where Isaac was standing rigidly, his chest and shoulders tense, almost at attention, with an acute sense of awareness that made every detail seem painfully vivid. He did not consider himself high-strung or easily flustered, but a calf muscle in his left leg had tensed up nearly a half dozen times this morning, something that had never happened before.

Isaac gripped his shotgun harder than usual, working out scenarios if the enemy attacked from the east, west or south. He wondered where Jacob and Levi, privates in the militia, had been stationed. He had not spoken with his brothers in nearly two weeks.

Finally, word came from George Playter and his son, Eli, that the Americans had not landed in the east.

"The only access they would have to the town would be across the old rickety bridge spanning the Don River," explained George Playter, "so they must have thought better of it."

"Then there is no longer a need to guard the eastern blockhouse," Isaac replied, "and no reason for us to remain here."

James Finch, who had served with Simeon at Queenston Heights, looked around and then whispered to Isaac, "I hear that we are to join General Sheaffe at the garrison."

Isaac had spent a good part of the previous night in conversation with Finch, who told him the details of Simeon's final days, dying of illness in the field. Isaac felt new anger rising in his chest. *My brother's life was cut too short,* he seethed, *and I will not rest until someone pays.*

Isaac's resolve to avenge Simeon's death heightened as the morning wore on. Images of his family living as peasants in Toronto under an American landlord filled his mind. He imagined his children working the fields alongside African slaves, and his land taken away from him by the Americans. *Who knows what would become of Fire Starter and his people,* thought Isaac, certain that the Americans would wipe out any trace of their homeland. His resolve to fight intensified with each passing minute. More than anything, he wanted to protect his home in the wilderness on the Humber, his solace, his solitude, his refuge.

Finally, word came that they were to march under the command of Lieutenant-Colonel William Chewitt to the garrison. They marched through the townsite while the fife and drums belted out patriotic songs that Isaac did not know. Just beyond the wharf, they stopped and waited under the cover of the forest, for what seemed like an eternity, everyone silent, listening for the enemy. The cannon fire became louder, more intense, and soon they could see some of the American ships tacking toward them from the west, still far off.

"They must have landed successfully," conjectured Isaac, "or else they would not be headed this way."

The Americans had reached the landing site west of Fort Rouillé before the Mississaugas. Fire Starter advised the warriors to stay behind the trees. "That way, we can scalp them with our tomahawks and charge them with our bayonets when they walk by." The Mississaugas were better known for fighting in the forest than in an open field with the white men's weapons.

Fire Starter glanced nervously along the shoreline toward the garrison, wondering why there were no British soldiers or militia to back them up. *I don't like this,* he thought, but put on a brave face. As the first line of Americans moved eastward, the Mississaugas fired a hail of bullets when they came within short range. Then they charged out of the forest with tomahawks, slaughtering a number of surprised Americans.

But the band of fifty warriors was no match for the 1,600 enemy troops. Fire Starter counted eight of his brothers already slain, one of them with his head flattened onto a boulder by a cannon ball. With no sign of the British army, Givens told Fire Starter to order all warriors to retreat.

The British Glengarries finally arrived high above the beach after being lost in the woods, too late to help the warriors. They opened fire as the last of the Americans were scrambling up the steep gravelly slopes. The Americans were taken aback, but only for a moment, then continued their ascent.

The Glengarries withdrew as they realized they were vastly outnumbered, while the Americans continued their organized landing, taking a full two hours to scramble up the steep slope. Before long, a shrill song was piped by the American fifes, to invigorate the troops for battle:

Yankee Doodle went to town,

Riding on a pony,

He stuck a feather in his hat

And called it macaroni

Although the song was originally a parody to ridicule British soldiers in the Seven Years War, the Americans had since added more lyrics and changed it into a patriotic ditty, one that they were proud of. The band continued to play as the Americans marched eastward along the Lakeshore Road toward the western battery and the garrison.

Hidden in the forest on the other side of the garrison, Isaac and the militia were frustrated beyond belief and anxious to join in the battle.

"Why is Chewitt keeping us here?" asked one of the privates, throwing his hands down to his sides, fists clenched.

"We should just march ourselves, there's no use standing here," said Finch, equally incensed. He was hoping to again prove his father wrong, and show that Canada would win the war.

"I cannot stand around one minute longer," said another with disgust. "Come on, let's go!"

Waving his arms and shouting, the young private almost started a riot as half of the militia wanted to join him, and the other half wanted to stay and follow orders. Isaac held back. Although he was now as motivated to fight as the next man, he also did not want to interfere with the British military strategy. What Isaac did not know was that at this point the British did not have a strategy.

When they arrived at the garrison, pandemonium was everywhere. General Sheaffe was nowhere to be found, and other officers were shouting out conflicting orders without consulting one another. The Americans, led by Brigadier-General Zebulon Montgomery Pike, had advanced close to the western battery. Cannon fire from the American ships hammered it, blasting holes through the stone walls and wooden palisades.

Isaac leaned over to George Playter and said, "Come on, let's make our way to the line of fire," and nodded in the direction of the western battery. Several others including James Finch joined in and a dozen or so crept away toward the fighting.

Boom! The breathtaking thump of a nearby explosion ripped the air. Clouds of smoke and dust shot up into the air along with pieces of stone and wood.

"What the devil could that be?" gasped Finch as the mountainous flame died to a flicker.

When they arrived at the western battery they encountered a tangle of bodies around an 18-pounder that had been launched off its mounting. Alexander Wood, a merchant in town, stood dazed and bleeding after being catapulted into the sky and landing on top of three men, two of them with stumps of gore where arms and legs had been.

"Someone must have jostled the gunner carrying the portfire and ignited the gunpowder before it was loaded properly," he explained. "I have never heard such a blast."

"And we have lost one of our weapons," exclaimed Playter, agitated that their meagre artillery was further depleted. The Canadians' biggest weakness was a lack of firepower. While the Americans had eighty-six cannons on the ships and eight mobile guns, the Canadians had only nine guns in total, two of them mobile.

Isaac, Finch and their companions cleared the dead and wounded away from the other 18-pounder to resume their defence against the relentless barrage from the American ships. Moments later, the first line of American soldiers appeared, poised to attack the western battery. Isaac helped turn the 18-pounder away from the schooners and toward the advancing Americans.

The British tried in vain to ward off the American fire, but the might of their enemy's artillery and navy was overpowering. In desperation, a small, portable 12- pounder was mounted on the carcass of the destroyed wall gun to fortify the defence. However, it was placed too high up and sent balls whistling over the heads of the advancing Americans, completely ineffective.

Isaac lined up beside Finch at the north end of the battery, drew his musket, rested it on the stone wall, and crouched for cover. He spotted a few Americans out in the open, aimed, and fired but to no avail. Go home, Yankees, go home, he muttered as he fumbled in his ammunition pouch.

Before Isaac could reload, a shot bounced off the rampart to his left, grazing Finch, who yelped and clutched his left shoulder. Isaac ran over and saw the young man's hand covered in blood, his face contorted in pain. Without thinking, Isaac removed his shirt, ripped it into strips and tied it around the wound, hoping to stem the flow of blood. Finch nodded his thanks, still grunting in pain, and indicated to Isaac to take his gun.

Lining up two shotguns along the ramparts, Isaac waited patiently until more Americans advanced. Reminds me of duck hunting, he observed nonchalantly, except that I don't dislike the ducks. Anger and resentment burned inside of him. Simeon would not be dead if the Americans had not declared war, and Fire Starter's way of life would not be threatened.

A Bluecoat suddenly came within view. Isaac aimed, fired, and saw the man fall slowly forward, like a tree toppling in the forest, the back of his head blown out. Isaac let out a war cry from the gut so loud and so strong that it reverberated throughout the pines, and shot out across the water. Euphoria, elation, guilt, raced through Isaac's mind, bouncing off one another, fighting for dominance. He had never killed a man before, and it felt eerily gratifying, like a forbidden pleasure, but at the same time utterly wrong and indecent.

A shot careened off the stone wall a yard away, and he ducked for cover.

That almost got me, he exclaimed to himself. The fear of his own mortality engulfed him and heightened his determination to kill the enemy. The only law out here is kill or be killed, he told himself, and I do not intend to die. He peered back over the top of the wall, aimed again, and shot another Bluecoat in the chest, blood spurting everywhere. Got him, he whispered, feeling a rush of satisfaction spread.

The battle raged on for another half-hour while the Americans continued to arrive in droves. Isaac and a dozen others kept taking shots and ducking behind the crumbled walls, successful in most of their attempts to wound or kill. For Isaac, the euphoria had worn off, replaced by a more subtle feeling of satisfaction, and thankfulness that he was still alive.

A messenger arrived instructing all troops to immediately withdraw to the garrison. After another volley of fire, the Canadians rushed eastward to the fort, leaving the Americans to take over the shattered battery. Isaac put an arm around Finch's waist and pulled him along to safety.

On their way there, they met Fire Starter who walked briskly toward them to join his brothers on the Humber.

"General Sheaffe is retreating to Kingston, and York is to surrender to the Yankees," he said. "The General does not want his officers to become prisoners of war."

Fire Starter followed the path to the Humber. Three privates came up and blurted out, "Stay clear of the Grand Magazine, it will soon be blown to smithereens." The British intended to destroy it so that the ammunition would not fall into enemy hands.

"Such a shame," said Isaac, shaking his head, imagining the cost of replacing such a large supply of powder and shot.

"Yes, we should not give it up so easily," agreed Playter, a plan forming in his mind. Moments later, he asked Isaac and a couple others to follow him to the Grand Magazine, where they encountered a Sergeant Marshall whom Sheaffe had sent to do the deed.

"Can you just hold off until we load some of this?" Playter asked.

Isaac helped Playter shovel the gunpowder and soot into two boats that Playter had found, then they rowed eastward, hugging the shoreline. There was nothing left for the British to do but surrender, so Isaac was happy to do something to lessen the spoils of victory.

Meanwhile, the Americans advanced and gathered just west of the Grand Magazine at Government House battery. General Pike saw the Union Jack still flying at the garrison across the creek, so he decided that they should wait until they see a white flag of surrender before occupying the fort.

Playter, Isaac and two others rowed away with the hidden ammunition just before the Americans arrived.

BOOOOOOOMMM!

A thunderous, ear-splitting clap exploded through the town of York as the Grand Magazine was blown into a thousand pieces. Isaac saw a colossal cloud, littered with stones, dirt, timber and bodies, burst into the air, then widen and spread out like a gigantic mushroom, the explosion shaking the ground like an earthquake.

Stones and logs from the walls of the Grand Magazine flew through the air and pelted down on the unsuspecting Americans, as if the sky was raining cannon balls. The soldiers had no time and no place to escape. Cries of pain from two hundred and fifty soldiers echoed in unearthly, horrifying screams of human suffering, as bodies were smashed to the ground by falling rock and timber. Isaac involuntarily shuddered, transfixed by the death scene.

Bodies were strewn everywhere, body upon body, stacked like a tray of salmon going to market. He later learned that General Pike was among the wounded and was taken to the *Madison* where he passed away. Most others died slowly in the battlefield, their wails and cries resonating throughout the town. Although the six-hour assault at York was not one of the longest battles in the War of 1812, with three hundred and twenty dead, it was one of the bloodiest.

Isaac sat still in the rowboat, horrified by the destruction and carnage, until Playter cried out, "The Yankees are after us!".

Two rowboats raced toward them with Bluecoats at the oars. The four men rowed away at breakneck speed to keep out of firing range. Any shot that hit the boatload of gunpowder would blow them to bits. They hurried past the town centre which almost looked like a ghost town. Most of the citizens, soldiers and militia were barricaded in their homes or scattered in the woods. No one was there to shoot the Americans on their tail.

They hustled past the *Sir Isaac Brock* moored in the shipyard, only a week away from completion. All our hard work, now to go to the Yankees? grumbled Isaac, appalled that his labour would now help the enemy.

"There's Eli!" shouted George Playter, surprised to see his son at the wharf.

As they got closer, Isaac saw Eli and some of his co-workers on the wharf with torches in hand setting the ship ablaze. Ten-foot flames shot up and through the portholes which Isaac had just finished smoothing the other day. Eli and the others stepped back from the fire as the heat intensified into a furious blaze. The stern of the ship was still intact and waiting to be completed while the bow was a mass of flames and blackened timber, its charred ribs showing like a skeleton.

"At least the Americans will not get it," said Isaac, hiding his exasperation at seeing months of hard work go up in flames, "and the *Prince Regent* left port three days ago." Damn the Yankees, he swore under his breath.

The men rowed furiously and finally reached the marsh at the mouth of the Don River.

Pop, pop!

Their stalkers had drawn closer and were shooting wildly, desperate to stop them before they slipped away. Isaac and Playter steered the rowboats through the maze of lily pads, logs and reeds, darting in and out of sight.

They easily gained some distance thanks to their superior navigational skills and familiarity with the marshland.

Isaac got out near the foot of the Don River, and wished them a safe journey.

"We'll bury it near my property," Playter said, "not too close to the documents. We don't want to arouse suspicion. Then we'll dig it up and fire it back at them, next time they come around."

He and the other men pushed off and rowed rapidly upriver hoping the Americans had given up the chase.

Isaac walked back to town and then along the Lakeshore trail in search of his canoe. He did not want the Yankees to take it, burn it or sink it. The roar of the cannons and artillery were silent now. He could hear the crunch of his footsteps along the trail and the wind rustling through the pines. If I didn't know better, I would never suspect that a battle scene lay before me, he thought. He felt strangely aware, yet numb at the same time.

He found his birchbark canoe near the wharf, noticing that Fire Starter's was still there. Laying his gun down, he grabbed his paddle and set off toward the Humber.

Paddling out into the Toronto Bay, he saw a bunch of Redcoats being corralled and led at gunpoint by the Americans throughout the town. Isaac did not have to surrender since he was not a soldier, nor did he have to abide by the soldier's code. He felt free to go on his own.

Strange that you would never suspect the carnage on the hill, Isaac thought, as he canoed by the remains of the Grand Magazine.

Hugging the shoreline, he rounded a rocky corner, and brought the canoe to an abrupt stop. He could not believe his eyes. There in a clearing on the shore, out of view of everyone except for Isaac, were two Americans with rifles drawn and pointed at a line of British soldiers standing shoulder to shoulder. The Americans were taunting them, hoping to stir up a fight.

"What's the matter, cat got your tongue?" one sneered.

The twelve soldiers did not move a muscle or say a word. They knew what the Americans were trying to do. If they reacted, they would be shot.

One of the Americans turned in Isaac's direction. He quickly lay down flat in his canoe, unseen in the falling dusk. Damn, he thought, wish I could have grabbed my shotgun first. It lay beside him, unloaded. At least his pistol was ready.

"Perhaps this will make you talk!" said the other, shoving the end of his musket into the gut of one of the soldiers. All the Canadians were unarmed, as per the agreements of the ceasefire. They had no line of defense. They are just standing there, like sitting ducks, thought Isaac.

"Or maybe you," said the gunman, pushing his musket into the mouth of a young soldier, no more than Simeon's age. "Tell us where it is," he said, shoving the gun farther. Fear was written all over the young man's face, his body trembled, his knees shook.

"Now!" screamed the gunman, shoving it farther down the private's throat. When the young soldier gagged, the gunman shot him, blowing his brains out, splattering blood everywhere.

Good Lord, Isaac exclaimed to himself, this is an execution line! By the sound of their voices, he knew that the canoe had drifted right in front of them, probably thirty feet away. I will only have one chance, he thought, as he quietly loaded the shotgun, hoping not to draw attention to himself. If I only get one of them, the other will get me for sure. I will be a dead man.

For a brief moment, Isaac thought of Simeon, so young and full of promise, dying in a senseless war. He wanted to avenge his brother, to make the Yankees pay. He would wait for the right moment, and shoot them both down.

Then he heard a familiar voice blurt out with fear, "We don't know where they put the documents, no one gives us that kind of information."

Jarvis! William Jarvis was in the line.

Isaac hesitated. Wouldn't that be sweet, he thought. All I have to do is lie here, silent, and no one will ever know. He will finally get what he deserves.

His mind took him back to the York jail, eleven years ago, lying in pain after thirty-nine lashes, wishing he would die. Then back farther to when Jarvis so smugly told him that his land claim was not valid, and every other time that Jarvis ridiculed, snubbed or belittled him over twenty years. Now *I am in control of your fate, whether you live or die*, he realized. *Sweet.*

"Silence!" he heard the gunman scream. "The only thing I want to hear is where the documents are. Do you want your head blown off too? Just keep quiet and you will get your wish!"

Isaac seethed with anger, every nerve on fire, every muscle tensed. *John White would not be dead if it wasn't for the likes of Jarvis and John Small*, he cursed. *Now I can avenge a good man's wrongful death. Jarvis deserves to die*, he concluded. *All I have to do is lie still.*

The gunman walked down the line, and shoved the end of his rifle at each soldier's mouth. "Maybe you will talk," he threatened, then went to the next soldier, "or maybe you will." Each time he pushed the gun harder.

Isaac breathed heavily, his eyes staring up at the darkening sky. He was amazed that no one had noticed the little birchbark canoe that Fire Starter had taught him to make so many years ago. *The sky is red now, the sign of war for the Mississaugas. Damn*, thought Isaac, *Fire Starter will lose everything if the Yankees win.*

The gunman came to a young soldier who was bleeding at the mouth from the last time. As the Yankee shoved the rifle into the man's mouth, he let out a cry of pain and fear, and Isaac heard the gun go off again.

Without thinking, he stood, aimed, and shot at the gunman, who staggered forward and fell. Isaac crouched low in the canoe to be less of a target, lined up his pistol and took a shot at the other Bluecoat, who had turned around and was aiming at him. Isaac's shot hit him in the leg.

The Bluecoat flinched, then took deadly aim at the canoe. Isaac ducked and lay still, hoping that the evening light was dim enough to misdirect the American's aim.

He lay there, drifting, not knowing if he would live or die.

Chapter 20 – April 27th, 1813

Images of Polly flashed by in an instant. Polly as a young bride, in her Sunday-best forest green satin dress with white lace at the throat, her auburn hair softly pulled back, her green eyes radiant, smiling with excitement. Then Polly bent over at the waist, pulling weeds out of the carrot patch, with Elizabeth strapped to her back in the cradleboard. Then Polly surrounded by their eight children, warm and snug by the hearth, as she read them a story on Christmas Eve. She was always so strong, so capable, so loving, Isaac thought.

Why am I thinking as if she is already dead, Isaac questioned himself. Maybe it is me that is dead?

A sudden jolt shook the canoe and knocked the senses back into Isaac. Looking straight up, all he could see was the pitch-black sky dotted with a mass of twinkling stars. How long have I been lying here, he wondered.

His arms reached out to feel the sides of the canoe. Strange that only my right arm moves, Isaac thought. Then a wall of pain bore down on the left side of his body. He reached across his chest and found a handful of soft, gooey flesh sticking out of his left arm, just below the bone. Reaching a little farther, he felt the bullet hole in the birchbark canoe.

The Yankee got me, Isaac thought.

But at least I got one of them. He tried to sit up, but as soon as he moved, blood gushed out of his wound. Jamming his arm against the side of the canoe, the blood flow slowed, then stopped from the pressure.

Damn Yankees! We must win this war, he said over and over again, as he drifted off into a deep sleep.

He awoke staring into the eyes of Fire Starter's wife, Mahima, who smiled and said, "at last you are awake."

Reaching over, he felt that his wound was dressed and bound up with a sturdy leather strap. Isaac sat up and saw that he was just west of Fort York. My canoe must have drifted here last night, he concluded. Isaac moved his injured arm around slowly, and saw that it wasn't broken. The bullet must have grazed the flesh.

Mahima offered Isaac some pickerel they caught the night before. After being nourished and feeling a bit stronger, Isaac asked to speak with Fire Starter.

"He hasn't returned," answered Mahima in a deadpan tone, not wanting to express how worried she was. Three of her sons were killed in the battle, and she did not want to add another death to the toll.

Isaac set out in the canoe around midday and paddled back to York to find his friend. He kept his paddle on the right side so that there would be less pressure on his wounded shoulder, but every stroke was painful. As he neared William Allan's wharf, three Bluecoats motioned with their weapons for him to come ashore.

"We need more Brits to dig graves at the blast site," one of them declared, pushing Isaac toward a group of Canadians at the end of the dock.

Isaac was handed a shovel, and told to walk along the path toward the garrison, single-file, like prisoners in a chain gang. I don't suppose we can refuse, considered Isaac. The citizens of York were unarmed and not permitted to carry a gun. Most of their weapons had been confiscated anyway.

They crossed Garrison Creek and hiked up the slope to a mountain of dead bodies lying crumpled in a heap where the explosion had left them. So much death, Isaac thought stoically, never having witnessed a battle scene before. Even during the War of Independence when he was a boy, there were no battles fought near his homestead. Isaac thought of how elated he had been to kill the Americans yesterday, how satisfying it was. Today, it seemed like something completely foreign, as if someone else had done it.

The smell of death was everywhere, an unforgettable, putrid stench. Isaac knew it from the back of the slaughter house. Here, with so many dead soldiers, it was intensified, rank, and thick.

Isaac could barely lift the soil that he loosened with the shovel, the pain in his arm was so intense. He stopped to rest many times, collapsing onto the ground, but was prodded with a musket to rise up and keep on digging. After an hour, a Bluecoat told Isaac and a dozen others to start filling the grave site with bodies.

Isaac glanced at the carnage on the battlefield. Many bodies were missing arms or legs, others with heads smashed under large boulders or logs, still others lying in pools of sticky blood with gaping wounds. Some had their eyes open and their mouth frozen into a painful, terrifying cry.

They started with the ones closest to the trench. Isaac nodded to the man closest to him, and they both bent down to lift the stiff carcass of a Yankee with a shattered shoulder and toss it down the hill into the grave. Isaac groaned and clenched his teeth, almost crumbling to the ground.

So many Americans, Isaac observed, and only occasionally did they come across a Canadian. It does not seem right to bury the Canadians alongside the enemy, Isaac thought, but I guess there is no time to dig another grave. He walked back over to the next dead soldier and heard a soft moan. Looking down, he saw a youth lying on his side, almost a boy, still breathing, eyes closed, letting out a pitiful moan every ten seconds, as if it was part of his breathing pattern. Two dead soldiers covered his legs.

"Come on, help me get the stiffs off of him," Isaac said to another worker.

They quickly rolled one of the dead soldiers to the side. As they picked up the second carcass, a stream of blood shot out of the boy's leg, no longer having the weight of the dead soldier to stop it. The boy's leg was ripped open to the bone, raw flesh showing from his hip to his knee.

Still in shock, the boy moaned louder, the pain excruciating now. Quickly, Isaac looked around for something sharp. Finding nothing, he grabbed a large boulder and threw it down at the boy's head as hard as he could, then did it again to make sure he was dead. So many were left in the field to die of their wounds, but he did not want to let the boy suffer. There had been enough suffering already.

"That's the kindest thing I ever did for a Yankee soldier," Isaac said to another worker, who laughed uncomfortably at the absurdity of it all.

Night time was approaching and there were still many more bodies to be buried. The American officers would not let them take a break and did not offer any nourishment. They just wanted the job done before dark. Isaac and the others were completely exhausted but were ordered to get one last group of dead soldiers, then return in the morning to finish the rest.

Barely able to walk, Isaac and his partner trudged over to the last one, and grabbed the shoulders and feet. Halfway back, Isaac's partner collapsed with exhaustion, dropping the feet with a loud thud, and fell back gasping for air. Letting out a long laboured breath, Isaac bent over to place the body down.

This one is not a Bluecoat, noticed Isaac, this one is wearing a ..... leather tunic? ...... no, it cannot be .... it cannot be .... Isaac collapsed to the ground, the dead man's head falling almost in his lap. No, Isaac moaned softly, almost gently, too weak and too bewildered to cry out.

The dead man's face had his eyes open, with a stern, determined look, as if he would not rest until his mission was accomplished. His chest was ripped open, his ribs showing on the left side, his stomach contents splayed all over his clothing. He must have died instantly.

Isaac looked away. He thought of the first time they met, so long ago, at the limestone outcrop along the Humber, the holy place for the Mississaugas. How he had chastised him for throwing away the birchbark that he had ripped to shreds while trying to make his first canoe. My first canoe, Isaac thought. Without him, I would have never known the river that I now call home.

He brought his hands to his forehead and pressed hard, keeping them there for a long time. I would never have survived the first few years in York without him, Isaac thought, or the last decade. When the whole town turned against me, mocking me, he was the only friend I had. When I lay dying from the wounds from the whipping post, it was his face I saw when I awoke, his wisdom and ancient remedies that saved me.

How many times did he tell Isaac to trust that the Great Spirit resides in every living being, every rock, every mountain, every cloud. That the Great Spirit will call you to join him in the spirit world when your life is fulfilled and complete.

No! Isaac cried out, pounding his chest in frustration. No, he whispered, shaking his head back and forth. There is not a finer person that ever walked the face of this earth.

Without a word, Isaac stood up and the two men carried Fire Starter's body to the trench. When they got there, Isaac said gruffly, "We will take him down to the river."

The two men walked down the steep hill but had only gone a short way before an American yelled over at them, "What are you doing? Take the corpse back to the trench at once!"

His partner stopped, letting Fire Starter's legs drop to the ground, but Isaac kept going. All alone, Isaac dragged his friend's cold body down the bank, with the American shouting at him to stop. Isaac did not notice or care. Fire Starter will not have his final rest in a grave full of white men, he vowed. He flinched when he heard the irate soldier fire a round up into the air but kept walking, and then lay his friend's body out of sight near the footbridge over Garrison Creek.

Without looking back, Isaac waded through the river and walked to the town, reaching the wharf in the harbour by nightfall. There was no one out that night. The shops, hotels and taverns were dark and lifeless. There was no sound of young couples out for a stroll, horse hooves clapping along or music and laughter coming from a tea party or ball. There were no children laughing, no choirs singing hymns at the church, and no drunkards brawling at the hitching post. All survivors kept to their homes, quiet and demur. Only the American soldiers could be heard, their boots tramping along the dirty streets, talking in low tones, patrolling for dissidents.

Muffled cries of the sick and dying could be heard from St. James church which had been converted to a hospital for the wounded. Looking east Isaac saw a cloud of smoke and the smouldering remains of the Parliament Buildings which were accidentally burnt to the ground by the Americans.

Isaac thanked the Great Spirit that there was only a quarter moon that night, enabling him to slip away through the enemy ships anchored in the harbour unseen, and paddle along the shoreline past the sleeping sailors. He carefully glided past the garrison full of noisy, raucous soldiers carousing about, obviously drunk and celebrating their victory. Hearing their reverie, he wished he could have killed more of them. Their loud, drunken laughter made a mockery of his comrades that were wounded and killed yesterday.

Paddling hard and favouring his right side, Isaac glided up to the footbridge and pulled Fire Starter's cold, lifeless body into the canoe, his head resting on the front seat, looking back at him. Isaac leaned forward and closed his eyelids, then pushed off and drifted back down the river, turning west along the shoreline. The pain from the gunshot wound had lessened now, overshadowed by the pain in his heart.

A few clouds blocked the moonlight, dimming his visibility as he paddled along. He could barely make out the remnants of the crumbled western battery, the place where he had satiated his urge to kill the enemy. He gritted his teeth and kept paddling, not allowing any feelings of remorse to enter his mind.

The wind picked up a little bit behind him, speeding his journey, making the newly sprouted willow leaves rustle and shake along the shoreline. That must have been the landing site, Isaac noted to himself a while later, when he saw a couple dozen bodies scattered along the beach and half-way up the steep slope leading to the highland. The brush was trampled to the ground, with bare patches of soil poking through. Someone will have to bury those soldiers too, he thought, but it won't be me.

We fought bravely, considering the Americans had twice as many soldiers, Isaac reflected, as he rounded the beachhead and entered the backflow at the mouth of the Humber, preferring only to think of the battle for now. It must be a few hours past midnight, by the position of the moon.

His injured arm began throbbing again, so he leaned back and allowed his forearm and stomach muscles to do the work. He paddled to the middle in front of a large boulder, then to an inside bend, expertly weaving his way from one hidden current to another. If only we had more artillery or ships, maybe we could have defeated them, he pondered, or at least weakened them a little more. Placing his paddle upright, he steered around a log floating towards him that appeared out of nowhere.

If only ....., if only ..... two such powerful, agonizing words. If only we had not lost all our possessions when we left Genesee. Perhaps then we would have had enough money to establish ourselves in Upper Canada, rather than chasing after Simcoe and his offer of free land in Toronto. And if we had stayed in Niagara, would Simeon still be alive today?

Isaac felt a crushing grip around his midriff, as if a giant hand was squeezing him tightly. Why am I letting myself think this way? he chastised himself.

If only Governor Simcoe would not have left. If only the Americans had not declared war. If only the British had not angered them. If only Simeon had not married Violet. Isaac racked his brain with hypothetical questions. So many decisions we make seem unimportant at the time, but when added together, completely direct the course of our lives.

With the moonlight reflecting off the water, Isaac paddled farther up the Humber to the old King's Mill that he helped Nicholas Miller build their first year in York. It was abandoned a decade ago when newer and better sawmills were built upstream. Who would have thought that the night I learned to fish from Fire Starter so long ago, right over there, would lead me to being tied to the whipping post? There is no way that I could have predicted that, Isaac concluded.

Trust in the Great Spirit to lead you on the correct path, Fire Starter always said. Whatever decisions you make, it is always right because the Great Spirit will not lead you astray.

But how can you trust the Great Spirit or yourself when even the smallest decision can have such dire consequences years later, and result in your demise or death?

Isaac paddled through the shallow east side, turned around a sharp bend, and then finally saw the limestone outcrop, his place of refuge that he discovered just days after landing in the Toronto Bay, just before Elizabeth was born, where Fire Starter had taught him to make his first canoe. He pulled over to the old rocky landing and tied it to a trembling aspen tree that looked younger than he did. New life was emerging all around the limestone boulders. The small chokecherry bushes that once enclosed it were now twenty-five feet tall and swayed in the wind. This place, sacred to the Mississaugas, always felt like home.

As soon as he alighted, he felt a wave of peacefulness wash over him. Squatting on the rock, Isaac stared out over the Humber, which now was a foot lower than when they arrived twenty years ago.

I really thought that when I came to Upper Canada that I could actually become somebody important, have an influence on how the province would be formed. Isaac looked down at a blackened reflection of himself in the smooth, cool waters. There was no room for an American in the government, contrary to the propaganda that led us here. You had to be born in Britain to receive any kind of recognition, to do anything important. It is still that way, even more so now, Isaac thought.

He glanced over at the spot where Fire Starter used to leave tobacco offerings before they went out to catch salmon at night. I don't think the Mississaugas knew what they were up against either. Now that Fire Starter and Kineubenae are gone, the only hope for the Mississaugas is Tecumseh. Only he has the foresight, charisma and knowledge to unite the native clans and fight for them. They also need the British to win, but now I am doubtful they will succeed.

Isaac walked up to the northern edge and glanced out over the trees to where St. John's trading post had once stood. Now there is someone who came from the river but abandoned it to join the high-wheeling backslappers, the upper echelon of society. It is hard to believe that such a voyageur succumbed to the demands of society. But I imagine that he achieved the wealth and prestige that he was looking for, that I was looking for.

His thoughts turned to St. John's wife, Margaret, a natural beauty, a woman of the earth. How had she faired as the wife of a diplomat, he wondered. I know that Polly would have preferred it.

He walked back to his canoe and kicked some loose stones into the river. I may have wanted to be a bootlicker at the beginning, Isaac thought, recalling his days of listening for hours to Governor Simcoe's visions for the settlement of the province, and his plans to stop the Americans. But thank the Good Lord that I did not get what I sought. I would have become just another puppet.

Look how being part of the elite society brought about John White's death. Many of Isaac's ideals died the day his friend was killed.

Exhaling full force, Isaac stared up into the black sky littered with tiny points of light, some of them twinkling, others stead-fast and sure, others fading away. He walked over to the canoe, squatted down, and put a hand on Fire Starter's arm, cold as the night air and stiff.

He finally allowing himself to mourn, and feel the pain. First Simeon, and now, Fire Starter, he wept quietly. Such a wise and brave man, a man of integrity, honour, and principle, with a kind heart and wise beyond his years. Death does not discriminate, he grumbled, nor is it just.

Finally losing his composure, Isaac bent over, his face contorted, his aching back and shoulders heaving with sobs felt deep within his soul. Fire Starter did not even want to take part in the war, he agonized. If only he had not gone to warn his people of the surrender. If only I had thought to warn him that the soldiers were going to blow up the Grand Magazine. Damn, I thought he would have walked past it with half an hour to spare. Maybe he turned back. Maybe he ..... ?

Downtrodden and filled with despair, Isaac stared out over the Humber, vaguely wondering if one could drown if tied to a canoe that was sailing down the river.

Gaining his composure, Isaac paddled back down the Humber and found Mahima and the rest of the Otter clan at the foot. They removed Fire Starter's body from the canoe, and laid it on a bed of leaves and twigs.

Holding Isaac's hand before he left, Mahima said, "Do not forget. Death is another part of the journey. The Great Spirit has called Fire Starter to join him. We must rejoice and be happy for him. His journey is only beginning."

Isaac held her shoulders, kissed her forehead, then returned to his canoe. He could not find the words to express his sorrow, or to comfort her.

Stepping into the river, he felt a cold rush of spring water soak his wool stockings. He stuck his other boot in and felt the same. The cold made him feel alive again. He stood there for some time, watching the river trickle past, so strong and forceful in the centre when the river dropped, slow and stoic on the inside bends, and so rich and full in the deeper pools. Every curve is different, every foot, every run …so many intricacies that together make the whole.

In two months, we will have lived here twenty years, he thought, looking far down the river. Simcoe's vision has been fulfilled. The untouched wilderness is gone, replaced by scattered woodlots, streams and swamps in a sea of rectangular farms with towns and villages peppered into the landscape.

Isaac stood and watched the birches sway in the breeze on the other size of the river. Tomorrow morning, I will paddle back down the Humber and take Fire Starter to his final resting place along the Credit. He will rest with his father and forefathers before him, he promised.

I will never feel like one of the British, he thought, as he climbed into the canoe and turned it upriver, and I no longer feel like an American. He watched his paddle dip into the river and pull himself forward. The water swirled around his paddle until he lifted it out again and took another stroke. The Humber is calm today, neither menacing or threatening.

Up ahead he saw the red maples on the river edge dip their branches down toward the water, the new yellow-green buds about to burst open and shade the cool waters of the Humber until they fall again in the autumn. I suppose I can call myself a Canadian now, he decided, since I fought for this country and was willing to die.

Alone, in his birchbark canoe, with no sounds other than warblers and the call of the loon, he steered past a whirlpool at the foot of a run, and drank in the glory of the sunlight as it reflected on the water.

Yes, he thought, the journey continues.

◇◇

The Battle of York was the first win for the Americans, which rejuvenated them and gave them enough courage to press forth with their campaign. They were again successful one month later when they instigated a two-day bombardment of Queenston and captured Fort George. The Americans had now defeated the Canadians on the north and south shores of Lake Ontario, controlling much of western Upper Canada.

One month later, the Americans sent some of their troops from Fort George to destroy a British advanced post at Beaver Dams. Fortunately for the Canadians, Laura Secord of Queenston warned them of the secret mission, and the attackers were ambushed by a force of Iroquois from the Grand River. Isaac heard about the attack from Fire Starter's wife who had come to ask Isaac to attend a memorial service along the Credit River near the Dundas Street bridge where they had buried him. With a heavy heart, Isaac placed some tobacco and sweet breads that Polly had made on the grave site to assist Fire Starter on his journey.

Despite these successes, the Americans and the British began a series of meetings to negotiate a peace treaty. The Americans no longer wished to continue the war since the British had already stopped interfering with the

French ships sailing to America, and stopped the practice of conscription. It was also crippling them financially. However, the war raged on throughout 1813 with the Americans winning all the battles.

The balance of power shifted tremendously in the summer of 1814 after Napoleon was defeated. The British Secretary of War for the Colonies, Henry Bathurst, ordered George Prevost, the Governor General, to abandon the defensive strategy and launch an ambitious counter-offensive. The British were now free to send a large contingent of ships and 28,000 soldiers to Canada, and they attacked America from the north, east and south.

The battle of Lundy's Lane in Niagara, in July, 1814, the bloodiest battle in the war, resulted in 1,600 wounded and dead in a small area the size of two football fields. Both sides lost an equal number of soldiers as they battled five hours in the darkness of night, sometimes firing on their own soldiers. The only outcome of such a fierce battle was that the Americans retained possession of Queenston Heights.

Later in July, General Robert Ross led a small British army in an attack on Washington D.C., defeating a much larger army led by President James Madison, Secretary of War John Armstrong, and Secretary of State James Monroe. The British burned the legislative buildings, military and naval strongholds, and the presidential mansion, which was later rebuilt, painted and referred to as "The White House." General Ross was killed two months later in Baltimore, when the British attacked Fort McHenry with artillery and rockets because they could not advance close enough to charge. A young American lawyer, Francis Scott Key, wrote a poem about the incredible display of fire and explosions that was later set to the music of an old English drinking song, entitled, "The Star Spangled Banner."

The British launched a massive offensive near Lake Champlain, Maine, on September, 1814, led by Governor-General Prevost, hoping to take the American naval base at Plattsburgh. Unsuccessful, the British were driven back. Perhaps it was the failure of their largest fighting force, with 10,000 army and militia, that made them more open to peace negotiations.

The war was finally over when the Treaty of Ghent was signed on Christmas Eve of 1814. It called for a ceasefire and reinstated all the prewar boundaries. The Americans managed to negotiate fishing rights on the St. Lawrence River as part of the deal. Even though the British had overpowered the Americans at this point, they did not gain any additional land or rights.

More importantly, the British did not negotiate for the creation of an Indian Territory in upper New York state or Ohio, Michigan, Illinois and Indiana. Tecumseh was killed one year earlier at the Battle of the Thames in Moraviantown. Without Tecumseh, there was no leader to represent the rights of the First Nations at the peace treaty talks. Each clan, Mohawk, Chippewa, Algonquin, Shawnee, Mississauga, remained as a separate entity and no longer would join together to fight for a unified territory controlled by themselves.

Both sides, American and British, claimed victory after the war. In York and the rest of Upper Canada, the idea of British imperialism was solidified, with many people claiming and reclaiming their devotion to the King. Fear of another attack seemed to reinforce the importance of having an elite group of British gentlemen to manage the country and provide for its safety. The elite group, which evolved from Governor Simcoe's formation of the Legislative Assembly, became known as the Family Compact.

Isaac Devins continued to serve as a spy for the British throughout the War, but did not see any American troops or militia along the Toronto Carrying Place Trail or along the Humber River.

March 16, 1856

Isaac lay quietly in his old featherbed, staring up through the window at the stars in the clear night sky. He pulled the woollen quilt up to his chin, then cussed as his toes stuck out the other end. Bah! he grumbled. He could never sleep with cold toes, but was too weak to sit up and pull the quilt back down.

His arm instinctively reached over to feel for Polly in the dark, even though he knew she was not there. She always knew what to do, no matter what we faced.

When I told her how Jarvis snickered and sneered the first time we met, even though he knew nothing about us, she remarked that taste does not always accompany the best apple on the tree. So even-tempered she was, my dear Polly. I was frothing at the mouth, sounding off, about to punch a hole through a hay stack while she took the insults without batting an eye.

John C. says the Americans are still arguing over slavery. The southern states don't want to give it up. Primitives!

Governor Simcoe abolished slavery before Toronto was even founded, that's more than sixty years ago. The Upper Canada Gazette writes that the slavery issue will probably lead to an American civil war — that is something I would not want to live through. I hope it doesn't spread to Upper Canada ... I mean Canada West. Damn, my memory fails me. I still refer to Canada West as Upper Canada even though it was renamed back in 1840. Why can't I remember that?

Times were different. Back then, you could speak with the Governor about any matter of interest, and debate the future of the country. Even the natives called him Deyonguhodrawen, "one whose door is always open." I guess it was because there was so few of us, especially when we landed in Toronto.

Now the aristocrats are unapproachable, sitting in their fancy parliament buildings, unwilling to acknowledge anyone other than their own. Isaac sighed, and thought of the river and his birchbark canoe overgrown with weeds.

Everything changed after the war. We defended our border, but did we gain anything for all that bloodshed?

The Mississaugas certainly did not. Some moved to the northern hunting grounds, and others farther west to Rupert's Land. The ones that stayed near Toronto went to the Grand River reserve. I haven't seen a Mississauga or spoken the language in thirty years. Isaac tried to voice some of the words, then gave up in frustration.

Toronto was still called York back then. It was trashed and burned by the Americans. They pillaged it and left a week later. We were safe up here. So were the rest of the Devins down in Weston, nothing was touched. But many of the townsfolk lost everything. Jarvis suffered most of all. His fine jewels, paintings and riches were gone. He deserved it, too.

A wry smile touched Isaac's face, then faded. He didn't get what he really deserved. Jarvis came though swimmingly, his fine reputation intact. Mostly because of the untruth that he spread. He felt a twinge in his stomach that automatically cramped when thinking about him.

A week after burying Fire Starter, Isaac went to William Allan's store, or what remained of it. Most of the stalls were bare, counters had been bashed in, windows were shattered, and the doors were missing. It looked like an explosive has hit it, thought Isaac at the time. On his way back to the dock, he overheard a disturbing conversation. Everyone was talking about Jarvis, the hero of the Battle of York.

At first, Isaac dismissed it, thinking that York was so badly defeated that people were desperate for someone, anyone, to call a hero. Then he overheard another young man say, "He single-handedly bore down on the Bluecoats, completely unarmed, and saved the remaining soldiers from the line of execution."

Isaac's face flushed and his heart started pounding. *That scoundrel, Jarvis, claimed that he saved everyone from being executed that afternoon, when I was the one who pulled the trigger. Everyone in that line of fire must have seen my canoe and heard the shots,* Isaac raged. But there was no mention of anyone other than Jarvis.

The next day, Isaac ran into Jarvis at the dock. Mockingly, Isaac taunted, "I hear that you are the hero of the Battle of York, what an astounding feat."

"Why, yes, Devins, I did step up when the time called for it." Jarvis tugged his lapels and nodded his head, proud of his accomplishment.

Shaking his head in disbelief, Isaac said, "How is it that you were able to take down two Bluecoats who were pointing their rifles directly at you?"

"Well, now, it was just a matter of timing. I waited until the precise moment, then charged them when they had their backs turned," Jarvis steadfastly replied.

"You didn't hear shots coming from the lake, from a lone gunman in a birchbark canoe, who happened to be paddling past, who shot at the two Bluecoats?" Isaac asked, his voice getting louder and more incredulous.

"Preposterous! Everyone there will tell you that I was the one who charged them."

Many times through the years, Isaac thought about trying to discredit Jarvis, but he hadn't recognize any other voices that day as he lay hidden in the canoe. There was no one who could verify the true story. Before long, everyone in the town claimed that Jarvis was the hero of the Battle *of York. There was nothing Isaac could do. He knew that no one would believe him.*

At least Jarvis didn't live much longer, Isaac thought. He died a few years after the war, broke and unhappy. Same as my father. He was only 70, but losing Simeon in the war killed him. He never got over it.

Why does Jarvis still bother me, after all these years?

I have kept this secret for so long. Would it have made a difference if anyone knew? Would my life have been somehow different? Perhaps I wouldn't die with nothing to show for myself. Isaac tried to lift his head but did not have the strength. His eyes became heavy.

Elizabeth came into the room after bidding farewell to her family at the end of the lane. She bustled about, chatting gaily, unaware that her father was becoming more and more agitated. Calm down, calm down, Isaac told himself. I must think of something pleasant.

He turned his thoughts to the nights spent with Fire Starter, fishing at night on the Humber in their birchbark canoes, with the fires blazing in the middle. I learned so much from him, Isaac reflected. It's funny that I grew up with a mistrust of the native clans, particularly after Little Star was taken, but then they became the only ones I could trust, other than my family.

Isaac sighed, contentedly this time. I was blessed to come to know Fire Starter, a true friend, warrior and a wise man. Blessed to have a loving wife and eight healthy children.

The only regret I have is that I didn't do something great, something that I will be remembered for.

Isaac closed his eyes, for one final rest. As he drifted into a deep sleep, he thought he saw Polly waiting for him, young and beautiful again in a white, flowing gown, standing in a patch of trout lilies and trilliums, beckoning him, her auburn hair blowing freely in the wind, arms outstretched, with dappled light reflecting off the flowing waters of the Humber, calling out and leading him home.

312

Epilogue

The Legend of Waabshkii Mnidoo

Many moons ago, before the earth was divided, there lived a white spirit who disguised himself as an ordinary man, who came to teach us the ways of the world. The white spirit was powerful, strong and wise.

One day, three warriors were walking through the woods and saw the smoke from the enemy's fire rising straight up from the maple trees. Starving and thirsty, they walked over to the fire and saw that everyone was asleep. One warrior said, "We are so tired, and they have three horses. Let us take them for we cannot walk any farther."

The warriors crept into the camp site and unhitched the horses to lead them away. One of them was black with a white star on its forehead. As they were about to leave, a young boy ran up to them and tried to stop them. One of the warriors grabbed the boy and rode off.

All the noise woke up the white spirit, who came out and was not pleased. The white spirit stood up on a rock, leaned back, and sent a cry throughout the land that echoed in the tree tops, bounced off the streams, and shook the mountain tops. The sound went forward and engulfed the warrior, causing him to drop the boy. The force pushed the warrior forward, all the way to the ends of the earth, where he fell off and is forever falling, falling, falling.

The white spirit, Waabshkii Mnidoo, lives to this day in the maple forest. When the wind blows hard, the trees bend over, waves ripple through the rivers and the mountains shake. Waabshkii Mnidoo is there to remind us and our children that contentment is the virtue that will set you free.

Made in the USA
Charleston, SC
14 August 2013